CW00687320

Colouring In

Nigel Stewart

Copyright © 2019 Nigel Stewart

The right of Nigel Stewart to be identified as the author has been asserted in accordance with the Copyright, Designs and Patents Act 1988.

All rights reserved. No part of this publication may be reproduced, stored in a retrieval system, or transmitted, in any form or by any means (electronic, mechanical, photocopying, recording or otherwise), without the prior written permission of the publisher.

Published by Purple Parrot Publishing

Printed in the United Kingdom

First Printing, 2019

ISBN: Print: 978-1-912677-06-1

       Ebook: 978-1-912677-07-8

Purple Parrot Publishing

www.purpleparrotpublishing.co.uk

Edited by Viv Ainslie

Cover Photography by Chris Nebard (chrisnebard.zenfolio.com)

Copyright © 2016

All rights reserved. The cover photographs, or any portion thereof may not be reproduced without express written permission of the photographer.

Acknowledgements

Colouring In is a work of fiction. None of its characters exists, and any similarity to any person, living or dead, is coincidental and accidental. Many locations and venues in the story do not exist and they are also not intended to portray any real places or businesses.

There is graphic language and descriptions of sexual acts and of physical illness. There is also a description of mild physical violence.

Throughout the book, characters use bad language and there is also terminology that was viewed as acceptable by some people at the time the story is set. That terminology does not represent the views of the author nor of the publisher.

Colouring In was originally self-published by the author in December 2016. This second edition, in conjunction with Viv Ainslie at Purple Parrot Publishing, is a wonderful reworking and enhancement of the book and its story. It nonetheless retains the essence of the original.

The author is indebted to friends and family whose help, love and encouragement during the weeks months and years of Colouring In being written were invaluable. Thank you all.

But a very special 'thank you' to Chris Nebard, who supplemented his amazing photography with unceasing support and guidance about the book's cover design. He is a big star.

You can follow me on Twitter: @menigestew

To

Amy Barron

For her constant belief that James Clifton's story would be told.

Part 1

Portraits Hung on Empty Walls

1
Another Fat Lady Sings
Christmas 1989

Taxi drivers were such a huge problem for James. They either talked when he needed silence, or they just didn't get his banter. That evening, the final few hours of Boxing Day, he sat silently surveying snowy streets.

Driver talked and didn't listen. 'Did you have a nice Christmas, sir?' A burring Herefordshire accent made this query seem doubly kind.

'It was fine thank you....'

'And don't call me sir.'

Driver took no notice. 'My two were in wonderland yesterday. They got one of these video games from the in-laws. Never saw them all day. Kids eh? You got any, sir?'

'No. I haven't....'

'You're still doing it.'

'Oh, well lucky you then sir!'

Once in a while a voice crackled through the car; the taxi controller, no less.

'47? Where are you?'

Silence. Static.

'Well he's getting more and more angry. What can I tell him?'

Static. Silence.

'I see. Right. Would someone else – anyone – please go to the Hearts of Oak to pick up a party name of Williams? He's been waiting...'

James perked up. This one way communication seemed to very neatly summarise things. Conversations at work or play ran on the same lines. People wanted and were given one side of every story.

It made the world go around.

The roads were quiet, clear of the snowfall from the last few days. James watched the meter as the fare clicked past five pounds. The trip seemed to be taking forever and Driver was still filling up the silence.

'Did you see that old Bond film on the telly last night? They are still great value. Great entertainment and action.'

His voice filled with the joy of Christmas slaughter. In the rear view mirror James saw the man's eyes creasing at the edges as he rambled on about cars that turn in to submarines. When James didn't reply, Driver half turned and repeated, 'Brilliant special effects; Bond films.'

'I didn't see it. Sorry.'

Silent.

Static.

At last, Driver was quiet.

The tiny dribble of guilt about his brusque manner evaporated when James saw the final fare. Driver provided an unsolicited explanation: 'Sunday rates today sir. Double fares.'

James didn't add a tip. Relieved of half the cash he had brought with him he watched the taxi slither away in search of more prey.

With a 360 degree turn he measured his surroundings. Large, nineteenth century houses filled a narrow, twentieth century road. James felt conflicting pangs of jealousy and regret, for he could not match this domestic splendour.

All around him, an eerie miasmic serenity prevailed. Still, cold air. Hazy, murky light from street lamps. Skeletal tree branches. James gazed at this vaguely festive, vaguely sinister scene and recorded it with a click of his artist's photo memory.

Cold particles, tiny chilly daggers, sprayed onto his face. A snowball had exploded on his left shoulder.

'You fat useless tosser.'

He turned to face a voice in the void.

'Paul?'

Another snowball hit him, now in the midriff. James giggled and set down his overnight case and a carrier bag of bottles.

'Come on knobhead; fight.'

James stooped and rolled a pair of snowballs. There was a guffaw from somewhere across the avenue. James retreated into the driveway with his baggage.

'There's no hiding place Clifton. My resources are limitless. My eyes are everywhere.'

This time, three snowballs splattered against him in quick succession.

'*Shit. He's got back up. Or a ballista. But never mind. Revenge.*'

With a whoop, James hurled a snowball in the general direction of the voice. Coarse, cruel laughter ensued.

'What the fuck was that? Come on. Surrender or die.'

James slipped behind the hedge marking the boundary of Paul's front garden. He glanced behind him at the house: fairy

12

lights blinked from one window; a glittering star adorned the front door, catching and reflecting occasional flickers of light. Time seemed to have slowed.

'I'll give you thirty seconds to surrender. Otherwise it's Armageddon Day.' On reflection, James realised he could hear a deranged quality in Paul's voice.

He leapt out from behind his cover, launched another snowball across the road then quickly ducked back into his bunker.

Absolutely nothing happened.

James called out, 'Paul?'

From the looming silence, a voice spoke right behind him and James jumped with fright.

'Happy Christmas! Come on, let's get inside for a beer.'

James was hyperventilating. 'What? How? I? You? Hap...py. Yes.'

'I was in a garden over there; the Mason's. He's a private dentist; doing very well. Your first shot hit me on the head. Over the fence and bang!' Paul slapped his head in emphasis. 'Lucky. When you hid – like a girl – for the nth time, I nipped across the road and into next door's driveway. They are away; Andorra, we think. Then into their side garden, through the bushes and tippy toes up behind you. In a war, you'd be dead by now. I therefore won.'

'Hail to the chief.'

Paul grabbed James' case and took it upstairs. His talking didn't stop during this ascent and, even once out of sight, Paul sustained a roaming dialogue. James lingered in the hallway on the threshold of the living room, wondering what to do with his assortment of bottles.

'I've put your stuff in the guest room; top of the stairs, turn right. Wends has probably... yes, she has put some towels out for you. Put that booze in the kitchen and find space in the fridge for stuff that needs to be chilled. Make yourself at home down there. Put some music on. I need a shit; back in ten.'

'Ten? For a shit??'

James took the wine to the kitchen then returned to the living room to collapse theatrically back on one of the two sofas. He jumped up and fell on to the other one. Satisfied that he had done no damage, he repeated these manoeuvres until there were man-shaped hollows in both sofas. Once settled, he inspected himself: around his knees there were damp patches the size of side plates.

'Attractive. Gorgeous.'

Moments later, a crescendo of stomping announced Paul's

descent of the stairs and his commentary resumed.

'I got yet another pay rise in November and I am minted. Do you still not like celery? How's Sally? Have I told you about Wendy's birthday party? Mid-January; you must come. I get my new company car soon, a shiny BMW 525.'

Paul stood by the living room door and, with finger pointing motion, indicated he was heading to the kitchen, purpose unclear. James stood to examine a long shelf of compact discs. His quick review of the titles revealed they were filed by artist, in alphabetical order and then by year of release.

James' preferred filing system for CDs and records was broadly governed by the rule *what am I listening to most often at the moment?* Albums filling that category lay scattered on and around his stereo, often with the disc or LP nowhere near its respective case or cover.

After more searching, James located a stack of LPs in a cupboard, hidden away like a luckless, awkward family member. He sprawled out on the floor to read the titles, extracted a choice and set it on the turntable.

'Do I need a mechanical engineering degree to work this stereo?'

Paul returned to the living room and pressed several buttons on several boxes. As he moved the tone arm on to the LP he said, 'It's a hi-fi system, not a stereo. And can't we have side one first? This side's very glum.'

'Leave it. I like glum. I want to hear *Your Silent Face*; in stereo, preferably.'

He winked at Paul, who half smiled in return.

Immaculately reproduced music ensued. Despite speakers the size of rabbit hutches, it was too quiet for James, but perfect for conversation.

'So, how's work?'

'Oh, the same as ever.'

James disliked discussing work at any time, but with Paul, it had become a mindgame battleground. Paul was a career animal, a rabbit to James' tortoise. They were on diverging paths of style, aspiration, commitment and drive. Paul spoke of his job now, and always, in a singsong incisive manner and with great clarity and confidence. He rarely paused to reflect. Everything sounded rehearsed and word perfect.

'You should get out. Look at me; I made a break from the corporate mainstream and I'm flying. I earn more in a week now than I earned in a month two years ago. I've made progress. I've got a great car. I've got all this.' He waved an arm around the room. 'My office overlooks the river and I've just bought myself three made-to-measure suits. I genuinely expect to be running the company as MD by the end of 1992. I'm bringing clients, revenue and growth to the business and everyone knows it.'

He droned on, revealing more of his plans for domination and success. Shortly, an evil smile spread across his face. This meant something awful.

'The slapper around our company is unbelievable. I was at a conference in Norwich the other week. A client over there did the whole thing as a kind of Christmas gift. I am now officially known as *Shagger*; which is fair.'

James' indifference went unheeded and Paul continued these smutty revelations to a predictable conclusion.

'Shit; we have no drinks. There's some Czech beer on ice.' Paul leapt up, soon to return with six green bottles. Two were about to fall. As he handed one to James, their eyes met and Paul zoomed in; 'What's up?'

James flinched. 'Nothing; why?'

'Come on; something's not right with you.'

'I'm fine, but so tired. Work has been busy.'

Paul needed a better answer and continued to burrow. 'I know this look, and it isn't caused by your gnomish little job. This is woman related.' He was still standing. James felt mildly provoked but said nothing and took a long draught of his pilsner.

'I think you've split up with Sally.' Paul's tone was triumphal, as if he had just guessed the profession on *What's My Line*.

James took another long suck at his bottle. 'True.'

At last, Paul sat on the sofa opposite James and narrowed his eyes. 'I thought things were good. What went wrong?'

'Rather a lot.'

'Such as?'

'Such as we spent most of this year apart.'

'What?'

Ownership of the conversation was now with James and his far less assertive style. He spoke in mumbled bursts: sentences of few words; sometimes just one word; difficult to listen to; a monotonous trickle that suggested a lack of belief or certainty.

'We spent the year fighting and arguing and not really doing the things lovers do. We split up for a while but got back together a couple of weeks ago. I thought things were right again.' It was many seconds before James concluded: 'But I was wrong.'

A too hasty swig of beer foamed up in his mouth and some ran down his chin. He wiped it away with the back of his hand.

Paul's steely gaze still indicated challenge.

'Well perhaps we should just stay at home tonight? Dinner will be good – as always – and there's a bucket load of drink here.'

'That's considerate but unfair on you and Wendy. We have to go out. Otherwise it might get to be a bit...'

Paul finished his sentence, '...introspective?'

James nodded and shrugged. Paul shrugged and nodded but he tried again.

'Well?'

'Well what?'

'Come on; let's hear it. I want to know why something that seemed good for you is over.'

'Why do you think it was good for me?'

'Don't dodge the question. And don't practice your elementary negotiation tactics here.'

James had been dreading the revelation of what had happened earlier in the day. He knew what to say but still struggled to say it. With minimal eye contact, he stuttered into his tale.

At length Paul interrupted him; 'And you mentioned a separation?'

'Yes.'

'What was that all about?'

'By the start of last summer, it was pretty strained between us. I was less and less convinced that Sal was right – that we were right – but I didn't know how to go about resolving things. In the end, my indecision pushed her into a corner.'

'What happened?' Paul's tone was calm yet detached.

'We decided to split. Not permanently, but a trial. It seemed the right thing to do.'

James breathed in deeply, looked up at his friend and was less hesitant as he explained that Sally had moved out and stayed with a friend leaving James to stew in his own juice for a while.

'That was fine at first, but I began to feel very lonely. Home felt empty and I missed her being there.'

'I'm really pissed off about all this. When you were here in August, you told us Sally didn't come because she was working. That was a lie.'

'Don't answer that. Say nothing. Drink some beer and keep going.'

'Things were not in any way good. Aside from being lonely and pretty derailed by everything that had happened, I was also on the verge of dying from McPoisoning.'

Paul smirked.

'I had a long chat with sis one day and she told me to resolve things one way or the other. I went to where Sally was staying and told her how I felt and that we should try again.'

James nodded an acknowledgement as Paul opened and passed him a second bottle. Renewed by fresh beer, James explained that his visit to Sally's had seemed to be a resolution; not a truce, or a trial. The build up to Christmas had been lovely.

'Sally had arranged to go skiing with her Mum so we parted on Saturday and I headed up here. We said we'd see each other soon and it seemed, at that moment, as if neither of us could stand the idea of being apart for a week or so.

But this afternoon, she phoned. Seems I am ruining her life. I'm A Nobody. I can't be her dream; I can't fulfil her dream. I'm still somewhat astonished by it. Can't believe it's over. I'm really not sure I will ever understand what's happened.'

Their eye contact during these exchanges had been limited. Now he'd stopped talking James held his friend's gaze; a signal that he'd said all he could say. But his eyes leaked sadness and he looked down again. For several moments, New Order's electronic Romanticism was the sound track for this scene.

Speaking more softly, Paul broke the silence. 'I don't know what to say. I mean I'm sorry for you, obviously.'

James barely noticed that Paul had stopped talking and jumped when his friend resumed; 'This comforting thing is supposed to have been consigned to history isn't it? Something we would never need again. It wasn't easy back then, but this seems much harder now we're older and wiser. I still remember when everyone was dancing around the fact that Julie Wheeler had dumped me. Everyone was being so precious and uptight about it. But not you. Why was that?'

'I'd been away with Mum and Dad; to my Grandma's funeral.'

'Yes, that's right. When you got back you were like a whirlwind of positive words and deeds.'

James smiled, despite his running eyes and dribbling nose. Paul continued: 'I remember you telling me to get to the Salmon and bring as much money as I could find because, just for a change, you were skint. You walked in to the back bar, downed a pint in one and with no preamble or hesitation said something like: *This will hurt for weeks and nothing can stop that. But she's gone. She doesn't count anymore, so you must stop her from counting because if you don't, you're buggered. The only people who matter are all around you and we're on your side.* I've never forgotten that.'

James sniffed, loud and wet. The past had this hold. It was a stronghold. It always pulled them up or down or through.

'I was such a precocious little turd, wasn't I? And not yet eighteen.'

'But you meant it and it mattered. And you know what? It still applies. She's gone, and all you can do is disengage. There'll be pain and anguish; but maybe instead of thinking that your problems have just begun, you need to believe they've just ended.'

Neither of them spoke for several seconds. James was assessing his friend's counselling, which was neither original nor good.

'It's a shame though. She was right for you. You have changed in the last couple of years, and I believe for the better. But you kept Sally from us. No one could play any part in helping your relationship with her to flourish.'

The merry men from Salford had moved on to less fraught matters. James stared at the stereo. He wanted sad songs.

Paul wanted nothing of the sort. 'Let's change the subject. How's your family? How's your gorgeous sister?'

It took James a few seconds to catch up with the conversation's new direction.

'Oh; Carol is very well thanks. Everyone else is fine, I think. How about yours?'

'Yes, the same. Fine. Dad's a bit mad, but you knew that.'

Paul seemed uncomfortable, as if he had someone in his house that was unwelcome and contaminated. He stood to gather up the four empty and two full beer bottles, then left the room. When he reappeared at the doorway he announced that he needed to get on with dinner, so James followed in mute admiration of furnishings, décor and tasteful *objets*.

There was an array of aromas in the kitchen and this prompted easy small talk about cooking, eating and drinking. James opened and tasted some wine and they were back on safe ground until a commotion in the hallway changed things. A door closed noisily; keys rattled; then a voice called, 'It's me. Where are you?'

'Kitchen.'

James was on edge as soon as Wendy appeared. Their relationship was fractured; something had never clicked between them. She was spiky and abrasive. There was no mirth about her. James had always felt that Paul's decision to marry Wendy five years ago had been a mistake. He felt his friend had been drawn to the gorgeous siren and missed, or been deceived about, the full extent of a cold, vacuous soul.

'Hello James. Happy Christmas. Are you well?'

He confirmed that he was and returned the seasonal greeting. He had barely finished those words before Wendy turned to Paul.

'Is the meal going to be long? I need to change and get ready.'

There was an exchange of domestic niceties, concluding that the right thing was for Wendy to change once Paul and James were enjoying the pudding she would not share.

'James has news.'

She giggled and held out a hand to brush James' shoulder.

'Oooh; good news I hope?'

He wasn't smiling and, before he could reply, Paul provided the details: 'Sally has left him.'

Wendy's smile did a cartoon change and she rounded on James with a noise that combined a hiss, sigh and bark.

'For god's sake, James. What on earth did you do?'

She seemed unperturbed by his shocked expression and turned to her husband with a look of exasperation. Paul blinked slowly and shook his head at her.

'James? Why don't you go to the dining room and sort a gin and tonic for Wendy? You'll find all you need in there for that.'

James wandered from the kitchen and heard Paul say, 'That was well over the top. She only told him today...' and Wendy interrupted; '...it's just so typical of him...' then her voice became a whisper and he heard no more.

In the dining room James was confronted by something almost as bad as Wendy's contempt. This was the only house he knew where there was what amounted to a cocktail cabinet. It was so remote from James' domestic experience. If he had spirits in the house, which was rare, he kept them in a kitchen cupboard near large bottles, half-full of flat tonic water or dry ginger. Here, there were three different brands of gin, two of vodka plus countless whiskies and brandies. He counted more than a dozen other bottles of obscure liqueurs.

It got worse.

There were small tins of tonic water, dry ginger, soda and cola. A small, lidded cask with *Ice* written on it had matching tongs. There was a bowl of lime slices with cling film stretched over it. The ice bucket, used earlier to keep their beer cold, was saturated with condensation.

'Jesus. When was all this prepared? Who has the time to do this? And why?'

'However, much gin you've put in that drink, double it now.' Wendy tapped him on the arm, then stroked between his shoulder blades. These were not affectionate gestures. James turned round to look at her, mistrust glowering, as she kept talking.

'I shouldn't have spoken to you like that.'

'No.'

'It's a poor excuse but I just feel so stressed. We've had my parents here and that's never easy. They left this morning and I seem to have spent a whole week running around after people. I don't feel like I've had a rest. Sally must be a very stupid woman. You're a lovely man.'

Her concern for James was a distant second behind her own anxieties.

'We should get back to the kitchen. I'm sure Paul will need some help. Here.'

James handed her a cut glass tumbler, fizzing to the brim. But Wendy didn't move and stayed near him, wiggling a finger in her drink to mix it.

'Do you think Paul and you are alike?'

James shrugged. 'Yes. I suppose so.'

She sucked on her mixing finger then tossed back her head with a snort. 'You're nothing like each other. You have connections and coincidences; some things join you, but you could not be more different as people.'

She looked into his eyes as if searching for something. He said nothing, and Wendy smiled, almost in victory.

'Anyway; enough of that. Tell me what happened.'

She smiled in encouragement, as if her insensitive behaviour had never arisen. He'd seen this smile before. It was the one she turned on for photos; a fixed replica; not really a smile at all. But James embarked on another version of his tale, interrupted by Wendy's occasional questions and observations.

The story ended as Paul declared dinner was ready, thus drawing a line under the whole nagging, inconvenient, regrettable problem of James' and Sally's failed relationship.

2

But dinner was convivial and fun. As time passed and the meal progressed, Wendy was marginalised by their merciless musing. Paul and James, apparently, were friends again. Wendy left them after the main course and when she returned more than an hour later, buffed and coiffed, there was no longer a stage for their tableaux of classroom delinquency and bedroom fantasy.

She smiled without joy at her husband. 'Have you booked a taxi?'

'Not telling.'

This provocation caused her eyes to narrow. The mood darkened by several glimmers.

'Don't be childish please Paul.'

Sensing her growing annoyance and the possibility of a scene, James confirmed that a taxi had been booked.

'Good, then you can help clear away these things.'

Paul protested and told James to stay where he was. His hosts left the room, at loggerheads.

James checked his watch and called out, 'Do we really need a taxi? It's a short walk to Graham's; they're only in Bodenham Road.'

There was a muffled exclamatory noise from along the hall, then Wendy returned to the dining room emphasising her reply with hand gestures and finger pointing.

'James, I am not ruining my shoes, hair and makeup by walking – even for ten minutes – on a freezing cold winter's evening.' She smiled, once again, without mirth. 'But you're welcome to; we'll see you there.'

James smiled back. 'I will walk. It'll clear my head. Who's going? Do we know?'

She walked off with some glasses and now Paul was back in the dining room to collect and clear things. These comings and goings reminded James of a sixties television farce. Paul picked up the discussion.

'It'll be the old guard plus some inevitable new people. You know Gerry can't stop acquiring friends. Tonight may well involve new-found chums from ante-natal but I suspect it will be mainly the troops, just like old times.'

He didn't look as if this filled him with elation and he excused himself to go and change. James followed shortly after. Any hope that his jeans and T shirt might be acceptable attire had been dashed by Wendy, who was dressed as for the Opera.

In the bathroom, James splashed cold water onto his face. A mirror revealed what the last few days of seasonal consumption had wrought on his complexion.

You look fat. And old. But that's fixable. Even so, slow down and stick to wine.'

21

He changed his shirt, trousers and shoes, assessed himself in another mirror then returned to the kitchen to drink two pints of water. When the doorbell rang he answered the door, but no one was there. On the avenue, plumes of exhaust filled the chilly evening air and a powerful sounding engine throbbed with throaty menace. James called out that the taxi had arrived, that he would see them shortly and could they take his wine for him. No one responded.

Pulling on his coat, he crunched off in to the night to slither along streets and avenues that had been his stamping ground for most of the seventies. At a small roundabout he paused to look at the Rose & Crown public house which was garishly over-illuminated. James had drunk legally and illegally in that public bar. He'd thrown his highest ever darts score (167) completely by accident in the smoking room and tried pork scratchings, with an initial disgust that turned gradually to fervour. The impact of rum and blackcurrant or vodka and lime had, too often, proved his downfall inside and outside those hallowed walls.

'Fuck this party. Let's go and grab a pint of Trophy. Or whatever has replaced it.'

But he was still moving towards his destination and soon the sight of Paul and Wendy disembarking from their taxi showed James where his responsibilities lay. He walked on, though not before recalling with a smile that it was also in the Rose & Crown that Jenny Mitchell had sneakily stuffed her tongue in his mouth for his first ever French kiss.

Yes: he'd tasted it all in the Rose & Crown.

He turned in to a driveway and his brief bright mood was dimmed. Something, and not the lure of over-carbonated, strangely brown beer, made him feel that he should turn around and run off into the night.

James sometimes hated parties: smoke; drunks; clingy dresses; unimaginative food; pretence; deceit; awful wine; warm beer. Any or all could conspire to ruin his evening.

Yet he knew that sometimes those things could transform parties into something special. And then it dawned on him that, for the first time in three years, he was attending a party as a single man. A smile split his face and it widened when he reviewed the house in front of him. It served as a reminder of the adolescent revelry that often took place in houses like these. Ones with cellars; safe places where parents could contain the gathering without risk to carpets and ornaments. Underground, undetectable and ungoverned, a series of conventions would follow.

At an unfeasibly early point some yob was being sick; uncared for and shunned.

A makeshift dance area was lit by a dodgy sound-to-light unit and one of those projectors creating karmic, oily patterns on a wall. The music was mainstream rock and the odd chart hit but, eventually, songs like *I'm Not in Love* or *If You Leave Me Now* would float from the speakers to encourage people to get it on.

Within an hour or so of the start, the drinks area was awash. A trestle table masquerading as a bar was littered with empty beer cans but full cider bottles. People took cider but drank beer – the inconsiderate bastards. This location was generally deserted after around nine, by when juvenile drinking capacity had been surpassed.

The place had sticky, stale smelling carpets and seemed to be filled by brash teenage braying, couples concealed in corners and a piquant haze of smoke.

'I wonder sometimes how we ever enjoyed them. They could be destructive in a way. Was it an obligation? There was that one where all I did was snog Sarah. It was perfect, yet everyone kept telling me I was missing a great party. What were they doing that I wasn't? Standing in rooms and corridors; drinking; shouting; making bold, elaborate plays. All I was doing was falling in love.'

As James reached the door it swung inwards as he touched it.

'Surprise, Surprise! Happy Christmas,' wailed various, numerous, laughing voices. He adopted a fixed, slightly insane smile and walked in, scattering greetings like gunfire.

'Hello. Hello. Hi. It's really good to see you guys. HI!'

James was never appalled by the ease with which he lied. This minor celebrity act had become part of the package.

Paul confronted him. 'What kept you?'

'Pavements were slippy and I spent too long yearning for the Rose & Crown's dubious delights. Where can I get a drink?'

'You can say hello first: come here.'

A splendidly pregnant woman had grabbed James.

'Hi Gerry. Happy Christmas.'

He kissed her right cheek self-consciously, then her left with more affection. She smelled nice. Over her shoulder, he saw an old friend.

'Graham. How are you, mate?'

'Good.'

They shook hands warmly. James nodded at Gerry's bulging tummy.

'Yours?'

'Probably. Sorry to hear about the thing with Sally.'

'Me too. How was your Christmas?'

Paul cut across the recollection and repartee. 'I'll get some more drinks then.'

James noted impatience in Paul's voice. Deranged during the snowball fight and impatient now; his old friend seemed full of something problematic and testing.

'I never cease to be astonished by this house, Gra. It's huge. You must need servants.'

He kicked off the conversation but, instead of listening or engaging, James took stock of the scenes around him.

'This hallway is bigger than my entire flat. Nice print over there. And well lit. Vaguely in the style of Matisse. Did Matisse do lighting?'

James sniggered aloud. It didn't interrupt his hosts' gushing narrative about the size, benefits and contents of their home.

'There's Claire Bracewell with someone young and barely able to shave. And Malcolm Brown, whose spots look even more pubescent. Extraordinary. I wonder if Philippa is here.'

Paul had returned with three glasses of wine clutched in his hands. James caught his friend's eye; 'You okay?'

'Yes. Bit pissed actually, so trying to take it easy. Got you a red wine.'

James took the glass and sniffed warily at its contents.

A drunk emerged from an adjoining room. 'Merry Christmas Paul! How are you? Everything all right at Horsley's? I heard you were in a... James! My dear boy! It's overwhelmingly splendid to see you.'

This apparition hugged James.

'Leo, it's lovely to have a hug and it's great to see you too but please don't breathe on me. Your breath is repulsive.'

'My privilege entirely. You're looking well; doesn't James look well?' He emphasised this question with a look around the gathered friends.

'And you look rat-arsed. Merry Christmas.'

James raised his glass. He still hadn't taken a drink from it. Leo continued with his Wildean pastiche, a social speciality he'd adopted at Cambridge and which no one had the courage to tell him was an absurd nuisance.

'Well yes; rat-arsed, rat-arsing. That's one of my deviant pleasures. Certainly.'

Now they shook hands and smiled broadly at each other.

'Up here for long?'

'Home tomorrow.'

24

'Ah yes, home; and how are things in the Smoke?'

'I don't live in the Smoke. You're being parochial.'

'In fact, I'm not. I said *The Smoke* mainly because you always used to smoke but also because I actually have no idea where you live.'

Paul moved silently away. Leo watched him go then pulled a funny face at James, who queried; 'What?'

'Nothing. Tell you another time. Too pissed to be indiscreet.'

'I thought being pissed was the perfect state for indiscretion.'

'Not for serious indiscretion.'

At last James gulped some wine. It was too cold.

'Bloody buggery bollocks. Why can't people sort red wine out and get it to room temperature?'

'It's a scandal isn't it?'

'Thatcher must act.'

'I think she does; A Tragedy of Errors.'

James smiled and looked at his old friend with great affection and then with twinkling eyes.

'You do know where I live. You stayed there a little under two years ago; that weekend when we went to the rugby at HQ.'

'Are you sure?'

'You were pissed and indiscreet. You shagged someone in my kitchen. It was terribly frustrating from my lonely bedroom.'

'She was a very horny lady.'

'I guessed.'

'She called me not long after that; at work and home. How did she get my numbers I wonder?'

'That's indiscretion for you.'

Leo smiled then touched his glass against James'. 'Well played. Anyway, come on, ditch the dirt: how's life, love and Linda?'

'Linda?'

Leo winked at James. 'It begins with L and sustains the alliteration. Try and stay awake. I meant Sally of course. I suppose I could have gone for Lassie, which is more or less an anagram of Sally. But a bit too dog-like, especially for one of your girls.'

James chuckled and emptied his wine glass.

'Life could be worse but could be better. For instance, I'm not as drunk as you.'

'Try this; it's dynamite.'

Leo handed James a glass with an opaque, muddy yellow

25

liquid. It smelled horrible.

'What is it?'

'Pernod, tequila, grappa and Lilt.'

'You bloody animal. I'll stick to wine.'

'So come on, how's your love life?'

'Not bad. How's yours?'

'Non-existent. How would you define *not bad*?'

'Not so good. I've split up with Sally.'

'No shit?'

'Uh-huh.'

Leo reached out his hand and squeezed James' shoulder, then rubbed his upper arm. 'I'm really sorry. I thought you were good together. And I liked her; she was cool about me visiting that time.'

'It was a good job she was elsewhere that evening. She would not have let you shag someone in the kitchen. Or anywhere within earshot.'

'Hmm. But still, she understood the need for our sporting life. Do you want to talk about it or forget it?'

'I don't know.'

Leo had moved closer. Their conversation became completely secret and intimate so no one would hear a word. It seemed to James that something had shut down any outside noise so he started the saga once more, this time with a more objective appraisal than he had shared with Paul. At the end, Leo was serious and unsmiling.

'I can see that you must be pretty traumatised. What are you going to do?'

'Don't know. Take stock I think. Nothing hasty.'

'Sensible. Well listen; you know where I am and where to call me.'

'I feel stupid. I really don't understand her change of heart.'

'That's women for you. They do that.' James frowned as Leo continued, 'Come on. Let's get another drink. We'll sort you out.'

They wandered away from their spot. James felt he'd been cut off and that Leo's concern had been superficial. Something felt wrong.

The party was in full swing and things had changed since those cellar days. People were enveloped in conversations about themselves. No matter what subject matter was started, it all came back to Me, Myself and I. Music was tolerated, not loved – an unrebellious, easy, imperceptible wash. Drinks were served in glasses and no one drank from a can, especially not from a Party 7. Gone were the vomiting, groping and dancing.

Yet a pervasive sexual tension lingered. Not the hopeful, youthful, vigorous expectancy of teenage nights but the despair of adults. Men gazed hopelessly at women beyond their reach. Women tried not to stare back. People looked ruefully at apparently happier people. Frustration and missed opportunity were constant. Nothing was new. Nothing seemed sacred. Ten years after the certainty of a successful future, all that remained was an insular, divided wilderness.

But, of course, some inevitable, happy, perfect couples made up the numbers.

When Leo and James reached the kitchen they found Paul and Graham and a sudden silence. Leo embarked on a long and increasingly foul joke that broke the ice. There was sustained laughter. After several more such interludes, they cast a vote of sympathy for James. Leo told the others that that was women for you. Graham and Paul nodded.

James said, 'That's a fucking stupid thing to say once, and you've said it twice. You aren't half a wanker Leo.'

Leo was unmoved and smiled benignly at the group. 'At least I don't have to dress up.'

He was reminded of another dubious joke that left the four of them in pieces. Soon they were evoking the past.

'Do you remember that party at that house in the country somewhere? 1978? I can't remember whose it was. The one... the one when that bloke... I can't remember who it was... got half the city round while his parents were away?'

The past gripped them. It was easy to recall and relive. It prompted a conversation in which, despite four people being involved, the dialogue seemed to be spoken by just one of them. They had probably had a similar conversation, maybe this exact conversation, every time they met. Yet this rendition seemed new and revelatory.

'It was at Withington.'

'The place got trashed a bit.'

'It got trashed a lot.'

'Pretty unacceptable really.'

'Yes, very.'

'You raided the fridge as I recall. A fry-up?'

'Indeed I did.'

'Some nutters were playing that game of going round the room without touching the floor.'

'An entire bookcase came over.'

'Someone was quite badly hurt weren't they?'

'I don't remember that.'

'Didn't matey, the host, end up in hospital with alcohol poisoning?'

'They'd dragged him off before I even got there.'

'And you were desperately trying to shag that woman. The lovely blond. Paula.'

'Pamela. It was Pamela Bell. She wasn't interested though.'

'It was payback time.'

'How come?'

'You were stupid enough to stand her up that time.'

'Pamela Bell. She was a dirty bitch wasn't she?'

'Not in my brief experience, no.'

'Someone told me she ended up known as Pamela Bell-End.'

They laughed. They smiled. They sighed. This always united them.

But it didn't last. Gerry dragged Graham away to greet more late arrivals. Leo saw someone he fancied and left the kitchen.

Paul looked at James with a wry smile. 'Are you all right?'

'It's good to be with friends and have the anaesthesia of all this wine and pointless recall.'

Paul offered no comment. James continued, 'You seem a bit less wound up now. What was wrong earlier?'

'Nothing to worry about. Look, sorry, but I've got to go and talk to someone from work who's here. She... I... we need to resolve something before work resumes next week. Why don't you mingle a bit? Wendy's somewhere. Or you could offer some skin care advice to Mally Brown.'

James laughed.

'Meet me back here in an hour. I'll try to round up Leo and Gra for more filth and a few gargles.'

'Mingle.'

James imagined a cloud of urine in a swimming pool. Mingling. Suddenly a hand smashed through the cloud creating several new clouds. Gradually the urine became part of the whole pool, diluted and made harmless by chemicals. Mingled.

He rejoined the hubris of the main event and looked in vain for someone to fool around with. It had been such uncomplicated fun with the lads in the kitchen. James wanted an extended bout of the nonsense. He tried talking to strangers but couldn't take them seriously. He briefly engaged with one or two minor acquaintances but soon lost interest. This was not a social success.

James returned to the kitchen for more wine. Once there he stood staring from the window into the deep December darkness. He could see nothing, but it was better than looking at something he didn't want to see.

He was agitated and anxious: about how things had ended with Sally; about his lack of empathy with a soulless, bland gathering; about the obvious and increasing lack of sincerity in Paul.

'Hello James. Are you avoiding me?'

He spun as slowly as he could, but still too fast for the rules of cool. A smile split his face.

'Philippa! Hello. It's incredibly nice to see you; and looking fucking brilliant, actually.'

He was stammering, blushing, rushing.

'Oh James; your poetic, romantic greetings never fail to make a girl feel spectacular.'

They laughed and walked into a hug that lasted until just before James had a hard-on.

'How long have you been here?'

'Less than half an hour. Been chatting to Gerry about babies.' She made a yawning gesture and smiled at him. 'But it's been a while, so let's talk. It's the end of the eighties in a week and I need to know how you survived these tortured times. We've hardly seen one another in a whole decade.'

'You haven't got a drink. And where's Adrian?'

'In London. He was unable to travel because of work commitments. I nearly stayed too but when I heard about all the snow here, I just had to get home. So I'm all yours.'

James couldn't conceal how pleased this made him. 'Good. So what are you drinking? Wine?'

'Yes. I had some white but left it somewhere. Something dry please.'

He looked in the fridge and soon selected an unopened bottle.

'Sancerre?'

'Yes, if it's white and dry.'

He rummaged around for a corkscrew and, having found one, opened the bottle and filled two clean glasses. As he poured, James looked at Philippa. An expert would probably claim she was no classical beauty, but in James' eyes she was perfect. The deep, wild sensuality he'd first seen when they were sixteen had never deserted her. She had dark auburn hair, big green eyes and the most kissable mouth. She was slim but curvy and sexy.

29

Now, as he approached with her wine, she held an imaginary microphone under his nose.

'James Clifton: artist; sex symbol; rock of our age. Let's hear it; how were the eighties for you?'

James affected a cod American accent.

'It was awesome. Totally awesome, and a wonderful thing.'

Philippa chuckled and picked up on the accent.

'Well viewers, there you have it. James Clifton gives the eighties an ultimate accolade. More after these words.'

She sipped some wine and her eyebrows indicated approval.

'But let's have a proper conversation. I'm curious about what's been happening. Paint some colour on to your silhouette.'

'Well, how do you mean? Big things or little things? Thatcher and Scargill? Or work and love? What are you after?'

This made Philippa look at him with such purpose and consequence that he knew he still loved her. He felt as if her look was lifting him from the ground and spinning him around her head. It was like he had taken an E. Her gaze was mind-altering.

'I can relive all those big memories in the papers on January the first. Tell me about your love life since 1980. You have two minutes. Or can you manage for longer?'

The tease was lost and James launched into a tale that revealed how hapless his love life, relationships and self-esteem had been since he left Hereford in 1978. She held up a hand to stop him once he reached a seventh straight year of being single and onanistic.

'What about Sally? Was it Sally? I met her in the Grapes. That was the last time I saw you wasn't it? Year before last.'

'Yes, the Grapes; and Sally was with me. You were horrible to me.'

'Pure jealousy James; you know how much I fancy you when you're unavailable.'

'I'm available now.'

Philippa seemed bewildered. 'Really? How come? I thought you were altar-bound?'

'No; we've split up.'

The tiger eyes squinted, then flashed. 'Not a very nice Christmas present. Whose fault?'

'She says it's mine. I probably do too.'

'Tell me the truth. What happened?'

'I didn't do any of the right things.'

'Did you mistreat her?'

'I just didn't open up to her.'

'You always had that; being closed and remote with people. The way you did that with other people put me off you, when I should have been on you.'

A group had come in search of drinks and Philippa nodded her head to one side indicating a new location outside the kitchen. James grabbed the wine bottle and followed her to some seats in the hallway. They sat side by side.

'So sex and love need a new direction in the nineties. What about work and, more especially, what about your art?' Philippa looked with great curiosity into his eyes. 'Tell me about the last painting you did.'

As had happened with Leo, it seemed as if something now closed in around them. James felt that he was in a vacuum with Philippa and they were completely alone.

'It's a still life, as yet untitled, mainly because it's unfinished. There's a tree in the small garden at our office. It's surrounded by paving stones and gravel and gets little or no care. I think someone tends it every month. It's standing there and all around is corporate concrete; mirrored glass. Around September time, there was a re-shuffle of desks at work and my team ended up on that side of the building with a view of this tree. And I realised how extraordinary it looks.'

'What kind of tree is it?'

'Well I wasn't sure, and you can guess that no one else had a fucking clue. So I took a photo, went to the local Wyevale and found out it's an acer. It's got these leaves that are deep maroon and it's incredibly frail looking. After a few days of seeing it from this new angle, I just thought it would be cool to do a kind of serial: four paintings; each with three segments; one segment for each month. I've done October, November and December. January will get done sometime in the New Year. I've done each segment in the third week of each month and will keep doing it that way. The first three months look different because October was warm and sunny, November was cold and windy and December was a misty, damp day. And of course, the leaves wilted and died in those months.'

'How are you taking home the memory of the way it looks on each specific day? A photo?'

James explained that it is all in his head. To keep perspective and tone he'd done a base sketch showing the tree alongside its environment.

'On the days that I decide to do the painting, I get a sketch pad and do a kind of cloak showing the colours around a line, which represents the tree. Back at home, I work it up into a full image – a kind of draft – using pastels. Then, as soon as possible, I convert that into an acrylic painting.'

'It sounds wonderful James. I'd like the January to March one please; my favourite time of year.'

James smiled. Someone was listening.

'You can have all of them. I'd like you to have something I've created.'

'Thank you. I'd like that too. But what about the last ten years? Where have you been successful with your wonderful skills?'

'Nowhere.'

'That's ridiculous. You've just described something incredible to me. Something anyone with eyes in their head would want to look at. How come you can't convert any of your great strengths as an artist and creative spirit into something lucrative?'

'I just can't. I have a drive to do the paintings and drawings. I just don't have a route or mechanism that takes them away from my home to a marketplace.'

'That's sad.'

Philippa licked her upper lip and looked pensively at James. 'I thought about you the other day. We needed someone to do graphics for the title sequence on a training video. The project lead was desperate for something new and different by someone who wasn't just one of the usual suspects. I so wanted to name you. But where were you?'

'At home watching telly and scratching my balls. Sorry; it's just never going to happen. And now it's your turn, but first, I need another glass of wine. Here.'

James topped up her glass.

'Thanks. This is lovely. What did you call it?'

'Sancerre.' He spelled the word. 'It's French, from the Loire valley. So are you still carving a niche in the film world?'

'No. That wasn't going anywhere. There was work but it was infrequent. I'm not patient enough to be a part-time earner. Even though the money was brilliant when I got it, it was just too scary. So I decided to step back into something less fulfilling but more secure. I've joined a firm that provides all sorts of creative services to clients. I'm doing things for television, radio programmes, adverts. It's sort of an insurance policy being with the firm but, strictly speaking, I'm freelance. Anyway, some of my stuff's being used. You know that advert for KitCrunch, the cat food?'

'You wrote that music?'

'Absolutely.'

'It's awful.'

'It's awful. True. But it's earned me plenty.'

'Not giving a tinker's cuss for the struggling artist.'

She chuckled. 'You might be the only person I know who still quotes Monty Python. You're funny.'

'I try to be.'

'But it's terribly passé James. You should probably stop doing it.'

'Right.'

James listened as Philippa talked about her current project and then about how she might soon be ready to settle down permanently with Adrian.

'She must love him. What a shame; he sounds like an arsehole.'

'James?'

'Sorry; I was miles away. I had floated off listening to you. I haven't talked with someone like this for months.'

'Not even with Sally?'

'Not even with her. Maybe at the start. But somehow we...'

'Hey, stop. I don't want to know. But I'd like some reminders about things I've forgotten, and I'm a bit drunk now so this is just fun. When's your birthday?'

'April 14th.'

'Year born?'

'1960.'

'Of course. Where are you living now?'

'Richmond. Surrey, not Yorkshire.'

'Favourite colour?'

'Violet.'

'Lucky number?'

'Mmmm, six.'

'Why?'

'No idea; why did you ask?'

'I'm asking the questions, James. Where was your last holiday?'

'Haven't had one for years.'

'Really? How bizarre. Favourite food?'

'Prawn Cocktail. Sirloin steak, chips and peas. Black Forest gateau.'

Philippa dissolved with mirth. For what seemed like several minutes he could get no sense from her and it was the last of their private discussion. Gerry came by, curious about Philippa's helpless laughter and soon others had burst into their enclave. Twenty minutes or so of precious, tender, real conversation were over.

Some time later, James realised that he and Philippa hadn't said goodbye.

Wendy laughed aloud. 'I wish you'd seen them. It's so transparent and he thinks I'm blind to it.' Her laugh was a coarse, rasping sound; false and insincere, like her smile. James didn't get the joke; he'd had enough and wanted his bed. Wendy wanted talk; and a nightcap.

They'd all left the party together shortly before two. Paul was uselessly drunk and it took James ages to get his friend into the taxi. To help things along, Paul was speaking what was left of his mind. It started with drunken, slavering affection; 'You're my mate you are. I love you.'

And expressions of how fortunate he was to have Wendy. 'She's gorgeous my wife; gorgeous; and fucking perfect. She'll do anything.'

But soon the gloves were off. Throughout the short journey, Paul berated the taxi driver for leering at Wendy. And, as he dragged the useless form from car, to door, to bedroom, Paul's ire was fully directed at James who smiled amiably as he was abused. For being a nothing. For not coming to the wedding. For being useless with women.

'You're a fucking loser Clifton. You've blown it. All of it.'

James threw this bag of bile onto a bed at which point Wendy entered the fray. She started to scream at Paul who, by now, could only drool expletives. He soon lapsed into an alcoholic coma. His wife's words were wasted.

James thought about slinking off to risk a bollocking for waking his parents; it would be a picnic after this. But, as if the scene had never happened, Wendy turned to him and told him to make them a coffee while she assured Paul's comfort and safety. James' watch showed that it was two forty-five. He would be driving more than one hundred and fifty miles in about eight hours. With a sigh, he trudged down to the kitchen and brewed up some instant coffee; the ideal accompaniment to the *ersatz* conversation he knew was coming.

And here they were in the living room where he and Paul had listened to New Order the previous evening. Wendy's litany was unaccompanied and as she went off to make some drinks, James stared drunkenly at her, admiring her very lovely figure. When she handed him a glass of brandy she leaned over, presenting the opportunity for him to look down the front of her frock. She was pretty drunk too and tottered as she stepped away from him. He thought about standing up to offer support but remained seated. Something was nagging at him: he kept imagining that Paul would appear in the doorway, like Nosferatu the Vampyre. He liked the look of Wendy's body but he didn't want his throat torn out.

'So now you know how it happened. How Paul ended up with this woman. The skin-deep appeal of that body is hard to resist. And if it would stop her talking you might well be tempted. Fool.'

'So, James; what about my prick of a husband and his monstrous bullshit?'

'That's just the drink talking isn't it?'

'Do you reckon? I'm not so sure. He goes off on these business trips and simply drowns himself in alcohol as if it's part of the deal. I've tried to point it out to him, but he just laughs and denies it's a problem. Yet it's reached the point where just a couple of drinks make him turn nasty. God knows how much he had tonight, and it wasn't the first time I've heard him talk as if I'm some sort of whore. I dread to think what he's said behind my back. Tonight was horrible. He ruined my evening. In fact, I hardly saw him all night. He barely spoke to me after about midnight.'

She was getting agitated and chewed at her bottom lip. 'If you hadn't been here when we got back, I might have killed him.'

James sat up, startled. 'Hold on. That's just preposterous. And very wrong.'

She looked sorrowfully at her drink and hiccupped, then sighed theatrically. Tears sprang from her eyes and her voice became thick with emotion.

'I didn't mean that the way it sounded. I still love him; he still means everything to me. But this affair he's having is just killing us. He's more or less ignoring me when we're here alone. That's why I was late for dinner. I just had to get out somewhere. He only talks when he's fired up with drink. I don't understand him. Why is he so incapable of hurting others, but I get all that?'

James didn't know where to put himself. This wasn't his old friend. Paul had always been sex mad, impulsive and completely incapable of fidelity. But he wasn't cruel, or vicious, as it now seemed Wendy was saying.

'Forgive me; poor James. You must be so sad and all I can do is to tell you my problems. I wish I could do something for you.' She looked sluttily at him. 'You can do much better than Sally you know. But keep right away from Philippa; she's bad for you and definitely not the answer.'

James sighed and began a defence of Philippa that lasted until a noise revealed Wendy had fallen asleep. A large amount of gin and tonic had spilled all over her, the sofa and the carpet. Her posture also revealed that she had nothing on under her frock.

'Go on: shag her. It's all there and the talking has stopped, so there is no boring, shallow dialogue to endure. No, fool; go to bed. Now.'

3

As he set off for Richmond, he waved to his family and pushed The Cure's *Disintegration* into the cassette player. He'd been playing it constantly since its release, and now it seemed ubiquitous.

The roads were clear and the music was soothing so he had time to get his head around all that had happened in the last few days. Initially, he was concerned with the telephone which, chez Clifton, was not supposed to ring at Christmas. External intervention was viewed as invasive and un-Christian, so the two calls made to James during Boxing Day were momentous. His mother always answered the phone and, on this occasion, her West Country accent became guarded. This meant the caller was a stranger. She motioned with the receiver to James saying, 'It's for you.'

He took the call in the study along the hallway. He was glad of the interruption.

'Hello, James speaking.'

A woman's voice said, 'Hello James.'

He had no idea who it was.

'If I said *This is Laura Drysdale speaking*, what would you say?'

'I'd say *Hello Laura Drysdale-Speaking*.'

'An old one; but okay; this is me; Laura Drysdale.'

'Hello Laura Drysdale; how are you today?'

She laughed and James was mesmerised.

'I'm fine. Except don't I ring any bells?'

'You made my phone ring.'

'We were at...'

The pips went. He said, 'What's your number? I'll call you back...'

This drowned out her saying, 'I've run out of change, call me back on...'

He frowned at the receiver for a moment. This Laura knew

stuff: an ex-directory phone number; that he was there; that he is James Clifton. He made a mental note to ask someone about Laura Drysdale-Speaking.

Back in the sitting room someone had managed to get the television switched on, but it didn't stop Mother from talking.

'So James, you are going out tonight?'

'Yes. Heading to Paul Thomas's at around five, then on to a party at Graham W's place.'

Conversation moved on, the siblings quizzed about old haunts, friends and acquaintances. James picked up a sketchpad, flipped over a page and began to draw a gallows.

When the telephone rang again, James was sure it would be Laura calling back. He leapt up, but his mother beat him to the phone.

'And a Happy Christmas to you too Sally.'

He didn't hear his mother's next words. He felt guilty that he had so wanted this call to be Laura.

But why on earth was Sally calling him? They had spoken late on Christmas Eve; she was supposed to be on her way to France; they had agreed that communication would be difficult, but unnecessary.

'Here's James for you now.'

He was back in the study where a fluorescent orange gloom filtered through the window. He breathed in and picked up the phone.

'Hi Sally. I thought we were incommunicado.'

'Hello James. Mother and I delayed our departure. And I'm... I've been... James, I've decided to call it a day for us. This time it's got to be a permanent end. All the weeks apart hurt, and our reunion was good. So this isn't easy. But after you drove off to Hereford, I realised how many questions remain unanswered for us.'

There was silence for countless seconds.

'What we have isn't sustainable. I can't live in stasis and I won't live with a reality where your past means more than our present. You're trapped in a rut and I don't think I have whatever is needed to get you out of it. You won't let me in; you won't let me take us to a better future. I want to be in a close, real, human relationship. But you know what? There's just this truth that you're cold, unfeeling and uncaring. You simply don't give anything. And I can't go on like that.'

Her voice cracked slightly.

His voice was low when he spoke. 'So what was the point of

even pretending that we were back together?'

'I know. I know. And yet I don't know. Maybe I was trying to convince myself that we could work. But you left me alone. You drove off and I looked at that and thought; this is it; this is how James will always be; heading off to a place I don't belong; his past in little Hereford.'

'I offered to stay. I wanted to stay. But you had your fucking skiing in Chamonix to go to. I'd have been on my own.'

'Don't swear at me.'

'Why the fuck not? Jesus Sally, this is unbelievable.'

'Goodbye.'

Once again James was left holding a buzzing receiver. He lay back and the chair reclined with him. After several moments he found that he couldn't hold back his tears.

....

A car raced past him and James dropped a gear to take up the challenge. He soon caught up with the chase, but then backed off. It wasn't out of the question that he was still over the limit from yesterday's revelry. Better to attract no attention.

....

Carol had taken him and the dogs to walk in the frosty evening air. Their exhaled breath created clouds of steam, like halos, and the snow was hard and dangerous underfoot. The dogs slid about, searching for smells and territories.

'What are you going to do?'

'Nothing.'

'Oh? Why not?'

'Because I don't think there's anything I can do.'

'Is that for the best?'

'Don't know. Don't care. I'll sort something out.'

'Come on James. Talk to me.'

'There's nothing to say. Probably, and isn't hindsight a wonderful fucking thing, this was always going to happen. I'm not going to over analyse. It's over. She's done it. '

Carol squeezed his arm. 'Surely you can't just let her walk away.'

James shook his head. 'There's nothing to fight for. Something has changed since I left to come here. So forget it. Change the subject.'

Their pace slowed and they soon turned for home. Carol had stopped digging and they spoke of trivialities. Cold and silent, they arrived at the gate leading into the back garden.

Carol brushed her brother's face with her hand. 'How do you feel now?'

'I feel nothing.'

....

He jumped on the brakes. His race opponent was stationary ahead of him and James had seen him very late. He swore quietly, told himself off then slammed the gear lever to second, smashed a fist on the horn and roared past the other car. The adrenalin rush and banshee howl of his engine made him feel better.

....

Many people had seen Sally's influence on James as positive. There was a facelift, then re-branding, toning and smartening. Layers had seemed to be stripped away to release a spiritually altered James Clifton.

Till their meeting three years earlier, James had been introverted and charismatic by turn. Anyone who cared enough to evaluate him found him confused and confusing. Though he was generally not loved, few people genuinely disliked him.

He was easily bored by mass male company and preferred the friendship of women. Yet, despite a degree of charm, he was painfully shy so lasting relationships were few and far between. This made him accept easy, short-term girlfriends and a weakness for infatuation with disinterested remote women who left him obsessive and grasping.

James drank and smoked more than was good for him. But he balanced that with a sensible diet, running, squash and football. Those physical activities also fed his competitive needs but he didn't carry that drive and determination into any other endeavours, especially his skills as an artist.

He'd been able to copy and draw almost as soon as he could hold a crayon and it was a delight to his parents until they realised he lacked essential skills. His reading and writing abilities developed slowly and he was awful with figures. His creativity was therefore discouraged in favour of the basics.

By his teens, James had begun to produce exciting things; but this still prompted his parents to talk of art as a useful hobby, to sustain him in adulthood. Despite passing A-levels in Art, English Literature and French, James was tainted by this indifference and was left with just one ambition: life in the real world. He declined the option to go to university and within four months of leaving school had a job as an assistant buyer with a printing firm in Slough. He rented a small flat in Datchet, started earning, and waited for the sex and drugs and rock and roll to overwhelm him.

But he was in a new, challenging and unexpectedly sober world. His life to that point had been simple, middle-class, protected and relatively privileged. Hereford had been like a big village: sedate, rural, and of a different era. Suddenly, he was in a diverse, complex environment, unprepared for the different value streams he encountered in people. It was 1978, and England was changing, but James was more or less apolitical. He couldn't follow arguments that changed nothing, remained unresolved and became bitterly entrenched. During that winter, and the discontent that swept the Conservatives and Margaret Thatcher to power, James realised he hadn't a clue about the root causes of the Callaghan Government's problems and about the alternatives posed. Within a single day at work, he was called a *rich cunt,* and *red scum.* James knew he was neither, but couldn't understand why anyone would think it of him. This drove him away from such people, their debates and any engagement in activism. Instead, he sought solace and found it in his art.

His home was tiny and became cluttered by his work. Unable to afford the alternative properties he saw at the rental company, James searched jobs pages, registered with agencies, and attended interviews. There was limited return from this and he found that the small number of offers he received were accompanied by an inadequate package.

He persevered and finally received a good deal that increased his salary and made him senior buyer at an insurance firm. James commuted for six months then moved to Richmond, where he was much closer to the company's Chiswick base. Savings and cash scrounged from various sources, plus a tiny trade in on his car, created the deposit for a two bedroomed flat near the town centre. He could just about afford the mortgage but needed a significantly more modest standard of living as a result.

For a year or more James worked hard and progressed well in his job. Otherwise, he spent most of his time painting, drawing and sketching. Cocooned in this life, he lost touch with people and became something of a loner.

When he finally crawled from under that stone in late 1981, he was pleased to find that he had more friends and money than he thought. He bought an old Triumph TR6, engaged in a mainly office-based social life and had occasional brief affairs. This reduced his creative outputs to little or nothing. Instead, with material things to comfort him, he played hard and partied whenever he could. He found no motivation to achieve anything more than just making it through the week. He also fell in line with the times and, over the next eighteen months, developed a lifestyle grander than his resources could sustain. The ensuing level of personal debt didn't trouble him; it simply added to his burgeoning sense of being a failure.

He met Sally in a pub, unplanned and unexpected, on New Year's Eve, 1986. James and a small group of work mates had boycotted the formal company party and ventured out to the pubs and bars around Richmond.

Sally was sitting in the bar, dejected and diminished by a failed engagement. James caught her eye a few times and she never looked away. As the midnight hour approached, he was standing close enough for an opening greeting and small talk. When he mumbled a suggestion that they both deserved a New Year's kiss, Sally agreed. Before James' astonishment had subsided, she demanded another kiss and it was a long one.

They left together when the pub closed, after some determined snogging and a conversation containing many platitudes. They were both drunk and talked nonsense as they walked to the taxi rank from where, eventually, a cab whisked her away to Kingston. Before she left him, James suggested they meet the next evening for dinner.

Six months later, they were co-habiting but with no permanent arrangement. Her family and home were in Winchester and since leaving university and starting work in London she'd been sharing a house with friends in Kingston. She'd commuted every Monday and Friday to and from Hampshire but as things evolved with James, they spent most weekdays and weekends in his home.

Sally's arrival in his life caused a new James to materialise: assured; competent; productive; responsible; restrained. He stopped smoking and his drinking was pared back. Sally became his drug of choice. All of this began during their early courtship, but the pace of change soon accelerated. They compromised and haggled; it was tough and sometimes wasn't pretty. Sally had a wealthy background, an expensive education, easy graces and big ambitions. She was dominant, extrovert, confident and strong. At twenty-eight she had a successful career, positive ideas and well-argued opinions. James liked all that. He took it in his stride, calmed down, smartened up and enjoyed eighteen months of being part of something wonderful.

He no longer felt so worthless.

Change had happened.

When the relationship passed its second anniversary, James started to feel that Sally had lost interest. This was completely wrong, but James contrived to feel hurt and miserable and to

41

sense doubt in every situation. He shared none of this and it became like a millstone; dragging him down; confusing him and making him emotionally shrivelled. He didn't discuss it because he dreaded confrontation. He believed that he didn't want a solution. He became convinced that it had to end. Occasionally he stayed out till the very early hours with neither explanation nor notice. He wasn't sinning; he was just stupid.

Sally, who sought commitment and stability, tried to get James to engage. But whenever she tied him down in a discussion, he was content to say everything was fine and she shouldn't worry. Sally kept trying, but they were drifting away from one another. James' home and household remained as an anchor where they were civil and shared exactly what they had always shared. But Sally stayed less and less.

He soon turned full circle and became desperate for things to be right again. But he couldn't communicate it to Sally. Her frustration deepened into incomprehension and, six months before this present Christmas, she said they had to separate then find a way to reunite. James agreed. He was shattered by his inability to resolve this and by the experience of watching Sally remove her things back to the house in Kingston. James blamed himself and viewed this not as a separation, but as an end. Sally's plans for them to maintain communications and to work hard on a solution didn't really register with James as something with which he was required to participate.

As if released from prison, James embarked on some nonsense. He realised how many beers, kebabs, curries and nights out he'd missed. He indulged himself with drugs, nightclubs, raves and some clumsily cute flirtations.

That phase lasted until James realised he missed Sally. He stared from windows wondering why and how he could have caused such a mess. But nothing changed and, after five months of separation, he was resigned to the fact that he had lost. He felt alone and exposed. He was almost completely disinterested in the Christmas festivities around him and resented the fun others were having. He received greetings cards addressed to Sally & James which hurt his feelings. He wanted someone to share the magic. He really wanted to be back in her arms.

One evening in mid-December he got home from work, changed and collected a bottle of wine before crawling through the Friday traffic to Kingston. When she saw James, Sally smiled and let him in. He was relieved to find that her friends were already out for the evening and, without pre-amble, James told Sally he wanted her back. She hugged him and agreed that she wanted it too and they both started to shed tears. They went to the pub to talk, had a few drinks and, later, made love with great passion. James believed, instantly, that his life was back on track and in the days before Christmas it seemed their relationship was renewed.

Until Boxing Day.

James was interrupted again and spent five minutes terrorising a small car, demure at forty-five miles per hour. He was concentrating so hard on staying within fifteen feet of the car's bumper that he missed at least four passing opportunities.

The events of Boxing Day, and the heavy irony linking his attendance at a reunion of school friends with Sally's condemnation of his outlook on past, enveloped him in silence. As he drove between Cheltenham and Oxford, the sky deepened to a silvery charcoal. More snow was coming so he quickened his pace when possible and made his thoughts dive down.

At Oxford he took a break, parked in St. Giles and grabbed a coffee and cake at a café in the High Street. At Magdalen Bridge, he gazed down at the Cherwell and its punts tied up in rows, unused for the winter. James mused on a collective noun for punt, settling on a shortlist of: *Woolsack*; *Cantab*; and *Brothel*. Somewhat cheered, he turned to stroll back. It was very cold and, when he reached the car, some half-hearted snow was flurrying.

Back on the road, stuttering through more purposeful snow and increasingly tentative traffic, James started to feel much worse. He had resisted Sally's words from the previous day and blocked out the criticism, bitterness and sorrow of her message. Staring from his car at the snow, the blackening sky and blurring red glow from the car he was following, he felt trapped. He shuddered with sadness. The lights around him exploded like fireworks through the tears in his eyes.

Nearly three hours later he turned in to the small car park at his block of flats. It had been a terribly slow and increasingly treacherous trip down the M40, and even worse in the London area. Grabbing a small bag of Christmas presents, James hurried from his car to the communal main entrance where he found his mailbox contained a dump of unsolicited deliveries.

He let himself in to his flat, threw the junk mail on the floor and the bag of delights on a chair. He needed two trips to retrieve more bags and it was seven o'clock when he lit the fire and slumped down on the sofa, cursing all over again his decision to buy first floor accommodation.

When he woke up at eight, the room was snugly warm. He'd dribbled down one side of his chin leaving a gooey mess on his shirt collar. He switched on the television and, as he made coffee, realised there was a small white envelope perched on the kitchen window sill with two other letters. Sally's handwriting, classical and navy blue, had inscribed the word *James* on the envelope.

'James,

Please don't hate me for what's happened. I've hurt you, I know, and it isn't what I meant to do; but I couldn't really do this any other way. It's much better that we should part now than go on fooling each other that there's something round the corner that marriage or children or simply being together will solve. You aren't getting on; just along. I want my life to be a changing fluid life. You can't provide that. But please don't hate me. I will always love you for what we had and for what you have given me.

I stayed here after you left and it's been cold; so I had the heating on full. I used the phone a lot too. I put some things in the freezer so there's something for you to eat. I've left my set of keys in the bathroom cabinet, except for the deadlock one which I will post back to you soon.

Take care, and be good to yourself – Sally.'

James slurped his coffee and, for the first time in a long time, fancied a cigarette. He tried to reply to Sally but gave up when five attempts contained nothing but invective. So he sprawled on the sofa and, while watching television, opened the two less consequential mail items. He soon took out a box file with *Personal* scrawled on the spine and filed away this post.

Sally had made James organise his life when she discovered his levels of fiscal and domestic negligence. With her guidance and discipline he had no overdraft, no credit card debts and no unpaid bills. She got him to save and invest; to buy rather than spend. She made him use a set time, usually each Saturday morning, to maintain that control.

Now it seemed the legacy of his life with Sally was a bulging box file and a schedule of administration.

A second folder caught his eye. *School* was scribbled on it and inside were two rolled up photographs, letters, certificates, copies of reports and football awards from two successive seasons in the First XI.

His very first day at that school was seared on his memory and he easily evoked the scenes. A mass of life, grey or black peppered with green and silver. Towering teachers with mortarboards, flowing gowns and coloured furry hoods stalked the school like automatons. The Autumn Term of 1971 began with a series of processes and ended with a label. A violent, hateful ducking process was ignored by anyone in authority and resistance was momentous. James got a torn shirt, his tie knotted so tight it had to be cut off him later and his ear full of cold water. But he smiled at his assailants to show that he had enjoyed it, that he had been blooded and was now part of the gang. One of them hit him on the nose. Another kicked his shin. James' smile faded to a quivering lip.

He flicked through the documents, a dismal compendium recording for posterity his perceived lack of achievement and wasted talent. On each report the Headmaster was judge and jury. The man had been a Classicist at Magdalen College, Oxford and, even though he was relatively young, his time had passed. At a 1950s prep school he would have been a great source of learning. But he was completely lost in a 1970s school that was slowly becoming co-educational and that crackled with that decade's changes in youth culture and needs. From parkas to platforms, Slade to Kraftwerk, mullets to mohicans this Headmaster was out of his depth. And, winning out against a number of candidates, James had been a primary bête-noire, a fact that dripped from summaries like this:

'James seems to have given up. No one can get it through to him that he has only ten weeks to organise his life for its supreme effort so far. On a personal level, he seems oblivious to the impression he gives to the world at large. He sometimes seems to care and to want respect. But his behaviour, thoughtlessness, immaturity and above all his bizarre set of values set him aside. I fear greatly for James' chances in these coming exams.'

James' parents gated him because of that, crystallising into certainty his suspicion that he didn't belong in the school and had no empathy from parents who couldn't bend towards his feelings. He always proved everyone wrong by getting good exam results, yet these O and A level certificates were symbols not of success but of conflict; stiff paper, marking triumph and achievement, from which nothing had resulted. James knew his decision to walk away from education was a reflex, and badly thought through. He sighed heavily. This was still a memory that tormented him.

James unravelled the two school photographs and cheered up. The first was one of those two feet long ones taken with a camera that scanned the rows of kids from one end to the other. James still loved the fact that Colin Nimmo was smiling from both ends of the picture. The second was taken in the spring of 1978 and he knew the precise location of everyone that mattered: Leo, Paul, Geraldine, Philippa, Graham, Sarah; and others. The faces smiled back at him, as they always had.

With a tiny smile in return, halfway between love and regret, James packed away the folder and headed to his bed.

4
The Art of History

He woke a little too early, troubled by an internal skirmish between sloth and vitality. Lying snugly inert, he wanted to sulk; disconnect the phone; stay indoors and stew in his self-pity.

But another side favoured action.

'Do something. Get out of this bed, eat, dress and spend some time painting. Use how you feel. Make it count.'

After some dozing and contemplative genital manipulation, James decided walking and fresh air were needed. More overnight snow had created a picture book winter's scene in the park near his apartment block. Trees held the eerie iciness that James adored about winter landscapes and the snow was unspoiled by footprints or other tracks. Like a child eager to romp, James donned a warm coat and wellies then headed out into the chilly morning air. He sensed inspiration and enjoyed an hour trudging in the snow, recovering some equilibrium.

He returned home with a newspaper, milk and a frozen pizza. The walk had sharpened his senses and he was ready to get on with something. For an hour or so, he sat in an easy chair sketching ideas. He worked with energy and was a study of control. His activity was interspersed with frequent reviews when he held the pad at arm's length squinting at its contents.

Once he had completed an initial group of ideas, James returned to his files and soon found a photograph of Sally smiling happily for the camera. He studied her for several moments; shoulder-length dark hair framed her face perfectly; brown eyes looked sexy but challenging. The challenge was maintained in her smile.

James discarded this and filtered through more photos, then stopped when another attracted him. It showed James and Sally arm in arm; she was gazing at him with great affection; he was looking benignly at the camera, seemingly embarrassed by her attention in public. It was a perfect reflection of their early relationship.

In the spare bedroom, James propped this photo on a shelf then started to assemble the tools of his trade. He chose some tubes of paint and mixed them until a flesh tone appeared on his palette. Soon he was at work with brushes.

It was evening when he took a break. He ate the pizza, lukewarm and greasy, with the television as company. There was nothing on of interest but he sat changing channels and swearing gently at the programmes. When the news started, he said *bollocks* after each headline then switched channels. A celebrity interviewer, also lukewarm and greasy, was talking to a non-entity on a chat show sofa.

James yelled in fury at the telly. 'And YOU can fuck off as well.'

Now he hit the remote control's buttons at random, smothering them with cheesy smears. He switched to teletext and checked the schedules. There really was nothing on.

Back in his studio he turned on an angle poise lamp and directed it at the canvas. It gave the painting a garish, dazzling quality and James felt deflated. There were two arms with hands reaching towards each other. The hand on the left was gentle and soft; smooth, slender and manicured with polished crimson nails. A simple gold ring banded a finger and a silvery bracelet dangled from the wrist. The other arm and hand were rougher and sinewy; a ragged, dirty bandage swathed the wrist and thumb.

Overcoming his sense of doubt and dismay, James pressed on and it was past two o'clock when he finished.

He was up at first light and running on streets free from snow and ice; a thaw had started. The exercise left him shaking; every muscle kicked and screamed at the punishment and negligence of an over-indulgent Christmas. He used all his hot water in a twenty minute shower that refreshed and revived. James was ready to review yesterday's work.

The two arms stretched towards each other, hands touching obliquely. A stone wall ran diagonally across the canvas, behind and underneath the arms; it looked strong and forbidding but it was broken at the point where the hands met. The overall effect was pleasing and James liked it. With his doubts forgotten, James congratulated himself aloud. The image was exactly what he had set out to achieve.

He was rejuvenated and talked out loud about what to do next. He paced the room energetically and made many notes on a flip chart. The project needed another part; another section; another painting. James began a new search in his files.

The photograph he needed was soon found. He studied it closely and dispassionately. It showed a group of people chatting informally with Sally and James in the background. They were deep in discussion and the topic was clearly an unhappy one. He stuffed it in the back pocket of his jeans before returning to the studio.

With the previous day's work on a spare easel to the left of his working area, James prepped his equipment and began a replica piece. For the whole morning and most of the early afternoon, James worked uninterrupted. There was urgency in his efforts, as if this was a purge.

He was relentless and, by early evening, felt confident he'd done the best he could do.

After a thorough clean up, he drove off to a supermarket. The crawling traffic made his temper fray. His creativity and exertion had caused damage, not therapy and, when he arrived at the shop, something was boiling up within him. He began to cultivate frantic views about shops and shopping. The aisles were congested, as if the whole world was here, buying reserves for the New Year festivities. Trolleys full of drinks, snacks and happiness rolled along like a production line. PA announcements rent the air every five minutes, chirpy and glowing with the season's greetings. James condensed what he heard in to four key messages: you're our customers; take our bargains; spend your money; make us profitable.

James stormed around the shop grabbing unfocused inessentials. He didn't know what he needed and the combination of all the noises, the retail environment and the intense concentration from earlier had made him forgetful and distracted. Instead of generating a shopping list, he composed a hissing, vitriolic letter to the store's management. It contained many insults, but as he completed this snort of mental sal volatile, he was packing his carrier bags and feeling a little better.

The second painting rested on its easel and was, in many ways, a duplicate of the first. It was generally softer and a closer inspection revealed marked differences. There was a pale, harsh background and both hands were closed. Each finger of the left hand had a ring on it and had lost any gentility. It was withdrawn from the other hand which was still stretched towards the middle, its bandage clean except for a small patch of red near the palm. Both arms were tense, straining down towards each wrist. And this wall was solid; an unbroken barrier filling the middle of the painting and completely separating the hands.

James was mute during this inspection. He took in the whole scene; the starkness; the bitter end that it illustrated. He was totally wrapped up in the image.

'Isn't it too obvious? The wall is wrong. It's all wrong. Don't work so quickly next time. The hands are good. Nice detail. Perfect colour. But who will ever know?'

He looked out of the window.

'Maybe we need to fix this whole problem about doing art for no reason.'

5

After a long lie-in and a larger than necessary breakfast, James had a productive Saturday. He managed mail, did rudimentary accounts, generated a meal plan for the week and itemised the people he needed to speak with. Then, in a T shirt and shorts, he started a deep clean of each room. He swept carpets, changed bed linen, polished windows, wiped and washed things. Any mess, like discarded clothes, piles of magazines, records, books and CDs, was thrown into cupboards or drawers. This order was less than skin deep.

Just after lunch, James made the first call on his list and confirmed that his team's match the following day was definitely on. He glanced at the still snowy park opposite his flat and doubted there would be football at any point in the coming week. But he made his next call and set up a lift for the following morning.

He called his parents and his brother David, none of whom answered. But Gary Greig was at home and ready for a chat. Gary was one of the few people he worked with that James considered a friend and their opening greetings led seamlessly to Christmas recollections, drinking boasts and general gossip. James told Gary, almost as an afterthought, that he had split up with Sally. Gary expressed sympathy but sounded confused and James didn't want to dwell on the subject. It was their company's New Year's Eve party the following evening; a heavily subsidised event in gratitude for a profitable and prosperous financial year. Now it was definite that he would attend, James needed a drinking partner and was delighted to hear Gary was up for it. The call finished with James grinning; it was going to be a much better night than he'd have had with Sally, alone together at a restaurant or at some event involving her yuppie friends. It would have been their third anniversary.

James still had calls to make. He booked a taxi for the following evening and, finally, called Carol.

'Hello brother of mine, how are you?'

'Not bad; you?'

'I'm fine. Glad to be home.'

'It gets more painful every year. How was your journey back?'

'Awful: snow all the way; trains running late. I am never doing that journey by train again. What are you up to?'

'I did some paintings yesterday.'

'I love your paintings; tell me how they look.'

James described them.

'They sound great. Take photos and post them. How was Boxing night? You sneaked off with no report. Who was there?'

James reeled off a roll call and recounted events from the party, focusing on Paul and his harem rather than his encounter with Philippa.

'I'd love to have seen Wendy and Paul's bust-up. Those two are such a match.'

'I don't know what to do about them. I got the distinct impression that Gra was ready to give Paul a slap at one point. Wendy, at face value, just takes it all in her stride. Yet she was very mournful when we spoke back at theirs. And I'm afraid I think she wanted me to make a move.'

'Paul has always been like this. You've just chosen to ignore it. I've heard from plenty of people about his total lack of reliability and fidelity and I think you need to be careful. Wendy is a victim; she dug gold and struck oil.' Carol giggled. 'That's quite clever isn't it?'

With perfect timing, James had completed all of his work and interaction by three o'clock and in time for Saturday's main event; the football. For nine months in every year, this consumed him for around two hours every Saturday afternoon. James rarely went to live matches. Instead he ignored all other distractions to sit and watch teletext updates with whatever sport was being broadcast as a distraction. Rugby League maybe; even horse racing.

He opened a can of lager and immersed himself in Grandstand. He'd soon consumed three cans and was grumbling aloud that the backup was ski jumping, which he would have watched more happily if it involved snipers and land mines. With a sigh of frustration, he turned off the sound, switched over to the text pages and waited for something to happen. He wanted it to be Hereford United taking the lead against York City. His team wallowed in the fourth division and had been stuck there for too long. This didn't change his loyalty and he always announced with great sporting and civic pride that he supported the club. But he never got in the car and travelled to matches; the bond was conceptual rather than obsessive.

The first scores of the afternoon were appearing on the text screens and he felt the buzz he got from this strange virtual world of sport. He was mainly silent but uttered an occasional tut; or sighed; or shook his head. Some score updates prompted exhalations of disappointment or snorts of sneering joy. By the time results were zipping up on the vidiprinter, James had finished a six-pack of large cans.

Hereford lost and he was broken by it.

It was past six when he emerged from a mildly drunken stupor and immediately sensed the horrible taste in his mouth and fuzzy buzz in his ears. He lurched to the kitchen and drank two pints of water but the foul mouth and thirst remained. Ten minutes brushing his teeth, and another pint of water made no difference. He felt dreadful. That dehydrated, numbed, incoherent shittiness that is the aftermath of daytime drinking sessions was on him.

Generally, his Saturday routine ended with some form of social event. A trip to the pub, or a party. Some combination of drinks, people and dancing. Even Sally had not changed that. But James' state was such that he didn't feel up to much, not even a few beers at the pub. He was left with his thoughts. Sitting in silence, he folded his arms and wondered what he would do now Sally had left him. The wounded pride he'd felt and brief tears he'd shed since Boxing Day were real enough. But there was a missing ingredient from the recipe. It wasn't killing him and he could measure this against something historic.

When he was seventeen, James had a small cohort of good friends – half a dozen of his peers at school – and with these people he always felt secure and happy. After an angular, gawky adolescence he grew in confidence and the previous long hot summer of 1976 had seen a great deal of noise, fun and experimentation. He'd learned how to be attractive but his diffidence, uncertainty and abstract manner were often a barrier.

In the autumn of 1977, as he started his final school year, several young women joined the sixth form causing ripples that became waves for James. One of them was Philippa Fletcher, who James had met the previous year. They'd become close, notwithstanding that she was part of a reasonably long term relationship.

Another was Sarah Smith, an altogether different proposition in James' eyes. Like an amphetamine, she caused an acceleration of cocksure sensationalism amongst his peer group. Graham sped fastest at the front of a chasing pack, spurred on by anecdote and rumour. He was completely wrong to assume that he was the subject of all that, but he still embarked on the ritual chase and it ended badly.

During an interminable October afternoon, James and Graham sat revising English literature in an otherwise empty school library. As the bell sounded to mark the end of lessons, they were joined by Philippa who smiled at James then turned to Graham.

'I need to tell you something.'

Sensing good news, Graham puffed himself up; this was what he had been waiting for.

'What you've heard about Sarah is true; there is someone in

the Upper Sixth who she fancies.'

James was only half listening but sensed his friend's agitated expectancy.

'It isn't you, and Sarah would really like you to leave her alone.'

Graham's tension erupted in a wordless exclamation; defeat and rejection wrapped in an overcoat of disbelief. He gathered up his books and belongings, then departed. Revision was over.

James looked at Philippa and said, 'That was pretty uncompromising.'

'He'll survive. What I didn't tell him is that Gerry is crazy about him and fully intends to turn that to both their advantages. So all he needs to do is make a slight adjustment of direction.'

She was still smiling at James. 'And you'll survive, too; especially since the rumours involve you.'

Philippa looked at him, her smile broadening to a grin. James frowned back and, as a smile of recognition and glee split his face, she bounced her eyebrows suggestively and they laughed. Without another word, Philippa picked up her bag and also walked from the room.

So, from nowhere, James and Sarah became a couple. It was his first ever boy/girl relationship. He hadn't really taken much notice of how she looked or what she was doing in school. He'd been behind the pack, a solitary nine behind the knaves and kings. She'd been a nice addition to the scenery, he thought. But now she was the answer; to every question.

James felt wonderful and projected this like a beacon. She had chosen him, ignoring the stack of alpha males buzzing around her space. He repaid this by focusing all his attention on her. They saw each other every day at school and stole time in the city together during breaks. They spoke every evening by phone, sometimes making three or four calls back and forth. Sarah lived two miles across the city and James walked there to see her, especially at weekends. They went to parties, to the cinema and even shared a meal that he couldn't afford, but insisted on buying.

The socialising was fine, but it was the moments alone that affected him most. Each touch was like a bolt of knowledge; each kiss breathed new belief. James came to the conclusion that this must be love. But some days she was irritable and off-hand. Instead of leaving her alone, he persisted with enquiries about her mood and what made her unhappy with him. His naive manner generally caused her to smile and kiss him, and once, as they passed in the schoolyard, she slipped a letter into his hand. It was chatty, loving and grateful that he was her boyfriend.

James felt more special than he had ever felt.

The door to Love and Affection had opened, with more than a little dedication. He planned presents he would buy, dreamed of what it would be like to be in a relationship at Christmas and eventually decided to move things forward.

One chilly afternoon, as they broke off from a kiss and looked at each other affectionately, he said, 'I love you!'

Sarah's reaction was instantly vehement and angry, as if he had insulted her. It felt like a massive, indelible mistake and she climbed on to her bus leaving him rooted to the ground and speechless.

With no words to back up her reasons, she started to avoid him; the breakdown left him desperate for information. It took several days and all his energy and emotion to get her to agree to see him and let him accompany her to the bus station. He could see and hear that she was struggling, possibly more than he. But her struggle involved closure, not repair. He pleaded with her to talk to him and she spoke a few cold, unfeeling words. She wasn't sure; she needed to think.

Next morning, he tried to talk again but Sarah turned her lovely head away and, unable to look at him, said it was over. He begged for this not to be true. She looked further in the opposite direction.

James left the room oblivious to people and surroundings. He had never felt this. The school bell beckoned him to learn but he ignored it. He went and locked himself in one of the toilet traps to hide from the new day and then, when the opening rush to lessons was over, sneaked out and into his house common room.

With his mind functioning at an almost feral level, James picked up his coat and walked out of the school. It was a dull, damp November day. The confusion and pain turned to a kind of shock. It seemed like he was grieving, and this made him cry. Walking through an almost deserted city, he couldn't stop sobbing with anguish. When he reached High Town, people glanced in concern but marched on by. After another aimless walk, he found himself staring at the Times in the city library's newspaper room. Nothing made sense; the words in front of him were jumbled and broken. He was constantly overwhelmed by tears. A librarian asked if he was all right. James shook his head, got up and left the building.

He walked from one end of the city to the other, trying to cope; hoping to recover. By lunchtime he was soaked and returned to school. He spoke in mumbled monosyllables to the few that addressed him. In the cosy closeness of Mercia House common room, he made a coffee and sat steaming miserably by the ancient iron radiator.

It was Leo that found him. 'I'm sorry about what's happened. Why don't you go home?'

This empathy made James feel no gratitude. He turned to stare out of the window, the view of the old cathedral slowly misting, blurring and dissolving. He felt a pat on his shoulder that became a gentle stroke and then the door closed. James shuddered with pent up emotion.

After lunch, he went to a lesson and tried to listen. He scribbled notes that later proved illegible. Then, between lessons, he bumped into Philippa who smiled sadly and gave him a small embrace. They agreed to meet for coffee after school and he wondered, with quiet desperation, if this could mean Philippa would once more bring good news. Another bell sounded, and James ignored the attention of his friends, threw his books into a locker and rushed to the local coffee bar. Philippa sat smoking a cigarette and sipping from one of the two cups in front of her.

For an hour they drank espressos and smoked. Philippa told him what she knew of Sarah's motives: it was all too public; she felt tied down; James was too possessive. Philippa told him Sarah had known all this for some time but still felt bad about hurting James.

He didn't contribute much to the discussion. The odd exclamatory tut or sigh was the best he could do. At the end he felt washed away and could only sniff and snuffle. Philippa held his hand across the table and told him to open up; to say something; to get it all out before it became ingrained.

He tried, but didn't know how to say what he was feeling.

Philippa was cross when she left the café.

When James arrived home that evening, he went straight upstairs. This was easily explained for he had masses of homework. He emerged for dinner and controlled himself well then, with revision as an excuse, returned to his room and did nothing.

Several days passed and the feelings of desperation and hopelessness were such that he didn't know where to turn. His parents weren't party to the relationship so he couldn't talk with them. Philippa knew and cared, but there was a block between them that wouldn't move. Carol gave him all she could, but her kindness and comfort were insufficient. His male friends, the whole gang of them, were so concerned for him that none seemed able to help or support. This group of bright, gifted, strong people could do nothing for James. None of them said, *Stop this; get a grip on yourself; she's not worth the self-destruction and self-indulgence; no girl is; find someone else; you're worth it.*

With no external support, James was left with an internal dialogue. Small voices within him cried that he didn't want, and never would want, anyone else. He had to have her back. The exposure of his feelings was a horror; it was driving him over an edge. Nothing in any of this experience was madness, but it was much more than sadness.

The worst of it was over in a couple of weeks, but it spiralled into a much longer period of frail insecurity. His social life became a nightmare. He lost his place in the school football team. He did drawings and paintings but these outputs were too furious and bleak to be therapy. It was only when he stepped back and became more reflective that he created a crystal clear honesty about what had happened. This eventually created healing, and taught him something he never lost: that the way to resolve conflict is to resolve it on your own; no one should contribute; no one should be part of the process.

During this period of havoc, James and his friends went to a Christmas party that offered hope and charity. In spite of himself, he enjoyed the early part of the evening but he couldn't sustain the positive. James found the scenes of couples and coupling made him feel excluded and lonely. He sneaked out, intending to go home but, instead, roamed the chilly streets, smoking and agonising.

When he got back to the party, he found it transformed by new arrivals. He also found that a girl he half knew had noticed his absence and expressed delight that he was back. She was Deborah and she told him she had heard how sad he was. From this opening, they proceeded to beguile each other. Wrapped up by the spell of a pretty girl with glittering eyes and lovely legs, James became overwhelmed by the need for her to hold him and kiss him and make everything better. They talked into the early hours, sometimes touching discreetly but avoiding full contact. He walked her home and listened as she told him to move on; to forget about Sarah; to see her – Deborah – as his safety net. And he agreed. She was just what he needed; a chance to forget. They kissed on her doorstep and agreed a date.

But the date never happened. When Philippa learned about James' liaison she called him and took less than ten minutes to talk him out of it. She knew Deborah, didn't much like her and convinced James that he would be dominated and nagged. He was too weak to fight with Philippa.

Deborah, and the chance she embodied, was consigned to history.

Denied the possibility to forget, James embarked on a different path. Petty and childish, he sent unpleasant, bitter, jealous letters to Sarah. He phoned her to try to be nice; but ended up being cruel.

This was halted by the arrival of Christmas and distractions of family traditions. The festivities made him happier, as if an anchor had stopped him drifting. When school restarted in January, James adjusted his behaviour again, turning his oblique sadness in to a weapon, challenging girls with the absurd notion that they owed him affection because he was so wounded. This betrayed an inherent, childlike weakness yet it could be an attraction; as if he deserved tenderness and a kind of protection. He repaid it with scorn and a hard, ruthless, dismissive malice that left a mass of unhappiness bobbing in his wake.

Without either of them requesting it, he became friends with Sarah. James didn't analyse this; it just seemed natural, and while he sometimes knew he would have her back in an instant, he felt free from the need to fight. He was also heartened by the knowledge that, despite what had happened, it was possible for them to be friends. He clung on to hopes and fears but, two and half years later, accepted it was over. A large-scale unofficial school re-union in Cambridge drew several dozen schoolmates to visit friends in the city's colleges. There was pubbing galore, then a party and when she tapped him on the shoulder and asked him to dance, James was delighted to see Sarah. They spent the evening talking, laughing and reminiscing. She asked him to walk back to the house she shared and they linked arms, mused some more and James realised there was nothing there. Sarah was an acquaintance; a fleeting encounter that had been nothing more than a teenage rite of passage. Even though he could still evoke the conflict and misery she caused, James felt a kind of peace.

Now, more than a decade later and with the benefit of hindsight, he saw clearly that Sally had not created such powerful sentiment. Sally and Sarah: relationships that ended because of something he hadn't been able to provide. One had lasted six weeks, the other just short of three years. Both women had declined to face him when breaking their news. Neither had loved him enough to paint over the cracks in his character, real or perceived. There was a single, hard-hitting and undeniable truth: these were James' only serious relationships; two women; one constantly broken heart; one decimated ego.

James was suddenly overwhelmed; not by the sadness of another broken relationship; but by the certainty that he was a dreadful failure in love.

6

He woke because a noisy engine rumbled outside and his entry phone buzzed. He looked bleary-eyed from the living room window to find Wayne grinning up at him and pointing theatrically at an imaginary wrist watch. The entry phone buzzed again and James opened the intercom.

'Pedro! Come on mate. Twenty to ten. Leave the old girl for later.'

'Ten minutes. Come up for a coffee while I get ready.'

'Got any light ale?'

'Probably somewhere.'

'Look, just get down 'ere.'

The intercom went quiet then the rumbling stopped.

James rushed to get ready, pulling on track suit bottoms, trainers, a sweat shirt and a hooded sports coat. He packed football boots, a change of clothes, a towel and toiletries. In something less than the predicted ten minutes, he was out of the flat and in the back of Wayne's fearsomely customised Sierra. The interior held a melange of smells; vaguely revolting, yet strangely comforting. On top of the mud and grass from football kit and a hint of alcohol, there was something else; James couldn't quite place it.

'I wonder if this is the very essence of Man Smell?'

Wayne drove faster than should have been wise on potentially icy roads. This was made more disturbing by his posture; one hand on the wheel; head turned constantly to talk to Jason or James; seat reclined some way past sixty degrees.

'Should be a cracker today Pedro. This lot are second. A win and we go third.'

James was staring in horror at the speedometer. His team mates continued to pepper him with chat.

'Did you do much last night Pedro?'

'A quiet night, resting before the storm...'

James paused as the car's rear slipped out through a mini roundabout. Wayne expertly corrected the glide to avert disaster.

'...the storm tonight. It's our office party at the Studbury Manor.'

'Knock out. Nice drum for a party too. I've heard some stories about these office parties. Untold shagging; married women off the hook that absolutely love it. Hey Jas, perhaps we could go along with Pedro?'

'No. I'm seeing Letitia. Going to some fucking arse hole with her folks. New Year's Eve in a restaurant eating pasta; shit on a plate.'

James sighed with relief. Wayne and Jason at a work event was a nightmare scenario. He shuddered at the prospect and to reduce his pounding heart rate, had a look around the car. A discarded, presumably used, condom and pair of knickers nestled under the driver's seat.

'You should have come out with us last night Pedro. The Coach and Horses early doors; a few light ales then on to the Barleycorn where the delectable Cindy and Maureen agreed to join us for the rest of the evening. On to Albert's and, after about twenty minutes in there, Wayne starts with this bloke at the bar. In come the lads. In come the oppo. What a laugh. The bouncers didn't know what had fucking hit 'em. I couldn't stop bloody laughing, how about you Wayne? So then it was back to Wayne's gaff for a night cap and a bit of blow, but not before a spot of mobile shagging with C and M. You'd love these two by the way Pedro. Both right goers: Martini girls; any time, any place, anywhere. Careful where you sit Pedro!'

This caused a great burst of prolonged laughter from the front seats and, as he now understood the nature of that other smell, James laughed too. He listened to these stories every Sunday and never knew whether his laughter and engagement were real. They had irrepressible optimism that he possibly envied. He certainly begrudged their extreme promiscuity. Things seemed so simple for them and he could look at that and wish it was the same for him. But there was other stuff: violence; racism; blockbusters; celebrity; the fake sophistication of black tie nights which neatly combined all four. His involvement, even on the margins, was something he didn't know how to reject. This was part of his life. He couldn't run away from it.

All of the snow had been cleared, the pitch looked surprisingly playable and flapping flags confirmed that the game was on. Several kids hung around the changing block; Dads, brothers or theft victims inside. James dropped his kit bag in the away team room, put on his boots and jogged out onto the pitch. His body was just about all right but he made a mental note not to overdo things. It was still only a few days since a vast Christmas lunch and lake of alcohol on Boxing Night. He went through his long-standing routine; stretching; warming-up. He was the only one who did this. But he was the only one who had been forced, almost as a punishment, to do so at school.

Back in the changing room, their manager called the team to be silent.

'Play the fucking game. Don't let the opposition have the fucking ball and they can't fucking beat you. Pass to any fucker in the team who's in a position to receive it. Don't thump the fucking thing into the next century. Again; play the game. Win; we go third. Lose; well it's only a fucking game of football.'

As the other players clattered into the cold morning air to confront a perky, eager opponent, the manager spoke a few final words to James.

'Keep them tight at the back son. Get yourself forward if you can and always at corners. You take all free kicks around their penalty area. Keep an eye on young Kevin as well; he's got a fast fucker against him today. We can beat these if we play like we practice. Get 'em going son!'

And as James jogged off, the manager called out, 'And I could do with a fucking goal from you Pedro; preferably two.'

No one could remember why he had been named Pedro. Everyone at the club used the name and he didn't mind it. The alternative was some derivative of James, which he absolutely hated.

Young Kevin got roasted and James, sweeping up at the back, quickly realised he was physically out of sorts. They conceded after thirty minutes; a sloppy, slack, avoidable goal. Things looked and felt ominous. Half time oranges soaked in rum and honey failed to cheer and a second goal caused heads to fall. James did as he was told and surged forward whenever he got the ball. The second time up field, he smashed a shot past the keeper. Ten minutes later, Jason scored a second and suddenly everyone had their heads up again. With time to spare, they took the lead and James was happy but hurting. Shortly before the end he managed to forget his stiff muscles and sore shins by heading in his second goal.

The overall view in the pub was that they had played a game of two halves. The more thoughtful amongst them discussed how to rectify that, but the Christmas club money was behind the bar and soon it was just another post-match piss-up.

After a couple of hours at the pub, James accepted his manager's offer of a lift home. They talked about the game and discussed the coming week's match and its ramifications. They only knew each other because of football and it was enough for them to concoct a twenty-minute, non-stop discussion. They couldn't have strung together two sentences about anything else.

While the bath filled, James stuffed newspaper into his soggy boots and put kit and towel in the washer. This was another of Sally's imposed rules. Before her time in his life, these things would have been left to stink and decay in his bag for a few days, possibly until the following match.

James lay in his bath with a mug of strong, sweet tea and reflected on his performance that morning. Two goals; a couple of good runs up field; a pinpoint pass to Jason for the third goal and a few telling tackles at the back. Not bad at all. Man of the match.

He smiled. Football made him happy and helped him forget.

As he dried himself down, James' anticipation of the coming party grew stronger. He surveyed himself in the mirror. With a towel wrapped round his waist, his figure was satisfactorily shaped. He turned side on and the devastation of Christmas was more apparent. A slight bulge in the tummy caused tuts and a shaking head. He dropped the towel. His legs, arms, buttocks, shoulders and chest were in good shape and he reckoned a week of care would soon reduce that gut. A closer look at his face brought more tutting. The mouse-brown hair was tangled and damp and in the absence of gel or mousse, it sagged down over his eyes and ears. Greying lines swept under his eyes; with the crow's feet at their edges and the cynical dullness of the pupils, those eyes made him seem very old. A scar on his cheek, as it always did when he was warm through exercise or bathing, showed vivid pink.

He stood back from the mirror and, after dismissing the temptation to have a wank, moved to the wardrobe.

'Wear that new shirt and jeans. Suede shoes. Leather jacket. You'll look vaguely hard yet endearing.'

James told people he was disinterested in his appearance, but this kind of debate always preceded a night out. He had clothes that appealed to him and he tended to look good in them. Equally, it wouldn't really have mattered if he had looked like a tramp, so long as he was comfortable and unadorned by fashion.

'New shirt, chinos and smart shoes. And your blazer.'

James shook his head angrily.

'It's an office party, not a regatta. What about a suit?'

He rummaged through his wardrobe and threw out a hanger with a recently purchased, charcoal grey suit on it. Then he pulled out a plain black shirt and laid it inside the jacket.

'You'll look like Mussolini. That just won't do. Try the maroon shirt instead; with black Oxfords.'

He put another shirt inside the jacket and examined the effect.

'Fine. Sorted. You'll look perfect.'

It was already dark outside when he switched on the radio and settled on the sofa to pencil sketch a face on his pad. It was a girl's face; a stranger, but after a while he decided to call the face *Laura*. This caused him to revisit thoughts about who Laura might be and where he'd heard or seen the name before. He ticked himself off for not asking someone at Gerry and Graham's party.

But James had no inspiration for his drawings and needed other diversions. He grabbed some books and sat to flick through them. The first was a big colourful anthology of paintings that he looked at, dismissing, appraising and smiling. He rotated one painting and confirmed his view of several years that it looked better that way. With a contented shrug he turned to a collection of poetry. It confused him, but he tried to like it and read aloud some examples; once in a normal voice, then in a silly one.

Finally, he turned to one of the books he had pinched from his school. He still had no shame about the fact that he never bothered to log library books in and out. When he wanted to research something, he went and found the right book, then took it away. No one noticed because Art was such an academic non-event that few people were remotely interested in books about it. Eventually, he had all the library's art section in his house common room and, on his last day, James put most of these in someone else's locker and stole the rest.

Here was one of those books and he opened it with a reverential air, smiling at the school crest and nameplate. It was old, donated to the school in 1908 by an eminent Old Boy whose signature and epithet scrawled across most of the first blank page.

The phone interrupted this browsing; it was Paul.

'Hello mate. All right?'

'Yes. I'm really sorry about the other night. I was well out of order.'

'You were well pissed. Forget it.'

'Well look, to make up, why don't you come to Wendy's birthday on the 20th? We're having people over for a party. It'd be great to see you.'

'That's nice of you both. Thank you; I'd love to come.'

'Great.'

'Is everything all right with you two?'

Paul's voice changed. 'Of course. Why?'

'Oh, I dunno. It's just little things. Like all the shit you were spouting in the taxi.'

'Like you said. I was drunk.'

'Right. How did you get on this morning?'

'Drew 1–1. Dreadful game. Listen, can't talk for long now. I'm on my way out. Bye.'

'Fine. See you soon.'

James tidied up the books and as he closed the old Art book something caught his eye. The latest list of borrowers and withdrawals ended in late 1976 and was stuck on top of several others, forming a small plinth in the middle of the page. He noticed his name:

NAME	RETURN
Clifton J – 3b	21.4.74

So he scanned the list above and below this entry. Shortly, he answered a question he had been asking himself for several days. His name appeared once again and then, below it, there were two more names one of which was:

NAME	RETURN
Drysdale L – 2a	2.9.76

7

James felt regally essential as his taxi pulled up at the hotel's entrance. But a uniformed commissionaire was unimpressed and completely ignored this arrival. He clearly intended to get not one blemish from rain, snow, salt, grit or ice on his shiny black shoes.

Undeterred, James skipped across the pavement and gazed, with many doubts, through the hotel's revolving door. He knew he would probably enjoy it. He guessed that it would be a few drinks, a few meaningless flirtations, a bit of a dance and a few more drinks. He fully intended to drink a lot of beer and expected no more than to leave drunk, but fulfilled. Yet there was this sense that none of that mattered and he should be elsewhere.

The hotel foyer was busy and he saw colleagues loitering and chatting so he moved through the revolving door and nodded at whoever noticed. There was a fabulously attractive woman behind the reception desk, taking a call and smiling her way through responses to whatever was being asked. She looked up at James and her eyes lingered.

A greetings and information board directed him and his workmates to The Orchid Ballroom Suite. James followed the signs and soon heard the noises of fun and celebration. Indecisively, he opened a door and found himself in an anteroom with chairs around the walls and, to his left, an attended cloak room. There was muted music, a murmur of conversation, laughter and a babbling hubbub. With ten paces he reached another set of doors and when he opened one, those sounds became a noise.

He was in a bar area where someone had got their act together in a big way. A battalion of uniformed staff was serving drinks to keep waiting times short. The free bar, with its 10pm curfew, also assisted the overall process of ordering and serving. Notwithstanding these benefits, James ordered two pints of lager and stood at the bar to drink them. Hunched at the counter, with a foot perched on the rest, he resembled a middle-aged man taking a lunchtime constitutional. He downed a pint in one and the second was gone within another couple of minutes. He ordered two more and took these through open partition doors to the main ballroom where dozens of large tables were occupied. Leaders moved among their charges, some with spouse in tow, scattering praise and appreciation. The music was loud but no one engaged with it and the large square of tiled floor was mainly unoccupied. Occasionally, a small group would reel out for the right record, goading friends to join. James tapped his foot and watched one of these ensembles strut around to *I Wanna Dance with Somebody*. No men were involved in this and James reflected that he'd once read that the only thing that will make a white English man dance is the drug Ecstasy. He looked around. The whole cosy, middle class, middle-aged gathering would have run a mile from the offer of drugs. And the younger players, who probably ingested their fair share of chemicals, seemed clean and spotless. James laughed quietly to himself, concluding that what might get these white English men dancing was the prospect of a good, hard shag.

'What's so funny?'

'Gary! I must owe you a pint.'

They shook hands and returned to the bar. James ordered two lagers then watched appreciatively as his friend swallowed his drink in one draught and slammed the glass on the counter.

'Another of those I think.'

'Let's get two or three mate. Saves waiting and the freebies stop any time.'

Some moments later, the two men each had three pints lined up in front of them. Gary raised one of his glasses; 'To lost love.'

'Very funny, you bastard.'

They supped but suppressed laughter prevented them swallowing. It took a while for order to be restored.

'Sorry I'm so late. Rehearsals today ended later than intended and with the usual frank exchange of views.'

'All not well in the rock and roll stakes?'

'It's terrible. We've slung out Helen, so I'm now the singer while we search again. She apparently had no image; in other words she didn't look great every moment of every day. This revelation came from Marcus who apparently saw her in Twickenham last Saturday looking – and I'm quoting here – like a bulldog sucking a wasp. It pisses me off. They're just so blinkered about image and making it, whatever that means. They can't see that we've got something really good; strong songs; good playing; a following. I can't make them understand that and I might have to leave.'

Gary sighed deeply. James smiled at him then raised his glass; 'To fame and fortune.'

'Touché; bastard.'

They emptied their glasses and started on the next rank. Gary lit a cigarette. With neither hesitation nor temptation, James helped himself to one. He hadn't smoked for nearly three years but his cravings were irresistible. They stood at the bar, uninterrupted, for nearly an hour as the music got louder and the party came to life. Around them, the ballroom filled with people who would be dancing the night away, not to mention the year and a decade. James and Gary simply got drunk, exchanging jokes, anecdotes and observations that left a very great deal to be desired.

'You two look in need of a drink.'

'You're not wrong Miles. Two lagers please. Each.'

The pair dissolved in giggles. Miles smiled indulgently in the time-honoured fashion of managers confronted by idiot employees in a social setting. He bought their drinks and wished them well. It was the only intervention to their gross drunken sniggering and behaviour. They laughed so much that on occasions it seemed to cause pain. They didn't stop when the food was served and stood in the queue loading up their plates almost as an aside. Some fleeting iota of empathy with others made them realise that they were an irritation so they sat alone at a table, eating greedily and maintaining the flow of mindless mirth. It didn't stop them being an irritation and they even spoke and ate through the short address made by their Managing Director.

It was Bridget's arrival that halted this horrible filth. She gave James a caring smile and lingering embrace but took Gary away.

James returned to the ballroom where the scene was transformed. Prompted by more useful music, the dance floor was packed with a heaving mound whose collective rhythm belied any component discord. Contemporary tunes were rocking the house. Overspill dancers grooved around their tables and near the bar. The DJ had finally got them moving.

For five or six songs, James leaned on a doorframe, drinking and smoking. He didn't engage; he didn't appear to have any link to this event; he didn't even observe the scenes, colours and textures that might produce a painting. He was effectively switched off and shut down. All he could do was to let the whole place make him laugh with contempt, unaware that he was standing in isolated judgement, sneering at the things around him.

'It's getting a bit out of hand isn't it?'

James turned to his left.

'Ah-ha! You are Tracy Miller and I claim my free glass of lager.'

Tracy smiled lasciviously. She had spent most of the last eight months smiling lasciviously at James across their desks, monitoring all the indicators of his failing relationship. She took his arm, pecked him on the cheek and walked him back to the bar area where she gave him a lengthy appraisal. 'You look very smart. I didn't recognise you. I love that shirt. How was your Christmas?'

His tale received another airing and he took the opportunity to wind his self-pity around this new audience, not realising it was music to her ears.

'I'm so sorry James. I think I knew things weren't good but I never realised you would end up available. Sorry, that is completely the wrong word; but you get my meaning. Anyway, is there anything I can do?'

There was a bawled request for silence then the noise of Big Ben going through the quarters. Glasses were charged and, as the first massive clang erupted from the speakers, the ritual began. For ten minutes or more, people leapt with joy at an incoming year's arrival. They rushed around hugging and kissing, slapping and squeezing, smiling and laughing. No one in the room cared that this New Year meant another birthday; another career move; another holiday; and another step down life's ladder. All the things they'd all done every year since time immemorial would be done all over again until, twelve months from now, they'd all be in a sweaty clinch somewhere. To make matters worse, there was also the whole sorry arrival of a new decade. People seemed happy to see the back of the eighties but portrayed no obvious optimism for whatever the incoming nineties might bring.

James and Tracy had not spared a thought for any of this. They were standing as close as two fully dressed people can stand.

'Happy New Year, Tracy Miller.'

'Happy New Year, James. I just have a feeling it will work out better than last year did for you.'

They clinked glasses.

James kissed her lightly on the cheek. Her hand brushed his

arm and shoulder and now their bodies touched. She played an opening card.

'Why don't you give me a proper kiss?'

The Queen of Spades, in fact.

'I might be tempted; but no tongues.'

Tracy sniggered. 'Don't be ridiculous.'

They walked to the dance floor and it began. Had they been birds James would have inflated his throat or flashed gaudy tail feathers. But they were merely human. *New York, New York* boomed from the speakers and they danced close. Tracy got the kiss she required, on her terms and so everyone could see. James clung on and returned each squeeze and gentle thrust. He was a good dancer but in the arms of this woman he kept it all low-key. After a couple more songs, Tracy bit his ear lobe and whispered that they should find somewhere to sit down.

The event was subdued now. Many guests had left within fifteen minutes of the New Year chimes; duties done; lines toed. The music had been turned down a couple of notches and the ballroom was brightly lit, so Tracy and James headed off into the hotel where they soon found a lounge area with sofas and subdued lighting.

'What did you think of the party?'

She shrugged. 'I've been to worse and better. It would have been nice to have more time with you and slightly less just talking the corporate talk.'

'And where were you all evening? I honestly don't think I saw you.'

'I don't think you saw anyone anywhere apart from your little friend Gary. I spent most of the evening with the finance crew. They're all going on to another party and spent ages trying to convince me I should go and get you to come too.'

'But you don't want to go, I'm guessing.'

'No, I don't. I'm staying here in the hotel tonight.'

James had drunk a lot but was clear-headed enough to calculate the significance of this news.

'You're staying here?'

'Yes, I am. Booked it ages ago and they offered me a great B&B deal. It's made everything nice and easy for me. I drove over here at around seven and checked in. Got into some tantalising lingerie and this frock. Had a couple of the drinks I brought with me, having completely forgotten the bar was free, then just sauntered down here in time to see you and Gary lined up at the buffet looking like Dastardly and Muttley. Except you both looked like Muttley.'

James watched her while she spoke. Tracy was around six years younger than him but seemed somehow older than her twenty-three years. She was wearing a simple outfit: black sleeveless dress, sheer stockings and shiny strappy shoes. James had surreptitiously always admired Tracy's figure but in this clothing it was simply sensational. He knew she played netball and squash and she looked fit and lithe. Her jet black hair was pulled back in to a small ponytail and she had applied makeup so that her eyes, cheeks and mouth looked perfect. She seemed very desirable indeed. Yet, as he evaluated his colleague's appearance, he realised she was still talking; still putting people and places and subjects in to compartments; still cross referencing everything to a fixed point that generally lacked substance. She did this at work. Tracy was rarely silent and often terribly shallow in her judgements and thinking.

Eventually he got a word in; 'Whose party is it? Where is it?'

'At Jacqui Scott's place. Miles away. Have you got any cigarettes?'

James passed her one, put another in his own mouth and moved a lighted match between them. They talked about work and play. Every now and then, Tracy leaned over and touched James on his arm, or shoulder, or face. They smoked and drank, sharing glances and smiles. These were seemingly uncomplicated exchanges, but they were a means to an end.

After a while, James suggested more dancing so they headed back to find encouraging tunes in the ballroom. Dancing in silence, swaying and clinging, they looked like a very happy couple. James whispered the words from one song in her ear and this seemed to help Tracy arrive at a decision.

'How are you getting home?'

'No idea.'

'Didn't you book a taxi?'

'No. I just kind of assumed someone would give me a lift or, failing that, I knew I could walk. It's only three or four miles; which would sober me up actually.'

'That's stupid. It's too cold and dangerous for walking.'

'I guess it is.'

They fell silent again. Tracy rested her head on his shoulder but the song soon petered out and they returned to their sofa. James watched Tracy gulp down more gin, staring ahead as if contemplating some great philosophical dilemma. James lit two more cigarettes and passed her one. She took it with a small, tight smile.

'Why don't you stay here tonight?'

He looked at her. She raised an eyebrow in support of the question and gave him a compelling smile.

'That could be nice.'

'Good. The party's over. Finish your drink and we can head back to my room. I've got some wine if you feel like more to drink.'

She reached out to hold his hand then planted another kiss on and in his mouth.

James drank up and they headed back to reception. Tracy took his hand and led him along a short corridor then up a flight of stairs. As they turned in to another corridor she turned to face him. James hadn't expected this and jumped theatrically. This made her giggle and laugh. The laughter became infectious, but was subdued in to a smile, and then a look, and then a kiss.

8

James was in an empty bed and lay staring at the ceiling. He realised it was light outside, but not much else was making sense.

'It's nearly eleven and I've missed breakfast. Do you want some tea?'

Tracy was holding a kettle and was naked. James was too blurry-eyed to take in many details. She made his tea, put the mug next to him then returned to bed and cuddled up.

'We need to check out by twelve thirty.'

James gulped some tea. 'We better get moving then.'

She turned to face him. 'We had, but I need you to fuck me again. At least once. It will make my day go more smoothly.'

Tracy said this in a matter-of-fact way; business-like and transactional. James glanced at her and smiled. She'd untied the ponytail so her hair swung loose. The makeup had gone too and James saw her unpainted, natural beauty.

'Well Happy New Year to you, Tracy Miller.'

'You already said that last night.' She smiled at him. 'But thank you. Let's hope you mean some of the other things you told me last night.'

Something started to nag at James. He racked his memory for what he might have said. The only thing he could recall with certainty was that he had murmured that song in her ear while they danced.

Tracy got up to walk to the bathroom and James gazed evenly

69

at her firm, perfect arse. He sipped his tea and felt better for it, surprising given the amount of lager he'd consumed. He reckoned he'd drunk no less than ten, but potentially as many as fifteen pints. Avoiding the export strength stuff was probably the only sensible decision he'd made all night.

Clothes were scattered around the room and he reached across to where his suit's jacket and trousers lay. They reeked of smoke and James grimaced at the realisation he had relapsed in to a filthy, deathly habit.

'And is Tracy a filthy habit too? It's not going to lead to anything remotely rewarding. Apart from the shagging.'

These were new doubts. Before they had finished kissing in the corridor, Tracy had undone James' trousers. Somehow they got in to the room and, once inside, garments were discarded – all but the tantalising lingerie. It lasted for a couple of hours and it was close to five when they fell apart to sleep. Tracy was new, exciting, vigorous and adventurous.

'James, can you come in here for a moment?'

He got out of the bed and went to the bathroom. As he walked in, she turned to face him and pulled him in to an embrace.

'Like I said, you're going to have to fuck me again. Here; now.'

They left the hotel just after one and drove towards Richmond. Tracy had an old XR3i, drove like a lunatic and looked like a man while she drove. The way she gripped the wheel and gear-lever, and the way she ran her arm along the window frame were really masculine.

'So all this time you've been sitting opposite me and didn't realise I was a total slut. Did you ever wonder?'

'Can't say I did, no.'

She ran her hand up his thigh and massaged his groin.

'The ultimate male fantasy. A woman who just wants it.'

James was perplexed and hushed.

'But no strings. We work together and I'm too young to settle down. I like you a lot and I'd like to know if you can fuck for two and half hours on a regular basis. I'm up for that, but nothing heavy or permanent. Just you and me in the sack, once every few weeks. What do you think?'

'I had a good time last night.'

'You had the best time.'

'And it was a nice surprise to find out that you are...'

'Such a goer?'

'I was going to say *interested*. I think you're right about work. So let's see.'

Tracy declined the offer to join James for lunch. When they reached his flat, she leaned across, kissed him hard and mauled the front of his trousers. It wasn't really that nice and James felt she was over-elaborating.

He went straight to bed and the afternoon, like most New Year's Day afternoons, disappeared in sleep. By early evening, James could manage no more than to get out of bed and slump in front of the television. He was soon unable to focus on anything other than the doubts he felt about Tracy. She had been a vigorous and exploratory partner and James was pretty sure he'd never had sex quite like it. He saw that as an opportunity to move on and consign Sally to history.

'But it isn't is it? No one starts a relationship with someone purely on the basis of top-notch sex. Do they?'

9

Meet the New Year (just the same as the Old Year)

James returned to work on January 2nd, relieved that a trying, emotional few weeks were behind him. The mundane routine of work and business would help him settle.

That first morning was uneventful and James spent most of it avoiding eye contact. The office was slightly more than half full and slightly less than half productive. A collective, enduring hangover seemed to excuse this loafing. No one appeared to have anything to do and mostly sat around talking about their holidays, their gifts and the crap on the telly that was getting worse, year on year. It was the same basic conversation James had heard every New Year since at least 1980. It had probably preceded that, for all he knew.

But the slacking slowed and the gossip died and, by lunchtime, work was being done. James caught up on letters, memos and announcements and found that his in-tray contained new things, needing his attention and skills. Slowly he formed a plan of action, with documents scattered around his desk, then with notes and diagrams on a flip chart. As he filled each sheet of paper, he tore it off and stuck it on a wall. This was just what he needed: distraction; routine; irrelevance.

After a long day, in which all that he needed to do had been done, he tidied his things in readiness to leave. He felt good that he'd been diligent, but was fretting about Tracy. She'd said there were no strings and he believed her. He was drawn to the notion that he could enjoy a healthily excessive sex life, and that he deserved one. It had been there in front of him all along and Tracy had cut to the chase, with no demand to be dated or wooed. She just wanted it.

But this was fantasy and James wanted reality. There would be a catch, he decided, and he should err on the side of caution.

Later in the week he met Miles about the plan James had compiled. His boss proposed changes and they reviewed several aspects in fine detail. The result was a new version of James' plan: it was the right approach; it would deliver a result. This led in to a longer discussion about workload for the coming year.

'You and Tracy are doing well as a team.'

James' mind flashed to New Year's Eve; a swirling collage of smiles, lips, tongues, breasts and flesh with a soundtrack of moaning pleasure.

'Thank you. I agree.'

'How do you find working with her? Could she do more? Is there leadership quality there?'

'She's one of the best we have. Her skills are strong and she really can negotiate. I'm sure she could run a team.'

Miles changed tack.

'I bumped in to Gary Greig yesterday. I'm sorry to hear about the end of your relationship with Sally.'

James looked out of the window, blinking repeatedly.

'I'm also sorry you didn't feel able to let me know, on a personal basis, that you'd been having problems last summer. Or is there some reason why you would avoid discussing a personal issue with me?'

James was suspicious. This sounded like dangerous territory, so he switched to defensive.

'Was there a problem? Is that where you're going?'

'No. But telling me about your separation would have been sensible. Wouldn't it?' His words seemed gentle, but there was a steely, implied threat.

'I suppose so, but I just wanted to focus on my personal life. There was no conscious decision to avoid discussing it with you, or with anyone. I'm private; you know this; I saw no reason to advertise what was going on. The situation wasn't easy, but I had it under control. Work came first all through that period. I worked bloody hard. But I take your point; I should have let you know.'

'Tell me about you and Tracy then.'

'What?'

'On New Year's Eve; you seemed involved.'

James was being lured to unsafe terrain. His mind worked quickly to counter it.

'We were drunk. A lot of things had not gone my way. But we're not *involved* as you put it.'

'Right; okay James; I hear you.'

Tracy returned to work a week later. James briefed her about their programme of work and targets for the coming quarter but during these discussions found her aloof and reticent; she didn't look at James when she was talking; she just sat opposite him, listening in silence broken only by the need to clarify assumptions or verify progress. They were working, but something seemed to need repair.

A week passed like this and it was lunchtime on Friday when

something broke through the ice. Tracy stood and stretched then asked James if he needed anything from the canteen. He said he didn't, but as she walked off she dropped an internal mail envelope in front of him.

He opened it to find a G-string and a hand-written note:

James, this is killing me. Trying to make things seem normal isn't working. What are we going to do? I can't cope with having to sit here watching you and needing you. It's killing me. Come down to the canteen and talk to me.

James stuffed her underwear into his bottom drawer and folded the note away in his trouser pocket before following her to the canteen. She was sitting alone at a table picking at a sandwich she didn't seem to want. He bought himself a cup of coffee and joined her.

For the first time that week, Tracy looked at him and held his gaze. At first she smiled, but this wasn't the lustful beam she'd turned on him during and after the office party. Her eyes held a level of emotion that made James anxious; that she might have feelings for him; that the things she did on New Year's Eve, and said to him on New Year's Day, had been a smokescreen; that something less lusty lurked behind all her actions.

'What are we going to do?' She was staring at her lunch.

'About what?'

'Don't be stupid. I've had a whole fortnight of you not calling me and I was expecting your attention. I think I earned that.'

She looked up again and her face seemed torn by shattered confidence. James held her gaze, and saw that he was being played; so he played back.

'You can have my attention. We agreed that on New Year's Day.'

She smiled. 'Did we?'

'Yes. But now I'm confused. You said there were no strings and we were going to focus on other things; so what's all this playing about?'

'It's most definitely about other things, as you so quaintly put it. And I wasn't playing, I...'

Before she could finish, two colleagues sat down at the table with trays and plates laden with chips and unspecified breaded things. James made some pointless remark about work and, glancing quickly at Tracy, got up and went back to his desk.

Late in the afternoon they were alone in the office. James was ready to leave but Tracy asked him to wait so they could walk together to the station. 'Why don't we catch up this evening? What are you up to?'

'I was planning a curry and a bottle of wine in front of the telly.'

'So you weren't going to call me?'

'I wasn't.'

'Any reason for that?'

'None. But listen, why don't you come over? Don't make out like I'm in the wrong here. I'm sticking with the script; no ties, but the occasional interlude.'

'So you're taking me for a curry. Do I like Indian food James?'

'I'm guessing you do.'

'Really? Why?'

'No idea.'

'In fact I love curries; they make me even hornier than gin.'

James performed a cartoon gulp that made Tracy laugh.

'What time do you want me?'

'When can you get there?'

Tracy glanced at her watch. 'Five fifteen now; I'll be home by six; shower; dress; pack. I reckon I'll be back at yours by eight thirty. Okay?'

James lay in a hot, foamy bath swigging from a bottle of cold, foamy lager. He had formed a smugly certain view that he was completely in the right and should take advantage of Tracy's promiscuous offerings for as long as possible. Whenever he questioned his own logic, or fretted about the wisdom of embarking on any kind of relationship with someone he managed, his mind very quickly reverted to the uncomplicated and basic truth: she was a very, very easy distraction.

He finished the beer and ducked his head under the water. He knew, deep down, that he might regret taking things further with Tracy. He havered about whether the coming evening was a good thing. As he surfaced from these thoughts, the warbling of his telephone filled the flat. He reached the phone just as it switched to answering mode. A voice he didn't expect to hear crackled from the speaker.

'Hi James, it's Rachel.'

James waited, unsure that he should answer.

'I thought I'd give you a call to see how you are and whether or not you've heard from Sally. Maybe you're still at work so I'll try again in a bit.'

James squinted at the handset as the talking stopped. This was a very strange turn of events and he wasn't at all sure he wanted or needed to hear whatever Rachel might want to say to him. He switched off answering mode then jumped back in to his bath, took a deep breath and submerged.

'What did she mean? Have I heard from Sally? They share a house.'

He exhaled in to the water and lifted his head through the bubbles.

'I really don't want to talk to her. Or to Sally. It's over and done.'

The phone rang again and James sighed.

'You should answer. Tell Rachel to forget it, whatever it is.'

With a towel wrapped round his waist, he ambled to the living room and picked up the phone.

'James speaking.'

'Hello, it's Mum. Happy New Year to you.'

'Oh, hello.'

His mother laughed. 'You sound disappointed.'

'No, sorry; I was expecting someone else. Happy New Year to you too. How are things? How's dad?'

'He's out this evening. They had a big sales conference today and there's a bit of a do at the Green Dragon to celebrate.'

James looked around for and found a pack of cigarettes. He didn't hear most of what his mother was saying about plans for the weekend. His head was still wrapped around the things he'd intended to say to Rachel. He lit a cigarette and realised a question was hanging in the air.

'James? Are you there?'

'Yes I'm here. Sorry.'

'Are you feeling all right? After what's happened with Sally?'

'Yes, I'm fine. Back at work now, so plenty to keep my mind on. I think I might be up in Hereford in a couple of weeks. Been invited to a party.'

'Well let me know your plans. It will be good to see you. Whose party is it?'

James explained it was more of the same at Paul's house and that he wasn't sure whether it was worth the trip.

'Well it's a long way to travel just for a couple of hours at a party.'

He tutted. Both his parents saw travel as part of something epic, planned and full of purpose. They would take weeks to organise a simple drive out to a pub for lunch.

'I've got a few days to decide. So I'll let you know.'

His mother changed the subject and started a tale about their neighbour's car parking habits. There was a buzz from the entry phone. James checked his watch; it was just before eight, so Tracy was early.

'Mum, hold on please; someone's at the door.'

He answered the intercom and Tracy's voice announced her arrival. James told her to come up and un-latched his front door. When he got back to the phone, his mother was still talking. She so rarely listened to him and he had to interrupt to say, 'Mum; I have a visitor so I need to go. Can we talk on Sunday?'

'No, we have people round for dinner on Sunday.' She continued with a schedule full of reasons why they might not get to talk for most of the next week.

Tracy had found James and smiled at him, then pointed at the towel wrapped round his waist, indicating he should take it off. James shook his head with a grin then turned away from her.

Mother was still talking.

James felt the towel being unravelled from around him. He interrupted his mother again. 'Okay Mum, I really do need to go. I'm running late.'

She sounded offended. 'Well if it's a bad time then you better go.'

Tracy had started nibbling at his buttocks and running her hands up the front of his thighs.

'Oh Jesus.'

'Pardon?'

'Nothing. I really need to go now.'

Tracy giggled audibly.

'Well obviously you have company.'

'Yes. But we'll talk soon.'

'Weren't you listening? I just said there's really not many days we can talk next week...'

By now Tracy had turned him round and was probing and licking.

'Goodbye Mum.'

He put the phone down just in time.

10

It was still early when James found Tracy gazing impassively down at him. No movement or noise had disturbed him, but here she was already dressed in a track suit and trainers. James asked, dozily, if she wanted a drink or some breakfast.

'Sorry lover, I need to be somewhere else.'

'That's a shame. What's the rush?'

She sat on the bed to tie her laces.

'I'm going to a wedding. An old school friend is getting hitched to a guy she's known since we were all teens. Sweet, eh? Sweeter still for being a winter wedding. So I need to get home and changed, then off to the church by two.'

'What time is it now?

'Just after eight fifteen.'

'That's far too early; and whereabouts is the wedding?'

'Mortlake, but the reception is near here at that American Franchise Enorm-o-tel.'

'What a shame. I thought we might spend some time together today.'

'Sorry, but no can do.'

Tracy expressed no curiosity about what James might have had in mind. She stood and left the room.

'Why didn't you mention this last night? Are you leaving, like, imminently? No time for any morning afters?'

He heard her laughing and she shouted, 'I can't believe I'm saying this but I think you've actually worn me out. I'm so sore this morning...'

News of Tracy's premature departure meant the glow he'd started to feel was weakened and cooled. She was still talking to him from the bathroom but James felt detached and let down. He didn't pursue answers to his other questions and, fifteen minutes later, she was gone. A cursory kiss on the forehead was all she left him with; no grasp of his bollocks and no whispered invitation for more of anything.

James soon got up and without getting dressed spent the morning sketching on an A3 pad. Greys and greens were foremost and by early afternoon he'd created something he felt had merit: a man, skeletal and haggard, with a wry smile of optimism directed at whoever might view the picture. This figure sat in a boat with an oar lying askew in its bracket. The boat was half full of water and waves swelled around it. Each wave held a face and each face had a different expression. James began to like this idea, and worked hard on it for most of the afternoon.

But he lost momentum when he stopped to make some tea. Until that voicemail from Rachel, James had found a place to conceal all he felt about Sally; he'd walked quietly away. Now there was a new dimension; someone who should know all the details was looking for clues about Sally. It made no sense.

Without conviction, he picked up the phone and called Rachel. There was no answer and he left no message. So he called other friends but no one was home. He sipped at his tea cup and wondered what to do for the rest of an evening he'd hoped might be spent with Tracy. It was almost certainly too late to arrange an alternative.

He switched on the television, flicked through the channels then switched it off within a minute. Nothing in the previous day's newspaper captured his interest and it ended up on the floor. He hit *Play* on the stereo's remote but the system flashed *No CD*. He poured more tea and retrieved the newspaper to have a go at the cryptic crossword. For fifteen minutes, he concentrated hard on the clues and confidently completed two answers. Another quarter of an hour proved less fruitful and James realised it was impossibly complex. Not to be outdone, he filled in some entries with words that he liked: *outwith*; *apse*; *moist*; *deluge*.

In the studio he gazed at the piece he'd started and felt it was ineffective, limp and meaningless so he tore it up. His boredom and apathy could not be driven out and he decided he might as well just go back to bed.

When the telephone rang, James wanted it to be Tracy saying she was sick of the wedding and needed some company. They would get to talk and maybe learn something about cerebral as well as physical aspirations. His disappointment at hearing a man's voice was tangible, but short lived. Gary had finished rehearsing to find Bridget was out with friends; so did James fancy a drink?

Gary arrived in less than an hour and they were soon face to face at a table in a town centre pub. A conversation started, scattered with tacit admiration of the women around them. They drank quickly and chatted as they always did, the idiocy of their discussion developing exponentially with their beer consumption. They also swore more progressively and loudly, which was neither complicated; nor big; nor clever.

Gary eventually opened an inevitable topic.

'Right James, from the horse's mouth; did you shag Tracy on New Year's Eve? This is important and I am tasked with finding the truth.'

'Why? By whom? For what purpose?'

Gary remained silent but raised an eyebrow. James sighed melodramatically. 'Well we sat around till late, and I ended up staying at the hotel. Tracy went to bed and I went to bed. No horse was involved.'

'Together?'

'As I was saying, we went to bed and slept.'

'Bullshit. You shagged her. Come on. Admit it.'

James said nothing but, after more prompts, he smiled and moved his head in a gesture that might indicate affirmation. He was careful to admit nothing.

'I thought so. You lucky bastard; I bet she's a right goer.'

James said nothing, but was surprised and intrigued by this display of jealous lust. In feigned disgust, Gary threw a fiver at James and ordered him to get another round in. With a fresh drink Gary became more serious.

'So are you officially in a relationship?'

'Not sure. There is a corporate angle.'

'What? How do you mean?'

James recounted his discussion with Miles and how a company radar was tracking whatever existed between Tracy and him. He blamed Gary for discussing things with Miles.

Gary objected. 'What did I discuss with Miles?'

'He told me you told him about me and Sal.'

'Well okay, yes I did mention that when he asked me. But I've said nothing to anyone about you and Tracy, not even to Bridge. Did he really say I'd said something? Or is this just your habitual self-obsession mate? Either way, it's none of his business.'

'Well fine, but regardless of who said what, do you think company relationships work? Because I'd say neither of us is interested in anything long term.'

'You mean you don't fancy her?'

'She's okay.'

'Okay? She's fucking gorgeous; beautiful. A sizeable majority of the men, and possibly some of the women, in our company would give their left legs to sleep with her. And you say she's okay?'

James was suddenly overwhelmed by images of one-legged people having sex. Gary brought him to attention by rapping his beer glass on the table. James continued, 'Well, all right; I suppose I do fancy her and I suppose it could be good news in some ways.'

'Isn't the whole work thing manageable if you both want to make it work?'

'Possibly, yes.'

'I think you need to see her again.'

James hesitated then decided to own up.

'We had a drink and a meal last night.'

'And?'

'It was nice, you know? Although, I still kind of feel that right now, I just need some breathing space and possibly I'm using her as an easy option. With hindsight, I probably shouldn't have got involved. But these things happen. And I've enjoyed the attention; and the company.'

Gary was looking at James with a smile.

'Mate, I don't think I've ever heard you talk like that. I think you're in love.'

'Don't talk bollocks.'

'Seriously. All the time I've known you, you kept the detail of your relationship with Sally tightly guarded. But two nights of lusty rogering with Tracy and, Bob's yer uncle, James is like a character from Brideshead Revisited; but not a poof, obviously.'

'Obviously. And who mentioned lusty rogering?'

'I just know that look. The one you had on your face when you described Tracy as *interesting*. Your mastery of understatement can only mean that *interesting* means *shagmonster*. Well, I hope it works; you seem happy.'

'I'm not. Anyway, how's Bridget?'

He led Gary away from the topic with a succession of diversions. The evening reverted to drinking, swearing and ogling; except that, at one point, Gary seemed troubled by something he saw over James' shoulder. It was still only around ten thirty and James was surprised to hear Gary say, 'Come on mate; drink up; let's go and eat.'

'You've got more than half a pint there. You're off your feed.'

'I just think there's a situation brewing here and we should go.'

James looked at his friend closely to gauge the seriousness of this and, realising Gary was sincere, downed the rest of his lager and grabbed his jacket. As he stood and turned to go, James learned the nature of the situation. There was Tracy, almost literally wrapped around a man who clearly had every intention of taking that to its logical conclusion. James stopped and stared but Gary began to propel him towards the exit.

'Come on mate; let's go for a bite. My shout. How about that nice Punjabi?'

'Good call. Yes, but hang on; I need a piss.'

'Do it somewhere else. Come on James. I can see it in your eyes. Don't stay here.'

'See what in my eyes?'

'Maaaaad Maaaaan.' Gary accompanied this with eccentric hand and facial movements. James laughed, then stopped laughing too quickly and Gary missed the nuance of that change.

'Don't worry. I really do need a piss and I won't do anything stupid. No point. Give me five minutes. Sort a taxi. Go on.'

Gary went to the payphone while James headed for the gents. His mind was reeling but, as he stood at the urinal, the need for revenge boiled up inside him. When he returned to the saloon, Tracy and New Man were standing straight ahead of him; she smiling seductively and talking constantly; he listening and nodding. New Man never acknowledged the frequent strokes Tracy gave his arm, shoulder and face. She was drinking a tall fizzy drink; the usual, for sure. New Man had a bottle of Mexican beer with a wedge of lime in the neck.

James walked to the bar and ordered a large gin and tonic. Turning around with the drink he got closer to Tracy and affected a beaming smile.

'Tracy! Bloody hell! Thought it was you, so bought you a large one. There you go.'

He handed the drink to her and smiled at the man, saying; 'Hi. James Clifton. I work with Tracy; when she's up for it.' He gave a massive wink to the man, who said nothing and glanced nervously at Tracy.

'James. What are you doing here?' Her voice held fear. 'I thought the Crown and Cushion was your local.'

'Ha, did you? Do I like the Crown and Cushion Tracy?'

Her face fell. Really fell. And her voice dropped quite low as she replied; 'I suppose so.'

New Man was on a white steed. 'Look, I don't know who you are or what you're up to, but we're just here for a drink after being at a friend's wedding. Leave us, yah?'

'Sure, yah, no problem. Tracy; I'll see you on Monday. And make sure everything you promised me is ready, okay?' Now his voice was a bit shaky and he was relieved to see Gary walking towards them.

'James, don't.' Tracy had tears in her eyes.

'James, leave it. Come on; cab's outside.'

'Excellent! Well, great seeing you. Hope the gin does the trick for you. And for you mate.' He smiled crazily at New Man and succumbed to Gary's tugging for him to leave the scene.

The taxi was there and carried them to the other end of town. James gazed from the window, a cruel smile of satisfaction on his lips. He'd resolved nothing whatsoever, but Tracy's tears felt like a reward for his actions.

James and Gary were shown to a table and ordered a lot of food and several drinks. But they struggled to rekindle any joy or find a way to discuss what had just happened at the pub. Instead, they stuffed food and beer down their necks and watched the restaurant fill up with other drunks. Tensions were high. Drink-fuelled banter turned to abuse, which turned to shouted racist insults, which turned to gratuitous violence. The police soon arrived and within just a few moments appeared to make matters considerably worse. Things were almost completely out of control, so Gary paid the bill and the pair sneaked out of a back door, parted and headed home.

James was in no mood to play football. He had a fuzzy head, indigestion and a powerful reminiscence of curry, garlic and onions. He drove to the match, in which his team thrashed hopeless opponents whose regular goalkeeper had let them down and who caved in resoundingly by half time. James substituted himself and resentfully watched twenty minutes of the second half before going home. Gary's car was still parked across the road and James wondered briefly if his friend got home safely. Then he pondered Tracy's actions and whether it might be a world record to be jettisoned from two relationships in a fortnight.

As he closed his front door, James felt sullen and morose. He threw his sports bag at the living room floor and slumped down on the sofa. A wave of pity and dislike swept over him. He blamed himself, entirely, for being unworthy of everyone then spoke aloud.

'You utter fucking whore.'

He stuffed his head under a sofa cushion to block out the frenzied jabber about Tracy that ricocheted inside his head. But it didn't stop and James sank deeper into a profound, darkened place and remained trapped there. He went to bed before eight and sleep broke this hex until he woke at around two, bathed in sweat and shaking with terror from a ghastly dreamscape. He didn't sleep properly again and got up before six.

He arrived at the office to find there was already a note from someone saying Tracy had called in sick. He smiled at this, crumpled up the piece of paper and settled down to his day. Her absence was convenient. It left him with time to review how to have her removed from his team.

By mid-afternoon he had a scheme that he knew would work and that Miles could not ignore. He wrote it all down, read through it then tore up the paper. He wrote it a second time. It would work. He was pleased and delved in to other activities that kept him occupied till after seven pm.

His post box contained a crisp, white, high quality envelope. His name and address were neatly inscribed; he didn't recognise the handwriting. The post mark was barely legible, but he could make out that it was probably from Hereford. The letter 'J' written on the reverse of the envelope completed the mystery.

James perched the letter against the toaster while he made a pot of tea, then carefully slit the envelope with a carving knife. It contained two pages of pale green paper and as he unfolded them he found the same handwriting. It was rather characterless, but the blue ink looked nice on the green paper.

'Westwick Lodge
Hampton Bishop
12th January, 1990

Dear James,

When I spoke to you on Boxing Day, there were a million things I wanted to say. I thought the hard part would be picking up the phone and asking you out. But in the end, the hard part was my poor fiscal management.

I haven't seen you much since you left school. But on Christmas Eve you were in the Lichfield Vaults and when I saw you across the bar I was reminded of so much. Some of it was probably forgotten; but I quickly realised all of it was still important.

You plus me. All my school friends said I was mad and a fool. Every day, I watched you stroll into the cathedral as if you owned it. Every day I watched you play football in the yard as if your life depended on it. Every day I sat and day-dreamed about you. I used to cut out the drawings you did for the school magazine. Owning something of yours was life-saving to me. I wish I'd kept them.

It was a hopeless crush; the very worst sort. You were four years older and that feels like a lifetime when you're twelve or thirteen. I suspected it was a dream that could never, ever come true.

Then, one fine day, I got you to myself. I slipped and fell down a couple of stairs in A block and you were there. It was like you were waiting to catch me. You helped me to my feet and carried me to a chair. I nearly fainted with excitement and I played hurt, even though I wasn't. You were so nice; much nicer than people said you could be. You were caring and kind, but never asked me my name. You kept asking about the pain, and whether I wanted to see Matron.

We had one more encounter. That same week we were next to each other in the lunch queue. You briefly paid all of your attention to me and asked if I was all right. I could only nod and you told me to sue the school for negligence. You were smiling and laughing and I was smitten. Love's young dream. And your attention evaporated as you turned back to your mates. You still didn't know my name; and I never told you; and I never spoke with you again. I just watched and learned, like I had for years. Then one summer's day, you went away forever.

It's almost impossible to describe how I felt when I saw you in the Lich. It was as if I'd met an old friend, yet we'd never spoken properly so I was still just watching and learning. And I did it all night, which really pissed off my friend. You seemed very, very unhappy. The guy you were with seemed to make you laugh and smile, but it seemed your laughter was over in an instant and your smile was not a smile. I should have come and said something, but I just wasn't sure it would have been welcome.

What's gone wrong? I hope it's not something that can't be put right. I hope you're not too sad. Above all I hope, one day, that I can make you laugh and smile like you mean it.

I'm sorry if this all seems improbable but I simply had to let you know that someone cares and would happily go on caring if it helps. Please call me. You won't regret it.

Laura x

PS – I phoned you to see if you would go to a party with me. Improper etiquette, I realise, but I really wanted to see you. When my money ran out I nearly went mad because I had no more change. I didn't go in the end but heard you were there after all. Typical. Anyway, when you said you didn't know me I was really put off. But then I thought I maybe ought to persevere.

PPS – deciding to write this letter has nearly killed me, L.'

James re-read the letter. He didn't believe a word of it and quickly assumed that it was a wind up. Leo would be at the root of this. He read it twice more, then scanned it for a phone number. There wasn't one and he picked up the telephone to dial 192.

'Drysdale. I don't have an initial. The address is Westwick Lodge, Hampton Bishop. No, Herefordshire.'

The number was ex-directory.

'Laura, how do I call someone who leaves no number? – James.
PS – you can phone me on 01 222 5656 or at work on 01 536 1211, ext.
402.'

He made his writing neat and scribbled a cartoon bear after his note.

She called that Thursday afternoon and he remembered her voice. It instantly made him smile.

'Hello? Could I speak to James Clifton please?'

'This is James.'

'Hello. I feel a proper arse about not putting my number on that letter.'

'A proper arse?'

'As opposed to a false arse.'

'A false arse. Now that is an interesting notion. How can one tell the difference?'

'Well a false arse lacks gravitas.' She laughed. James felt a swell of hope.

'I suppose it must. My older brother has a suitcase with a false bottom. There must be similarities.'

'No, that is entirely different. A false arse can't be carried, unless worn.'

'Good point. So how are you? Where are you? Who are you?'

'It's all in the letter. I leave you to draw your own conclusions; proper or false. Say something.'

'Plimsoll.'

She giggled. 'Have I interrupted your busy executive schedule?'

'No, I can talk. You picked a good time. You didn't miss much at Gra and Gerry's party.'

'Oh? I heard there were all sorts of shenanigans.'

'Shenanigans: good word.'

Her giggle was tight and controlled. It sounded intriguing.

'Your switchboard person is terribly nosey. Getting through to you appears to require some sort of security clearance.'

'There are three of them and they are the only people in this company with any idea of what's going on. They will be listening right now to check up on us. Are you doing anything this weekend?'

'I might be. Why do you ask?'

'It's just that I'm in Hereford for a party on Saturday. Maybe we could get together tomorrow evening? Or at the party; or both. You can tell me more over a couple of light ales.'

'That would be perfect; although I'm a bitter man myself.' She had made her voice sound like a yokel. It made James laugh.

'Great; tomorrow night then. You choose where to meet. I'll be there.'

'Okay, Bogart's. Eight o'clock. How will you know me?'

He suggested she should wear green and black.

'Do you mean that?'

'Why not?'

'Perhaps I should wear a school scarf?'

James realised he might be on difficult ground. 'Well, look: I don't know you, but you know me. So you can seek me out and I will suffer a frisson of fear and expectation every time someone walks by.'

'Meet me in the downstairs bar, and do not wear a comedy mask to confuse me.'

'Damn. But all right. And, sorry, but I have to go now.'

'No problem.'

'Bye Laura.'

'Bye James.'

He had completely forgotten the trick questions he'd lined up: to prove that this was all a wind up by Leo; and to find out how Laura knew his home address. So far as he could remember he had never seen her and had no idea what she looked like. Since its arrival, James had read her letter over and over; he'd looked at the school photo, racking his memory for the incident she mentioned. And although he recalled nothing, he had begun the process of massaging Laura, and the incidents she described, into his own history. It never once occurred to him to pick up the phone to someone and ask who she was.

During an unmemorable meeting at work, he drew in his organiser and made doodles in his head. Her voice and giggles were playful but she sounded strong and confident. He imagined a face and figure. Laura became real.

Work got in the way of this fantasy and he was drawn into questions and debate. As the meeting ended Miles asked James to stay behind.

'James, I've been thinking about your proposal to move Tracy onwards and upwards. I agree with your analysis; she should be managing more and will grow with her own set of responsibilities. You've done a good job there. She's ready, isn't she?'

'Absolutely. And I think there's nothing to gain from waiting; we do this soon. What about her replacement? Are you comfortable with moving Maxine to my team?'

'Yes, definitely. Maxine is well-qualified in theory but I think she'll benefit from your coaching. So I've cleared it all with HR and you can get on with it. If you need my authority for anything, just ask.'

James left the meeting with something approaching glee. Tracy was back at work and very, very pensive. Since her return they'd spoken disjointedly and ineffectively; and only about work. Now, with his plan approved, James asked to speak with her in private and they walked away to a meeting room. He had practiced this moment and the speech he would make. He had been certain Miles would fall for his plan.

'Tracy, I really wish I could pretend this is about work but we both know it's not. We can't work as a team any more. So I've agreed with Miles that you're going to head up your own team supporting purchasing for Finance. It's a good role and you'll do it brilliantly.'

Tracy was evidently stunned by this. 'Thank you James. I thought... I was expecting...'

'You thought I had the same lack of loyalty and sensitivity as you? You were expecting what? A trumped up disciplinary?'

'No, but I...'

'Well actually I do lack loyalty to you and really don't care what happens to you.'

'Who are you replacing me with?'

'At work? Or in bed?'

Tracy gasped but before she could speak, James continued, 'Sorry. I didn't want to say anything like that. Please ignore it.'

But she was crying.

'Anyway; new role effective next Monday. No need for you to hand anything over; I can do all that. Thanks for everything.'

James walked out of the room almost overwhelmed by anger that hadn't dissipated when he got home two hours later.

There was a voice message from Tracy. It began with thanks for his efforts but ended with her sobbing apology after apology and how she wanted to make things right between them. James hit delete then hit it again and again until he broke the button. At last he smiled. This pointless destruction and violence against an inanimate object actually made him laugh. In a better mood, he packed a bag for the coming weekend, then phoned his parents and Paul to conclude arrangements.

Without formal explanation or notification, Tracy was absent the next day. James was unmoved and by mid-morning had arranged to take the afternoon off. The early departure meant he avoided the worst of Friday's traffic. A blast up the M4 to Swindon and cross country to Hereford got James to his parents' home by five, in the shower by six and nervously preoccupied by seven.

Bogart's was already packed when he got there at seven forty-five. Despite an entrance charge and a house rule about smart clothes, the atmosphere was tense and vaguely threatening. James ordered a Mexican beer with lime in the neck and drank from the bottle. The noise was staggering; a loud hailer would have aided and abetted anyone trying to order drinks or chat someone up. Perhaps that was the idea? Perhaps the reason for this noise was to accustom couples to a lifetime of not talking to each other?

But the music suddenly dimmed and an announcement boomed out that if there was a Mr James Clifton in the house, he should go to the main entrance.

When he got there, James nodded affably at the muscle-bound security personnel. One of them glared back as if James was recently scraped off his shoe; the other smiled, revealing that one of his front teeth was the colour of pewter.

'Mr Clifton? This gorgeous lady says you will pay for her to get in.'

He nodded towards his left.

James looked at the woman who kept smiling at him.

'Yes. She's with me.'

11

She was tall; about five feet eight, he guessed. She had shoulder length blonde hair and eyes that seemed to be blue, but in the dim light of the club's entrance could just as easily have been grey. Her face was slender and she had a tilted up nose that wrinkled slightly when she smiled. Laura's mouth was large, like a model or a film star. She wore subtle makeup and golden earrings matched by a neck chain. A silky green blouse with black trousers met his identification requirements.

James listened to her excuse that her cashpoint card had failed, leaving her with just £1.50. It was an odd conversation to have on a date and by the end of it she looked worried and pursed her lips. James changed the subject.

'Did you sue the school in the end?'

She laughed. 'I didn't. Aren't you going to buy me a drink?'

'Yes, come on. But let's not stay here long. It's horrible.'

Laura fell silent as they walked to the bar. When James asked what she wanted to drink she ignored him.

'What's so bad about it?'

'Well aside from the clientele, it's just not my kind of place.'

'You should have said that when I suggested it.'

James turned to her and smiled. 'I didn't know; I've never been here before.'

'I feel like I've messed up.'

He made his smile warmer. 'You haven't. So, tell me; what would you like to drink?'

'Jim Beam on the rocks. And for making me feel stupid, you can pay for a double.'

'Deal.'

They shouted to each other for half an hour and James ordered more drinks. The loud music and tumult of conversation meant that they needed to stand close and lean in to one another to be heard. It created an inevitable instant intimacy. During one of these clinches, Laura took James' hand and squeezed it as she spoke in his ear. She was ready to leave but needed to powder her nose.

He watched her go then scanned the club and the animation around him. The combination of sounds and movement turned in to a collage in his head. He closed his eyes and saw sweeps of colour zipping randomly around inside a cube. Then he smelled and felt that Laura had returned and was next to him.

She said, 'A penny for those thoughts, Clifton J.'

James' eyes opened. The idea he'd just formed was made complete as he explained it to her. She smiled the way a mother would at a precocious child.

But he changed the subject. 'Tell me what perfume you're wearing.'

'It's *Eternity*. Do you like it?'

'I do. It's lovely.'

'How do you feel about Bogart's now?'

James thought about suggesting they stay, because he loved being so unavoidably close to her.

'Well I think there are some people here from our respective pasts.'

'That's difficult to avoid. But I bet you can't name anyone in the house.'

James pointed across the room with his bottle. 'Over there: blue top; tan chinos; Russ Hughes. Looks about forty but in fact was in my year at school. Used to frighten me; now I'm not sure why because he looks lame, unfit, and slightly sad. Notwithstanding my pacifist tendencies, I reckon I could have him.'

Laura smiled, nodded and said, 'You're good.'

'There's more. Up on the mezzanine; Claire Adams; went to the girl's high school and shagged more or less everyone in my year; except me; not sure why. In fact, I think she's just spotted me and is pondering the same question.'

'Shit; then we better go. Come on.'

Laura grabbed him by the hand and they walked off to the exit. James, giggling and laughing in tune with this woman, finished his beer as they walked in to the night.

'I'm really hurt that you don't remember me. Or were you just pretending on the phone?'

'I wasn't pretending. Sorry, but I don't remember you.'

'It explains why I had to wear a badge. But top marks for honesty.' She stopped and turned to face him; 'Don't ever bullshit me, will you?'

He felt a jolt of something and couldn't tear his eyes away. She held his gaze and repeated; 'Will you James?'

'I won't.'

Satisfied, she turned and led him away. 'I knew you'd be honest. We must explore that comment about Claire Adams.'

'Oh no. Is she a friend of yours?'

'She's not; no. But I'm intrigued to know if she did shag everyone in your year. Such information can be helpful for a girl, even twelve years after the fact.'

'Well more or less everyone. I think she probably ignored the most obviously gay boarders.'

Laura laughed heartily, then feigned concern.

'But could that mean that you are also gay? Which is why you were left off her list?'

James snapped his fingers decisively. 'That must be it. I always wondered, and thank you for outing me.'

They strolled along Broad Street past several pubs that were rejected as venues. Laura tried her card again at two different ATMs and showed James a screen message saying *Service Temporarily Unavailable*. He took a twenty pound note from his trouser pocket and told her to take it. She planted a lingering kiss on his cheek and they stayed close in an embrace.

When they reached the Saracen's Head, James looked quizzically at Laura; 'It better be here then.'

She seemed pleased. 'It really has to be. I'm too cold and if we walk any further we'll be in another country.'

They grabbed a table close to the fireplace and as James bought more drinks he looked at the place where an old juke box used to stand. It had held such treasures back then.

In the relative calm of the pub they seemed to relax into a round of small talk. James reeled off the basics about his job then learned that Laura was a Pensions Advisor at a bank and didn't really like it.

'Why don't you like it?'

'I'm short of experience and feel like I'm a nobody. I've done no real work. Since I left college I've drifted too much.'

'What did you do at college? And where?'

'English; at Exeter. I never really knew what I wanted to do. Never had a career in mind. But then something stupid happened, and I didn't finish my course.'

'What did you do?'

'I was just stupid. You don't need to know how or why.'

Whoever was talking tended to make no eye contact. Whoever was listening watched intently while the other spoke. They were sitting opposite one another, but leaning forward so their faces were close. At one point, Laura made as if to touch James' cheek but then withdrew her hand and searched his face instead.

'You've hardly changed. The hair style is different, in that you've got one, but I see no grey; unlike under your eyes.' She searched all around his face. 'You look as if you might be growing old gracefully.'

Her wicked laugh didn't stop him from pouting.

'I loved that bear you drew on my note. What kind of paintings do you do these days? I remember how some of what you did at school seemed really complex; dark and destructive.'

'I paint quite a lot, but I like working with pastels and charcoal. And, yes, what I do is still dark and destructive.' He paused for a swig of beer. 'In many ways I prefer drawing to painting.'

'Why?'

'I like the simplicity and roughness; and the way a drawing can be incredibly good at portraying depth.'

Laura squinted her eyes. 'But it's all just a hobby for you.'

James looked wistfully back. 'It probably is, yes.'

An awkward silence ensued; James felt admonished.

Laura switched subjects again. 'Whose party are you going to tomorrow?'

'It's Wendy Thomas' birthday. Paul invited me. I'm not sure I really want to go.'

'I heard he was a disgrace at Gerry's do.'

'Yes, he was. How come you heard that?'

'I keep in touch. Living here means you're touched by all that history. I suppose you don't see it, as a visitor, but it's very insular and vaguely incestuous. Maybe you noticed at the party?'

'Yes. I did. It's inescapable.'

'It was fun for a while but it feels false now; I mean it's been so long since school. But I have my spies. I heard all about you and Philippa.' She smiled triumphantly.

'And who are your spies?'

'I can't reveal that! Otherwise, what would be the point of having spies?' She squinted her eyes again. 'You like Philippa don't you?'

'Yes.'

'But?'

'How did you know there was a *but*?'

'I just did. Go on. Tell me about you and her.'

'There is no me and her. We used to be close and should still be close; our very short meeting at Gra's proved it. But in fact all we have is... back then.'

'Well *back then* has been unexpectedly kind to you and me, so let's not dwell on it. Another beer?'

When the small talk ensued, James spent time trying to convince Laura she should join him at Paul and Wendy's party. Her excuse, that a family dinner party would make it difficult, didn't stop him persisting and eventually she said she might be able to join him later in the evening.

'But that's very late, and you said you don't really want to go.'

'If you are there it will make everything right.'

'You old charmer. You should be in a smoking jacket.'

This made them laugh; like old friends would laugh.

'Like you said earlier, parties can be false so let's make tomorrow's real.'

Laura nodded, and seemed to have been persuaded. 'All right then; call me at ten thirty. I will know what's possible then.'

They switched track again to discuss their homes and what they liked about them. James talked disinterestedly of his two bedroomed flat near Richmond town centre, close to assorted parks, and how he'd been mainly happy there. Laura still lived with her parents in Hampton Bishop, a village about two miles east of the city.

James said, 'Do you think you'll stay in Hereford?'

'I don't really know; and that's linked to my uncertainty about what job I want. Being at home makes it too easy to just roll along.'

'Come and see the bright lights some time.'

'I haven't been to London, or anywhere near it, for ages. But – yes – it would be good to come there, and hopefully spend time with you. If you'd like that?'

'Are you free next weekend?'

She feigned shock and put on her mock yokel voice. 'You aren't proposing that I come alone to your chambers am you Squire Clifton? Why, I hardly knows 'ee. I could be in grave peril alone with 'ee.'

'You will never be in peril with me Laura.'

Their eyes met and James was hypnotised by the cobalt blue of her stare. She held his gaze. 'What was the huge heartache on Christmas Eve? I thought you looked suicidal.'

'On Christmas Eve there wasn't really any heartache. I was with David, my little brother, for a reunion beer or two.' He hesitated but the cobalt blue kept him talking. 'I'd had a rough few months; my then girlfriend and I had separated and even though we got back together just before Christmas, I wasn't sure about things.'

'Your girlfriend? Is that something I should know about?' Her voice held a strange combination of threat and sorrow.

James smiled and touched her hand. 'Hey, lighten up. I said *then girlfriend*.'

'Go on.'

'She is called Sally and she left me for good on Boxing Day. A phone call lasting two minutes drew a line under our three years together. I don't really know why she did it and, if she hadn't, I guess I was looking forward to seeing her again. But, it's over; and I really don't care that much.' He laughed, which seemed to relieve the tension.

'What's funny?'

'I actually had two very short phone calls on Boxing Day. One worked out bad, the other has confused me but it might be all right.'

Laura smiled at him. 'So you are single?'

'Yes, I'm single; which might just be the best way for me to be.'

'I know what you mean.'

'Really? Well it sounds like we're perfect for each other then.'

Her smile broadened. 'I've always thought that. Do you think I was a bit pushy; the call and letter and everything?'

'When you called on Boxing Day it made me curious. I didn't really know what to think; but it was only a few minutes later that my ability to think straight got crushed. I almost certainly should have asked about you at Gra's party.'

'My spies would have known.'

'Your spies; yes. It would have been risky to mention your name wouldn't it? Anyway; when your letter arrived I honestly thought it was a wind up.'

'In what way?'

'It's the kind of thing that well-meaning people would do to cheer me up, while also inflicting a cruel joke. Anyway, if you hadn't been pushy we wouldn't be here now. You needed to be pushy. It's made me fascinated by how you've retained this...'

'...obsession?'

'Are you obsessed?'

Laura held his gaze again; he saw truth and honesty and felt a surge of warmth and captivation.

'I think it's very much an obsession. Like a stalker.'

'Should I be afraid? Have you got a knife?'

She ignored the question. 'I know it must seem improbable, but it's true. Every word in my letter.'

'Good. It's important for me to know people, places and events from my past; I'm very nostalgic about those times. So it bugs me that I don't remember you. It really, really bugs me.'

'I don't care. I was terribly spotty and ugly then.'

'I can't believe that.'

'Oh I was. Too tall, nerdy and angular.' She swigged back some bourbon; 'I was very, very infatuated with you and my punishment was lots of spots. I remember being so jealous when I saw you with other girls.'

'That can't have been very often.'

'And I reserved a very special dislike for anyone who hurt you. Like Sarah Smith. I hated her.'

James felt another rush of affection for Laura. She really was part of his sacred past. 'All that is forever ago. It only matters in retrospect.'

'Is *forever ago* a real phrase? I don't think it is.' James laughed again. She had an assured humour; like someone with total certainty.

'I remember how much I wanted to hug you in those days.' She paused, apparently planning her next words. 'I still want to hug you, obviously. But, then, it was different. I wanted you to share my spots and whatever sweets I was sucking. You never had spots but I would willingly have shared mine.'

Laura kept extracting these memories from her compilation of his deeds and it made him feel that she was reading from his biography. But she sometimes revealed things he didn't recognise, or were different versions of his own recollections, or that he had conveniently forgotten. It was mesmerising, yet there was a sense of being on the outside of this, looking in; as if he still thought the whole thing was a game; that she was simply a well-briefed charlatan who might be causing him to revise his own history.

They left the pub shortly before eleven and walked hand in hand through the Cathedral Close and on to the taxi rank.

'Is that our first and last date, or will you be calling me soon to ask me out again?'

'I'm calling you tomorrow at ten, remember? That's our second date.'

She pulled a funny face at him and nodded. 'Okay; but please call me anyway; whenever you can.'

James said he would, and she pecked his cheek before getting into her taxi.

He said: 'See you tomorrow.'

'Yes, hopefully. Bye.'

As the cab drove away she turned and waved at him through the window. He waved too and watched the car until it was lost in the traffic.

Walking and thinking, he could reach no conclusions about this meeting. More things troubled him than helped him. And what troubled him most was the extent to which Laura knew him. He found that complicated and unnerving. It felt wrong.

But her beauty, eyes and smile, and her inescapable physical charms, felt very right indeed.

12

By as early as eight thirty James was fed up with what was a travesty of a party.

He'd arrived early, hoping to resolve and fix things with Paul. Wendy didn't come to greet him and sent a muffled welcome from upstairs; various noises from above suggested significant struggle.

Paul was almost constantly on the phone and, about forty-five minutes before the party's scheduled start, grabbed his car keys and left the house. James wasn't invited along for the ride, so he read that week's Hereford Times, sipped some beer and felt like a cuckoo in the nest. Nothing got fixed. When he returned Paul seemed to be at arm's length and there was no attempt at rapprochement for Boxing Night.

Eventually, the house and party became populated with guests. These were strangers; people James didn't know and had never met; a mixture of work and business associates plus friends of Wendy and relatives of them both. Paul was a smiling, cordial host. He floated from guest to guest like a bee to flowers, solicitously confirming people had enough to drink and soaking up their enthusiasm about the house and everything in it.

On one of the occasions that he buzzed past James, Paul introduced a woman called Helen. Before she spoke, James had already made up his mind that she was unpleasant and desperately overdone; like the indulgent birthday cake of a spoiled seven year old. She told them about her Porsche; her love of the best champagne; her bi-annual holidays in Barbados and her Christmas skiing in Aspen. She only stopped talking about herself to take a swipe at things like living in Britain and how much she hated foreigners, especially the French. Her makeup was immaculate but had made her grotesque; her hair was gelled to the point that it looked like a shiny new bog brush. James found it wonderful that, despite all her projected excellence, she had a speaking voice like a honking goose. She also had a habit of using big words that were often not the right words. At one point she said she intended to *extrapolate myself from that situation.*

He couldn't understand why this person was in the country, let alone in Hereford, and when she finally stopped talking James said, 'So you must be the heir-head to a massive fortune.' The insult flew over her and she smiled back at him with dazzled incredulity. Paul glared at James. Once, he would have joined in an assassination of this character but he led her away in search of less cynical eyes and ears. James found he was alone once more, but slightly cheered.

Other guests wandered by with opening remarks and introductions. But they discovered James was someone who didn't talk about his work or family, was disinterested in what others do and who didn't fit in. What James wanted, more than anything, was someone to say or do something spontaneous rather than act out this pre-scripted masque. People drifted away from him with haste; he was not a player; he had dangerous and impulsive tendencies and those didn't fit with the pervasive culture of success.

When Paul announced that food was being served, James queued up with a plate and shortly felt a sharp poke in his ribs. He turned to find Wendy gazing boldly in to his eyes. She seemed pleased to see him, but sad and dejected.

'Hello Mrs Thomas. And are you enjoying your fabulous party?'

She didn't register the implied rudeness of James' greeting.

'I can't say I am. I'd be amazed if anyone is. Look at all this food; Paul has gone completely over the top and it's just so obviously a guilt trip. What about you? Have you been all right since the break up from Sally? I thought you seemed a little helpless at Christmas. As if the whole thing was what you expected.'

'I'm fine, and I will be fine.'

'Well that's good. Paul always tells me that you are a survivor and mentally very tough. But that was in the days when he talked properly to me.'

'So things are still bad?'

Wendy looked around. 'Get something to eat and we can find somewhere to talk.'

He piled food on his plate. Wendy picked some salad and chicken. Grazing among the numerous nibbles he'd accumulated, James followed Wendy to the dining room and they sat at one end of the table.

'The answer to your question is *no*. Things are not going at all well between us.'

'Is there anything I can do?'

'The only person who can do anything to resolve this problem is Paul.'

'But surely you have to work with him?'

'We've gone beyond that; I really can't see us making it.'

James concentrated on eating. He felt he had to avoid looking at her. He didn't think this sounded good and created a diversion.

'Does Paul have a problem with me? Has he said anything? He's like a stranger this evening. I kind of hoped we could discuss the stuff he said to me at Christmas.'

Wendy nodded towards the door. 'There are a lot of important people here tonight; clients mainly, but Paul's boss too. He's out to make a good impression. So I don't think he's necessarily being terribly nice to anyone other than those select few.'

'So your birthday is effectively a networking event? Charming!'

'Yes and, worse still, I am instructed to be the loyal, willing, adoring wife.'

'Of course you are! Shall I get us another drink?'

'Let me get you something. I'm not drinking tonight. I dare not risk another loss of control.' Wendy was blushing as she walked away.

She returned with an open bottle of red wine with gold coloured netting around it. The bottle was around half full. 'I don't know if this is what you like but Paul has been reserving it for his special chums. You should be on that list; not just tonight; always. So I'm putting you on it.'

James poured a glass and sipped gently at it. Then he took a gulp and examined the bottle. It was vintage Rioja; a significant improvement on the plonk Paul had served up on Boxing Night.

'Is it good?'

'It's sensational. You should try it.'

Wendy shook her head. James smiled again, realising he had the whole lot to himself.

She interrupted this vinous reverie. 'I do need to talk to you about Boxing Night, even if Paul is avoiding the topic.'

'Go on.'

She lowered her voice to little more than a murmur. 'Well, this is difficult. After Paul had been so utterly vile to me and pretty horrible to you, I... I came downstairs and really, really intended to seduce you.'

James hesitated. His next words needed to be chosen with care.

'Why did you want to do that? What would that have solved?'

'I don't know, but I took my knickers off and I honestly had it in my head that I wanted you to make love to me. On the living room floor; or on the kitchen table; or anywhere; anyhow.'

James glanced at the door. They were alone and no one was in earshot. A mild panic was rising in his tummy.

'God James; I know that sounds terrible and what makes it worse is that the whole thing was just a stupid childish reaction to Paul. I don't harbour any particular feelings for you. I just wanted to make myself feel happy that, for once, I had got him back for being such a bastard.'

James remained quiet and drained another glass.

'And then I woke up at god knows what time, still in the lounge with gin all over me, and you weren't around. I thought: *how could he leave me like that?* And I just had to talk to you about it. I mean it was completely wrong of me to think like I did and to be so brazen, but tell me; how could you resist? I was out of control. In the same circumstances, Paul would have gone ahead and shagged someone who did that, conscious or not. But why not you? Don't you fancy me?'

James realised he couldn't remain quiet.

'Well for starters, if I had done anything to you while you were in a drunken coma, it would have been rape; and that is not something either of us would want is it?'

Wendy shook her head.

'Second, it isn't a question of fancying someone or not fancying them. You and Paul are married. I believe that is important and I have no right to disrupt it. Things might not be great for you two right now, but I was not and am not prepared to be part of the problem. I'd prefer to help you both patch things up.'

Wendy had filled his glass and James took another slug of wine.

'Third, you and I aren't close are we? Since we're talking openly, let's admit it. I don't think you've ever particularly liked me and I've always felt as if I'm somehow an intruder on your relationship with Paul.'

'I can't think of anything I've ever done to make you feel that way. I like you and I like the influence you have on Paul.'

James couldn't tell how true any of that was, but chose not to challenge or correct it.

'As for whether or not I fancy you, you're a beautiful woman; a highly desirable, sexy one too. But I can't ignore what you are; my friend's wife. And that makes you someone I can't desire. Your beauty and physical charms are inescapable, and I would be lying if I said I didn't think about going for it on Boxing Night. It crossed my mind. But the right thing was to walk away. I can't shag someone who is my friend's wife. It's just not in my make up.'

James thought she was about to snatch his glass and throw wine in his face, such was her look of perplexed, broken disbelief.

'This is awful. I feel so shut out, like I'm a castaway. All this: what Paul is doing with all these women; the fact that I can't tempt a man to have sex with me; this horrible loneliness. I have to see a future in which, if Paul and I are to part, there is love and sex. And happiness.'

'Wendy, you can't think like that. But equally, you can't mix up what I did or didn't do with your ability to attract a new partner should that come to pass. Boxing Night was neither the time nor the place for me to take advantage of an upset and confused woman. That doesn't make you a spinster.'

She looked at him, a tear growing in the corner of one eye. There was affection in her gaze, something James had never seen before, and he couldn't understand what was causing it.

'I'm glad we've spoken. Everything you've said has been a tonic. I know you think I'm shallow and a gold-digger; but I'm not. I am in such despair though and, as you say, I need to resolve that openly and honestly with my husband. But thank you for your honesty. I really did need to know that I have something to cling to; to know that I might have a future in a relationship if everything with Paul just fails.'

She sobbed, and wiped away more tears with a serviette. Again, James looked to the doorway; but they remained alone and unobserved.

'I am not the answer to your problems. I really do want to be someone who repairs what you and Paul have and who values you jointly as my friends.'

She got up and, with her head down, left in a rush. James picked at a chicken drumstick and downed another mouthful of Rioja. He licked his fingers extravagantly and stayed at the table to finish off the bottle. It tasted amazing and it felt good to guzzle it down knowing Paul had never intended him to have it.

Unfortunately, James had now consumed a lot of beer and wine and when Paul flowed suavely into the room with a couple in tow, James' condition was somewhat regrettable. After a glance across at his disintegrating friend and friendship, Paul said something to his guests and they departed.

Paul's voice was raised; 'Where did you get that wine?'

'Kitchen. It's nice. Lovely.'

'How much have you had?'

'Not much; a couple of glasses.'

'Bloody hell. That's proper wine; expensive stuff. Not for necking back like a wino.'

'Oh well pardon me your Right Honourable Judge Mental.'

Paul stormed off with the empty bottle.

James tittered to himself and made a V sign at his departing friend. He stood unsteadily and set off to survey the party. Moving from room to room, watching a house full of people he now loathed, James made a decision. He staggered from the house and stumbled off in search of a phone box. With each step he became more hopelessly drunk.

'Cud I spik to Laura plis?'

'This is Laura.'

'You sound diffrnt tnight. Or is it the phone? You sound worried. Ptight.'

'And you sound drunk.'

'Say mname. Please?'

'Whatever for? I know it's you.'

'But mname: sounds snice when you say it. Go on.'

'You are very drunk.'

'"course I'm fuckin drunk.'

'Please don't swear at me.' Her voice was lowered and James, even in his tricky condition, noted a sudden anger.

'Sorry. Didn't mean tswear. Slipped out. Sorry.'

'What do you want?'

'Aren't you going to come t'thparty?'

'I can't.'

'But y'said y'would.'

'I didn't. I said it would be difficult. And it is. I can't come.'

'But I wanna see you. I HAVE to fuckin see you Laura. I need to tell you summing.'

'I need to tell you something too: but not while you're drunk. And I don't want to hear whatever it is you have to say so long as you're drunk. Please, James, just go home and be safe.'

'You seddit! SHESEDDITEVRYWUN! But 't sounded bett bfore.'

She emitted a tiny laugh. 'Do you get like this all the time?'

'Only when I wantsee you.'

'Oh shit. Look, I've got to go now. Call me again soon. Is there someone with you?'

'I cudrive round? The party's shite. Why dun I do that?'

'No James. It's late and you mustn't drive under any circumstances; promise me.'

'Y'seddit again. I love it when you dthat.'

'I hope you mean that.'

'Yes.'

'Got to go. Say goodbye.'

'G'bye.'

'Bye.'

It was nothing more than a whisper.

As the phone went dead he started singing a song about not hanging up. This barely remembered ditty was soon replaced with another loved love song which he was still drooling in to the receiver when, of all people, Leo walked by.

'Ah, the indestructible James Clifton Esquire. Indestructible, despite years of self-abuse and hatred. How are you?'

'mpisssafar.'

'Surely not? You seem fine. Who were you yelling 10cc at just now?'

'No one that matts.'

'I'm just on my way to Paul's party.'

'Yornorrinvited.'

'I'm not, true. But he'll let me in. I've got his balls in a very large vice just now.'

'Really?'

'And anyway. I'm with you.'

'Correct. Hoorahhhhh.'

James seemed to be welded to the phone box door and could hardly stand.

'Come along with me. I'll tell you all about the people he's shagging and all the shit he's in at work.'

During their short walk, Leo unveiled a series of revelations about Paul's extravagantly corrupt business practices. This was interrupted with a variety of exclamations from James.

Mainly, he yelled, 'NO!?!'

Sometimes, he squealed, 'Get the fuck outta here', as he had once seen in a film.

Sometimes he stopped dead to emphasise these exclamations.

'Here's the house.'

'sluvvly house init?'

'Yes. It is. I'm going to have a quick spliff. Want some?' Leo extracted a joint from his jacket pocket and lit up.

'Han't hadenny... fkin ages.'

'Sally didn't approve?'

'sright. 'n wa she know? Eh?'

'She has a degree in Modern Languages, I believe.'

'ExACTly. Eggs-fuckin-zactly.'

Leo handed him the joint and James drew a lungful of the

smoke. He choked and spluttered.

'So you don't feel that your ex was too bright then? Because she wouldn't let you take the odd spliff?'

'Bright'sa button, Sally. 'sabuttn. But... in the real world... Leo... lost.'

'You're talking bollocks James.'

'sagift.'

'Come on. Let's get inside. I want to wind this bastard up a bit.'

'Wha? Why? sgoinon?'

'You'll see.'

After grabbing a bottle of wine and a couple of glasses, Leo and James arranged themselves on a sofa and began a sort of conversation. Essentially, Leo made a proposition of some kind and James swore, mumbled and gestured with his increasingly flaccid head. Shortly, Leo took out another joint.

'Leo? Yurra top man. I really fkin enjoyed seeing yat Gra's party.'

'It was a good night. I enjoyed it. I even enjoyed seeing Paul. But that was before New Year's Eve. Why are you so pissed?'

'sisparty. ss shite. swurznat. etsgo. c'mon. 'sfuck off to a club or summing.'

He stood up and knocked into another guest who called him a piss artist. James fell over then leapt up and spun round. He stared unevenly at the man and belched.

'Piss artst? PISS artis? You cun. ooo the fuck are you nyway?'

Leo stood up. 'James; leave it.'

'No.'

James punched the man in the mouth.

Leo grabbed him and Paul was soon on the scene, looking furious. James yelled at the prone figure of his opponent.

'Pisartist? No mate. Shit artist. Yes. SHIT. ARTIST.

I carn paint, draw, nuthin like at.

I AM a shit Artst.

But don't you ever, EVER call me a pissarst again.'

It was like a scene from a budget English gangster movie.

But now the bloke was on his feet and he was a bit big. Paul was trying to corral him out of the room and had instructed Leo to remove James to safety. All seemed well.

Then James leapt past Leo and Paul and hit the man again.

'Don fuckin' lookit me like at you twat. Come on.'

And the man did. He worked diligently for a local Estate Agent making a solid living by ripping off clients with unwarranted fees and dubious pricing mechanisms. So he wasn't having this. He kicked James in the knee then pulled a punch into his midriff. James crumpled a bit and took another hit on the chin for his trouble.

The man knew how to fight.

Leo winced and moved between the duellers. But James, with his mind in a muddle, thought he also knew how to fight. He leapt at the man and grappled him to the floor, managing an inexpert head butt as he did so. There were screams and shouts now from other guests, some of whom were suddenly not so sophisticated.

'Stop him.'

'Hit him.'

'Kick the shit out of him.'

The music, like the piano player in a Wild West bar, suddenly stopped. Wendy arrived looking upset and flushed. She started to cry and Paul got mad; he shouted at Leo; he shouted at James; he shouted generally to the room. The other man was glaring at everyone and a couple of his mates were lined up, ready to broaden the conflict if needed. Leo made a placatory gesture with his hands and pulled James towards the door.

'Come on mate. Let's go. You can stay at my place.'

Paul was still furious. 'Tell him I want to see him in the morning. I want an explanation. I want...'

'Go fuck yourself Paul. And fuck your secretary while you're at it.'

Paul was shocked into silence.

James wasn't to be outdone and picked up on Leo's lead. 'Yeah. Gwon. Shag 'er in u bthrm while everyone's dancin dnstairs. Or't work 'nthgents eh? Or 'ntha train. Always 'nth bog in'it?'

Leo grinned maliciously at Paul who glared back in horror.

'Get out of my house.'

'Gladly. t'sa pss por ouse anyway.'

Leo was laughing openly now.

'Come on James. Let's get some fresh air.'

As the door closed behind them, James heard Paul say: '...pissed as a fart. Stoned too. Delirious. Needs treatment.'

James yelled back through the door; "eeza fucker', and vomited down the door and onto the step.

'Oh great,' said Leo.

It was around half a mile to Leo's house but the journey lasted more than thirty minutes. James was not at all well and was sick several times. He also kept roaming into gardens. As they reached the house, James was silent and morose. Leo's efforts to understand what might be wrong were met with incoherent mumbles.

'I've never seen you hit anyone before. You hate violence. And you behaved dreadfully back there. If I wasn't so ashamed of myself, I'd be utterly ashamed of you. You're not yourself. What is it?'

'Dunno. Just feel. I dunno.'

Once inside James became a tearful, sobbing, hysterical wreck incapable of speech. Leo got him onto a bed, threw a duvet over him, placed a bucket and towel and jug full of water by his side and left him there. Ten minutes later he returned to the room and turned James onto his side.

Leo's spare room faced east and James was woken by bright wintry sunshine; an unwelcome start. He was sweating profusely and sat up to drink some water. He buckled under the onslaught of a pounding head and churning stomach. He tried to relax, to lie still and think himself better. But there was trouble ahead. He rushed to the bathroom and stuck his head into the toilet bowl. He heaved away but these were gulps of nothing. Then occasional lumps of inexplicable yellow matter filled the gaps: then a mouthful of something revolting. This went on for some moments, his efforts accompanied by stentorian bellows and pathetic whimpering. Things calmed and James drank water from the cold tap. When he stood up straight, another sensation gripped him. Now, instead of clinging to the bowl, he sat on it. A great thundering fart rent the air; then another. Then a long, drawn out, melodious one. He laughed at this but that made him feel sick. He leapt up from the seat, twisted round and plunged his head into the bowl. The residual gas smelt so absolutely vile that it prompted a prolonged bout of lump spitting.

Leo's voice filtered through the bathroom door; 'You okay?'

'Yeah, sure; I'm fine. I'll be out for the 100 metres final in about four minutes.'

'Tea, sir?'

'Yes. Eight sugars; twelve sugars. And don't fucking call me sir.'

Leo laughed loudly. 'Yes sir. Take your time. There's fresh water out here for you.'

James shut his eyes. He felt absolutely dreadful. A mess; out of control; shaking and raging hot. He clung to the cold, comforting china.

Gradually, he arrived at a place where he no longer felt likely to be sick. He stood and waited, clutching the bog roll holder for support. He steadied himself in stillness. Taking small steps, he opened the door to find a reassuringly large mug of tea and more water. He picked up the mug and winced at the violent thump in his head. The tea was acidic and lukewarm; he gulped it down in one then sipped the pint of water. Again he waited. Once he felt safe enough, he spent several minutes cleaning up the bathroom and squirted bleach around the toilet.

Leo was waiting for him in the kitchen. 'Well, well: The Laughing Cavalier.'

'Remember 1977 Leo; we promised.'

'Yes. I know.'

'We swore that, no matter how bad the mess... '

'Yes, all right.'

'...no matter how dreadful the behaviour...'

'Yes.'

'...no matter how utterly terrible the aftermath, we would never make fun of a friend's hangover. Maybe the odd post mortem. But no, positively no piss taking.'

'But, like many of those adolescent vows, it's incredibly balanced in your favour. No one else ever got into quite the same state as you did; and still do apparently.'

James felt well enough to defend himself. 'That's not fair. What about your behaviour at John Morton's 18th birthday party.'

'Hmm. Although I have to tell you that you do look and smell particularly lovely. Come on then; post mortem time.'

James sat at the table. 'Right. Damage?'

'Extensive: one good friendship, one fading friendship, one carpet, one pillow, one nose, one mouth, one smart shirt, some vintage Rioja, one marriage.'

'I hit someone didn't I?'

'Yes. Why?'

'What did he call me?'

'A piss artist.'

'That would have done it. And did he hit me?'

'Three times: knee, tummy, chin.'

'That explains why I've been so sick. I never normally get so ill.'

'That, my friend, is a preposterous thing to say in the circumstances.'

James examined his knuckles.

'I've never known you get violent. I mean it was quite funny, especially when you started calling Paul an adulterer in front of both his wife and two of his lovers. But you were like an animal; real Saturday-Night-At-Bogart's stuff.'

'Oh shit.'

'Oh yes. Another cup of tea?'

'Please. And have you got any medicinal drugs and some very cold, fizzy, sugary drink?'

'Behind you.'

'You've thought of everything.'

'You'd do the same. Take a shower if you like. Please; take a shower. I'll put a clean T shirt in your room.'

Leo poured out another mug of tea and shovelled some sugar into it. James took it back to the bathroom where he undressed. His shirt stank of sweat, stale wine and vomit; it was ruined. The shower revitalised him and the fresh shirt, even with yesterday's underwear and trousers, also aided his revival.

'Who had you been calling when I met you?'

'A friend.'

'And not the Prime Minister? Well there's a surprise.'

James was struggling to open a bottle of aspirin. Leo eventually took it from him to help out.

'Your sarcasm has never been appealing; you know that don't you?'

'Who was it James? Tell me.'

'A woman; someone new. She phoned me on Boxing Day, at which point I'd never heard of her; but she, it seems...., knows me like the back of her hand.'

Leo smiled and said, 'Go on.'

James was munching the tablets and washing them down with tea.

'Said she knows me from school. Had a thing for me. Wanted to see me. Saw me in the Lich on Christmas Eve. Called. Wrote.'

Leo laughed. 'Who is it? Tell me the truth.'

'She's called Laura.'

'Laura Drysdale.'

'How the fuck do you know that?'

'Let's call it instinct.'

'Sounds more like inside knowledge to me.'

'I suppose it is. But don't be so defensive.'

James, in spite of his hangover, was slightly puffed up with indignation. 'I don't understand how you know, and what you know.'

'Well everyone knew at school, but no one had the courage to tell you. At the best of times you could be touchy and unreceptive and to make things worse, all this came to light during Sarahgate.'

'Right.'

Leo beamed at his friend. 'Come on, calm down. If you're so concerned about it being real, how come you were on the phone to her in an appalling drunken state?'

James sighed. 'I just feel as if it's some sort of manufactured outcome. Too convenient and close to the end of things with Sally.'

Leo gave him an avuncular smile. 'That's nonsense. Get a grip.'

James swigged down another half pint of tea then opened a can of fruity pop.

'How come everyone knew and nobody told me?'

'Like I said, we lacked the necessary mettle.'

'Well shame on you all.'

'What's the worst that can happen?'

James shook his head disconsolately but Leo changed the subject. 'Are you up to a bite of breakfast?'

'No. Nothing.'

'Not even an undercooked fried egg and some lukewarm tinned tomatoes?'

'Oh you bastard.'

James wretched and dashed from the room.

An hour or so later, as they sat yarning about old LPs and picking through the football pages of various Sunday papers, James managed to munch some toast and jam. He felt increasingly strong enough to broach a complex subject.

'Tell me why you suddenly started on Paul like that.'

'I'm getting sick of him. He treats Wendy like a doormat. He thinks there is nothing at all wrong about lying that he's away on business when he is, in fact, rogering some slapper somewhere. I dislike that and all that it signals. They've been married for less than six years, and so far as I can tell not much is working. Far be it from me to judge him or her, and I suppose if their marriage doesn't deliver the goods for Paul, I don't really mind if he has a fling. But this is a succession of women and a trail of lies. Wendy is a friend who I want to remain my friend.'

'Is she? Really?'

'That's a strange question. Tell me more.'

James explained his lack of empathy with Wendy and then recounted the events at the end of the Boxing Night party.

'Paul said that to you? The bastard. You should have slapped him around, not the beardie.'

'Well it gets more bizarre. Before you got there, and in spite of our poor relationship, I had a long discussion with Wendy. She is very mixed up. She made it quite clear that she wanted me to shag her on Boxing Night and was disappointed that I didn't.'

'That is such bad news. You didn't fuck her, did you?'

'No. I didn't and I wouldn't. I told her this last night. It made her terribly morose; not because she wants me per se; just because she wants someone. So she can hit back at Paul. I think she thinks it might stop him.'

Leo shook his head in disgust. 'It won't. I honestly think he's close to being beyond redemption. We both know he's always been a serial shagger. But now there's another dimension. He's also up to his corporate armpits in deep, reeking shit. Dodgy deals, dodgy clients, dodgy outcomes. It all points to someone who is unbridled.'

'Maybe we need to do something?'

'No; we must not. He won't listen because he is driven by his own sense of righteousness. The end of the line with me, because I've tried to be understanding and a loyal old mate, was finding him at the Sports Club New Year's Eve party getting what looked to be a very persuasive blow job from one of the catering staff in the gents changing rooms. I mean anyone will do. Well, I told you this last night. And then you told everyone else. Brilliant; you were brilliant James.'

'I do try. Seems that he isn't capable of repaying loyalty is he?'

'No. He doesn't deserve any from me or you and especially not from his wife. Tell me about the drunkenness. You've always got like that for the wrong reasons. What was it? Sally?'

'Sort of.'

'Bad answer.'

'Not sure there is a good answer. Right now, I should probably be feeling positive about this Laura. We met for drinks on Friday and it was a good evening. She's... we... she seems to be right. But something just clicks in my head and I lose it.'

'You're so selfish. It's wonderful. I wish I had an ounce of your absolute self-importance and indulgent egoism. Let's go and have a beer. I'll try to tell you how to turn that self-importance into self-belief, because I am a man of considerable counselling skills. Anyway, you owe me lunch for making me have to clean up your mess and sing you lullabies at two am this morning.'

'You're a great man Leo. Thanks for looking after me. And thanks for the loan of this T shirt. I will return it laundered and smelling gorgeous.'

'Keep it; I won't miss it. What had you been eating which was a sort of fluorescent orange colour and smelled of minge?'

'I had a lot of smoked salmon pâté. It was lovely.'

Their conversation progressed as they walked to the pub where they stayed for an hour. Leo drank a couple of beers and James gulped down several pints of iced cola. Leo put a few things to James which he knew would be ignored. His counsel had been routinely disregarded by James since they were fifteen, but Leo persevered.

By mid-afternoon, James had collected his car from a street near Paul's house, called in to say goodbye to his parents and set off on the long drive home. Despite an enjoyable first date with Laura, a rubbish party, a fight and a potentially fatal drunkenness, James mysteriously concluded that it had been a good weekend.

13

Maxine slammed down her phone and it interrupted James' daydream about how badly he was dealing with Laura. He'd reached the conclusion that his call the previous Saturday evening would cause most people to walk away. This was consuming him.

But he realised that Maxine looked angry and that had never happened before. Until now she had been a smiling, attentive colleague who volunteered to do things James should have been doing. He liked that enormously. She was clearly very irate and the things she told James also annoyed him. Someone was stepping on their patch. James' phone started to ring and he asked Maxine to take it while he made another call. He stabbed four buttons on his phone.

'Martin? Can we get together about this print tender? I want to know who's doing what.'

Maxine scribbled on a yellow sticky and held it up for James to see.

'Laura Drysdale. Hold? / call back? / not available?'

James pointed at *Hold* while continuing his conversation.

He was in a complex situation; Maxine must see him being

decisive and firm, but he was talking to a senior manager whose reputation for shafting people was legend. The call didn't last long and ended with another slammed phone.

'Bastard; he said...'

'Wait; there's this call for you.' Maxine transferred Laura to his extension.

'Hello?'

'Is this a bad time?'

'No. Yes. No. Sorry; definitely not. How are you?'

'I'm fine. I wanted to say I wasn't that nice to you on Saturday night.'

'I deserved it.'

'Maybe, but I didn't want to leave you with the impression that I don't want to talk to you.'

Maxine waved, pointed at her watch and nodded at Miles' office. James began to rush.

'I didn't think that.'

'You sound cross.'

'I'm not. Laura, I'm really sorry, but I have to be in a meeting. Can I call you this evening?'

'Of course you can. I'm glad you're not cross with me.'

'And I'm glad you still want to call me. I have to go. Bye.'

He grabbed a file and rushed off. Within minutes he was back for his organiser and a mug.

Maxine looked up at him. 'You need to calm down.'

He looked at her, breathed in deeply and exhaled slowly.

'Being calm won't change what's happened. But while I'm gone, get hold of Sue Bailey. Find out if she knows who Martin's been talking to. Sue owes us a favour. If you get a company name give them a call and find out what they're charging us; or what their standard rates are. See what they've been asked to do. Chances are that Martin has done this one to one with a buddy somewhere which means we won't get much. Worth a shout though.'

Maxine nodded and James concluded; 'We'll have him for this.'

'We will. Leave it with me.'

An hour into the meeting James had neither said nor done a thing. He scribbled a cartoon showing the man sitting opposite him with an axe instead of a head.

'James? I gather we have an outside consultancy doing our work on this?'

He hoped his short silence, caused by the fact that he hadn't been listening, was taken as an angry pause.

'Yes. Martin Castle has done it again. I'm seeing him on Wednesday morning.'

'Can you do it sooner? Has he explained why no one was consulted?'

'He says that he has a steer from Norman Calderwood. And he says Wednesday's his earliest window.' James hated himself for this descent in to corporate bullshitspeak.

Miles looked around the room. 'Big Marty is rapidly becoming a pain in the arse. James? Spend the rest of today finding out what has been done and what can be done to undo it. Come back to me by six with whatever you've got. I'll speak with Martin's boss.'

James was excused to be a bloodhound.

That evening he sat with the phone on his lap, unable to compose the killer opening line he needed to impress Laura. Her call earlier in the day had been reassuring but he still wondered if his demeanour on two successive calls was going to result in another rejection. In this irresolute state he kept lifting the receiver, knowing he had to call. In the end, she beat him to it.

'Hello, James here.'

'Hello. You don't sound drunk and you don't sound grimly focused. Do you think this means we can talk?'

He laughed. 'Yes. But I was supposed to call you.'

'A girl can't wait forever. So here I am.'

James smiled. He liked it when people made things easy for him.

Laura was still talking. 'How are you?'

'Good. Had a bust up at work and I'm coming out on top.'

'What's the problem?'

James explained the situation he and Maxine were trying to resolve.

'Maxine answered your phone. She has a nice voice.'

'She's a very good team mate. How was today for you?'

'I had a nice day; although.. this man I really like kept me waiting, then wouldn't speak to me and then didn't acknowledge who I was until the last sentence of our call. But I managed to spend the whole day looking forward to speaking to him again. In fact I've looked forward to speaking with him ever since a very sweet call on Saturday night.'

'I'm so sorry about all that and I'm simply amazed to hear you call Saturday's conversation *sweet*. I'm crap on the phone aren't I? It isn't always easy to speak at work and it was like that today. Saturday was worse though. I was very drunk indeed and ended up horribly ill. I also ended up fighting with someone and losing a friend.'

'You like fighting?'

'No. I was falling down drunk.'

'You were sober at the office today.'

'True. Different sort of fight. But if I hadn't been legless on Saturday I probably wouldn't have called you. Sometimes I think more clearly when I'm drunk.'

'There's always some boast about what men do better when they're drunk. I've never heard thinking on the list though.'

They floated off into a series of anecdotes about encounters with PPE students. Laura had met a few at college; James while visiting Leo at Cambridge; neither had been impressed. James reminisced about his numerous visits to friends at their universities, much of which caused Laura to laugh long and loud.

'It sounds as if you lived the dream at university and have first class honours in something terribly grand. How on earth did you accrue all this experience?'

'One visit each term to my mates. Mainly to Cambridge where Leo and Graham were at Corpus Christi and Downing respectively. I caught up with Paul too, at Sheffield, and a couple of other guys who were at Lancaster. That was a very strange place to visit.'

'A shame you never made it down to Exeter; we might have met sooner. But I suppose by the time I was there, your visiting days were done.'

'They were. So can you forgive me for the fact that I'm handling this so badly?'

'Why do you think it's bad?'

James squirmed. He didn't like to be challenged. He just needed conversations to be conducted at face value.

In the absence of a reply, Laura continued. 'I can forgive you for Saturday and today. Boxing Day was bad though. You were very sarcastic so I'll have to make you sweat for forgiveness on that. Anyway, on Saturday you said you had something to tell me.'

'I did. And so did you.'

'You first.'

He faltered, then spoke clumsily. 'I'm confused by you and can't grasp why you've hung on; it doesn't really make sense. I'm flattered; but I keep wondering if it's some sort of practical joke.'

'It isn't.'

'That's it really. When I'm confused I fall back on what I know. In your case, what I know is that I can't place you in my past, which makes me doubt you and it. That sounds terrible. Anyway on Saturday, in a drunken haze, I realised I really wanted to talk to you, and see you again.'

'Is that all?' Her sarcasm was clever and subtle. She used it sparingly to great effect.

'It's all you're getting. I'm a wreck now and need a drink and drugs cocktail. It's your turn.'

'Well I wanted to say the same; that I want to see you whenever it's possible. It won't be easy because we live so far apart, but I think we can make it work. None of this is fiction; and, of course, whatever we have is incomplete and some way from being a certainty. But I'm for real and I always will be. What I have to know now is when we can see each other again.'

James was impulsive and direct. 'This Saturday. I'll come up to Hereford. It means an early start on Sunday so I get back to play football.'

'I wouldn't want you to miss that for me.'

'It's fine, I can easily travel in my kit.'

'I'll pay for dinner then.'

'Well, okay. Where shall we go?'

'There's a new restaurant in the Palace Hotel. It's central for both of us.'

'And perilously close to our alma mater. Is it any good?'

'It is, apparently, very good. Meet me there.'

'Can't I collect you?'

'Please don't drive. Let's relax and get quietly drunk together. You said something rather nice when you were drunk on Saturday.'

'So why don't I pick up a taxi and collect you.'

'That's plain stupid; it's miles out of your way and would cost loads. Seriously James, meet me there. I'll book a table for eight.'

In the next few days, James became gradually hopeless. His expectation of the coming date with Laura was overwhelming and the only decisive thing he did was to make himself unavailable for that weekend's football. Otherwise, he messed up many simple things and his crushing ineptitude continued right up to the moment when, from his window seat in the hotel bar, he saw Laura get out of a taxi and walk in to the hotel. She smiled happily as he stood to welcome her, then took off her coat to reveal an electric blue sleeveless dress. James couldn't stop his jaw from dropping and after the Maître d'hôtel had taken her coat away he confessed; 'I don't know what to say.'

'Try starting with a kiss and a hug and then saying *what would you like to drink*? Then you can commend me for my dress sense.'

A waiter delivered menus to their table and after a few moments surveying the options, James was impressed but overwhelmed by choice. 'This menu is fantastic. And you look utterly sensational.'

'Thank you for noticing. I think you're worth it.' She raised her glass with feigned seriousness. 'You're right; the food does sound great. Are you a foodie?'

'Yes and no. I like to eat but don't like to cook; I think that's a bad combination for anyone. I prefer eating out; you get surprises; I like to be surprised.'

'Well like I said the other evening, this is my treat. You've spent a lot of money driving up here twice in a week. Have whatever you want.'

He didn't protest and opened a new conversation. 'Tell me about your family. Got any brothers or sisters?'

'No, none. I'm all Mummy and Daddy need and a spoilt singleton, which you can tell by the fact that I'm twenty-five and still call my parents *Mummy* and *Daddy*. You've got a huge family haven't you?'

'Some of them are quite small.'

Laura sipped her drink and shook her head. 'Don't over-do the samrt-arse quips.'

He grimaced. 'There are four children but I'm now the only child.'

She shook her head again. James took note and realised he was on a warning.

'I came second, Carol last, David's in between us and Simon's the eldest. We sort of get on as siblings except for Simon who's a difficult man to love. David's married to a wonderful woman called Annie who's about to produce the first of our next generation. Carol lives in Bath with an old hippy called Alex who my mother and father don't like. He's much older than Carol which my folks see as a waste. They are wrong, but whatever anyone thinks, Carol is happy. Simon's divorced. My folks are becoming old and grumpy, argumentative and very forgetful which is funny and sad by turn. Which reminds me; Carol's having a party on the third of March. Will you come along with me?'

'In Bath?'

'Yes. She's got a place close to the town centre. Or is it a city?'

'Not sure. I'll let you know.'

'I can find out if it's a city on my own. I have an almanac.' He pronounced it *orlmunac*, making Laura laugh.

'You see? You can be funny without being a smart-arse. But your description of your family told me everything and nothing. For an artist, you don't especially embellish things while you're talking, do you?'

'I'm a man. I give information in sufficient detail to answer the question and move on.' He smiled triumphantly at her. She poked out her tongue.

James wasn't finished. 'I don't really do detail. You need to know that.'

'That sounds very shallow.'

'It is. I am.'

'Not doing detail sounds like an excuse for not listening. I'm prepared to bet you are very good indeed at detail if it involves your own thoughts and feelings.'

He knew she had scored a direct hit so he closed down the discussion with an inconclusive, 'Maybe.'

A bustling, efficient waiter arrived, introduced himself as Armand and escorted them to their table in the dining room. When he returned with their starters, he wished them Bon Appétit and strolled haughtily away.

James watched him go with mounting suspicion.

'You look troubled James. What's wrong?'

'I'm really not sure that man is French. Or from any French-speaking nation.'

Laura chuckled. 'He certainly isn't. He's called Mark Williams.'

'I knew it. I'm going to complain.'

'No; don't. Let's eat.'

For some time they ate in silence; the food was very good indeed. James watched Laura; she ate with a kind of care, testing different combinations of tastes. She caught him looking and her eyes creased at the corners. James felt an impulse to dance and suggested it to Laura.

She said it wasn't possible.

'Shame, because I'd really like to dance with you.'

Laura stared across the candlelit table and wiped her mouth with a napkin. 'I'd like to dance with you too; slowly and sensually, but alone; just you and me. Not in a club or restaurant or anything. You, me, maybe a bottle of wine. Sexual Healing as an accompaniment and a warm fire to lie beside at the end.'

James loved that record; he loved the fantasy she had shared; he told her it was perfect.

He said, 'One day we must have that perfect dance.'

She shook her head. 'What I'm hoping is that it will be perfect on many, many days.'

Laura and James were locked in to something now. The low level flirting and exploratory wondering had generated this; a place in which they knew what would be. It seemed hard for them to switch back in to a basic mode and their efforts to discuss what had happened at Wendy's birthday party were vague and disinterested. Sitting opposite each other, their agenda was quite formal, as if some unwritten rules about dating made them players in a series of scenes. But outside the chat and polite conversation, there was now an underlying sense that they should express more about how they felt.

Instead, they ordered more wine and by the time their main courses were finished they were cosily drunk and chattering away about many things: favoured and detested books, music, films, food, art, drink, things, places, and people; and they still wanted to dance.

Then James reverted to his summary of what had happened at Wendy's party, and how Leo had been so hospitable afterwards. As he spoke, Laura slipped off her shoes and glided her feet up and down his shins. Then she pushed her left hand across the table towards his right hand and began to stroke it.

'It sounds like you and Paul aren't so close any more.'

'We go back a long way, but that isn't a guarantee of anything. I've known Leo much longer and he and I have such a simple, easy relationship. Paul and I just seem to be broken.'

'Perhaps you should try stroking Paul's hand. It can be very calming.'

James snorted a laugh. 'I wouldn't wish to stroke anything of his: not even his wife.'

She raised both eyebrows quizzically and said, emphatically, 'Excuse me?'

'Do you know Wendy?'

'Not really; only by reputation.'

'Which is?'

'Never mind; tell me what you meant just now.'

James explained what had happened on Boxing Night and Wendy's review of it the previous weekend.

Laura scoffed at him. 'You're making this up. I don't believe you.'

'I'm deadly serious.'

'No knickers? And she just collapsed on the floor?'

'Well I don't think *collapsed* is quite the right word. She just kind of fell asleep and revealed all. But her intentions were pretty blatant.'

'So did you think about giving her one?'

James chortled. He hadn't heard that expression for years and was pretty sure he'd never heard a woman use it.

'The drunken, male-ego-beast within did consider it for several seconds. The rational, slightly lonely ascetic strolled off to bed and slept. An untroubled sleep, as it goes.'

Laura was looking closely at him now and he thought she looked cross.

'What's the matter?'

'James, you must be mad. From everything I know about Paul, he would certainly have done it to your wife in the same situation.'

'Funny; that's what Wendy said. But life isn't about mimicking the faults of others just because they're ahead of you in some sort of race. I don't care if he would do it. I do care that I saw no justification in shagging someone in those circumstances; nor in shagging Wendy in any circumstances. They are... they were my friends. I think I might never see either of them again.'

'Maybe they deserve it?'

'It shouldn't be that simple, but the whole thing is so artificial these days.'

'In what sense?'

'In the sense that I don't really share much with him. For example, when I was with him on Boxing Night, I didn't really open up about what happened with Sally. He got a basic version of the facts.'

'Perhaps that's all he needed. How did he react?'

'With his usual efficient lack of empathy.' James paused to reflect and made a small noise of resignation. 'I don't know; there was a time when our problems were shared. Now it's just easier to keep them inside.'

'It sounds like your treasured friendships are in need of repair. Is it you that has changed, or them?'

'I suppose we've all changed.'

'Yet you seem to have a need to cling to those days and memories.'

'Do I?'

Laura smiled broadly. 'Yes James. You refer to it often, as if something about it comforts you. If everyone's changed, maybe you need to move on?'

James was flabbergasted.

Laura sat back in her chair and said, 'I wish you could see your face. I think I've hit a very raw nerve.'

'Well yes. In my mind, those days are special; sacred even.'

'Which is fine, but you can't keep living in them.'

'Is that what you think?'

'It's what comes across. But hey, let's change the subject. I feel bad that I've made you uncomfortable.'

Laura switched topics, but James wasn't listening. She had thrown this challenge in to the conversation like a grenade. Was she right? Did she have the right? He admired how she'd done it; but he ached from the criticism.

His mother knocked at just after ten and brought in a cup of tea. 'Are you going to lie there all morning?'

It was a question using a tone that could easily spark an argument between them. But not today. James sat up, took his tea and smiled benignly at his mother who told him, 'Come along to the conservatory when you're ready. You can have breakfast in there; it's nicely warmed up now.'

He showered, shaved and dressed and, as James walked into the conservatory, his father looked up from his newspaper. 'Good morning. Head all right? How was your evening? I gather that's a fine restaurant, with an excellent wine list.'

'Hello Dad: head fine; evening lovely; food very good; wine comfortingly expensive.'

Mr Clifton nodded, unperturbed by his son's economical responses. Small talk ensued in which James avoided most questions and any form of detail.

It was a beautifully sunny day and the conservatory was too warm. After wolfing two rounds of bacon sandwiches, James took another cup of tea into the garden and sat, burping, on a garden bench with his sketch pad and pencil. Half an hour later he had drawn several small monochrome scenes. The crisp, fresh air was energising.

'That one's really lovely.' His mother stood behind him.

'Why don't you have it? You could put it in a frame and hang it in one of the bedrooms. Have these others too.'

'Yes. I think I will. Thank you.'

She touched his arm but a silence enveloped them. It always did. There was a reticence about their relationship; a mother and son who could only share a cold, cloudy life. But they strolled around the garden looking at plants, James trying to imagine how it would look in the coming summer.

'Why don't we go to the pub?'

'You take your father. I've got a million and one things to do and, if you two are out of the way, I'll be done quicker.'

He couldn't remember the last time they'd all enjoyed being at a pub or restaurant. It was a way of life the family no longer lived in. But James and his father soon walked to the local and began one of the father/son chats they sometimes had, exploring issues of the day. There were times when James couldn't bear it but today he was happy to feed the right lines to his father's sentiments. Inevitably, the discussion ended with a topic James had hoped to avoid.

'Your mother and I were both very sorry about Sally leaving you. She was a good influence; a settling influence.'

'Why does everyone say that? What the fuck is going on?'

His father continued, 'Are you coping all right?'

'Yes. I think so. Let me get some more drinks.'

'No; first tell me about how you are.'

'I really am fine. It was tough when it happened and it might not have been what I wanted. But, on the plus side, I've met someone else.'

'This would be last night's date?'

'Yes.'

'Good. Well done. You can get those beers now. And I'll have a scotch too.'

When James returned with these drinks, he felt determined to talk to his father about something real: an emotion; a feeling; a sensibility. But it didn't happen. Both his parents, but especially his father, had an innately artificial view of their children's feelings. So long as they could see or hear a level of stability and control, this was a parental union that just let the kids get on with things. So they reverted to Mr Clifton rambling on: about the price of ale; about how to sell things; about why farming is down the pan.

When last orders were called they returned home, where

a large mound of egg and cress sandwiches sat next to a note saying: *Taken dogs to Queen's Wood. Back around 4.* Within an hour, both men were asleep in front of the telly.

14

The Cinema Show

James' trip to Bath was a fast, energising blast along the M4 with unfashionable rock music for company. He arrived just before eleven, parked in a street near Carol's flat and when a knock on her door revealed no one was home, set off for Bath Spa railway station, where he knew he would be happy waiting for Laura.

He loved wasting time in stations: there was something endlessly uplifting about the scenes of greeting and farewell; of the sense of an impending adventure; of smiles and tears; of struggles with luggage, children and timetables.

James cajoled the man guarding the entrance into letting him go to the platform without a ticket. Once there, he sat on a bench to watch the theatre unfolding with each departing and arriving train. A father, cases festooned with tags, nearly knocked flat by onrushing, adoring kids. A proud Grandma waving goodbye to a bemused toddler who timidly waved back. A young gun opening and then hanging from the still moving train's door to greet his girlfriend, a can of lager raised with a sardonic smile to show he just about cared. A crying teenage girl, leaving someone behind who was herself so overwhelmed by tears that she couldn't talk.

But a noisy, chanting, swearing gang of football fans – opposite, on the Bristol bound platform – tore up the magic sequence and then dissolved James' recollection of it forever.

When the train bearing Laura began its approach to the platform, James gazed with appalled curiosity at the massed dead insects smeared on its wedged, yellow nose. From a pie-shaped section of clean windscreen a slack-jawed, mouth-breathing driver seemed to have no part in the business of controlling the engine. He was just a head and shoulders. James moved along the platform and spotted Laura walking towards the exit, a rucksack on her back bounding in time with her steps. She hadn't seen him. James quickened his pace in her direction and called out her name. She turned, beamed, then diverted into his path to grab him in a hug.

'Have you ever travelled from Hereford to Bristol by train?'

He confessed he had not. He then confessed that he only went on trains if lives were at risk.

'It is absolutely gorgeous, especially the bit between Hereford and Abergavenny. I felt quite uplifted and all pastoral.'

'How long has it taken?'

'Too long.'

'I wish you'd let me come to pick you up.'

'We spoke about that; it was a silly idea.'

Their relationship was nearly two months old and James had been in Hereford with Laura every Friday evening and Saturday since their meeting at Bogart's. She had rejected his proposal to collect her on a round trip from Richmond to Bath via Hereford.

'Shall we get going? We can drop off your stuff at Carol's then grab lunch. I'm starving.'

'The reason it was so long, since you ask, is that I've had to change trains twice. Once at Newport, which I would prefer never to see again, and then again at Bristol Temple Meads, which ought to be a firm of Quantity Surveyors.'

'You're annoyed with me.'

'A little.'

They had descended to the concourse and reached the street. James realised that he had almost certainly compounded whatever was making Laura cross by failing to offer to carry her rucksack.

'I came by train to prevent you driving all the way to Hereford to collect me. I offered to get to and from here by myself, which I was happy to do. I thought coming by train would make a change, so the least you could do, James, is check on how it went.'

'I see. Why don't you give me your rucksack?'

Laura removed the pack and passed it over. James grabbed it and was shocked to find it nearly pulled his hand off the end of his arm.

'What's funny?'

'This rucksack weighs a ton; what the fuck have you got in it?'

Laura switched on her plummy accent; 'A girl must be prepared when she is spending time alone with her man.'

James wrestled the pack on to his shoulders. Laura stayed with the accent; 'Home, James. Is it far?'

'About half a mile that way.' He pointed down the road opposite the station. 'Then right, over the river, then left and right again. Where do you want to go for lunch?'

Laura quickened her pace so she was ahead of him. He heard her say, 'I can't believe you're so selfish.'

'What have I done now?'

She stopped and turned to him. He thought she might stamp her foot but she poked him just above his left pectoral in time with each sentence.

'Your sister is hosting a party this evening. We're both guests in her and Alex's home. We, well at least you, are family and not some hanger-on. So any plan you have to just drop in, drop out and do bugger all is not an option.'

'Why?'

'That's outrageous and we're doing nothing of the sort. When we get there, I want you to check what we can do to help and then offer to go out to collect anything she might need. Also, what have you brought as a gift?'

'Some wine and beer.'

'Yes, but what gift did you bring?'

Now James moved ahead with his head down and muttered, 'Nothing; we don't do that sort of stuff.'

Laura jeered at him. 'Don't be ridiculous. Right; when we reach your car, we'll leave my rucksack in the boot...'

'It's an Alfa Romeo GTV6. It hasn't got a boot.'

'...and then go in to town to find a suitable present for your sister. And you're paying.'

There was silence between them as they carried out these instructions. James stooped under the weight of the rucksack and felt a growing resentment that he had been attacked; and worse still, attacked with the truth. They didn't exchange another word before reaching his car but as he stuffed her luggage on to the back seat, James muttered something about the risk of it being stolen by smack heads. Laura grabbed him, turned him around, told him to shut up and kissed him. He pushed her away, but she grabbed his lapels and dragged him in to another extensive kiss. It left them smiling lecherously at each other, and giggling.

'Now you've stopped sulking and know who's in charge, tell me how far it is to the city centre.'

He pointed back in the direction they'd just travelled. 'About another half a mile back that way. Or I could throw you in the river and you could swim for it. We will walk past several of the pubs I had lined up as lunch options.'

'I'm going to force you to walk past all of them and suffer. We can go for lunch tomorrow by which time you will have done all the right things.'

They were soon in the city centre and Laura identified the perfect gift, which was eventually enveloped in perfect wrapping paper.

It transpired that Carol and Laura had met and didn't need the ungainly introductions James conducted when they returned to his sister's flat. While the two women chatted amiably, James was asked to *do something artistic with the table decorations* which he agreed to do as it meant he could keep track of the football scores on the radio.

When Alex arrived home he poured two half pints from a barrel of real ale, hoping for James' approval. This tempting sample soon degenerated and by the time James needed to change in to party clothes he'd had several pints.

It turned out to be a very good party. There was plenty to drink, too much to eat and the twenty or so guests were all funny, lively, unpretentious people. Above all, James had his first chance to publicly reveal that he and Laura existed as a couple and this seemed doubly satisfying in the presence of almost total strangers. When they weren't chatting quietly to one another they dived in to the conversations of others. And when they were separated, James happily talked to anyone and found no one remotely unpleasant. And if no one was talking to him, or engaging him, James didn't care; he just watched Laura as she smiled at, laughed with, and listened to people. He was amazed. Her smile showed sincerity and a depth of joy at whatever was making her smile. When she laughed it seemed controlled, as if she couldn't commit to a full belly laugh. And she listened to people with such intensity, absorbing what was said as if programming it, sorting it and then measuring her response. She never seemed to give an instinctive answer to anyone and never interrupted people.

What amazed him most was the way that, every time she glanced at him, Laura's eyes glittered with affection and friendship.

It was such a good party that its hostess had to retire quite early on. By eleven thirty, a few guests remained and most were huddled around the scraps of food, picking at them like bored vultures. James was on the sofa with Alex, talking bollocks about music and occasionally refilling his glass from a bottle of red wine. Laura was cuddled up to James and giggled at some of whatever the two men were rambling on about. To illustrate a specific point from their discussion, Alex got up and put on *Grace and Danger*. Then, after less than two tracks, he mumbled that he was too pissed to stay awake and shambled off to a bedroom. The heart-wrenching love songs, filled with the almost unbearable torment of their composer, made James cling very tightly to Laura.

They sat like this, chatting, until they realised everyone had left. The only sound was gentle snoring from Alex and Carol's room. Laura started to stand but James pulled her back to caress and kiss her. Then James held up his hand and said, 'Wait.'

He stood and began a search through a shelf of CDs. After finding and opening a case he pushed buttons. Clicks and slides preceded a familiar tune.

'There's no fire to lie beside but here's Marvin and here we are and there's some wine. Shall we dance?'

Laura smiled and stood up and walked to him. She rested her head on his shoulder so her cheek was touching his neck. She held one of his hands and for a moment or two they just swayed like this, the song weaving its spell. Slowly Laura moved her free hand up and down James' back. He felt tingling bursts of sensory joy from his coccyx to his scalp and held her tightly round the waist as they kissed. Their first dance ground to a halt; Sexual Healing was complete.

James broke the silence. 'Time for bed.'

'Yes please.'

Laura disentangled herself and padded off.

He bolted the front door and went to the kitchen where he nibbled at some of the scattered remains on a cheese board. After drinking two glasses of water, James filled a third then switched off all the lights.

It was dark in the bedroom but James could make out a shape in the bed. Laura's clothes were all over the floor. He started to undress and stumbled about in an attempt to do so quickly without making it obvious that he was virtually ripping off his things.

Laura said, 'Be quiet but hurry up. It's lovely and warm in here.'

He soon slid into the bed beside her.

'I want you James.'

She kissed him lightly then, as he moved closer, with passion. He kissed her neck and throat and began caressing her buttocks. She ran her hand up his leg from knee to groin. Once there, she brushed his balls with her finger tips, then stroked down the other leg. He mimicked this and soon left his hand between her legs and began to probe.

After several minutes, she grabbed his hair and pulled his face up to hers and said, 'Have you got a condom?'

James seemed to turn to stone.

'Oh. I'll take that as *no.*'

'Sorry; I didn't think. I mean it never occurred...'

'What did you expect James? I'd be the ready-made shag who'd have simple little things like contraception all lined up?'

James rolled on to his back and sighed deeply.

'No, that's not what I thought.'

'Did you even consider the possibility things might just be best if you came prepared?'

James swung his legs out of the bed as if to stand up.

'Don't go off in a sulk; I want to talk about this like grown-ups.'

'Right.' James didn't sound convinced.

'Cuddle up close to me again.'

James obeyed, but was desperately racking his brains for what he could and should say about the situation.

'Have you always had unprotected sex with new partners?'

'Yes, although there haven't been many.'

'Well that's a different discussion. Do you agree that it's fair for me to expect you to be completely and utterly free from any potential risk?'

James nodded; 'Of course. Laura I'm sorry if it looks like I made an assumption. That is definitely not the case and I didn't expect anything. Well maybe I did make an assumption. But more to the point, I just made the mistake of not thinking it through; which I'm very good at.'

Laura pulled him closer and stroked his chest. 'I really, really wanted you to fuck me tonight.'

He laughed. 'Really? It hadn't even crossed my mind.'

Laura slapped him hard on his stomach. 'Don't forget James Clifton, I do the sarcasm in this relationship. But maybe we need an alternative.'

'What do you have in mind?'

James woke with a start the following morning to find Laura standing at his side. She was wearing his shirt and offered him one of the two mugs she was holding.

'Looks like Alex and Carol are not around.'

'They run miles every morning. It's a big part of their lives, even with a debilitating hangover.'

Laura got back in to bed and they sipped at their reviving brews.

'I'm curious about that remark you made about not having many partners.'

'It's true. I haven't.'

'You mean sexual partners or just girlfriends.'

'Both.'

'Oh dear. Feel like answering more impertinent questions on the subject, or shall I shut up?'

James gulped down his tea and discarded his empty mug.

'Laura, there is something you need to know about me. If

anyone asks me to talk about, or to explain myself, I am almost always likely to oblige. I am my very own favourite subject.'

He expected Laura to find this funny, but instead she frowned. 'I want me to be your favourite subject. But let's go back to your love life. When I saw you at Christmas, you were in a relationship but it was effectively over.'

'Yes.'

'We've never discussed it in detail have we? Tell me what happened.'

James told Laura the story, omitting nothing.

She remained impassive. 'Did you think it was a serious relationship? Was she *The One?*'

'I think I made a mistake believing I could be part of her life and lifestyle when basically I was a bit of an oik alongside her set. Our first few months together were great. I can't say they weren't just because the relationship has finished. But with hindsight, we did too much too quickly.'

'Maybe we are too.'

'Why do you say that? Is it all moving too fast for you?'

'No, I can't get enough of you. But I don't want you to feel pressure.'

James said he felt nothing of the sort.

'Did you love her?'

'I did. And she loved me. It worked.'

'Would you have her back?'

'Not even if my life depended on it.'

Laura raised her eyebrows; 'Bloody hell James, that's a very final position. Is it because she chucked you?'

'No. It's because all she did was blame me.'

Laura looked in to his eyes, searching for something, then perhaps found what she was looking for because she grabbed his head in her hands and kissed his forehead.

'Am I her replacement? Are you on the rebound?'

James thought about Tracy, and whether to mention that unhappy affair.

'You aren't replacing anyone, or anything. In the six or seven weeks we've been together, I've come to think of you as someone who changes things.'

'That's rather a bizarre thing to say, but I think it sounds positive. Tell me about before Sally.'

'I wasn't in a single serious relationship for around ten years.'

'You're joking?'

'Am I smiling?'

'But surely you had something?'

'Yes, I occasionally did. But there was never a situation in which I felt I had a girlfriend.'

'Right; and these... encounters involved unprotected sex?'

'Not always, but usually.'

'But you still showed up here expecting to have sex with me, and without a condom.'

'Actually I didn't expect to have sex with you. I sincerely hoped it would happen, because you're very sexy and desirable. I didn't bring condoms because I didn't want to assume it would happen. I didn't want to tempt fate, even though I'd like to make love to you... forever.'

As he said all this, Laura had picked up her cup and was looking at him over the rim. He thought he detected anger or suspicion in her eyes, but saw that she was suppressing laughter.

'What's so funny?'

'You are. Last night you heard me tell you that I want you to fuck me, so you know that I'm completely open to that kind of base language when discussing sex. I don't require it to be hidden behind some prude euphemism. Yet you used the phrase *make love*.' She stroked his cheek. 'You're really rather sweet, aren't you?'

'I'm really not.'

'So you had no relationship of any kind after leaving school until you met Sally.'

James nodded.

'But surely you were at it like a ram in Hereford?'

'I wasn't.'

'Don't believe you.'

'I definitely wasn't. There were opportunities that I didn't take and I was determined not to demand anything that wasn't truly available. I needed to be led.'

'Poor James. I can't believe one of the various girls around your scene didn't help out. Some of them were very, very dirty indeed.'

James raised his eyebrows quizzically.

'Don't even think about asking me for names. But go on. Tell me more.'

'There's not much more to say really. I just had a very

unexceptional teenage time and discovered, too late, that I spent too long chasing the wrong people.'

'Well it doesn't matter, so lighten up. Let's get up soon, have some breakfast and get out of here. You can take me for lunch before I catch my train.'

'No. You're not going on the train. I'll take you back to Hereford.'

'I've been dying for you to offer to do that. Thank you.' Laura looked lasciviously at him. 'When will Carol be back?'

'No idea. Why?'

'Well we didn't get all that dirty last night, but I think a shower is in order. Let's get clean.'

That intimate interlude served as a catalyst for their relationship. Despite its long distance characteristics, it was evolving; fizzing with chemistry; becoming a bond. Their remoteness from one another was never a complication and they seemed to revel in the challenges it posed. The fun and joy of what they shared became the driving force for surprises, changes and new knowledge.

All three were generated one spring afternoon when Laura and James were shopping absent-mindedly in Hereford City Centre. Their minds were on the coming evening, in which they would be celebrating James' birthday, and they literally bumped in to Philippa. The two women greeted each other with small whoops of joy, then a hug and a kiss. Perplexed, James joined in with the hugging. The two women spoke in bursts of information about what they were doing and what they were looking for and what they had bought; and then about their parents and how things were going between Philippa and Adrian. James was on the margins of this conversation but, before she rushed off, Philippa grabbed him and planted a kiss on his lips by way of a birthday treat. Then, with a suggestion they must catch up soon for drinks somewhere, she was gone.

When they resumed their shopping, James asked Laura why she had never mentioned her friendship with Philippa.

'You've never asked me and it's a stupid question.'

'No, it's a sensible question, to establish facts. We've been seeing each other for three months and spoken of Philippa many times. You've never mentioned she's your friend.'

'Well has she ever mentioned me to you? And I mean ever?'

The question stopped James in his tracks. He knew that the answer was no, and in turn that he had learned next to nothing about Laura. Something had to be done; this chance encounter had revealed his hopeless lack of curiosity about two people who knew him inside out.

James vowed to spend time, much more time, asking questions; and listening properly to answers.

During his birthday celebrations, they agreed it was overdue for Laura to visit James in Richmond. A date was fixed and she said she couldn't wait for them to step out in his world.

James took that Friday off work and completed his standard household chores twenty four hours early. Sitting in the tidy splendour of his home, James reflected on how he would feel when Laura was there. It was less than a year since this had been a home he shared with another woman, and James fretted that this could be a test of some kind. He knew his home retained no lingering memories or mementos of Sally, but he felt a tug of concern that this place might never be special for Laura.

She arrived that Saturday, just before eleven. James watched her VW pull in to the communal parking area with a lurch of joy, bounded down to meet her and carry her numerous bags inside. Laura sliced through their habitual reunion of hushed hugs and kisses by handing James a medium sized, gift-wrapped box with a grinning insistence he must open it. It contained two tall crystal tumblers and a note from Laura saying: *Surprise Gift, Part One.*

Before James could express any thanks, or question the note's meaning, Laura had jumped into a cuddle and series of kisses that distracted them for several minutes. James peeled himself away and told Laura to make herself at home.

'Aren't you going to give me a guided tour?'

'That would be presumptuous in the extreme and an overstatement of the size of my estate. In the time it takes you to look round, I can boil the kettle to make drinks. Off you go.'

They set off in opposite directions

'Coffee or tea?'

By now Laura was in the bathroom, opening and shutting things.

'Tea please. This bathroom's unnaturally and suspiciously clean. I expected rings around the bath and great jumbo jet skid marks in the bog. You disappoint me.'

James took their drinks into the living room where she soon reappeared, pointing at the small bookcase.

'You, James Clifton, are a bloody thief. Those books; school property; stolen property. I'm lost for words. I'm not really sure I can stay here with all this plunder.'

He explained that he'd found her name in one of the books and took it from the shelf. She looked in the book with a sigh of recollection then insulted two of the people listed as borrowers. While sipping her tea, she surveyed the rest of the bookcase, his music collection and finally the view from his window. Small noises of approval were made throughout this review.

'James, you're deceiving me. This simply cannot be the normal condition of the place where you live. I refuse to believe it.'

He confessed the details of his diligent housekeeping.

'That sounds like some sort of compulsive problem. Do you also spend a lot of time silently rocking back and forth for no reason?'

'No, but I do buy bleach in bulk and throw away shirts if a button comes off.'

'So none of this pristine, scrubbed loveliness is for my benefit?'

'It's not. And actually, it's a wafer thin deceit. I simply put all my clutter in to cupboards and drawers. It's a shabby illusion.'

She curled up her lip.

'I need to see the bedroom; come along; show me.'

Laura walked straight to his wardrobe, rustled through the hanging contents and pointed to several items of clothing she'd never seen. She also took out the suit and shirt she wanted him to wear that evening.

'Which reminds me; I've got something else in my bag that I brought for you to wear.' She soon extracted an envelope which had *Surprise Gift, Part Two* written on it. 'Open it.'

James slit the envelope to find a condom.

'It's time we made lerve. Come on.'

It didn't last long and afterwards she turned to James with a wide smile and said; 'That was lovely James. I think I might want to do it more often; possibly once or twice a month once we're married. Why are you blushing?'

'I'm slightly ashamed.'

'What? Why?'

'I don't feel like you got a great deal out of that.'

Laura slapped him hard on his thigh. 'Don't you dare dictate what does and does not constitute good sex; it was perfect, because it was you and me.'

By mid-afternoon, James and Laura were in the spare room looking at a picture he was painting. This led to an appraisal of a selection of his works, old and new. Laura commented occasionally, but didn't say much until she summed up with;

'You're very good you know. I like the drawings more than the paintings. You're too self-indulgent and self-destructive in the paintings; all those hands and nails and bandages and faceless heads; and this fixation with wounds. But the drawings and charcoals and some water colours; they're just lovely. Simple, dreamy, strong and provocative; like you are.'

Very few people had seen what was stored in this room. Laura's feedback revived a feeling that had become submerged. James had forgotten how to enjoy the pleasure of praise. And he liked the negative as much as the positive.

'But what you've created can't stay locked away in here like this. You know that, don't you?'

'I'd like to believe it.'

'I'm going to help you, one day. I'm going to stop you playing at this and take it seriously. Above all, I'm going to stop you being the gaoler for all your works of art. They need to be set free.'

They walked into Richmond and mooched around shops and cafés for a couple of hours. They didn't buy much, but Laura insisted they find limes, mint and soda water. Once back at his flat, Laura revealed *Surprise Gift Number Three*; a bottle of white rum. She made him go to the living room and he heard noises; stirring; bashing; chopping; more stirring.

Laura joined him carrying the two crystal glasses filled with effervescence and greenery.

'Ever had a Mojito before?'

He confessed that he hadn't.

'No, me neither. Salud!'

They joined Gary and Bridget at a restaurant for what turned out to be a low-key company event arranged by Bridget's boss. It was a sober occasion in which unrestrained drinking and laughter were frowned upon. So, as soon as it was courteous to do so, they left the venue and installed themselves in a pub until closing time. Not long after midnight they were at Bridget's house with takeaways and vodka and Gary was playing songs on his guitar. They had a righteous sing-a-long and, during breaks from the songs they knew, they listened to and admired Gary's own music. It was nearly four when James and Laura got into a taxi and returned to his flat.

James was incapable of playing football the next morning. His team won but he delivered nothing. During the drive home, Laura questioned him about why he played football, especially on a morning when he had a hangover and could have stayed in bed with her. James started a well-practised speech about keeping himself fit and being part of a team.

'But some of those people are genuinely horrible. I mean in your team.'

'Football is like that.'

'I think I'd prefer you didn't play if it means you're being dragged down into that environment. What possible benefit can you derive from being part of a team made up of such thugs?'

James remained silent. Laura hadn't just hit the nail on the head; she'd driven it clean through the wall. Eventually, he muttered that the season would soon be over and he'd think about what to do during the summer.

'Please don't ask me to come along to watch again. I'd rather stay at home, or even go home. It doesn't actually give you anything you know.'

James shook his head and was about to argue, but his head throbbed dully.

They spent the rest of the afternoon preparing dinner. Before, during and after this meal they were full of their school day memories; an apparently inexhaustible subject which resulted in James dragging out his rolled-up school photos.

'Bet you can't find me,' she teased.

James pored over the more recent of the two photographs and was on the verge of pointing at someone vaguely of the right age and appearance when Laura said; 'You know, I've seen this photograph so many times and always wanted to ask you about your face. What on earth was going on?'

'I was just about to burst out laughing. Someone just near me – Gareth Young; remember him? Posh voice; had a proper motorbike – yelled out that Harry Hutton was a wanker. I couldn't stop myself and there's the result: a combination of Bugs Bunny and Fu Manchu.'

James scanned the shot and tutted.

'So where are you then?'

'Ha ha. Trick question. I'm not on it; off sick that day with a tummy upset. You really don't remember me do you James?'

'I really don't. And now I realise with certainty that it's because you're not on this photograph. It explains everything.'

By early evening, James was almost asleep on the sofa so Laura packed him off to bed and soon slid in alongside him. James was fast asleep. When he woke the next day she had gone. A note sat on his bedside table.

'Darling James,

You snore dreadfully. Well, actually, you snore really well but it's dreadful to be nearby. I had to leave before the noise and vibration drove me to some terrible act with a cheese grater.

You look rather sweet when you sleep. Not like a baby; well not like a human baby; a bear cub, maybe. Anyway, I'll call you later today and we'll arrange next weekend. Can I come to yours? I had such a good time this weekend, even if I do have to drive back at the crack of dawn. But so do you.

Give my love to Gary and Bridget. Can't wait to see you again. This weekend was so special.

All my love – Laura xxxxxxxxx'

15

He arrived home from work, excited and ready for Laura. She would be back with him by eight thirty, just five days after leaving him. James was thrilled by that knowledge and it had sustained him all week.

His new answering machine blinked a light at him and Laura's voice said; 'James. I got away early. It's four o'clock and I'm on my way. Should be with you... mmm... seven fifteen or maybe seven thirty. Bye.'

She didn't seem convinced about her arrival time, but James' excitement wasn't quelled. Things were looking up. He felt good. Time spent with Laura always created a conduit to better times, past, present and future.

When Laura hadn't arrived by eight, James was almost disabled by a combination of panic and drunken indecision. In the space of a few minutes he thought about calling Laura's parents, the police, the fire brigade and even a local radio station to see what might have happened. He was increasingly concerned that the lack of news or an update from Laura meant something serious. He considered the possibility that she might have been killed, and what that would mean. He lit a cigarette even though there was one burning in the ash tray.

The phone rang and Laura's voice crackled in his ear.

'There's been a big holdup on the A40. Some sort of road works. I'm going to be pretty late. Sorry.'

'How long do you think you'll be?' His voice was shaking.

'Another hour, I suppose. I'm through it all now, and stopped here just outside Oxford before I get on to the M40.'

'I'll cancel the table for dinner and make something instead.'

'Are you sober enough? You don't sound it. I need to go James. Do whatever makes sense. Bye.'

Abruptly, the line went dead.

Laura arrived to find James standing in the car park waving at her. He jumped in the car and kissed her. 'Sorry, but you need to stay in the car a little longer. Chinese takeaway, ten minutes up that way.'

'Good; and perfect timing. How did you know I would be here at exactly this time?'

'I didn't. I've been standing outside since about nine fifteen.'

'You silly bastard; I mean that is the stupidest thing I've ever heard. What's wrong?'

'Nothing's wrong, I'm just relieved you're here. I'm pretty drunk too.'

'You smell like a distillery, and you look really upset. Why?'

He looked at her in a panic. She didn't look at him as she drove. His voice shook.

'I got so scared when you weren't here on time. I didn't know what to do.'

'I was all right. It can be busy. You know that.'

'Yes; and you insist on taking the slow road.'

'Then why the gloomy face?'

James stared out of his side window, sighing repeatedly. 'I jumped to the conclusion you'd had an accident. And I realised it would be horrible and I might not cope if it happened.'

'Tell me what you thought.'

'All sorts of things: who to call; people telling me the news; sympathy from strangers and friends and family. I was thinking only of me.'

She made a cold laughing noise. She didn't seemed amused. 'That's nothing new James; and if I was dead there'd only be you to think of. Sorry, that is such bad grammar.'

He frowned. 'That's not true.'

'No, the grammar was awful; trust me, I nearly got an English degree. And I'm not dead. I'm here. One of us has to travel, or one of us has to take drastic and decisive action involving a change of home. Let's get this food, get it home and get it eaten. Stop worrying; everything's fine.'

The phone rang as they were preparing to go out for lunch. James was ready to ignore it but Laura made him answer. It was Mr Clifton.

'Hello Dad. How's things?'

'Good morning James. We're both fine; one of the dogs is a bit sick but nothing serious. I spoke with David last night and thought I should call to have a chat about the baby.'

James pursed his lips and snorted impatiently. He noticed Laura watching him and signalled with a nod that she should sit down.

'David hasn't asked me to call. But he is very upset.'

'Dad, it's really simple. I've told both of them I don't want to be the baby's godfather. David told me he understands. We really did sort all this out at Christmas. They're fine. There's no debate.'

'Well actually he is upset and he thinks there is a debate and it would mean a great deal to your brother and Annie if you would do the decent thing. You know David gives in to you. Really James, what's so terrible about being a godparent?'

James voice was rising with a combined impatience and frustration. 'Dad, I'm not going over it all again...'

'You need to speak to David and Annie. The baby is due any time and they need support, not worry.'

After a curt exchange of farewells, James put the phone down and sighed.

'What's up?'

'I'll explain in the car.'

While driving, James took a couple of minutes to explain his dilemma. Laura listened, then said; 'Explain this to me in more detail. Why can't you be a godparent?'

James fiddled with the handbrake lever. 'I think you know why.'

'Oh, this is your rational atheism.'

'Correct.'

'You're being incredibly selfish. I know you like David and adore Annie. I'm pretty sure you will love your nephew or niece. I don't understand how you can relegate all that below your views about gods.'

James' voice was whiny and strained. 'They're going through the motions. They don't go to church; they don't have a copy of a bible or a prayer book; they won't be taking this baby to church.'

'You're extraordinarily pompous sometimes. It's not very endearing.'

'Laura, I don't care if people have faith but I won't be dragged into it for the sake of an excuse to dress up. Because that's all it will be and I'm not going to be godfather.'

'That's pathetic James.' Laura's voice had risen a couple of decibels.

'No, this is me saying I'm not going to join a parade and pretend to be what I'm not.'

James looked ahead again and ground the car forward a few feet.

'So your refusal to be a godparent actually comes before your family?'

'I put plenty of things before my family.'

'Oh right.' Laura was glaring at him.

James glanced at her briefly; 'Look. What is this? Why the sudden lurch in to confrontation?'

'I'm trying to understand your position. So far, you're not making any sense at all.'

James revved his engine and pushed the car into a space in the next lane. That queue immediately stopped moving; he thumped the wheel.

'It sounds like you want everyone else to accept your view, but you refuse to accept that it will hurt people; which, incidentally, is not what rational people do.'

'You're twisting what I'm saying.'

'Because you're not saying anything.'

James sighed crossly. Even though he resolutely detested consensus, he just wanted everyone to agree with his point of view.

Laura started to laugh and poked him in the side. James grunted by way of an appeasement. By the time they had done some vague, disinterested shopping, they were arm in arm and smiling. But when they reached a pub for lunch, James re-opened the discussion.

'I'm sorry we had that row.'

'That was a row?'

'A disagreement.'

'James, it was nothing. I was just testing you.'

'You seemed cross with me.'

'Don't be silly.'

'You seem cross now.'

Laura shook her head in bewilderment. 'No. But since you mention it, there was something about your manner that I didn't like.'

'Go on.'

'Well, it's several things actually.'

James laughed.

'I'm serious. One: it's not the first time you've given me your views about religion and at no time have you ever asked me for mine. You've never bothered to see if I might be offended by your opinions, which I'm not. But it would be nice to think you would respect whatever I might feel.'

'Right.' He strung out the vowel sound.

'Two: I need to know that we can have, and live with, different views.'

This time, James' laugh was exasperated. 'All I did was say why I don't want to be a bloody godfather.'

'Yes. But you did it in a way that was intended to show that your view is authoritative. You wanted to give an opinion, not answer my questions. You have this tendency to air opinions without invitation and then expect compliance with your view. I argued with you because you sounded so self-righteous.'

'Oh.'

'Don't get left with nothing more than your opinions James and don't expect me to agree with everything you say. I am never going to be submissive and bow down to you.'

The people at the next table stopped talking and started to listen to what might be a looming storm. They were disappointed.

'Oh.'

'Stop saying *oh*. Try another vowel.'

'Ah.'

'A consonant please Carol.'

'What?'

'Please don't believe that because I'm crazy about you I will automatically think everything you say is sacrosanct. It's not that simple and neither am I.' She took a sip of her drink. 'What are you thinking?'

'Nothing.'

'Tell me what you're thinking; please don't withdraw from the discussion just because it isn't going your way.'

'You're criticising me for being me.'

'I don't believe, not for one moment, that how you behaved earlier is the real you. This insensitive, arrogant, argumentative, opinionated person is not you. You didn't used to be any of those things.'

'Didn't I? How do you know?'

'I just do. All this is new, and it's a charade. I think it's caused by your shyness to an extent; but I think it's manufactured and above all, it's a kind of shield.'

James had been trained about the negative aspects of body language, but it didn't stop him folding his arms and sitting back in his seat. 'I haven't manufactured anything.'

'I think you have.'

'It sounds so calculating and cynical the way you say it. Nothing I say or think is made up.'

'It's not what you're saying that's the problem James; it's how you say it. That aloofness isn't really you. The way you treated me in that conversation was appalling, as if I'm some sort of imbecile. You're not doing it now; this is a grown up discussion.'

'You make me sound like I'm a thoroughly egocentric maniac.'

'Well that's within you and you need to be more careful about when you let it rule your head.'

'I thought you didn't want me to change.'

'I've never said that. But what I do want is for you to try harder; to be free from pretence and tell the truth; to behave with dignity and a sense of purpose.'

'I think you've just called me a liar.'

'No. I know what you said earlier was the truth. What I sense though is that you sometimes aren't truthful with yourself.' Laura stretched her hands out to him. 'Smile for me. This isn't damnation. I want to make sure we're going in the same direction on the same road. I want to be with you; the you that is trapped somewhere.'

Their eyes met and James had to suppress a shiver, because suddenly he knew something inexorable was at work and he couldn't step off this train.

But Laura's eyes lost their lustre and the crow's feet of her smile transferred themselves to a frown and a hint of anxiety.

'What's wrong?'

Laura was looking out of the pub window. 'I don't really know how to say this and I've practised the moment time and again since we've been together. But I really can't put it off any longer.'

'What are you talking about?'

She looked into his eyes. 'I'm married.'

'You're what?'

'I'm married; well, I was. No; I am married; it's over but there's no legal break.'

James looked at her in astonishment. 'Why have you waited till now to tell me?'

'Truly, I've wanted to since the start. Today had to be the day.'

James was silent.

'You're upset. Shit; I knew I shouldn't have told you. Or found some other way to tell you.'

'It's why you wouldn't come to Paul's party.'

'No, it isn't. I'm not a prisoner because of this. '

'I don't know what to say.'

'Well, perhaps we should get out of here. Where can we go that isn't your place but is private and a good place to talk?'

James was numb with uncertainty. 'Let's go to Virginia Water. It might be busy but there's usually space and privacy where we can walk and talk.'

The journey took an hour and neither of them said much. James parked the car and they set off into the woods. Laura put her arm through his.

'I'm sorry.'

'For being married?'

'For making the whole of the last few months seem like a lie.'

James took time to collect and structure his thoughts about what to say. 'That's not how I see it. Nothing we have has been a lie. But I do feel a bit let down. I'd made up my mind, and created a wonderful picture, that you'd always been waiting for me. I saw your love as unique; a one way street of emotion coming my way. Now I find that you're sort of second hand.'

She wrenched her hand away and looked at him in horror. 'That's a terrible, hurtful thing to say.'

'I know, but you made me say it. It's horrible to find that someone you feel wonderful about has omitted to tell you something so fundamental. It's so disappointing; not the fact, but the secrecy.'

'I never meant it to be like that but it's why I've struggled to tell you.'

'It's only an hour or so since you lectured me about being truthful and honest. That seems a bit hollow now.'

They were facing each other in a stand-off. She said, quietly and sadly; 'I suppose it must do.'

James reached to her, put a couple of fingers under her chin and lifted her face up.

'Anything else I need to know?'

'Like what?'

'Skeletons.'

'No, there are no more. This was the big one.'

James tugged hard at her hair causing a look of outright alarm.

'What are you doing?'

'Checking you're not wearing a wig.'

Laura laughed, but the sudden release of pressure didn't stop her eyes from seeming almost terrified. 'This changes nothing about how I feel.'

They walked on and James took her hand. 'Tell me then. I want to know what happened.'

'Are you sure?'

'Fucking right I'm sure. This is more important than anything we have; if that dignity and sense of purpose you want is real, then I need the facts and the truth.'

'Can we sit down? Look, there's a picnic table; I have to say this to your face.'

They brushed away some leaves and twigs and found the seats were dry. Laura spoke with less conviction than he had ever heard.

'After I left school I took a gap year. For six months I was in Brittany working as a nanny and when I got back I just did whatever work I could get in Hereford. In the summer before I went to Exeter I was waitressing and I met Steve. He was visiting Hereford with his parents and they all came in to the café one day. I served their table and I couldn't stop looking at him. Then, completely by chance, we met up a couple of days later in the Grapes and started dating. I really fell for him and after he went home we had a couple of weekends together before I went to university. He lives in Bridgewater, no distance from Exeter, and everything took off. We were an item.

Not long after my final year started I became pregnant. I was using no contraceptives and he always wore a condom; but one time we were stupid.

I still don't know why but it made me want to leave college, so I did. I was in a panic and while I know I could have stayed on, it just seemed impossible for me to study and sit exams while I was pregnant.

I was in love with him; he was in love with me. So we made hurried arrangements to marry. Told our parents what had happened and asked them to work with us on an accelerated wedding schedule. Neither of us was bothered about it being the full thing. But we had this weird kind of rush to make it right for our baby; for him to be borne to a married mum and dad. I think we were grown up and honest about it rather than living through a disaster of lies and secrets.'

145

Laura stopped suddenly. She was pale and looked even more uncertain and sad.

'The baby had a heart defect and he was still born about a month before our wedding. It was horrible; just the most upsetting thing I've been through. It was so much like an omen for me and from that day I began to doubt the need for what we were doing. I started to think I no longer loved Steve; that the baby's death was his fault.'

Her voice trailed away to nothing. James took her hands and squeezed them.

'But we went ahead because I couldn't or wouldn't explain any of this to Mummy and Daddy. It would have been like throwing all their work back in their faces. And in the end, despite the awful tragedy, our wedding day was pleasant enough. Steve wanted to try again for a family. He thought it would be a good way of keeping me occupied. I wouldn't do it. In my mind, we needed to go back to being a young couple with lives to lead, and love to get right. I thought I might go back to university but nothing worked out to my benefit. He had a very well-paid job so I didn't need to work, and fell in to being a housewife. It was all so wrong.

We'd been married less than six months when the arguing started and over time the bickering turned to disputes that were sometimes quite violent; verbally, not physically. It could get thoroughly unpleasant. At first we fought through these episodes and seemed able to kiss and make up. Then I began to realise that he wasn't interested in me anymore and not long after our first anniversary, I found out he was seeing someone else. It was a relief. He left me in our house and I hung on there for a while, but really there was no need for me to stay.

Mummy and Daddy were furious and insisted that we had to make something of the marriage. Steve's folks were the same so with guidance from all our parents we were reconciled. This was about two and a half years ago and we got through a year in which things seemed all right; but this wasn't love any more. It was an obligation; a capitulation. Steve appeared to be happy enough, but I was almost frantic with the sense that I had no way out.

Yet he wasn't happy. It turned out he was just playing a part and, in the end, he made things easy. He'd promised he wasn't seeing his girlfriend any more, but he was. One night, I came home from seeing friends and there was a note on the kitchen table saying he was leaving me for good. He wants a divorce and he will accept culpability. That was more than eighteen months ago.'

She looked in to the trees as a man walked past, a dog scampering around him waiting for instructions or a stick to retrieve. There was a backdrop of birdsong.

'I hung on in Somerset for a while, then just headed to Hereford and moved back in with Mummy and Daddy. I got my job, settled down and became very boring, but happier than I'd been for more than three years. My parents are still concerned, still exuding this need to be doing what is right. They struggle to balance their need for me to be happy with their view of divorce as a scandal. One day, and in the nicest way, it can be just like I'm a debutante; eligible, single, an opportunity for someone. Other days, their disapproval and guilt about my situation are so hard.

I've largely eluded people I know in Hereford and until I saw you in the Lich, was actively avoiding men. I'd heard nothing from Steve and had occasional bouts of unhappiness that it all failed so miserably. Not because I want him back but because it somehow reflects so badly on me. But on Christmas Eve, when I saw you, I was dumbfounded by a whole load of feelings about where I'd come from; good feelings; great feelings. Seeing you opened my eyes to the possibility that I was missing out on something. James Clifton was standing there at the bar, and I knew my future had to involve him.'

She looked longingly at him. James stood and went to her. They embraced and after a moment, James whispered to her; 'I'm truly sorry about that remark I made. If I'd known what a terrible tragedy you've been through with your baby and how much you've suffered I'd never have said anything so stupid and selfish. Please forgive me.'

She withdrew her face to look at him. 'It's me who should ask forgiveness. I've hated myself for concealing this from you.'

'Well I'm glad you've told me and it's changed nothing.'

Laura smiled at him; her open, lovely, sincere smile. 'I can't believe you're so kind and understanding. I'm shattered by telling you. I thought it would make you hate me.'

'Nothing you can say or do would ever cause that.'

They stood in each other's arms and James realised Laura was shivering.

'I'm so cold. Can we go back? There's something I need to do.'

'Not another surprise gift?'

'Sort of.'

Back at James' flat, Laura took hold of him and kissed him. She began to whisper obscenities in his ear. Her hands pulled at his clothing with increasing urgency and she unfastened buttons and zips before pushing him on to the sofa. James tried to move away, saying; 'I need to get a condom.'

Laura shook her head and looked into his eyes with a smile before climbing onto him.

Later, they lay in bed and gaped at each other.

'Tell me why you pretended I needed a condom that night, and ever since.'

'There was no pretence. You did need one. You just didn't need to wear one. I would have fucked you if you'd shown me you'd thought about it. I just wasn't prepared to let you do it as if it didn't matter.'

'And this afternoon, you think differently?'

'I do. Everything has changed. There can be no more deceit and pretence.'

Much later they took their seats at a theatre and James relaxed to watch the play. He glanced occasionally at Laura and saw she was absorbed by the drama in front of them. James ended up watching her more than the stage, but shouts and screams regained his attention. Then the curtain dropped and the interval was announced.

They went to the bar where a half bottle of chilled champagne had their name on it. Laura tried not to look impressed by this but her smile was a giveaway. 'What do you think of the play?'

'I've been looking at you for most of it. Sorry, but you're the best thing on view here.'

She told him not to be stupid.

'You tell me about the play. You're the English scholar.'

She paused for a moment and sipped her bubbly.

'The main characters symbolise Love and Death. Love meets Death on a train. They speed towards a destination that they need to reach. The very noisy bit at the end was a crash; clever the way they did that. I think it's a good story of two people who fall in love and end up separated in the most final way possible. Some of the ideas and the dialogue are beautifully constructed. So far the leading actress is brilliant.'

Laura spoke a while longer about the play and the playwright. She concluded her thoughts with; 'But really, it's just another play.'

James laughed out loud. 'What? Just another play?'

She finished her champagne. 'Yep.'

'So all that stuff about nihilism and finely crafted tragedy and powerful imagery and timeless allegory is not how you see it?'

'Nope.'

'Then why did you say it?'

'Because I knew you'd be impressed by it. You treat art and life like that. The cleverer the aspiration of the creator, the better you like it. The less you think that the proles at the office are able to understand it, the more you want to know about it. If a poem has no verbs and doesn't rhyme, you love it. If a musical piece has no melody, form or structure, you love it. If a painting of a blue square is called *White Circle*, you love it. So I described the play like you would have if you'd studied all that bollocks. I'm sorry if you feel deceived but I couldn't help it. You're an easy target.'

James laughed again. 'Do you really think I'm such a pseud?'

'I didn't say you're a pseud. What I mean is that the ordinary doesn't interest you, especially if it's obviously ordinary. This play is a good, down to earth drama-tragedy. If I'd said that earlier, you'd have switched off as quickly as if I'd said it was an ITV sitcom or a song by Neil Sedaka.'

'Oh.'

'Don't start saying *Oh* again. You know what happened last time.'

'Oh, oh, oh, oh, oh. OH.'

'James stop it. The champagne was a lovely surprise. I'll have to seduce you more often.'

'It won't work. You'll get brown ale in future. Here; we'd better get back to the timeless allegory.'

As they walked side by side down one of the corridors leading to the stalls, Laura suddenly stopped and faced him. She took his arms and put them round her, kissed him on the mouth, stared into his eyes and said, 'I love you, James Clifton.'

Her cobalt eyes sparkled and her smiling face lit up. As James stumbled around this disclosure, she turned and led him back to the story of Love and Death.

When the play finished, they sat in their seats while the rush died down, then went out to hail a cab. They soon arrived at a live music venue where Gary's band, *...and so it seems...*, was headlining. James and Laura fought their way to the bar, then stood to watch this new entertainment.

James had seen the band before, but not with Gary as lead singer and clearly he had become the leader and focal point. His rapport with the audience surprised and fascinated James who quickly felt the new set up was better than before. Laura tugged his sleeve and shouted, 'They're bloody brilliant. Gary's a star; you never told me.'

'I always knew Gary is good, but this is unbelievably impressive.'

'Is the band going to make it?'

'Who knows? They are big enough and happening enough for a venue like this to put them on. Usually this place only has bands with deals, but maybe that's changed.'

'Who are the other guys?'

Instead of shouting over the music, James pulled Laura to him so he could relive the instant intimacy from Bogart's.

'I met most of them once after a rehearsal. They're all younger than Gary, intend to make it big and let nothing stand in their way. Dale, the drummer, is funny and a really nice guy. The bass player is Steve; the driving force in the group; unemployed, time to burn and he does lots of work for the band. He's a great player too. I don't know the keyboard player but, apparently, he and Gary write most of the songs. The other guitarist is Marcus. I didn't like him at all. I'm not sure that Gary does either.'

'Is Bridget here?'

'Later, possibly; she hates Gary doing this and says it interferes with everything.'

A song had just finished and, amidst the background of tuning up and drum hits, Gary was introducing the next. 'This is a new song which we hope you like.'

Someone yelled something.

Gary laughed. 'You could be right mate. Anyway, this new song is especially for a good friend of mine called James Clifton. Are you there James?'

James yelled that he was.

'Good. Lager please. Anyway, this is *Ambition*.'

The music built around a pattern of rhythms entwined with two synthesiser chords. Gradually the other instruments joined in, building on the pattern. The chorus was a sudden shock of action and a chanting, *woah yeah* refrain.

I've got something to show, I've got somewhere to go
I'm in love with myself, I won't be left on the shelf
I've got a story to tell, I'm gonna give them hell – Ambition.
I got a job with a man, got a pension plan
I got a GTI, don't have to try
Got a BUPA card, but that ain't hard – Ambition

What a waste say the people who know
As they live on in the ebb and flow
'You could be' says a voice in my head
But I never hear a word that's said any more
There's a fortune to earn, there's a lesson to learn
There's a book to read, there's a system to bleed
There's a talent to use, and I know I can't lose – Ambition
What a waste...

As the second chorus started, James was frowning. He didn't get it. He looked at Laura and saw that Bridget had arrived and the two of them were listening intently. He looked back at the band. He had no idea what Gary's words meant or why they had been dedicated to him.

During the interval, James handed Gary a pint.

'Did you enjoy your song?'

'Nice experience. Can I see the words some time?'

'I guess so.'

'I'm really enjoying the show. Is it a show? Or a gig? You sound so professional. You can sing. I mean really sing.'

'We'll call it a show. The sound's shite. We've only got about thirty per cent fold back and someone's feeding back like fuck. The second half should be better though. Someone's on the case.'

James nodded knowingly but none of this meant a thing to him and Gary was too distracted by others for James to dig deeper. He was like an onlooker and their relationship was lost in the strangeness of these roles.

The show resumed. James stood with Laura and Bridget who were now deep in a conversation. He moved closer to them and tuned in to what they were saying. James heard Bridget express her fear and resignation that she was distant behind Gary's love of writing and performing music. Her solution seemed to be that she must leave him because she couldn't compete.

James cut in; 'Gary won't be launched to stardom from places like this.'

'Yes, I know that. But it's not what I'm saying. I'm not willing to be the third love in his life.'

Bridget walked off and after a quizzical look at James, Laura went after her. James returned his attention to the band who were powering their way through Roxy Music's *Out of the Blue.* When Laura returned she told him Bridget hadn't changed her mind.

'She will, and before the evening is over. Laura, keep out of this.'

'What? Why?'

'On this particular subject I'm afraid Bridget has form. She's said all this to me before, and has clearly forgotten that she did. Meanwhile, Gary has mentioned to me that Bridget gets like this whenever they've argued.'

'She just told me they had a row earlier about where to go on holiday.'

'Well there you go. We should keep out of it; nothing we do or say will change anything, mainly because nothing is going to change. It's their problem; not ours.'

'You make it sound like you don't like Bridget very much. Or that you don't trust or respect her.'

'I like Bridget a lot. But on this specific point I don't respect her at all. It's like she's got a short circuit.'

'I've never known you be so blunt.'

'Let's change the subject. Same again?'

The atmosphere revved up to a very enthusiastic, noisy commotion that resulted in three encores before the band finally stopped for good. A DJ took over so James and Laura danced. Gary and Bridget joined them briefly, but when James declined an invitation to a party, they said goodbye and left. Their dances resumed, with great energy and passion. It left them sweaty, but joyful. When the slow songs started, James looked for a table while Laura went for more drinks. A recent hit boomed from the sound system.

Tomorrow seems a life away, do I want to live today?

Laura tapped her fingers and looked around to find James. She located him, sitting hunched forward at a table, gripping a cigarette just away from his lips. His attention seemed trapped.

...you never gave me a chance, you never let me off the hook,
not even a sideways glance, you never took a second look.

Laura put the drinks down and he barely noticed. She put her arm round him and whispered in his ear. He seemed to suddenly leave a trance.

'What's wrong? You look so sad.'

James smiled weakly and said, 'Nothing.'

'No; I was watching you from the bar. People who go from smiley to abject misery like you just did don't say *nothing's wrong.*'

He looked at her. She gazed back at him with a mix of concern and suspicion. James explained that the song that had just finished had made him feel sad and he wanted to leave.

'Do you mind if we walk home? It's not far. Twenty-five minutes.'

'If that's what you want, I don't mind.'

'We can talk.'

They downed their drinks, collected their coats and walked into the night. It was cold, with the moon occasionally peeping from behind clouds. Neither spoke for a while then James broke the silence. He looked ahead or at his feet. Laura waited, patiently pensive.

'That song; what's it called?'

'*Left Behind*, I think.'

'When I first heard it, things were a bit out of shape. It was the day after Boxing Day. I was sitting in the car at Oxford and the whole of my life seemed to be summed up in those words.'

'It's just a song James.'

'I know.'

'A song can't ever be a life summary.'

'It brought me down with a bump just now. It's wonderful being with you, and these last two weekends have been magical; but that song reminded me that nothing is forever.'

Laura was holding his arm and looking across at him every few paces. 'You need to stop thinking that.'

'I think I thought Sal would last forever right up to the point when I stopped trying to guarantee it.'

'How do you mean?'

'When I met Sally, there seemed to be instant chemistry. We got on so well; it was brilliant and refreshing. But I began to feel that I would lose her if I didn't start to think like she did. I left some stuff behind. Nothing she ever said or did prompted me to change; it all came from within.'

He expected Laura would ask another question, but when she didn't, James carried on. 'I started to take my job seriously and call it a career. I revised some of my beliefs so we didn't argue or fight. I kind of cut off the people from my past, even my family. It felt like my big chance; the big break I had given up on getting. I also began to see it as my last chance. Sally was worth working for; someone to succeed for; someone that made me look good. All I'd had was loneliness and celibacy; I had to make this work, otherwise nothing ever would again. Sally wasn't massively controlling, but she did sort me out; financially;

socially; spiritually. It was great; it really was. But we ended up with a single irreconcilable sticking point: marriage. I'm certain we both wanted the relationship to remain intact, but Sally wanted us to marry and I didn't. It caused arguments and ended up as a barrier between us. It got really tough.'

'What do you mean by *tough*? Unpleasant? Violent?'

'No, nothing extreme; it just got entrenched. Sally's method of getting her way and winning arguments was to keep chipping away at the subject; never letting it go; bringing it up in company; almost shaming me in to agreement. But I dug in.'

'Would you never have married her, even if it was an absolute condition of staying together?'

'She never once said: *marry me James; because I love you so much that I can't imagine not being married to you; I want to show you that you could grow to love it that way too.* All she did was make it out to be what people do; a tradition; something that showed the world how much money would be thrown at it.'

They took a few dozen steps before James continued. 'I converted my resistance to that into a lie: that she didn't love me anymore; and vice versa. We drifted apart, and you know the rest.'

'I do know what you've told me. But I still don't understand why some song lyrics can plunge you in to the despair I saw earlier.'

'I heard that song about twenty-four hours after she dumped me. The words didn't hurt because of her rejection. They hurt because deep down I am terrified of being alone; and my shortcomings as a partner or boyfriend, or whatever the fuck I was, had caused me to be alone; and without her I would revert to being what I had been before.'

'Are you crying?'

They stopped so she could see his face. There were tears streaming down his face and he could only speak in between sobs.

'She rejected me and I just accepted it on the basis that she was right; I am crap; it was all my fault; there was no point in patching things up or papering over the cracks. I assumed responsibility for the failure.'

Laura brushed his face and tears, then pulled on his arm so they resumed the walk. 'How come none of that was discussed when you got back together?'

'It should have been, but it wasn't. Our reunion was a sham: good, but lacking substance; it may well have been mainly about sex. Then Christmas got in the way and we parted too soon. When you saw me in the Lich, I was in a massive turmoil. I was happy we'd reunited; but I knew I shouldn't have been in Hereford. I shouldn't have been without her; there was no future while I was in Hereford and she wasn't with me.'

'But why does that make you responsible for her decision? You mean that if you'd stayed in Richmond, she wouldn't have chucked you?'

James puffed out his cheeks then exhaled. 'That was what I thought. But as I drove home that day I got my head around the fact that she was always going to end it. Because I was the cause and effect of a failed relationship. Then that song came on the radio and that stuff about second chances really hit hard; and yes I know a pop song can't be a design for life. But at that moment it felt like it was; as if someone had written a song for me.'

'They really hadn't though James.'

'I know. And the truth is simple; what hurt most was not rejection, lost love and a broken relationship. It was simply that I was and am a failure; a sad little man with nothing to offer; nothing worth fighting for; not good enough for this priceless princess who'd picked me up and shaken all that out of me and who couldn't be arsed to tell me why she couldn't be arsed.' James looked across at Laura. 'Does any of this make sense?'

'It doesn't. But keep talking about what matters. Even if it doesn't make sense to me, it must make sense to you; so we have to discuss it.'

James was quiet. He was thinking he should tell Laura that he loved her. But there was still some way to go.

Laura's voice cut in on his thoughts. 'What worries me a little is that you have such a negative view of yourself. Where has that come from?'

'From being alone.'

'That's stupid. It really is.'

'By being me I caused someone to leave me.'

'Nonsense. You told me less than fifteen minutes ago that you changed – and from what you said, you changed a lot – to maintain your relationship with her.'

James frowned in the darkness. Laura was confronting him with things that he didn't like. Things that demonstrated the stupidity of some of his worst idiosyncrasies.

'Either you changed to be what she wanted, and something was still wrong. Or you changed and she didn't really like you that way. Or you actually didn't change, and she didn't like that. Which was it?'

'I don't know.'

'Then your argument is rubbish. You were in a relationship where both parties contributed to its failure and the two main factors were poor communication and almost no shared tastes or feelings or beliefs. You're both to blame for that.'

James was silent. This was the truth he had always run to avoid. He had clung to Sally and the trappings and potential of her lifestyle in spite of that truth. His pretence had been absolute and he had ignored the nagging doubts because he wasn't brave enough to admit there was a chasm between Sally and him. He'd known it for at least two of their three years together. And now he wasn't brave enough to admit it, even to Laura.

'James? Are you ok?'

James turned to her and they kissed. Small voices were still telling him to say he loved her.

But he didn't.

16

James had talked enough. His fractured revelations dried up and though Laura dug for more, he just wanted sleep.

Much later, past noon on Sunday, they were still in bed; James lying on his back staring at the ceiling, occasionally turning his head to talk; Laura alongside and facing him with her head propped on a pillow.

She was keeping conversation simple. 'Gary's band were excellent, weren't they?'

'Good. Very good. But it was all a bit weird.'

'What do you mean?'

James took a deep breath. 'I found it hard to feel I was part of it. I didn't feel like his friend; just an onlooker; maybe even just a customer. In that world, Gary's no longer the bloke anyone works or lives with. I felt a bit jealous; because he's using his talents and skills; and is adored.'

'Is that what you want?'

'There is a part of me that has always wanted – really wanted – to be loved for my creativity; to have fans. Last night I saw someone delivering and it showed me that I don't even try.'

'If you want your pieces to be loved, why do you hide them away?'

'I don't know, but that's my point. I'm doing nothing.'

'Right. So what's the answer?'

'I don't know. Let's get up and do something.'

Laura pinned him back on the bed. 'No. If this is how you feel, there's a simple solution; sell some paintings. It will fulfil your needs.'

'But it's hard.'

'That's a very bad reason not to do it.'

'And it's soul destroying. It frightens me.'

'Fear of rejection? Or failure? Or criticism?'

'It's all of those.'

'This is crazy.' Laura sounded frustrated and she was still pinning James to the bed staring in to his eyes with mounting annoyance. But she saw defeat and her tone of voice softened. 'According to Daddy most small galleries will display an unknown artist's work. There must be a couple of places like that around here.'

'I suppose so. Yes.'

'Yes what? Is that an agreement to do something? What are you going to do and when?' Laura was trying to be a fan and enthusiast; someone who would pull James away from his malaise.

She was disappointed.

'I meant *yes* there are places around here, but I always think they look crap. I bet they charge massive commissions...'

Laura snapped. 'Oh for fuck's sake James. If you're just going to whine on like this, forget it.'

She bounced out of bed and slammed the bedroom door, then the bathroom door, then the bathroom cabinet door a couple of times. James got up too, and crept in to the kitchen to make drinks. Laura spent ages getting ready, declined the offer of coffee and toast and engrossed herself in the Sunday paper and some writing.

There was a heavy sense of an implacable dispute that hung on until Laura was packing her things to leave. James came to the door and, when she didn't acknowledge him, moved to stroke her shoulders and apologise. He felt her sigh then turn to give him a *what am I going to do with you?* look.

'You say you're sorry; but I don't need an apology. I need you to stop being so utterly inert. Will you do that?'

James nodded, but looked away.

'Cut out the am dram and for once in your life try to grow up. This is important and I am deadly serious. Did you mean it when you said you're jealous of Gary?'

'I think so.'

'You think so; you made quite a lot of it earlier.'

'Okay, it makes envious; it's like having my lack of success with something I can do well thrown in my face.'

'Well I'm sure that isn't Gary's intention. There's no conspiracy; no queue of people standing on your life support tube, watching you expire. The only person between you and your future is you.'

James tried to look away again but she took his face in her hands. 'I'm not going to let you wallow in this place. Either make a serious effort to use your talents commercially, or accept you never will. I don't care which you choose so long as I don't have to be on the receiving end of this self-pity. Because there is nothing I can do to make you any better as an artist and there is nothing I can do to make shops sell, and people buy your pieces. And you have no right to make it my problem.'

'I didn't think I was.'

'I'm afraid you were.'

She was still holding his head like a ball between her hands, but now smiled crookedly and kissed him.

'I've got to go otherwise the roads will be terrible. I'll call you tomorrow at work.'

She got up to leave and James carried her bags to the car. After Laura's closing words of encouragement and love, they kissed and she drove off. James stood in the road staring at her car until it turned out of sight. He gave a last wave to the space it had recently vacated and blew a kiss she would never catch.

On the kitchen worktop he found an envelope. He looked at it fearfully, then slit it open and paused again before unfolding the paper.

'Darling James,

I had a wonderful, wonderful weekend. You are everything I dreamed you would be.

I hope talking about all that stuff last night got something off your chest and that you feel better for letting me in a bit. I'll always be there to listen; you must always tell me if there's something troubling you.

And I'm so glad I told you about my marriage. Now we can really begin to make this whole thing perfect, the way I've known it would be since that night at the Palace. I hope you really are able to forgive me for being secretive. It was unfair of me. But I feared that you might never have been interested if I'd told you straight away. And we were having such a fantastic time that I didn't want to break the spell.

This thing about your paintings is destructive. We can't have it hidden away, and you need to get a grip on whether or not you can take a commercial view of the problem. I didn't like being so cross and blunt with you earlier, but your sulks gave me the opportunity to write this. And it's left me with just this to say: I think that what you create is very interesting and could attract buyers if that's what you want. I can't decide what you want any more than you seem able to do but at least I can see a way to move forward. You said that deep down you want to be loved but I think that remains submerged because of this fear you have of being a failure, or being rejected. If you try, and no one cares, what have you lost? Nothing; but you'll have gained my pride and respect because you tried. I think it would do you good to have the pat on the back. To sell a painting might release some potential and frustration; might move you to better things. I'd love you to try James. But if you don't that must be the end of it because I won't ever try to help again. I will not live in a permanent state of 'what if?' with you.

I'll see you on Friday night and, by the way, I can't wait. Don't forget the dinner party on Saturday – you'll need a DJ.

I love you – Laura xxxxxxxxxxxxxxx.'

The early May bank holiday gave James time for research and planning. From Yellow Pages, he found four shops or galleries within twenty miles of his home, then noted the addresses and phone numbers for each. From a drawer in his studio he took out a small exercise book with his handwriting all over the cover and across most of the first twenty pages. It looked a mess, but was a comprehensive reference system of every painting or drawing he had ever created. He flipped back and forth through the pages. Titles came and went; some meant nothing; others he recalled after reflection. He grabbed a biro and scribbled on his hand: *Simple Cell/Shoot Street/Cubism-ism*. He soon found the three pieces – two paintings and a drawing. He put one on his easel and stood back from it.

James had painted *Simple Cell* in 1985. The foreground was a cage of prison bars. Behind these were wispy, shadowy figures in ragged clothes, some sitting on benches. None of these people had faces but, between the bars at various heights, several faces were jammed tight. These all had the same expressionless eyes and open mouths, as if calling to those beyond the bars.

He nodded. It surprised him how good it looked.

He swapped this painting with the drawing. *Shoot Street* was slightly older and James had drawn it with no initial inspiration. Originally he'd intended to develop a painting from it but the effect had pleased him so it stayed as it was. It showed a street corner, apparently in a run-down place; litter lay on the ground; there was a boarded-up window. Blank street signs gave no clue about the location. He wondered now, years after creating this piece, if the streets should have names.

Leaning on the wall of one street was a naked man; his nakedness unexceptional; his head bowed; one leg raised so its foot rested flat on the wall.

Around the corner was another naked man, standing with an aggressive demeanour and pose. His hands stretched towards his groin where, in place of standard genitalia, a pump action shotgun was aimed and ready to be fired from the hip.

He took it down and placed the second canvas on his easel.

Cubism-ism was one of the last paintings James had done before leaving school. On a plain white background it showed three cubes in perspective. Three sides of each cube were visible and contained a face. Each face was perfectly drawn, beautifully shaped, coloured and defined except at the points where the edges of the cube prevented further detail. Each face wore a smile and a knowing look.

Having made up his mind to go with these three pieces, he searched in a cupboard to retrieve a cheap frame for the drawing. He hung them all on a wall and directed a light at them, then left the room. He waited a while then returned to view them, as if for the first time.

He thought they looked rather good.

The phone rang. Before James had said a word, he heard David shout, 'It's a boy!'

'What??'

'Annie's had our baby. It's a boy.'

'David! Brilliant! This is wonderful. I'm an uncle! Is everything okay?'

'Annie's fine and the baby's perfect. I'm not sure I understand how women can do all that. Watching it was absolutely horrible.'

'How big?'

'Seven pounds, six ounces.'

'Is that big?'

'No idea. You should have seen it James; such an amazing experience; it was just fantastic.'

'I thought you said it was horrible?'

'Well watching Annie, sort of in so much pain and screaming, all that was horrible. But once my boy appeared; I mean it's...'

'Well look, this is good timing. I'm up home this weekend. We can have a couple of lagers.'

'Abso-bloody-lutely. Friday?'

'Fine. I bet Mum and Dad are happy?'

'Yes. They're down here now. I'm at the hospital.'

'Laura and I will come and see you all.'

160

'Yes. Great. Got to go. Need to phone so many people.'

'But what are you calling him?'

'Bye now.'

It needed several calls that evening but James finally established that his nephew had been named Andrew.

Early the next evening, James stood in an art gallery talking to a man who he didn't really like, but who appeared to be marginally interested in the three items they were surveying. Hanging on the walls were paintings that James found dull and since opening the shop door he had started to resent the time wasted in the previous few hours.

The other three galleries had proved to be failures. The people running the first were rude to him. They said that they only accepted works by accredited artists, which they pronounced *artistes*. He had asked what that meant; the lady replied that she thought it was obvious what it meant and James walked out.

The second place was no better. This time two women confronted him and while one smiled, the other sneered at his pieces. 'It's not the sort of thing our customers would want to buy dear.' He didn't wait to find out more.

By then he wished Laura was with him. Wearily, he trooped to the next name on the list he'd scribbled down from Yellow Pages. When he left fifty minutes later he felt a little better. The couple who ran this one gave him the time to explain the three works and his philosophy and vision as an artist. They listened hard and sympathised with what he said. They talked about art the way he talked about art; but they couldn't oblige him by displaying any of the pieces.

Now, last on his list, he was talking to a very tall man called Roger Whitham who was arrogant to the point of disdain and who seemed to have been drinking. He was one of those people who, whether by fault or design, seem utterly affected. From his voice to his clothes to his deportment, James didn't think much of this expert.

'So how long have you been dabbling then?'

'I suppose I started for real when I was about ten.'

'Oh. A child prodigy.'

'I always did drawings and paintings. I wouldn't say much of it was ever prodigious. But it was always something I did well.'

'Fine; let's have a good look at these meisterwerks then.'

James sighed at the incorrect German and seriously thought of leaving. But he opened the case and took out his work. Roger examined them, sometimes closely through his half-rimmed glasses. James sensed that, despite the man's demeanour, he seemed to know his subject and was receptive. But Roger hummed and tutted, and made other sounds that James could neither define nor interpret. On a good day they might have signified approval, but James' glass was half empty.

'The cubes are a bit obvious; why that statement?'

Before James could think of a reply, the man said, 'You don't have to answer that. Because I actually think someone could be fascinated by it. I think it is possibly better sold as a poster. Perhaps it could be copied.'

James started to speak but was silenced with a wafted hand. More examination ensued. 'I love the penis gun. Or is it a gun penis? A nasty idea and nicely drawn. Charcoal?'

'No, black and grey pastels.'

'Ah, right. I see. Do you have any more like it?'

'Yes. I do quite a lot of that kind of thing.'

'I like the blank street names. Anonymity as the root cause of repressed male sexuality and threat. Unnamed. Unwanted. Unnatural.'

James laughed.

'I amuse you?'

'I was going to think up names.'

'Don't.' For the first time, Roger looked directly at James. 'Please don't change any of it.'

He moved sideways to view *Simple Cell*.

'I also love these prisoners. The faces between the bars are great. I like the blend of sadness and resolve there. This is a powerful piece. It rewards careful viewing.'

He continued to stare at the canvas for several moments. 'Well I can certainly display these, and suspect I can sell them too.'

James felt a swoon and needed to steady himself. Roger hadn't finished.

'But not yet. You see, in July I'll be exhibiting some work by Angela Tulley – you know her obviously – that these will complement. I can only use yours as a sideshow but I can promise you that they will be listed and will not be ignored.'

There was silence while James wondered what to say and whether or not he looked like a success or failure.

'Money. Shall we talk money? My standard terms are that I take thirty per cent of the sale price. But I won't take a sale for less than £450 on these.'

James mentally miscalculated how much that would earn. 'What do you think you'll get?'

'That depends on the punter. As I say £450 is my worst case. I won't sell for less. Otherwise, you are getting nothing for your, and my, trouble. Don't worry about the size of my fee. This is what I do. I expect to sell these for prices that will net you plenty more than you are probably expecting.'

James accepted the deal once Roger had agreed to get proper frames for each piece, and to take good quality photographs of them in case James never saw them again. He also made sure there was a no sale/no fee agreement and that no exclusive relationship was created. He made a note to himself that he'd done his best, but really he had no idea what he was agreeing to. He was just so astonished by the situation he could have accepted anything. This sense of helpless commercial oblivion had not left him as he worked through and signed some paperwork Roger gave him about the terms of their contract, Roger's insurance position, James' rights as the owner of the works, and their status as Parties in the contract. This was James' day job; and he more or less ignored all that he knew in favour of accepting his position in the deal.

When he finally left the gallery and walked to his car, James didn't know whether to laugh or cry. Slowly any nerves and fear turned to feelings of elation, and then to pleasure. He had done it. He had ripped something from the protection of its cocoon and tried it out on the world; and the world had said *maybe*.

17

James and David met as planned and got drunk. It was fun; a bond of brothers and, towards the end of the evening, they hugged. New things lay ahead for them, yet their celebration felt like a reaffirmation of something old and unshakeable. James told David he was proud of him for becoming a family man. David replied that he had always been proud of James and always would be.

Late the following morning, Laura met James in the city and they went to meet Andrew. James had never had any enthusiasm for babies, but somehow this little bundle of pink skin and blue clothes, making strange squeaking noises and smelling of something he couldn't define, moved him to tears. Here was the future: his first nephew; James was an uncle; everything had changed.

For the first time in his life, James was thinking of the part he might play in his own future.

Laura was equally besotted by Andrew, so they billed and cooed until the arrival of new visitors, which felt like an invasion on their territory. They retreated to a pub for a long chat over lunch and soft drinks. The conversation made James feel that something had been repaired, and a reset button pressed. The previous weekend had seen their relationship become complicated, complex and confusing; but now they seemed back to being young lovers.

Young lovers, in fact, on the verge of being formally presented to their respective parents. As they finished lunch, Laura indicated that they needed to go to her parents' house and get ready for the evening, which consisted of cocktails and canapés, and dinner with a myriad other guests. Worst of all for James, he must endure the unbearable discomfort and humiliation of wearing a dinner jacket, wing-collared shirt, bow tie and shiny shoes. He shuddered, but Laura had a warm up plan.

'If we go now, Mummy and Daddy are at the races and won't be back before four. You can do pretty much whatever you like with me, and in a variety of locations. By which I mean biological rather than domestic locations.' Her smile was licentious.

Later, they lay entwined and Laura said; 'Well I need to spring surprises on you like this more often James. That was your best performance yet. It was like a joust.'

'A joust? How? Where were the horses? And armour?'

'Well not a joust then. We didn't both have enormous poles.'

'Indeed we didn't.'

'But anyway; I need you to know that I spent the whole of this week looking forward to this and more or less since we got to the pub I was – to be blunt – wetter than a wintry weekend in Wick.'

James blinked and blushed; Laura laughed at him.

'Oh for fuck's sake James; please stop this prudishness.'

'I'm not being a prude.'

'You are. Come on; start treating sex as an act of urgent, intense, unstoppable necessity instead of this hearts and flowers love thing you seem to want it to be. Fucking, James Clifton, is what men and women do to keep things worth keeping.'

Laura had climbed on to him, and they were on the verge of another tilt when the noise of an approaching car caused pandemonium.

'Oh fucking, sodding, jesus-ing hell; it's Mummy and Daddy. Get out, quick; go to the room where we left your bags and in to the shower and don't come down until you're clean. Wear your chinos and a polo shirt. And take your horrible pants with you.'

James fled and, as he opened the door to his guest room, he turned to see Laura heading downstairs in a robe, a towel wrapped round her head. She flashed a breast at him as he closed his door. Clearly she had a plan to front it up with her parents.

With anxiety welling up inside him, James followed her instructions and took his time to get changed in to the desired costume. He really would have preferred a less challenging scenario for his first meeting with Mr and Mrs Drysdale. Aside from what had just been interrupted, and trying to guess whatever excuse Laura might have strung out to cover it up, James was still fretting over how her parents felt about what was left of her marriage.

At lunch, Laura had done her best to reassure him. 'Don't let that worry you. They know it's over. They have to live with the fact that I have someone new. You'll be fine. Don't let them intimidate you.'

'What do they know about me?'

'Very little.'

'Great. Is that good or bad?'

'Don't worry. It's neither. Just be yourself. Except for the hesitant introvert thing. And don't do your pompous voice. Otherwise, sorted.'

Twenty minutes later, James wandered downstairs. Voices were coming from somewhere, but standing in the large hall he felt isolated and even more apprehensive. Like a paranoid character in a Hitchcock movie, he darted glances at the various closed doors around him.

'Here he is.' Laura's voice was a soothing balm. 'Did you bring your dirty shirt and trousers down? I was just telling Mummy how baby Andrew was sick over you.'

He looked at her with comprehension dawning that he needed to link up the dots of this fiction. Behind her he could see a middle-aged couple preparing to join them.

'My things will be fine. I think I got most of the mess washed off...'

Laura was minutely shaking her head and flashing her eyes at him.

'I'll go and get them James. They need to be washed or they will smell dreadful. You might never get the stains out.' She winked at him and tripped up the stairs, out of sight.

'Hello James, it is a delight and joy to meet you at last. We've heard so much about you.'

James shook her hand and returned her greeting. Angela

Drysdale had passed considerable beauty to her daughter. She was polite and smiling and full of concern. 'What a shame that the baby was sick over you. But they are always a hazard; anything can happen.' She laughed; a tight, controlled laugh.

James was certain Laura's mother had seen right through the pretence.

Bill Drysdale was in plus fours, a tweed shirt and a deerstalker. James wondered if he'd been hunting rather than racing and concluded that, possibly, this might be someone who actually would hunt horses. He greeted James with a vice of a handshake and seemed very enthusiastic.

'Excellent to meet you James. Rather glad though that you've been able to change. Can't abide the smell of puke.'

'No, me neither Bill, and...' James considered the option of starting a man to man discussion about the specific aspects of puke that they hated most. Bill's gaze was so intense, as if he was seeing through James' thoughts to the very back of his head, that he made do with: '... good to meet you too.'

Laura was back with a large canvas bag which she declared full of things needing a wash. Bill, Angela and James were still clustered in the hall so he offered to help with the washing.

'No James, talk to Mummy and Daddy. Who wants some tea?'

'Good idea Laurie Lee. Bring it through to the sitting room. Let's go and sit down in there James, come on. Angela? After you my love.'

Over tea and digestives, they chatted about easy things. He found that when one of the Drysdales asked him a question, the other one watched him eagerly, nodding and making small assenting noises. Laura came back to top up cups, then announced she was going to continue with her preparations for the evening. Angela looked at her watch, decided she should follow suit and excused herself.

Bill resumed the discussion with questions about what James did, where he lived and what car he drove. He seemed impressed by the news of James' Alfa and mentioned he knew a former chairman of James' company. It was polite and restrained and James managed with a pretty straight bat. He was getting off to a decent innings when Bill asked for an opinion on something and beckoned him to come to another room. James crept fearfully behind Bill as they walked across the hall.

'This is going to be dead stuffed animals. Or he's got a trainset the size of Biggleswade. Or a prisoner.'

They arrived in a well-lit room with paintings hanging on three of the four walls, one of which had an alcove. Thankful that stags or horses weren't staring glassily down at him, James joined Bill in front of the first painting. It was a dreamy, nebulous landscape, evoking every cliché for its subject matter. Next to it was a classical portrait. Neither had feeling, nor depth, nor despair.

'I can sense you are underwhelmed James.'

'Well, really, they are just not my cup of tea.'

'Laura has been telling us that you like art; that you're an artist.'

James was hesitant; 'Oh. Has she?'

Bill was less tentative; 'Well, let's see. Come and look at these.'

He led James through the alcove to the next room, where the lights gradually undimmed as they crossed the threshold. Three paintings in plain frames hung on one wall.

'Angela's tastes are, I'm afraid, represented by what you've just seen. These are mine. I picked them up last week at a little place in Malvern. The young artist is called Vanessa Hunter. I'm very impressed. She has talent.'

James was enthralled by great washes of colour and light over menacing greys and blacks; animals; machines; people; surreal; bizarre. The kind of images he aspired to. He had no idea what might have prompted the works but each combined considerable fury with emptiness and dispassion.

'They're bloody brilliant.' He murmured it under his breath. 'And you bought these in Malvern?'

'Yes. Maynard's; you know the place? A modest gallery. They were listed at £400 each. I got the three for £900.'

James' heart sank at that news. A skilled buyer would easily defeat Roger, he was certain of it.

The mood between the two men had gained confidence and now they talked quietly and knowledgeably, like friends, about the pieces on display. Bill explained that the two rooms were being developed as a place to display their favourite works and that he had five or six other pieces in store that would soon be hanging here.

This bonhomie rolled on in to the evening. James was introduced to each set of arrivals as *Laura's new man, the artist*. He became the sole subject of a conversation with Jon, who sat next to him at dinner and plied James with questions and listened intently to all he said.

Some port arrived and those who wanted to smoke were invited to do so in another room. Bill invited interested parties to take a look at his new paintings, so James and Laura went along with three other guests. He enjoyed seeing the pieces again.

'So when can I expect something of yours up here James?'

Five pairs of eyes bore in to him. James spoke slowly and deliberately to hide his excitement, because now he had to tell them; to show he'd done it. He looked directly in to Bill's eyes; 'Well I've got three pieces scheduled to be on display later in the summer. A place near home will be putting them on. Perhaps you could buy one of those?'

'Perhaps I will. This is marvellous news. You must be thrilled.'

'It's a nice feeling. It's a modest beginning. But it is a beginning.'

'Exactly. Tell me about the pieces.'

James described the three works and was, once more, the centre of attention. It pleased him mightily but Laura soon took him to the sitting room, away from the limelight and curious eyes and ears.

'I knew you'd do it, but why didn't you tell me?'

'I did it because you created the setting in which I had to try. I didn't tell you because I wanted to show you instead, next time you're at my place.'

'Well that's sweet. But no, I didn't create a setting. What I learned last weekend is that you needed to take that step forward. It's something you've always wanted to achieve. I don't know what problem has stopped you, and maybe I don't care. Although really I should find the root cause somehow or I might always be pulling you from whatever trough it is. Deep down, you know that what you do is good and you know that others are attracted to it. All I did was to make you say it and see it clearly. Tell me about the paintings; did you show them to me last week?'

James described the three pieces again and Laura indicated that she had seen *Cubism-ism*.

'Yes, I remember the cubes; Daddy would like that one.'

'It'll cost him £800.'

'Anyway, enough of this. Your head is over-engorged with all this adulation and I am changing the subject. I had a call from Philippa; it slipped my mind completely till now. She's free next weekend and I really want to get together with her; we haven't had a proper catch up for ages.'

'But you're coming to me aren't you?'

'Yes.' She said it in a way that suggested a possible change.

'Well why don't you invite Phil down to my place?'

Laura seemed unsure; 'I think you'd have to ask her to do that, not me.'

'I will.'

'And you don't mind?'

'Not at all. You two can go off somewhere on the Saturday and maybe we can join up in the evening. It'll be good.'

'Well if you're sure. But ask her yourself; it's your home. I would feel wrong making that call.'

'Fine; I'll speak to her tomorrow. Make sure you give me her number.'

'Thank you. You really are a lovely man, aren't you?'

Laura stroked his cheek. Some profound, mysterious realisation must have struck her because tears had welled up in her eyes.

They said goodbye to Bill and Angela the following morning and drove to Hereford and the Clifton family home. His parents were at church, but Annie, Andrew and David had already arrived. When Mr and Mrs Clifton returned, Laura was introduced and in the nodding and smiling that ensued, she announced that James had something to say.

'Well, yes. Thank you Laura.' He looked around him; David was frowning; Annie was smiling; his parents seemed on the verge of panic. 'I've been a bit selfish and stupid and I want you to know that I will be Andrew's godfather if you'll still have me.'

David shouted his assent. Mrs Clifton muttered something inaudible and went off to the kitchen. Annie's smile became a beam of joy.

James' father had also disappeared but was soon back with two bottles of champagne.

'There is a very great deal to toast, so I won't reel them all off. Here; come on, have some.' He was pouring glasses to the brim and handing them to everyone. When they all had a full flute of fizz, and he had cajoled Mrs Clifton from the kitchen, he raised his glass and said: 'New Horizons', which everyone repeated loudly.

Shortly, a sleeping Andrew was removed to a bedroom and this left Laura as the sole centre of attention. She was repeatedly asked for her opinion on any subject and she responded assertively and happily. Mr Clifton was in an especially charming mode; showing Laura round the house; pointing at the garden through windows; politely enquiring about her parents and where she lived.

Laura was a hit, even with Mrs Clifton whose critical appraisal of clothes, hair and make-up seemed to be positive. It was an ordeal, but Laura coped and James was proud of her.

They had little or no time alone together. After lunch, as

they walked to the sitting room, Laura squeezed his hand and whispered to him that she thought his parents were lovely. He whispered back that they were barking mad. She whispered back that it explained a lot.

The following Friday afternoon, James met Philippa at Richmond station. She was clutching a bottle of Sancerre and a small suitcase. Their meeting was unrestrained and they chatted as if it had been five days, and not five months, since they had last spoken one to one.

After it had been chilled in the deep freeze they drank the wine with very little regard for its quality and price, then started on a second bottle of wine. Laura arrived to find two voluble chums, full of wine and a rediscovered friendship. To catch up, Laura made herself a gin and tonic and drank it down in one. She took another to drink while she changed. With these preparations completed, they all went to the pub to drink beer and were soon talking far too loudly about many pointless things.

Their drinking became unruly, and at one point Philippa grabbed James' hand and started a rambling monologue about how special he is. She then grabbed Laura's hand too, creating a circle. Droning on, sometimes incoherently, she squeezed their hands tightly and told them how much she loved them both and how they should take good care of one another. Towards the end of her outpouring, Philippa turned to Laura and said; 'You must never hurt James, Laura. He's a delicate, sensitive thing. He can be very easily hurt.'

James laughed. 'What on earth are you on about?'

'Shut up James.'

They demanded that he got the next round in and, while he waited at the bar, James looked over to their table and watched them talking. They were animated and laughing without restraint. Laura looked back at him constantly and, when he returned to the table, she stood to hug him.

James said; 'What were you two on about just now? Anyone would think you're in love.'

The two women looked at him with distaste.

'Shall I get my coat?'

Philippa giggled. 'No James. Please stay, we will need more drinks shortly.'

At closing time they staggered home and, once in the flat, Laura retrieved the vodka she'd placed in the freezer and something started that couldn't really be called conversation.

He'd had significantly more to drink than he could cope with, and an irresponsible mix of grape and grain, so James soon fell asleep on the sofa where he found himself in the early hours, disoriented and incapable. After a regrettable fifteen or so minutes in the bathroom, he drank three pints of water and went to his bedroom where Laura and Philippa were sleeping. He climbed in next to Laura, who stirred.

'James you smell horrible.'

'I've just thrown up; copiously.'

'You're such a lightweight.'

'Guilty as charged.'

'Well don't breathe on me.'

'But I want a cuddle.'

She snuggled up to him and within a couple of minutes they were asleep.

James woke up early, after less than five hours sleep. He felt awful, but sensed joy that he was lying in a bed with two amazing women. Laura stirred beside him and soon Philippa was awake. These three adults were shortly lying torpid and complaining that they felt shocking. They compared notes about how shocking they felt and after a dramatic description of his own shocking symptoms, James was voted *Most Sick Person In This Bed*.

There was a concerted effort to get someone to make tea and, in the end, Laura went off to the kitchen. Left alone with Philippa, James gazed at her with uncertain, slack-jawed amiability. She turned to him, winked and smiled, then mimicked his cretinous look. Laura returned with a tray of cups, spoons, and a sugar bowl. This collection made tiny ringing noises as she walked. The tea tasted good and soon provided James with renewed equilibrium. He went to make toast.

When he returned to the bedroom several minutes later he found Philippa was up, standing at the window in a T shirt. She smiled coyly, took a piece of toast, winked at him again then went off to the bathroom. James crawled into bed beside Laura.

'How do you feel?'

'Better than I should. Mixing wine with beer, and then vodka with anything, is lethal for me. From this day, Laurie Lee, it is your mission to stop me doing it again.'

'Don't ever call me that.' James caught the icy blast from her voice.

'Sorry; I thought it was a term of affection.'

'It's my father's term, not yours. I had a major go at him for saying it in front of you.'

'Don't you like it?'

'That's not the point. I just don't want you calling me anything other than Laura. Or perhaps darling; and maybe shagger.

The chilly tone had gone.

James smiled and said, 'Your preferences are noted.'

Philippa called out that she was going to have a shower. James made an assenting noise.

Laura leaned over to him. 'Your breath isn't so bad now. You smell toasty.'

'Toast is the answer on mornings like this. And more marmalade than should generally be spread. It remains to be seen if I will retain my current well-being. I don't see me doing much hearty exercise today.'

Laura kissed him tentatively and seemed satisfied that his mouth was acceptably cleansed. They started to feel for each other but when she grasped his cock, James couldn't stop himself from coming.

'I'm sorry.'

'Don't be sorry.'

'It's embarrassing.'

'It's not. It's a bit messy, and thank you for that. But I know you can do it right. Things sometimes don't work out.' She pulled his hand down between her legs and said; 'Why don't you do something for me?'

He started to kiss her but she pushed his face down to her stomach. He was soon kissing and licking all around her abdomen and legs. He vaguely heard the shower stop running and tried to withdraw, but Laura kept his head between her legs so he carried on nibbling and licking and sucking. After what seemed like an age Laura suddenly went tense and gave a deep, throaty groan.

'Would you two like some more tea? Or coffee?'

He heard Laura say, 'Mmmm, tea please'. James stayed under the quilt.

When he surfaced Laura appeared to be asleep. He lay next to her and felt a massive wave of embarrassment.

Philippa brought them a cup of tea each and smiled at James who looked away quickly. Laura opened an eye and smiled sexily at him.

'You should have said you're an expert at that.'

'I wasn't aware that I am.'

'Well you are. I have never come quite like that before. It better not have been a one-off caused by your hangover.'

'We will have to try it next time I'm sober. That could be a while.'

'James, how wonderful. You haven't blushed.'

They were both sticky and needed to be washed. Laura got up and went to run a bath and dragged James into the bathroom to share it with her. By late morning, James was squeaky clean but felt terrible and collapsed on the sofa. Laura and Philippa said they were heading out for the afternoon and he heard the door shut and their laughter fading as they left the landing. James was soon asleep and missed the whole afternoon.

They returned in the early part of the evening with carrier bags full of ready-made meals, fizzy drinks and a gift for James. It was a small painted wooden sign saying *Beer before Wine – you'll feel fine. Wine before Beer – you'll feel queer*. Except they had crossed out the last three words with a marker pen, and scrawled; *you'll vomit the lot you lightweight.*

James hung it in his bathroom.

He went running early the next morning and returned to find Laura alone. A phone call from work had given Philippa no choice other than to head back in to London to fix something. She'd left Laura with a hug for James, along with the suggestion that they should do it all again soon, and an offer for that to be at her place – perhaps dinner with Adrian.

With their plans for the afternoon torn up by this change, James suggested a walk in the park to get some fresh air, then some dinner before Laura's departure. She had a less rustic plan that started in the shower, worked through the confirmation of his newfound expertise and ended with them spending the entire afternoon in bed.

When she left at seven, James was exhausted. Too much to drink, a vigorous run and a harder physical confrontation with Laura had left him immobilised. He locked up, disconnected the phone and after drinking plenty of water, crawled into his bed.

18

A Wonderful Colour

As he fell in to the deep sleep he needed, James' final lucid thought was a realisation that he had fallen in love. It took him several weeks to share this news with Laura and, when he said, 'Laura, I think I've fallen in love with you', the words seemed to boom out like a klaxon. They were walking in the quiet lanes near her home and she had stopped in her tracks and searched his face through the gloaming. Then she held his face in her hands and kissed him lightly on the lips.

'And I love you too. You know something? You're all right.'

James giggled. He could not resist her sardonic humour. 'Are you sure?'

'Promise; super sure. Yes, I love you. Yes, you're all right. But tell me; when did you have this epiphany?'

They started strolling again and in a few sentences James mapped out the journey from their first meeting at Bogart's to the weekend with Philippa. Each meeting had created a step up.

'So is that it James? You've climbed to the top of a ladder and there's nowhere to progress to?'

'Not at all; I feel like we're on the same plateau, with more ladders to find.'

They walked on a while. It was starless, but the sky had a luminescence so they could see each other's features. He saw that she was smiling.

'James? Let's have a shag.'

'What? Where?'

'In a field somewhere. Come on.'

'No. Regrettably, but no. It's been raining all day. Our things will get ruined.'

She pouted.

'I suppose so. Not even a quickie up against that gate?'

'You only need to wait until next week.'

'It's the christening next week. You'll be up here again and we will not have space or time. Two weeks without your body: more in fact. That is a tragedy. But come here.'

Laura took James in her arms and kissed him. It seemed to last forever. When she broke off she said, 'Say it again James; look in to my eyes and say it again.'

He looked at her as requested. 'I love you Laura. I know I always will.'

Laura beamed back at him. 'Perfect. You're perfect. My James.'

Andrew's christening proved to be a stereotypical family gathering. Annie was an only child and her mother was long dead. This meant that it was to be a Clifton convention with only four of Annie's family present: her father; his brother and sister-in-law; and her cousin. Aside from Andrew's other godparents and Laura this was all about Family, whose key elements were assembled at the Clifton's house by nine that Sunday morning. They soon formed a convoy bound for church and the waiting arms of the pastor.

Seated on his pew near the front, James felt renewed doubts about the ceremony in which he would soon be ensnared. During the previous day's rehearsal, he realised he was required to make a lot of declarations and vows he might never keep. Looking around and behind him, he saw how the church had an overloaded look down the north side, where the christening party was in occupation. Opposite, on the south side, seven souls sought succour.

During a brief address, this swollen attendance caused the pastor to take an unrestrained swipe at people whose attendance in God's House is fleeting. Nods to the south; blind ignorance to the north.

The other godparents were a married couple, Sharon and Mick, who were friends of Annie and David. They looked shiny, keen and responsible, and very willing to take this thing seriously. James suspected them of being teetotal. He whispered this to Laura, who stamped on his toe and hissed at him to shut up. James narrowed his eyes at her and whispered that she was a very bad christian to cause him such pain. She spiked his other foot.

The Eucharist dragged interminably and when the baptism started it was a huge relief all round. Annie and David carried little Andrew to the font and there were some incantations and a bit of arm waving by the pastor. Then he took the baby and, falling in line with convention, Andrew started to wail at this bizarrely dressed man. James felt great warmth and love for his nephew and stepped forward with the other godparents to make some pledges and oaths. He spoke louder than the other two, for Andrew was still bawling away. More responses, commitments and vows: yes, I'll see he goes to church regularly; yes, I'll see he understands that religion is terribly important; no, I won't let him listen to strange rock music that encourages Satanism; no, I won't let him convert his neighbour's arsenal.

Finally the water was splashed, the cross was drawn and that was that. The service, and James' impatient fidgeting, were over and everyone poured out from the church with indecorous haste. Photos were taken in the churchyard during which people stood around in polite groups, smoking and making small talk. Then Mrs Clifton started to chivvy people into their cars; she was in her element; there was a platoon to feed; the kitchen and her apron were calling.

James and Laura took a detour with a view that a quick snog and a cuddle could be achieved. But it got out of hand and they ended up on the back seat of her car unable to contain their respective lusts. It was quick and, though hugely satisfying, had taken time that could not be easily explained. A viable excuse was established, tested and deemed watertight. They drove to Laura's house to collect a conveniently forgotten camera, a shawl for when it got chilly later and a fresh pair of knickers.

At the post-christening party, groups were formed and territories had been staked. Outside, in a pleasantly warm garden, were the proud parents, one proud grandparent and most of the younger guests. In the conservatory were Mrs Clifton, her youngest sister, their elderly aunt and two of James' teenage cousins. This group was minding the buffet, except for the two cousins who were gossiping openly about why James and Laura were late; they didn't buy in to James' excuse about cameras.

In the kitchen, Mr Clifton was sorting out drinks and swearing under his breath about some of his relatives. He was being helped with the drinks by one of his nephews and hindered by his younger brother and sister-in-law; they were keen to get some formal photos taken and seemed to need endless approval for this activity.

In the living room was the remainder of Annie's family with Sharon and Mick. The rest of the Clifton crew was encamped around the dining table. Several were getting tipsy, the men smoking cigars and going on and on and on about wetting the baby's head every time they took a drink. Simon was here too; not saying much but smiling distractedly at his relatives.

Away in a crib was the star of this show. Andrew was sleeping off his ordeal and looked, James admitted to Laura, rather wonderful in his silky, milky gown. Annie had asked them to look in on the baby and, as they looked down at him, it did seem that he was struggling with some great problem.

'He's probably having the usual mental anguish about the validity of religion in a modernised, rational society.'

'Sshh, James; you'll wake him up. And don't talk such bollocks.'

Andrew made a gurgling noise and they looked guiltily down at him.

'He likes his kip doesn't he?'

'He's so sweet. He's got Annie's eyes and nose.'

'How can you tell that? He's got no recognisable features at all.'

'Well he has. And he's got your ears. In fact he's very like you. I noticed it in the church when the Vicar was holding him and Andrew was screaming.'

Back downstairs, the party had become a kind of mass parlour game. In any given room, a minute didn't seem to pass without someone getting up to leave and being replaced by a newcomer. This almost seemed controlled, as if some secret signal was made to those who needed to switch rooms. The mountain of food had gone causing Mrs Clifton to bring in back-up rations. And Mr Clifton's supplies of beer and wine had been devastated. Simon was identified as the only person who hadn't been drinking and was sent out for fresh stocks, wherever they could be found.

Gradually, as afternoon became evening, the scene mellowed and each group settled into a room of choice. Mr Clifton organised a game of cricket in which the youngest guests were encouraged to join, even the ones who wanted to be allowed to drink wine and mix with adults. This contest was surprisingly competitive, but not enough to tempt James to get involved even after he caught a ball, one-handed, that someone had hit hard at him as he walked by.

Once she had given up trying to help with the tidying and cleaning, Laura joined James on a covered swinging garden seat where he had settled to smoke. There was a two-thirds full bottle of red wine on the ground between his feet, from which he now poured Laura a glass.

'It's been lovely to meet everyone. What a shame Carol is away. It's gone quite well I think.'

'Don't suggest anything like that to Dad.'

'Why?'

'He's a bit grumpy. They say that old family wounds never heal and, in our case, they tend to suppurate at weddings, christenings and funerals.'

'Oh dear. Anything I should know about.'

James thought about changing the subject and hesitated.

'Go on James. Tell me. I want to know.'

'Well part of it's nothing really. One of my uncles has never forgiven Dad for his success. Uncle Jack is not too well off and always makes Dad feel really guilty about having all this. It winds

Dad up like a clock. The other thing is not so trivial.'

He drank slowly from his glass and topped it up. The wine was nice and he checked the labels. While reading them he went on, as if telling the bottle these revelations.

'Annie and David got engaged very much against her parents' wishes. No one has ever understood why they objected and there's never been any nastiness or anything like that. They simply told her they wanted no part of the relationship and she was to proceed on her own. But, about a month after they got engaged, Mrs Thomson died from cancer of the stomach; sudden; terrible. David told me that Annie was really, really pressed to cancel the engagement. To her credit, she refused. She said her mother's death made no difference whatsoever to her love for David. It was all very sad. But in the end her father relented and came to the wedding and did all those fatherly things. It's all forgotten now really, except that my Mum and Dad never feel quite comfortable when Mr Thomson is here.'

'Tell me more about your family.'

'You know my family.'

'I know what you let me see, what you let me hear. Give me some padding.'

James looked around the garden. His father was running around like a dervish, yelling *howzat* and giving it everything.

'Dad's from Cornwall. He was brought up on a farm, eldest in a family of four children. He was to inherit the farm when he had gained the necessary experience. But he grew up with only one ambition: to play jazz. My father was an absolutely shit hot bass player.'

'You're joking.'

'No. Straight up.'

'Does he still play?'

'It's hard to encourage him. It's not the easiest instrument to haul out at parties, or during a winter evening. You can't accompany carol singing with one of those fuckers.'

Laura giggled. James smiled with her.

'Anyway, he played around in little quartets and even a big band in the years just after the war. Eventually he found a group that might make something happen and he announced one day that he wasn't going to stay on the farm. All hell broke loose, and Grandpa never spoke to Dad again.

So off he went with his bass and four mates. They did all right and started to make a few quid and a bit of a name for themselves. Their name was so cool: *Razzamajazz*. Then one day they descended on Cheltenham and, at some matinée performance or other, in the audience sat my mother. She was finishing her final year at one of the schools there and her parents had brought her to this club as a sort of pre-exam treat. Their eyes met across the room and that was that.'

Laura interrupted. 'Where is your mum from?'

'Patience, Grasshopper. Dad left the band and settled in Cheltenham; got himself a day job doing nothing much and worked every night in a club band. *Razzamajazz* was no more. Mum had one term left at school and exams to sit, which she was single-minded enough to get through despite his attentions.'

James watched his mother through the conservatory windows, deep in conversation with her sister; never smiling, always animated. As he spoke, Laura followed his gaze towards the conservatory and said, 'Is Linda her only sister?'

'No, there are four of them, but Aunt Linda is the only one here today. They grew up in Wells; a very middle class background; Gran was a doctor, Granddad was a big-wig in the county council. Mum was always the bright one and got a scholarship to the school. When her exams were over, she joined up with some girlfriends from school and rented a flat. This apparently had the blessing of all the parents who didn't know Dad was also a more or less permanent resident. She got a summer job in a shop and they became a couple. The crunch came when she had to make a decision about university because she had been accepted by several, having got the necessary A levels – or whatever they had then.

She ended up getting a place to study Law in London. Dad moved up there too and easily got work and gigs that supported them pretty well. To cut a long story short she qualified as a lawyer and they moved up here so she could start working for a local firm of solicitors. I have absolutely no idea why, with the whole world to choose from, they picked Hereford as their home.

Dad got a job with a firm of farm tool manufacturers and apparently did all right because he ended up as Sales Director, which he still does today. Mum didn't let the arrival of children stop her from working; instead, she set up her own firm and directed business from home while we were wee. About five years ago, Mum sold her practice to a much bigger firm. Did very nicely out of it.'

'How do you all get on with your parents?'

'There's a sort of fifty-fifty split. Carol and I are both on Dad's side. David and Simon are on Mum's.'

'All one happy family.'

'I don't think we've ever been that. There's so much tension and debate; so much contradiction. No one seems able to open up emotionally.'

'But you know so much about your folks; how they met; all that.'

'Oh, that's Dad's infatuation with history and tradition. He spilled the beans to me one night at the pub in one of his *it's time you knew son* speeches. It could be fiction and lies for all I know. Mum's never talked to me about their past other than the usual naff family anecdotes. I think the others know too, although we've never discussed it. This is not a happy family in the traditional sense.'

'Well you seem to be.'

'Hmm.'

'Why the feud with Simon?'

He caught sight of his elder brother through the dining room window. Simon was talking to their uncle who looked half asleep.

'Feud's a bit strong. Simon and I fell out because of the joint need to be parental favourite, but also leader of the other two. It worked out that we ended up as neither. We argued constantly about everything when we were in our teens and I was delighted when he finally left home to live with Sandra.'

'His wife?'

'His wife to be. They married very young and it cost them dearly. What happened wasn't nice. She had an affair, so Simon left her. Then they were reconciled but, and this is the difficult part, the evidence is that Simon really messed with her head. She had a major breakdown and ended up being sectioned.'

Laura said; 'Bloody hell. That's awful.'

'It was, and it is. Their marriage was eventually annulled because of her mental health and it's as if she never existed. She isn't in Hereford. Had a kid with some bloke and lives on social security.'

James looked again at his brother. 'Simon has a phenomenal brain. But he wastes it and has no interests or hobbies; works in a nothing job at the Town Hall. I think he punishes himself for what he did even though he was probably driven to it by her infidelity. It's very sad.'

'This is unbelievable James. He seems happy and normal.'

'Yeah; he's happy and normal. But he thinks he's a monster, which he isn't, and sometimes he just finds a way to really piss the rest of us off. Let's stop talking about him. David is the star of the show; not today, always. Got a two-one in Chemistry at Southampton University and is a successful pharmacist. I gather that university in the early eighties was the perfect place for a pharmaceutical career to begin. He is kind, sensitive and tolerant with a wicked sense of humour. I used to think we had nothing whatsoever in common but, as we've grown, we've realised how much we love each other and how our different personalities go together. So now we talk more, and try to see each other often and have forgiven each other for the fact that we hardly saw one another for several years.'

'How did he meet Annie?'

James laughed; 'An unbelievable story. The perfect male ego trip.'

Laura waved her empty glass at him, and he drained the bottle in to it.

'Are you driving?'

'Daddy said he would pick me up. I should call soon to make sure he meant it. Go on. Tell me the male ego trip.'

'David's always been attractive. Physically handsome but also a non-physical appeal. He was in his first job after graduating; a shop pharmacist, dispensing plasters, pills and pile ointment. David was there late one afternoon when he gets called through to see a customer. It was Annie. Basically, she said she wanted something for a very sore throat. Her voice was barely audible by all accounts.

So David provides a couple of options and she chose one. Then she looks pensively at David. This whole scene, by the way, has taken place with much staring and lip-licking, boiling trousers and the *Romeo and Juliet* overture swelling in the background. And she asks him for some condoms. David blushes to his roots and hands over the cock socks. Annie asks coyly, *Don't you want to know what they're for?* And David stammers, *I know what they're for.*

No you don't, croaks Annie. And she motions for him to come close and she whispers in his ear: *I'm buying these so that when my throat's better you can come round to my flat and fuck my brains out.* And she pressed her address and phone number into his hand and walked off; without paying.'

'This is a wind-up.'

'No. It's exactly as David tells it. I'll prove it; David, over here.' James beckoned to his brother.

'James, I believe you.'

David joined them. 'Hello you two. Have some more wine.'

He handed them another bottle, with a good few glasses left in it.

'Thank you. I was just telling Laura about how you met Annie.'

David blushed and smiled, then walked away.

'And did he?'

'What?'

'Go to her flat?'

'Well yes. He's not as sweet as he looks. They went out for quite a while, then moved in together. At that point, there seemed to be some early signs that her folks disapproved although no one has ever understood why. But anyway, after about a year they got engaged and here we are.'

James and Laura swung back and forth awhile, sipping wine, swapping stories and beaming at the sights around them.

'What about Carol?'

James thought for a while.

'Carol's my friend first, and sister second.'

'Really? That's an amazing thing to be able to say.'

'It is, isn't it? But we've always been close. We are very different people and there are several years between us, but we've done many things the same: a bit rebellious; straight from school in to work; bad career choices. But she quickly extracted herself from any dead ends and moved on and up. She is a very, very good photographer.'

'She told me at her party that she really idolised you when she was little.'

'Did she?'

'Yes.'

'I wonder why?'

'Stop it James; you know why.'

'She was always out playing with me and the lads when she was little. Then in our teens we became buddies. It felt like she was my only friend when Sarah Smith dumped me.'

'Oh not her again.'

'I can't help it.'

'Why do you hold on to it so tightly?'

'It's always felt like a defining moment.'

'But you know, deep down, that a teenage relationship that lasted a month...'

'...six weeks...'

'...and if you tell me the number of days, hours and minutes I will smash your face in James.'

'Easy tiger.'

They laughed, and James motioned for Laura to continue.

'Those things we all did as kids; they were perfect and lovely, but whether there was one or ten they were just building blocks. Your life didn't end in 1977 because of her decision to dump you.'

'I know. That is all true. But what is also true was the lack of any guidance about what to do. No one explained it to me, so I just made up my own rules. Philippa tried but just ended up pissed off with me. All the guys were next to useless. So like I said, Carol was the constant. Wise beyond her years. But her love and support didn't stop me making wrong choices'.

'I was your best friend throughout that whole period; bar none.'

'Well sorry, but I'll just have to take your involvement as read.'

James drank slowly from his glass then spoke very deliberately. 'You were lucky I didn't know you then. I behaved like an ogre and was really very unpleasant.'

'Really? Are you sure about that?'

'I couldn't stop myself. I just wanted to hurt people and fuck with their heads. And at the same time I idolised almost every woman I met because I was desperate for stability and certainty. But I had no idea what that looked like.'

'You didn't hurt me, ever, except when you looked like you wanted to die. You know; you looked the same that night in the Lich.'

'I didn't want to die. I didn't want anything, except the stability and certainty I have been searching for since 1977.'

Laura took his hand and smiled. 'And here you are; in love.'

'In fact here we are, both of us, in love.'

They clinked glasses but James couldn't look her in the eye. She pulled his face round and saw that his eyes were filling with tears. She set down her glass, hugged him warmly and whispered her love for him.

Away in the kitchen, James' mother watched this scene as her sister embarked on another tale of woe about her daughter's delinquency.

From the dining room window Simon stared at them, mesmerised by the image of a brother's love.

Fielding at second slip, Mr Clifton missed a very catchable ball as he noticed his son being comforted by a girlfriend he hardly knew.

It really was all about Family.

19

On June 26th, as he sat at work preparing for a meeting, James celebrated a semi-anniversary. Boxing Day had been the day Laura arrived in his life. In those six months, they seemed to have filled their lives with things that had never happened during the two and a half years James was with Sally.

Was that selective amnesia? A purging process? Was he shutting out the good things from those days in favour of now?

He scribbled *Laura* on his notepad substituting the last *a* with a heart shape. Whatever his mind was up to, James felt confidence and certainty. Despite living so far apart they had managed to do many sparkling, exciting, perfect things. Entertainment and eating out were woven in to their social lives. They tried to be cultural, knowledgeable and diverse but happily watched soaps if they chose. They had become accepted and embedded in each other's families and domestic arrangements reflected it. Laura was now spending more time in Richmond but at both ends of their lives was a busy and growing social calendar and it was as a couple that they filled it. Their roles as individuals were almost secondary. It felt as if they knew all that needed to be known about each other and they took pride in themselves and in what had happened. They wanted to retain it as closed and private; something locked in to their own hearts and minds that was no one else's business. However, they were incapable of suppressing whatever signals they broadcast. Everyone they encountered knew: Laura and James were a near perfect couple.

James was interrupted by the clamour of his telephone. It was Sue from Finance, who had never encountered the word preamble.

'Are you coming out tonight James?'

'I'm undecided.'

'You should come; it'll be a laugh and everyone's going.'

'Quite.'

He vaguely knew the script. Two colleagues were leaving the company and their celebration would start in the pub as soon as work was done. It would continue at a party once the pubs closed. This would involve low quality food, warm beer, cheap wine and dubious brands of vodka and whisky. He realised Sue had not responded to his last remark so he continued; 'Who's going?'

'Not sure. I think some quite senior people are expected but mainly it will be the cavalry; and they need their Generalissimo Clifton.'

'I'm sure they do.'

'Gary's going.'

'Really? He's usually gigging or rehearsing at the moment. Amazed he can fit us all in.'

'Well tonight he can.'

James made a noise that made him sound like a dithering old man and he said he would check Gary's plans. He rarely combined work and play. It had become frowned upon to be seen as a player in the social game and James generally needed a very strong reason to be part of it.

During his first few years at the company he had been the very model of a party-animal, sometimes with no stop button. With other twenty-something colleagues he craved lunchtime drinking, frantic celebrations of anything and endless office nights out. When the pubbing and clubbing had been at their height, he was lured into running the office sports and social club. He ran squash ladders, five-a-side football leagues, quizzes, raffles, wine tastings, and games nights. At the peak of his popular stewardship, James made the unwise decision to devise and distribute an office newsletter. From a tame start, it soon became rude and libellous. People loved it and each edition was eagerly anticipated. It was banned after three months and seven newsletters when a lambasted colleague threatened legal action.

Chastened by that experience, James withdrew to the margins and became largely remote from work and play.

Later in the afternoon he picked up the phone. 'Gary? How are you mate?'

'Fine. What's happening?'

'Are you going to this do tonight?'

'Of course. Aren't you?'

'Can't make my mind up.'

'James you have got to put the brakes on those grandma noises you make whenever you're confronted by your own uncertainty.'

'I know. It's because you're being very decisive.'

'Well stop it.'

'Yes master.'

'Right. Good. So listen; there's a change of plan you might not know about. I know you don't like the Tavern but don't worry. Me, Gaggi, Sue, Jacqui and Big Phil are going to Saints instead. I have two new team members and I wanted to make the early part of the evening about them.'

'Who are these people? What do they do, and why haven't I met them yet?'

Maxine looked up at him. For a reason he couldn't explain, he poked out his tongue.

'Rob, who has been poached from one of the banks, is a media buyer. Nice bloke. Supports QPR, but so far that hasn't proved more than mildly difficult. Petra has joined from a small advertising agency somewhere App Norf. Her husband has been relocated to our capital.'

'Petra. As in Blue Peter?'

'No James, she is most certainly neither a dog nor under the benign control of Valerie Singleton.'

James yielded. 'Well, I suppose Saints is a better bet than the Tavern.'

'So you'll be coming?'

'Yeah. Why not? See you in there.'

By seven o'clock, James had an inkling he would give the party a miss and, by eight, was completely certain of it. The whole event was without merit and James had given up the search for things that might cause improvement.

Gary was mainly drilling one of his new team with a manager's agenda. James, snubbed by this rejection, chatted briefly to Gaggi, but they weren't close and when Gaggi went off to score his fruit machine addiction, James stayed with the group. He was poorly equipped for gambling. Big Phil was getting drunk; this was planned and he had stated it as an ambition on arrival, since when he'd had three drinks for everyone else's two. It was funny at first but Big Phil had become a drunken, lecherous moron. Which left Sue from Finance and her chum Jacqui, who were mainly interested in the array of smart young men strutting in and out of the bar.

He sat in silence on the edge of a group he wouldn't join. There was an untouched drink in front of him that Big Phil kept eyeing covetously. James was tetchy, cross and wanted to go home. He hated the sense that the party later on was mandatory; something so special that it couldn't be missed; and missing it would mean condemnation. The conversation around him was really pissing him off; it was like a fight. No matter what the subject, someone had to be or have bigger, better, brighter, faster.

James just wanted to leave and get home in time for a chat with Laura.

'Petra! You made it at last.'

James turned to see this newcomer, then stood as she reached their table. There were introductions, handshakes and smiles before Petra sat down in the seat next to James and gave him a polite nod. She was soon receiving the same speech Gary had made to Rob earlier and James noted her lack of interest; she was paying more attention to the surroundings than her new boss.

Once his scripted welcome speech was finished, Gary turned to the whole group and proposed they should all take a crack at the pub's general knowledge machine. There was a murmur of approval, but James and Petra declined and offered to guard the coats and handbags.

Petra looked relieved. 'I'm glad you said *no* to that nonsense. I really hate those games.'

'No problem. I quite like them. But I prefer to play on my own.'

'Really? How strange. I need another drink. Want one?'

'May I have a pint of lager please?'

Petra arched her eyebrows and smiled; 'You like to play on your own, and you appear to be living in the 1950s. Extraordinary.'

Before James could speak, she went off to the bar.

A shout of rage from the quiz machine rent the air and an argument started about who wrote *Lord of the Flies*. James turned back just in time to hear a tuneful and apparently satisfying fart from Big Phil's prone, lumpen figure.

Petra returned and, after thanks and cheers, they chatted about things with no context or relevance. He looked at her closely, sucked in by her purple eyes. She had a Liverpool accent and it sounded lovely. He set himself a small challenge to get her to say *fuck*; that word always sounded special spoken by Scousers.

'So I'm curious. Why does a man in his late twenties exude such polite good manners? Where I come from, standing up to greet anyone and then starting a question with *may I?* is cause for actual bodily harm.'

'Well, you know, I think standards are worth maintaining.'

She acknowledged his sarcasm with a raised glass and a mocking nod. 'You are in a shrivelling minority there, la. But how come someone with such high standards is sitting all alone in this dump?'

James confessed he didn't really know.

'Are you still going to the party?'

He told her he doubted it. 'I should have gone with my instincts to stay at home this evening. But I thought something would invigorate me if I came along.'

'I'm only here because it felt like a duty; a team-building necessity. But I sense that the hope and expectation is for me to get drunk so some fat bastard like him tells everyone he shagged me.' She laughed, and looked at Big Phil with contempt.

James laughed too. 'The perils of men at work.'

The mood lightened and they chatted about why she joined the company, what he did there and what had brought her to the capital.

Petra pointed to his left hand. 'The lack of a ring suggests you're not married.'

'No, but I'm spoken for.'

'That's nice. Who's the lucky girl and why isn't she here?'

'She's called Laura and she lives in Hereford. We were at school together.'

'Tell me more. I love a good romantic tale, especially if teen sweethearts are involved.'

James spent several minutes outlining the course and cause of his relationship with Laura. Petra watched him intently, smiling and nodding as he spoke.

'You really love her, don't you?'

He blushed, and stammered that he did.

'Do you think you'll get married?'

James blushed again and said he didn't know.

'But this lovely woman has held a flame for you since you were kids. She's probably dreamed of walking down the aisle to you at least twice a week since then. You do realise that, don't you?'

He confessed it hadn't occurred to him.

'Laura has some challenges ahead. You're not going to make her life easy with your fear of commitment.'

He couldn't tell if Petra was perceptive or presumptuous. 'It's only been six months. What we have is special in its own right. So I'm not sure either of us needs to commit.'

'That sounds pretty fucking defensive to me.'

He smiled with the satisfaction of an objective achieved.

'I suppose you want to keep you options open; free to go off with other women.'

'No. I don't. In fact I think fidelity is incredibly important.'

'So you're not in league with the men at work you mentioned earlier.'

'I try not to be.'

'Full of PC and New Man sensibilities?'

'No; I just want my relationships to be real, and not a sham.'

'So you and Tracy Miller was what?'

James couldn't stop a deepening blush of burning pink covering his face. Petra laughed loudly. 'You really are easily embarrassed aren't you? You're like a small boy.'

He was rocked by the reference to Tracy. A complete stranger and newcomer had simply tossed it into the conversation.

'That was a one-off and wasn't behind anyone's back. I was single; I think she was too. It was also a colossal mistake.'

'By both of you.'

He didn't feel vindicated, but a prickly curiosity was welling up.

'What else do you know about me?'

She shrugged. 'Just about you and her. The New Year's Eve party and clandestine canteen trysts.'

James shook his head; 'This is really pretty bizarre.'

'It's gossip. It's what happens. You're a personality, and part of the grapevine. Stop worrying; let's change the subject. Do you think Gary will be really offended if I don't go to the party? I really don't want to, but is there a plausible excuse I can make?'

'Gary doesn't like bullshit. If you don't want to go, just tell him.'

'Oh, okay. Right.'

'But I'm also looking for a way out. Remind me where you live.'

'Barnes, for now.'

'Perfect. Why don't you just tell Gary you don't feel like it and you know I'm not going either and we're planning to share a taxi?'

'Is this how you started things with Tracy?'

James bristled; 'If you just want to take the piss then sort out your own excuses.'

He stood and walked off, wishing he was miles and miles away.

Petra followed him and pulled him back by the arm. 'Okay, okay, okay. I was out of order. Let's not end the evening in a dispute. You're the only person I've met since moving here who is remotely interesting; I'm sorry I offended you. Come on; forgive me.'

James withdrew his arm and kept going. He left the building and stood, looking up and down the noisy street. He wanted to go home but knew he couldn't do so without his jacket and briefcase. He crossed the road and walked a few yards to a phone box to call Laura.

No one answered.

His walk back in to the bar and return to the table felt like a massive defeat. Petra was talking to Gary and everyone else was trying to revive Big Phil. It seemed they were ready to move on.

James grabbed his things; Gary leaned over to him.

'Sorry you're not coming to the party mate. But thanks for offering to see Petra gets home safely. It's good of you.'

She already had her coat on and James looked at Petra with an ironic smile. They left together shortly afterwards and walked in search of a taxi.

'Please forgive me. It was rude and unnecessary. I'm sorry I said it.'

'It was; and you should be. Whatever you've been told about me it should have included that I don't like being confronted with my own mistakes.'

'No one told me that.'

'Thought not; and since that's not your fault, I accept your apology.'

No black cabs appeared and, when they reached the taxi rank, there was a queue of half a dozen clients. They had a short debate about what to do next.

Petra said, 'Why don't we go and have a bite to eat? I'm tempted to offer it as my treat since I've annoyed you so much. But you can talk me out of that.'

James thought this through. It was midweek, and he'd already drunk five pints. He didn't like working with a hangover which would be inevitable if he drank more.

She seemed to guess his mood. 'It doesn't have to be a meal. Come on; let me get you a kebab or something; you can tell me all about your tendency to break rules.'

In the queue at the kebab house, they chatted about the variety of things Petra had heard about James: that he was a maverick; that people were a bit scared of him; that he was difficult to get on with; a cold fish. And that other people said he could be amazing fun; a good drinking buddy; and loyal. 'You seem to score high on the loyalty and fidelity front. How does that sit alongside your creative free spirit as an artist? Deep down it's clear you're not conventional.'

James raised his hand to acknowledge that he had ordered the doner kebab, with extra chilli, that was being called out. He was relieved when Petra's order arrived simultaneously; he didn't want to talk openly in a queue full of drunks.

'I'm incredibly conventional. Painfully conventional.'

Petra had already taken a bite from her kebab and spoke with her mouth full. 'Bollocks James.' A small blizzard of shredded cabbage reinforced this invective. 'Your unnerving and rare habit of being honest and vaguely charming with complete strangers doesn't mean you conform. It's just one your little acts. A giant defensive wall.'

They were dawdling; small steps to prevent loss of balance while guzzling. James looked at the packed pitta bread with the welling dread of what it would do to him overnight. 'You make me sound like a fraud.'

'Don't forget; I'm a married woman; I'm confronted by a man's dishonesty and diversion on a daily basis. I can smell out deception.' She looked across at him, aghast, as he took a whole chilli and crunched in to it. 'I can't believe you're eating that.'

'Why? It's probably the only organic thing in the entire package.'

'It's horrible shite isn't it?'

'It is, but the company helps.'

Petra burst out laughing, and most of her remaining strips of meat fell from her grasp. She soon threw the rest in to a bin. James looked back at the tiny trail of sliced vegetables they'd left behind them.

'Looking for something?'

'Just checking no one who knows me is in the vicinity. I shouldn't be eating this. In fact I'm chucking it.'

'My husband would go mental if he knew I'd had that. But in spite of its unadulterated horror, there's something insanely special about eating a kebab: the cheaper the better.'

She said this as he dumped the remains of his meal into a waste bin and James instantly regretted his decision. She was right; it made him peer longingly down into the bin.

'Leave it in there; it's me who's supposed to be the bin-dipper.'

'The what?'

'You never heard that? It's one of the many lovely terms of abuse reserved for scousers. Mainly used by people old and smart enough to know better; but who just keep on wanting to cause offence. Twats.'

'Wouldn't your husband be more likely to go mental about a drunken roam around the streets? Especially at night with a bloke you work with?'

She bumped into his shoulder and made a vaguely affectionate noise.

'Ignore what I said just now; our marriage is a happy, trusting and intense relationship. He really would be much more upset about me wasting money on condemned meat served with week-old salad. Luckily he's away until the weekend, so he won't have to cope with how bad my breath will be.'

'Will you be all right getting home on your own?'

She bumped in to him again. They were both quite drunk.

'Are you chatting me up?'

'Are yer askin?'

Petra giggled. 'Decent attempt at the accent there, la.'

'It wasn't a chat up. Just concern, to be followed by an offer to see you get back safe if you need it.'

'I don't. Let's get back to the station and go our separate ways.' She frowned at him. 'You look relieved. You could have the decency to look disappointed.'

'Stop teasing me. I wouldn't dream of messing around with someone else's wife. Or with a comparative stranger.'

Petra smiled at him with affection. 'I think we will be great friends. But for the record, you're not my type.'

'Charming.'

'I don't think I've ever met anyone as utterly fucked up as you. You've a quite remarkable collection of hang-ups. More than one person should ever have.'

'Don't take this the wrong way, but I didn't need you to tell me that.'

They'd arrived at Turnham Green underground station where James could jump on the District Line.

Petra gave his arm a squeeze. 'Thanks for a lovely evening. Oh, good, there's a cab.'

James waited till she was safely in the back of the taxi. 'And thank you for being happily married and making me feel happily involved. We must do this again soon.'

When he spoke with Laura the following evening he decided to tell tell her about the social event and his discussions with Petra. Laura contributed very little to the conversation but soon began to ask him questions, slowly and deliberately. She made him go over the evening's events again then said; 'Tell me why you felt you should spend an entire evening with this woman James.'

James frowned down at the phone handset. 'The entire evening? It was a couple of hours with a work colleague. What are you getting at?'

Laura's voice was strained. 'I need you to be very clear about what you wanted from that encounter and what you hoped you would achieve by telling me.'

'I told you because I want us to have no secrets.'

'James, that's irrelevant. What matters right now is that you've done something so hurtful.'

'Laura. What is this? Come on...'

'Did you go out hoping to meet someone? To shag someone?'

'I didn't. I didn't even want to...'

'Well why didn't you just stay at home James?'

'Look. I wanted nothing more than what I got; a conversation with someone who is open and whose company is good. I told you about it because I hoped we would have no more secrets, which you might recall is what you demanded from me.'

At that point he almost put the phone down as a gesture of annoyance.

Laura's voice was raised; 'You are there and I am here James. That isn't going to change and, if we can't trust each other, this is going nowhere.'

'Laura, please listen to me. There was nothing in what happened that should cause you to distrust me. It was two adults who were bored by their surroundings and company.'

'And this Petra. Is she pretty?'

'What's that got to do with anything?'

'Attractive? Horny?'

'She's a married woman Laura. She's attractive, yes but not to...'

'Fuck.' Laura more or less shouted the word.

'Now what?' James' exasperation was turning to impatience.

'Well what do you think? Explain to me how you're supposed to be helping our relationship along by telling me this.'

'Laura, I simply had a couple of drinks with a colleague at work...'

'Who you describe as attractive. You just can't see it can you? You talk about trust and yet you seem to think you can just dispense with any sort of guilt or shame by telling the truth.'

'I've nothing to be guilty or ashamed about. I thought we agreed after your revelations about Steve that...'

'I don't care about that. Your ideas and notions of beauty must begin, exist and end with me. Just me. If I'm not worth holding out for then you can...'

She hung up. James rang straight back. The receiver was picked up and replaced. He called again and it was engaged. He was angry and snorted in disgust at a ridiculous over-reaction.

He called her at work the next morning but no one answered her phone. Ten minutes later, he rang again. Someone picked up and said Laura wasn't in the office. James called her home, spoke to Angela and confirmed Laura had left for work. He called the office again and this time a different person answered to say Laura was in a meeting.

'So she is there?'

'Yes. But she's in a meeting. Who's speaking please?'

'It's James, her boyfriend. Can I leave a message?'

The person sighed audibly.

'Tell Laura that I called and I need to talk with her as soon as she is free this morning. Please.'

'Does she know your number?'

'Yes. Thanks for your help.'

'No problem. She might be some time.' The last comment sounded like it had been prompted.

Later in the morning James had to leave for an offsite meeting. When he returned at one, there was a note on his desk saying:

'Laura called. She said thanks for the flowers. She will call you this evening.'

By eight, James was in a state. He dithered between two perspectives: that Laura was being utterly irrational; and that his honesty had let him down. Either way, he dreaded her call.

The phone rang and there were no formalities.

'James, I'm amazed that you made no effort to call me this afternoon. And that you haven't taken any action, other than to pester Mummy and my colleagues, to try to show some sort of regret for how you've treated me.'

'How I've treated you?'

'Don't interrupt. So anyway, I've decided to cancel my trip to see you this weekend. Philippa is here on Friday evening and I'd prefer her company. She doesn't tell me that she's happier being around others. She doesn't tell me a story of how she prefers someone else's company, with a smile – WITH A SMILE I COULD HEAR IN YOUR VOICE DOWN THE FUCKING PHONE JAMES – as if that makes it all right.'

James had never, ever been shouted at like that. He was shocked by it. 'Laura. Please. Stop this.'

'No James. You've made me SO upset.'

'Why?'

James winced because he knew that you never ask *why*. But she surprised him with no further shouting and no reiteration of what she'd already said.

'I've told you. See you when you've got your head around what this is all about.'

The line went dead.

He didn't like the half anniversary now. The last time he'd been left holding a phone after Laura was cut off, what followed was unhappy and difficult. He soon curled up on the sofa and stayed there for more than an hour. When he saw that it was midnight he shuffled off to bed, numb and uncertain.

The following morning he phoned Miles and got approval for a day off at very short notice. Nothing could have been more transparent than calling in sick on a Friday so he would just have to chalk off another day's holiday. As he ate breakfast he drew on a sketch book with a stick of charcoal: an apple suspended from a branch with snakes massed below; a large bird of prey on the branch, its talons clutching the apple's stem.

He tore off the sheet and threw it on the floor. Again his charcoal began to fly around the paper: hands held together in supplication at the base of a guillotine; a gnarled witch overseeing the scene.

Another sheet; another frantic burst of mental scorn converted to an image; another thirty minutes of slowly diminishing resentment.

By mid-morning, James had resolved this conflict. He dressed and walked in to town. At a florist, he arranged for a massive bouquet of flowers to be delivered to Laura's home. He bought a card and wrote:

Laura, I love you and I'm sorry I've upset you. Call me when you can. Sorry we won't be seeing each other this weekend. James. xxxxx

He paid a king's ransom to ensure the flowers would be delivered that afternoon.

When he arrived home, the answering machine showed a message was waiting. It was Maxine, asking for advice about a new contract they were working on. He looked at his watch; four fifteen on a Friday and the message was timed at one fifty. Maxine had probably sorted things and gone home by now and James decided not to call her. Moments later he decided the politically sensible course was to phone, even if all he got was switchboard telling him she'd left.

Maxine was still there. After less than ten minutes on the phone it was clear he would have to go and help. Something had gone quite impossibly wrong and he couldn't leave her to resolve it alone at this time on a Friday evening. He headed to the station.

By eight, they'd resolved all bar one of the issues and the outstanding item could wait until Monday. They were ready to leave and Maxine suggested a drink at the office local. James declined and headed home, taking in an off licence and kebab house once he was back in Richmond.

Laura hadn't called to acknowledge his flowers. He munched his doner kebab morosely and slurped his way through six cans of export strength lager. By eleven, he needed more food so he fried up some sausages and gorged them down between slices of bread. It would be wrong to describe these items as *sandwiches*. Then he hit the vodka and slumped in a chair to watch whatever was on the television. He was asleep by half past midnight. At around four am he woke up and soon threw up. He fell asleep on the bathroom floor where he slowly came to at around eight.

He'd been sick in the bath and it was a hideous, malodorous mess.

James undressed and propped himself in the shower. Then he drank a litre of water, put on some sports things and went out running. He was sick on the pavement half a mile from his flat and continued his run in a daze. When he got back nearly two hours later he was gulping for air and shaking with a kind of fever. He was shocked by the state of his flat. The lounge had beer cans littered on the floor and in a chair. There was a discarded kebab wrapper under the coffee table and bits of doner meat everywhere. The kitchen revealed a frying pan half submerged in some grease-covered water with great globules of congealed fat floating in it. A half-eaten sausage, which also appeared half-cooked, pecked out from the bread bin. And the bathroom – oh no.

He was shocked even more when he walked in to the bedroom to find Laura grinning at him from the bed. She was naked and had her hair tied back.

'You are a totally disgusting and stupid man. But I'm a sucker for you and everything about you. So you're going to give me an hour or so of your undivided attention and make me come as many times as possible. Then I'm going to supervise while you tidy your appalling and stinky mess.'

20

James enjoyed every moment of the build-up to their holiday. It was all done in a rush, with few destinations to choose from. They liked the look of Crete and booked a holiday there, leaving less than a fortnight to resolve the minutiae of passports, tickets, currency, logistics and packing. What thrilled James most was the knowledge that he would share fourteen days with Laura. They would be together, encased in a new world.

James wasn't well-travelled and had no fond memories of family holidays. The Cliftons had roamed traditional destinations in South Wales, the Lake District, Norfolk, and the English South Coast; places that, in the minds of the four children, were duller than ditch water. He recalled tension and bad feeling amongst the children and a sense that his parents were quickly fed up with them all and wanted to be alone somewhere else. There was no communal fun, no mass family cricket matches on the beach, no candy floss, no fish and chips on the prom and above all, no real reason for them to be where they were. Instead, there were just staid walks and tours of venerable buildings.

James' first independent holiday was a trip to Bournemouth with Paul, Leo, Graham and two other friends. They were all seventeen and the warm summer of 1977 was perfect for the adventure. Rites of passage ensued: experiments with cannabis; chasing girls; romping in the sea; getting drunk on illegally purchased cider; daring to sit boldly in the local pubs; learning new things about one another. Their shared domesticity enhanced and cemented a collective friendship. Any minor conflict was quickly suppressed by the joy they all felt about this independence and freedom. After eighteen months of well-established schoolboy brotherhood, their holiday created seemingly unbreakable bonds of love.

A year later the same six went to Newquay, determined to recapture those heady days. It didn't work. They'd now been close for more than two years and had assembled detailed knowledge of one another. But it felt like they had less to say. There were tensions and mind games. Affiliations began to sway in a diplomatic dance. Long-suppressed irritations were voiced, and they seemed to be splitting apart. James still found he could be shaken and broken by what had happened with Sarah even though it was eight months past. He often felt alone in the group, like an outsider who had something wrong with him. He found he only really enjoyed himself when they sat in pubs drinking beer, smoking, laughing and talking of the future. It was the end of their schooldays and something stretched out ahead of them all: travel; university; work; marriage; careers; children; love.

Things would never be the same again.

He told Laura all this as they sat in the departure lounge at Gatwick. Her curiosity was high and she kept digging for more.

'Tell me about other holidays. Where did you go last year?'

'Nowhere. Sally and I only went away once. That was two years ago. I had almost no money when we first met and she declined to pay for me. Last year we were apart most of the summer so a holiday was not an option.'

'Couldn't you have gone somewhere on your own?'

'Maybe. But I was too incapable of anything other than the routine of work and worry and wondering what do to about Sally.'

'Oh. And where did you go in 1988?'

'To Spain, away from the hordes; near a place called Valladolid.' James was being vague and hesitant.

'It really is okay for you to tell me about things that happened in your relationship with Sally. It doesn't have to be taboo.'

'I know. It's not because I don't want to tell you. It's a bit sad to think about it, that's all. It was fun. We were happy and both had jobs that were hard work. We needed and wanted that relaxation together. Before that, not much to report really. Eight years ago I went to the South of France with Gary and some other work colleagues. We had a laugh, but it was really just a very hot, sunny version of what we did every Friday and Saturday night; out on the piss; out on the pull. Nothing terribly highbrow or worthwhile. The autumn after I'd moved away from Hereford, Paul and I back-packed to Cornwall for a week and that was nice. It wasn't too busy and we were still close enough for it to be fun and funny. He was taking a year off before going to university. I was working.'

'Any romantic interest?'

'We were walking fifteen miles a day, eating crap and sleeping in a tent. We stank like shit so weren't terribly attractive propositions.'

Laura sniffed at him like a dog; 'Nothing's changed.'

'Lovely. Thank you.'

She licked his face. A couple near them picked up their bags and walked away.

'The only other holiday I've had was a trip to Italy in 1985. I went on my own. I was really down at the time, lonely and unhappy. I took three weeks off work, flew out to Milan and took buses and trains to wherever sounded good. I'd no idea where I was going half the time but I absolutely loved it. I didn't drink, ate very frugally and when I got back seriously thought of going to live there. I'd just utterly fallen in love with Italy and Italians.'

'You really are a loner aren't you?'

He smiled at her; 'I was.'

'Aah, bless you. I think that's meant to be a compliment.'

'It most certainly is. What about your holidays? Anything I need to know?'

Laura smiled at him. 'Up until I was ten, I think we mainly went to either Scotland or France. Then I think Daddy came in to a lot more money around my twelfth birthday so we started to go to the Caribbean and Mexico. My favourite holiday as a family was when we went to Austria for Christmas. I was fifteen and it was magical, like the final childhood gift.'

'I've always really liked the idea of spending Christmas in a log cabin, halfway up an Alp. Do some skiing, drink gluhwein, eat monstrously bad things.'

'That's our next holiday sorted then James. It's too late to book for Christmas, but you can take me for my birthday; can't wait and thank you for offering to fund it.'

They'd vacated the waiting area and were now inching towards the gate juggling their boarding passes, passports, duty-free carriers and hand luggage.

'Then, during my second year at Exeter, I went on a girls-only trip round Europe with five friends. It was all right, but too tiring and stressful and uncomfortable for my liking. I shouldn't admit it in these troubled times, but I really do not like hardship. I was almost an outcast among my somewhat sisterly companions.'

'Sisterly? As in sapphic?'

'Yes James, if that notion feeds your fetid imagination.'

They were finally at the gate to be processed.

'Steve and I had our honeymoon in Florida and it's fair to say that the destination was little more than a concession by me, because he and his family were paying. He behaved like a kid for the whole two weeks. It was rubbish really. With all that had gone on I knew almost before the end that this was someone I'd fallen out of love with. That's appalling grammar. My English is becoming awful. You already know about the time in Brittany which wasn't really a holiday.'

On the plane they were separated by the aisle. They drank gins with tonic and spoke quietly to each other, despite the steady stream of people marching up and down the cabin and occasional interruptions from neighbouring passengers. James was seated with a couple who introduced themselves as from Kent and who otherwise didn't have much to say. Mr Kent was clearly very perturbed in the build up to take-off and a moderately bumpy flight made him almost rigid with sweaty terror. James tried to speak calmly to him a couple of times but the man was thoroughly alarmed, gripping his armrests as if they were the plane's controls. Mrs Kent seemed blissfully ignorant of her husband's plight and maintained a commentary while staring out of the window at the miniaturised geography beneath; 'Amsterdam? Paris? The Pyrenees, no, the Alps. The Rhone delta? The Pyramids? The heel of Italy, definitely.'

The man looked out once and could only say; 'Oh fucking hell Lilian.'

When the plane landed at Chania, Kentish man leapt up and pushed his way past James to grab what he had in the overhead locker. His wife apologised with a smile.

Several times, as they queued to leave the plane, Laura made loud bleating noises.

Two hours later Laura flung open the balcony doors in their hotel room. After the stale air on the flight and the oppressive heat at the airport it was a relief to have cool air flowing into the room. They showered, made love, showered again and as midnight came and went, they sat outside drinking duty free brandy.

'This is perfect,' said Laura.

'How can you tell? It's pitch black out there and we are probably being quietly perforated by swarms of mozzies.'

'I'm trapped in a room with you and, if necessary, we can lock that door and not go anywhere for the next two weeks. Would you like that?'

'Can I go out for beer occasionally?'

'So we've reached that stage already? My charms in the sack are waning and you've become a beer troll.'

'Never. Your charms are intact. But we will need essential nutrients.'

'What shall we do tomorrow?'

James suggested that they have a long lie by the pool and then a long night in the bar.

Laura disagreed. 'You're in the right direction. But I've got a better idea. Let's stay up till dawn, watch the sunrise, get bonkers drunk in the meantime and go to bed after whatever breakfast we can rustle up from our various bags.'

When they got up the following afternoon, a hot sun blazed and the Mediterranean sparkled for as far as the eye could see. Small sea craft zipped back and forth like dragon flies, the minuscule buzzing of engines adding to the illusion. A paraglider flew serenely by and off shore a large ferry steamed away north. To the left and right of the hotel, white buildings topped with pale blue roofs were dotted all around.

James and Laura headed to the pool where chaos reigned. Children ran around, screaming and laughing and crying and affecting contortions as they leapt into the pool. Adults steamed and melted on loungers, turning many shades of pink and brown. Hotel staff, dressed in smart shirts and shorts expertly weaved among the static and moving obstacles, delivering drinks and food and smiles. A thin haze of charcoal smoke, laden with the scent of grilled flesh, wafted through the scene beguiling and nauseating in equal measure.

Their tour rep soon approached, severe and unsmiling. Her name badge revealed she was *Crissi* and she took no time at all to tick them off for missing the welcome party that morning.

'Aren't you interested in the available tours and activities?' she asked, clipboard gripped tight to her chest. 'And you missed the free glass of ouzo or retsina.'

'Well give us it now then,' said James. 'We'll try both.'

'That's not really possible,' said Crissi.

'This is a disaster,' said James.

Laura sniggered; Crissi stormed off towards the hotel feigning intense interest for something among her papers.

So they ate chips and souvlaki, washed them down with cold lager then lay in the sun belching garlic smells and watching The People.

Groups of younger tourists lounged about, planning sensational evenings. Some had tape machines playing music and one group of young women had a tape recording made from their local radio station. It made for surreal listening since they had edited out neither adverts nor news bulletins nor weather reports. Laura christened them *Those Stupid Girls*. A gang of miners, possibly the only ones left, strutted around; brown, beautiful men looking for a different kind of slag.

Occasionally, people spoke to James and Laura.

'Just arrived have you?'

'What's happening back home?'

'Did Liverpool win the charity shield?'

'Look at those fucking German bastards.'

Later that night they dived into the shrill night life of the resort. Music seemed to pound from every building and a mass of people spilled into the streets. Women in baggy white

T shirts and tight skirts, their limbs tanned and lovely, chatted coquettishly to men in tight shirts and baggy trousers. James and Laura selected a bar and went inside to drink the insanely cheap liquor. Music drowned any attempt at conversation and James shouted that they should move on after a couple.

A fight erupted. Lads from London and Lads from Leeds. Banter became disagreement, became taunting, and ended with punching, kicking and butting. The flurry of action lasted seconds as calmer influences seemed to prevail. But it was a false flag and a thrown bottle signalled a restart. Now all hell broke loose.

It was terrifying.

The police arrived with no plan, leadership or organisation. They lost control, hitting anything that moved including innocent bystanders. James and Laura, too far from the exit to make a dash for it, cowered in their seats and watched the systematic destruction. Around them were scared faces, smiling faces, faces scarred by rage and violence. Men shouted encouragement. Women shouted encouragement. Police battered away with sticks and one drew a gun.

It was a small town in Crete, but could have been anywhere. Anywhere with English people.

After several moments trapped in this mayhem, James spotted an escape route behind the bar. He grabbed the petrified Laura and pulled her to safety and they ran to their hotel, speechless with shock. It left James impotent and insomnolent.

After three days of routine relaxation, the dust of working life and the tensions of office politics were gone and they sought stretched horizons. They hired a small car and set off on a tour of the island looking for seclusion. In the larger towns they found a kind of hustle, which felt like life rather than a masquerade and when they arrived in Chania, James and Laura found it irresistible. They stayed for several hours, strolling the streets, drinking frappés, buying fruit and snacks and watching this world going by. Away from the madness of their resort, this place felt peaceful and trusting.

Towards evening, they set off back to the hotel feeling like it was somewhere they didn't want to be. About five miles from their destination, they took a right turn along a track and found a small, deserted beach. They sat in silence watching the sun descend into the Mediterranean and only spoke when darkness settled. Their day of discovery was completed when, much later in the evening, they found a small bar away from the front line serving cocktails and snacks, and where they were welcomed as people, not customers. This became their local.

The car was available for two more days, so they went back to

Chania to soak up the beauty of the old town and harbour. The next morning, they returned to the beach they'd found and it was still deserted. They spent an hour in the sea and made love in the shallows. By mid-afternoon they lay in silence, baking in the heat.

Eventually James said, 'Thank you.'

'What for?'

'For everything.'

Laura propped herself up on an elbow to face him. 'Like what?'

'For loving me the way you do. For making me love you. For having the nerve to chase after me.'

She kissed him on the forehead.

'Because I do love you. And in a way I've never felt before.'

'How?'

'I just feel positive. About you, about us. It's like a jigsaw and every piece fits. You understand where I come from and how important all that adolescence is to me. You loved me as I was, as I am. I think you love what I will be.'

'What will you be?'

'I suppose I'll be what I was and what I am. But with you. Always.'

'Yes. You will.'

'I always want to be with you. I always want you in my life. In all the things that make up my life.'

She sat up and looked out to sea and the breeze caught her hair. She smiled into the distance. 'When I first saw you, I was eleven. You were fifteen. I thought you were like a hero; a god; mythical. By the time I was thirteen, you were seventeen and neither of us was so naive and you were no hero. But possibly still a god; a demi-god.'

'Or a demi-john.'

'You'll always be a complete and utter John.' She looked away again. 'In those two years I'd seen changes that didn't really make sense to me. You grew up. You became more like a man, less like a boy. You fell apart but seemed to reassemble as something slightly different. Is that true? I think your brittle dreams were shattered, weren't they? Your pieces of art were always on display somewhere and I think they became more bizarre. Before, they were either comedy or something arty. By the time you left they were quite twisted.'

'So was I.'

This time she ignored the interruption. 'It wasn't a crush anymore and in its place was something simple; love. During the next ten years I don't think I saw you more than three times, and a great deal changed. I fell for other people; I thought I loved someone and married him. But I still had thoughts about you; I always did. I heard about you from Philippa and there was this constant nagging voice hinting that there may be just one love. All I had to do was wait, and it would stop being a fairy story and come true. Then on Christmas Eve, there you were and...' she clicked her fingers, '...happy ever after time. Now, after eight months with you, I can't imagine life without you. There's just one niggling imperfection.'

Laura was sitting and looked down at him with a vaguely troubled smile. 'Say those words to me again.'

'I always want to be with you. I always want you in my life. In all the things that make up my life. What's the imperfection?'

'It's not so much an imperfection as an irritation.'

'Your marriage.'

'My ex marriage, yes. It doesn't exist other than on paper.'

'I know. But I can live with it. It really doesn't bother me.'

'I'm glad you don't care. But sometimes I do.'

'Why?'

'I feel like it's an impenetrable barrier between us, even though it's not real. And while you can live with it, I definitely can't. I just have this terrible sense that because of him I might never get all of you.'

Laura took out a cigarette and offered one to James. She lay down again as they smoked. 'So I've done something about it.'

James looked warily at her.

'Just before we left I got Daddy's solicitors on the case; I'm filing for divorce. You have to be the only man in my life.'

Now James sat up and looked down at Laura. She smiled up at him. 'Say those words again.'

He repeated his mantra. She stroked his arm.

'Have you said this to anyone before?'

James lay back again. 'No, because I never felt it. Now, with you, it's the only truth that matters.'

'What about Philippa?'

James did a small double take at this,

'That's a funny question.'

'I know how much she means to you. It's not a threat in my eyes, and I know she adores you. I think, back then in Hereford, you two were something quite rare: a boy and girl that were friends, not boyfriend and girlfriend.'

'Maybe; maybe not. I think we probably liked each other, possibly fancied each other, but didn't want to break whatever spell it was that bound us. I wanted her to be more, and sometimes that felt frustrating. We were close but never became lovers. She said she loved me as a friend. Once she said *let's grow up first, and grow apart. Then we can get together when we're older and wiser, marry and have dozens of children*.'

'She said that?'

'Yes. There was always that kind of intimacy without anything physical.'

'Say the words again.'

'I always want to be with you. I always want you in my life. In all the things that make up my life.'

They lay gazing at the sky.

'I'm going to say them to you every time we have to part.'

'Are we apart now?'

'No. We're together. And it's perfect. Six unbroken days with you.'

James stopped talking.

'What are you thinking James? I am learning to be worried by your sudden silences.'

'I'm thinking that there is something between us that cuts through my relationship and commitment issues. I know I can create a difficult atmosphere and I was worried it might happen here, and you'd discover how troublesome I can be. But so far, it's perfect.'

'We'll always have to work at things James. Being happy together on a holiday isn't conclusive proof that there are no problems to solve. Don't be complacent.'

'I won't. But I do feel special. And this news about your divorce; it needn't have mattered and I honestly would never have pushed you towards it. But I'm so glad.'

They laughed in unison.

'I honestly, truly, madly and utterly love you Laura.'

She grabbed him, hugged him tight and he felt her tears on his face.

James had overdone it, ended up with sunstroke and suffered an uncomfortable night. All he wanted to do the next day was stay in the hotel, so Laura went off to shop for trinkets and mementos. James sat in the shade, wondering how he'd coped in all his years without Laura. It made him want to draw, so he grabbed a pad and pencil and moved on to the balcony to sketch things.

When she returned, Laura handed him a small bag containing a slim leather bracelet with *L&J* burned on to it. James gave her two sheets of paper; one showing the view from their room; the other a near perfect sketch of her face.

When it was cooler and James could face being outside, they took a stroll along the beach looking for somewhere to eat. The sea was calm, sending susurrate ripples towards them, as if it knew the beach was currently not in use by humans and it could risk this bold encroachment. As they walked, the commotion of holiday making was firing up, looking and sounding no different to every other evening, and every other resort. They found a place and ate chargrilled swordfish with salad and soon returned to their local for cocktails and backgammon.

They returned to England on a late evening flight and sat together. Laura rested her head on his shoulder and slept throughout the flight. James watched the deep nothing outside, occasionally broken by the dots of light that signified cities and people. He felt terrible about the fact that Laura was going to be leaving him in about twelve hours, and they would return to the routine of being weekend lovers. The two weeks together in Crete had bound them inextricably and James wasn't sure he could easily revert to being apart seventy per cent of the time. He looked at her; the pretty face was deeply tanned and her hair had bleached almost white. She slept, yet was smiling.

It was just before two when they landed at Gatwick. The airport was quiet; they were processed quickly and soon found James' car to head for Richmond. They had no desire to watch the sun rise on the day that would see them part. Instead, they cuddled up to one another, sighing with the sadness of their impending separation.

Laura phoned her parents and chatted excitedly to them while James sorted out some lunch, the last meal they would share for a whole week. At Paddington station, he carried her bag to the train. As she leaned out of the door she said; 'It was a wonderful holiday. Thank you. You look ever so sexy with a tan. I love you.'

He said; 'I always want to be with you. I always want you in my life. In all the things that make up my life.'

She smiled lovingly at him and stroked his face. He thought he might cry. As the train made departing noises, he said, 'Laura?'

'Yes?'

'Now that you're...'

'What?'

'Now that you're free, or nearly.'

'Yes?'

'Marry me?'

She said; 'Oh.'

The train started to move off. It gathered speed and he stood watching her recede, still looking back at him. She looked confused. They waved and she was gone.

Four hours later, his phone rang and, without introduction, she said; 'Of course I'll marry you James Clifton. Did you ever doubt it?'

21

There was now an awful lot to do and say. People to tell; places to be. Things to buy; ideas to float. Plans for almost every aspect, not only of their wedding and marriage, but of their current and future lives together. There were dreams to live in. And there was a new kind of love, like a giant arch over their heads, protecting and framing them. They now had love with a future.

Laura's divorce was moving across the desks of various lawyers. Steve was honouring his offer of culpability and the parties were agreed on a speedy, clean settlement. It was anticipated that there would be a decree nisi within weeks. In turn, that was driving plans for a spring wedding.

The weekend after their return, and while his proposal was still their secret, James travelled to Hereford. They had a dual alibi for this: it was Annie's birthday; and they could show off their photos and complexions. But the real reason was to make announcements.

When he saw Laura in the busy pub near her home, he realised with a jolt that, for the first time, he was looking at and would soon touch, caress and kiss the woman who would be part of his life forever. It made him feel something he couldn't express and he stopped just inside the door to ponder it. But his fantasy was interrupted as she turned to face him, and he knew instantly that something was wrong.

Laura had bad news. 'Adrian has left Philippa.'

'You're kidding'

'I'm not. He's a bastard. Four years ripped to shreds. You know I never really liked him. She's well shot of him; but I can't tell her that because she's so distraught.'

'Do you know what happened?' said James.

208

'He was very calculating and cold. She got home on Wednesday to find him there, with all his things packed in bags. He'd also brought all her stuff back from his place. He told her it's over and told her to hand over her key to his apartment. Wouldn't answer any questions; just kept saying *it isn't working, we can't go on being unhappy together*. Then he just walked out. Phil was on the phone with me for more than three hours last night. I tried to get her to come here this weekend but she didn't feel up to travelling.'

'Why didn't you tell me sooner?'

'I wanted to tell you face to face.'

James nodded. 'I'll give her a call now; here, get some drinks.' He held out some cash.

'I've got you a pint already. And call her tomorrow. She'd love to hear from you, but this evening I think she just needs time on her own. Tomorrow, she will need the comfort of a friendly voice, and you have the ultimate friendly voice. Your voice, on the phone, is almost perfect; like aural sex. Did you know that?'

'I'll call her tomorrow then. It will be like old times; Phil and I seemed to have these post-split-up comforting conversations a lot when we were kids. But, shit Laura; how do we tell her about us?'

'I know. It's a nightmare. I thought about telling her last night, because it might cheer her up. But I bottled out.'

'Once we've told our families, Philippa must be the next to know. We've all slept together.'

'You are a dreamy, romantic old fool aren't you?'

'I'm not. But you and I are telling Philippa face to face. And it will have to be next weekend, so you better come and stay.'

Laura agreed and crushed against him for a kiss. 'I know she's our friend and we love her, but let's change the subject. I don't want to eat here this evening; it's too busy and I fancy a cocktail. Daddy has found this Brazilian drink none of us can pronounce, which also makes a cocktail none of us can pronounce. But they taste amazing and, when you have one, it will blow your balls off. Then we can have dinner with M and D. Do you know how lucky you are to be marrying me?'

'I sometimes think I might never know.'

'Well I'll show you next weekend. But before anything else, there is the small matter of you asking Daddy's permission to marry me.'

'I...what?'

'You've got to ask his permission; it's traditional.'

'Now hang on.'

'There's nothing to it, but it has to be done.'

'But it's 1990. This stuff went out with the ark.'

Laura was not to be dissuaded and it made James petrified. He barely registered the short drive back to the Drysdales' house and the caipirinha he drank too quickly made him feel more terrified. Nothing he could say, and no excuse he could dream up, would make this horror go away. He sat through dinner, looking around his future family with a false fixed smile and it made him look insane. His contribution to any discussion was negligible, and two glasses of wine simply made things worse. When Laura took Angela away on the pretext of preparing dessert, James sat miserably as Bill waffled on about their holiday photos, and how delightful Crete can be, but that he preferred Rhodes. There was no opening until Bill got up to retrieve a wine bottle. James stood too and, looking his future father-in-law firmly in the forehead, said; 'Bill, I'd like your permission to marry Laura please.'

Bill looked at him impassively, then with dawning comprehension and finally a wide smile.

'My dear James, that's marvellous.' He lowered his voice, 'But, for fuck's sake, this is the twentieth century. You don't need my permission.' James had never heard Bill swear before but he soon had his hand grasped and shaken vigorously. 'Where have those women got to?'

'But Laura said...'

Bill looked sideways at James as Angela and Laura reappeared, each bearing a tray laden with champagne or glasses. Angela quickly put down her tray, rushed to James and hugged him tightly, planting a kiss on both his cheeks. Bill's angry voice cut through the euphoria; 'How dare you put James through that.'

Everyone stopped.

'And how dare you put me through it.'

Laura was staring at her father with incomprehension. Then Bill burst out laughing and grabbed his daughter and wife and future son-in-law in an embrace. It was, briefly, silent and emotional. Bill was first to break from the scrimmage.

'What champagne have you got there Laurie Lee?'

Laura, still looking admonished, held up a bottle to show him the label.

'Not good enough. Give those to me. I'll be back in five minutes.'

He returned with an ice bucket swathed in a napkin, with the top of a gold foiled bottle peeking out.

'I spent a fortune on this and it is therefore the only champagne appropriate for this celebration. It is also perfectly chilled and, best of all, there is more if needed.'

He expertly uncorked the bottle. Permission was granted.

The mood was more restrained but no less joyful at the Cliftons'. James' father hugged his son, then Laura, then his wife, then Laura again. Mrs Clifton kissed Laura lightly on the cheek, embraced her son and smiled wistfully on the scene. James produced more champagne and there was a round of clinking and drinking.

The arrival of David, Annie and Andrew created a competing celebration and Annie's birthday went top of the league. More toasts were raised and Annie was handed gifts to open. Once the merriment died down, the younger generation grabbed drinks and went to sit outside to discuss James and Laura's marriage. Mrs Clifton remained on point in the kitchen preparing everything for dinner with a small but seemingly permanently full glass of fino sherry. Her favourite backing track, The Gondoliers, rippled through the house from a CD player. Mr Clifton had been sent off to bed for a nap.

The dinner they all shared that evening was another happy family event.

James and Laura had made their announcement to universal acclaim; everyone heard it with joy and love; and no one expressed concerns or challenged them that this was all too sudden. Relieved of that burden, they stole time together the next morning by taking a stroll along the riverbank opposite the cathedral then round the old city. Their conversation was contemplative and reminiscent. James felt like he had come home.

When it was time for him to head back to Surrey, Laura was almost incapable of holding back overpowering tears. This had never happened before. She was speechless and held on to James as if she needed to restrain him from leaving. When he finally convinced her to let go, she blinked back more tears and simply waved her hands at him as he climbed in to his car. Two hundred yards along the lane, James pulled up. He stared out of the windscreen and into the rear view mirror, wondering why he was going instead of staying forever in this place with his future wife. He selected reverse gear to head back, because he'd decided to be with her until later in the evening. But lights and a car horn interrupted this and he had no choice other than to drive on down the narrow lane. By the time he reached the main road he'd made up his mind to keep going. His return to the house would only make Laura more upset.

He was soon speeding cross-country to the M4.

Six days later, Laura travelled to London by train and met James at Paddington station.

'I've been thinking all the way down here that maybe we should plan to live in London. Or close. What do you think?'

'I think you look amazing, and maybe you've done something with your hair?'

Laura looked at him closely. 'Another thing I've learned about you is that when you are evasive it's because you are planning to impose your own agenda. So out with it.'

James told her to put down her rucksack and as soon as she did, knelt on one knee and said; 'Laura Drysdale, will you marry me? And is this ring one you'd be good enough to wear for me?'

He handed her a small, red, hinged box and watched her face as she opened it. There was a broad ring of white gold, with three embedded amethysts.

'Stand up James Clifton.'

'Only if you say yes.'

Laura smiled down at him and then looked round at the small group of people who had stopped to watch.

'He really worships me,' she told them.

Now she was looking with astonishment at the ring and whispered, 'Of course I'll wear it James, it's beautiful. I can't believe you could have chosen something so perfect.'

James stood up at last, took the box from her, took out the ring and slid it onto the designated finger.

'You were on a train out of here when I asked you the first time, so I just wanted it to be here, in the same place; smelly, dirty old Paddington station that I asked you properly. And tooled up with the right accessories.'

Laura was watching him in disbelief as he said all this. 'My god James; I don't think I ever, in all my most feverish fantasies about what it would be like to be with you, thought you would do what you've just done.'

'I'm a talented boy.' He said this with a smile of such loving certainty that Laura simply took his face in her hands and kissed him on the mouth, longingly and passionately and with a smattering of applause from their audience.

'Shall I keep it on? Philippa will spot it straight away.'

'Good point. I'm sure you'll find a better moment to share it with her.'

Half an hour later, they emerged from the Underground and quickly located the bistro Philippa had recommended for lunch.

Once their restrained, sad greetings were over and the ordering was done, James saw that Philippa was barely in control. Deep, dark shadows under her eyes, and an occasional crack in her voice as she talked about what had happened, made it clear that her brave face was a frail mask. When it arrived, she barely touched her food and seemed to just want to drink, which she proceeded to do at a pace that Laura and James didn't pursue. But it helped her, and soon opened her up to tell of the unbearable difficulties she'd suffered in the previous ten days. She'd been unable to work and had stayed off. She said she'd been drinking a lot and eating binges of unhealthy, unworthy food. She revealed thoughts of such shadowy despair that Laura reached out to take her hand.

'Try to eat something Philippa; it's important. Please.' Laura's voice was low and insistent and filled with concern.

'She's right. Eat; and let's get some water.' James looked round for a waiter so he could order bottled water.

Laura encouraged Philippa to keep talking. 'Take your time, but just tell as much as you can.'

'I can't believe I didn't see this coming. He'd come and stay at mine as usual but then go for long nights *out with the lads* involving 3am finishes with lifts home in mysterious BMWs that he thought I didn't see. The sudden lack of him wanting sex unless I more or less forced it on him. The long solitary walks at weekends when we usually spent all our time together; he just disappeared for ages saying he was getting some light exercise. He claims there was no one else, but he was fucking someone; I'm sure of it.'

'Don't blame yourself. People who want to be deceitful will do it and hide things very cleverly. They will also deny it if challenged. I think you should just accept that he was wrong for you.' Laura looked across suddenly at James, as if she realised this was less than comforting.

James was quick to support her. 'Laura's right. You're in pain and it's clear you're suffering and it's horrible to see you so upset. But at the end of this, you will have to get your head around the fact that Adrian wasn't right for you.'

Philippa looked at James and took his hand. 'I know he wasn't and I'm upset because I've wasted nearly five years on the wanker, not because I feel I've lost something perfect. Yet I suppose I thought it was good; that it could be good forever. I gave up things I believe in to fall in line with his world view. I gave a lot more than he did. I set aside many things I didn't like about him because I thought I loved him, and could see a long happy future in which the good things would outweigh the bad; and we'd find a way to focus only on the best bits. I've been blind and stupid. I know he's not worth this pain, but I'm feeling there might be no one else I will ever trust or love. Or anything.'

During the long silence after Philippa stopped talking, they saw that she was shaking with pent up anger and grief. Laura stood and put her arms around her friend's shoulders. 'Come on with me to the ladies. Then let's get you out of here. James?' She gave him a look that he knew meant *pay the bill and grab our things; we're leaving.*

After settling up and gathering assorted bags and coats, he waited at their table. Laura re-appeared alone.

'Phil just needs a few more minutes to sort her face out. And by the way there is no way we can tell her about us.'

'I know. Let's get her to come back to mine. I think she needs us around, and I think we should give her all we can.'

'Yes, agreed.'

'And if by mid-tomorrow no opportunity has presented itself, we just write to her instead.'

Laura slapped his shoulder.

'Don't be trivial. But you're right about sticking together. Here she is.'

Philippa didn't need any convincing and they were soon back on the Underground headed for Richmond. Laura and Philippa cuddled together on the train and none of them spoke. James sat opposite and watched these two women with immense pride; that they could be so close and open and kind to one another; that they trusted and relied on him in these moments; that they formed a kind of triangle of love that had existed for nearly fifteen years. When she saw him gazing at them, Philippa gave him a tiny smile, held his gaze and cuddled up closer to Laura.

Once they were back at James' flat, sipping the strong sweet tea he always made for people in distress, Philippa helped them solve their dilemma by insisting they change the subject and stop talking about the travesty her life had become. Instead, she wanted to see their holiday photos and hear about Crete.

Over the course of an hour, James and Laura presented their pictures and told their tales. They watched Philippa relax and peppered the conversation with references to how well they had got on, and how much closer they felt, and how much they'd been upset when they had to part.

'Please, you two, stop this waffling. It's so bloody obvious you're trying to tell me something.'

Philippa had called their bluff. Laura stumbled through a few words; 'When I was heading back to Hereford from London, we... James...'

Philippa interrupted. 'James, have you proposed to Laura?'

James nodded.

'Laura, did you accept?'

'Yes. Well, not straight away.' Laura explained how she'd been caught off guard by James' proposal.

Philippa was aghast. 'What? The man you've been crazy about since you were twelve or something pops the question, and you make him wait four fucking hours before giving an answer? Jesus, Laura, that's shocking. But hey; come here.'

She was standing, smiling widely and with a sparkle in her eyes that would have been unthinkable three hours earlier. She beckoned them both to join her in a cuddle and, as they embraced, she kissed them both repeatedly on their cheeks and necks and heads.

'I've known you two would do this. I knew it that time we were all here. And I'm proud to know you and I just love the fact that you're going to get married.'

They all stayed in the hug. Laura said; 'James and I both agreed you had to be the first friend to know. Because you are like a link in our chain.'

'James said that?'

'No I did not. I said it was because we'd all slept together.'

'And we must do so again tonight. But maybe this time you could refrain from going down on each other the minute my back's turned.'

James' burst of laughter became contagious. This news had been difficult to give, but had been received with more joy than they could have believed. So drinks were now in order and, while James was in the kitchen pouring wine, he heard Philippa gasp at something and say; 'Laura that is simply stunning. When did the two of you find time to look for it?'

'James bought it. I knew nothing about it until around noon today. You'll never believe what James did.'

He heard Laura recount the scene at Paddington, prompting more sounds of disbelief and wonder from Philippa. When he walked back in to the living room with their drinks Laura said,

'Here's my man!'

'Laura? You make sure you keep that man safe from harm. He might be a borderline alcoholic, almost painfully self-absorbed, insecure to the point of comedy, indecisive, moody and a pompous prick when the mood takes him. But, fuck me Laura; what you just told me...'

Philippa was shaking her head as if the motion was generating her next words.

'Not only has he done the most perfect proposal to the most perfect fiancée, hearing what you've just told me has, at a time when I think all men are Adrian the Wanker, made me see that a man can be perfect.' She looked up at him as he handed her a glass. 'You, James Clifton, are one of a kind. But I'm going to find your double.'

Philippa raised her glass; 'A toast: to my oldest friends, united.'

They chinked and drank.

Philippa wasn't finished; 'A double toast: to my soon to be married best mates.'

It turned out that they didn't sleep together. The raw emotion of the situation had left them all disinclined to excessive drinking. It was still quite early when Philippa admitted she needed to sleep. Laura led her to James' bedroom and found some spare pyjamas and it wasn't long before James realised Laura wasn't coming back; he confirmed this with a quick peek in to the bedroom where the two women were cuddled up and sound asleep. This time, James didn't need or want to interrupt them and retired to the sofa to watch television. Eventually, he rolled up under a blanket and slept until Laura came and lay next to him.

'Make love to me,' she demanded in a whisper.

'Not that prude euphemism?'

'No James. Tonight, it really will be making love. I want to feel you; feel part of you; feel whole.'

She didn't stay with him and he woke alone to the sounds of breakfast being prepared. Laura appeared with a mug of coffee and a plate of toast and marmalade.

'Breakfast fit for a prince. And I mean a proper bloody prince James. Not a frog one or one with a horse. How do you do it?'

'Do what?'

She shook her head. 'Do what you do. This whole quietly-perfect-man routine.'

'If you think I'm perfect, loud or quiet, you're deluded.'

'If I say you're perfect, and if Philippa says you're perfect, it's a wrap. Deal with it.'

'Is Philippa all right?'

'She's still asleep. I don't think she has slept at all well for days. I had to stay with her. When we were getting changed she became so tearful and told me she needed someone to hold.'

'I understand. It was fine.'

'And so was our lovemaking. In fact it was sensational; the first time since you proposed and the first time wearing your ring.'

'I never thought that it was possible to have sex without making any noise.'

'We must do it like that again. It really, really turned me on. But to more important matters. My train is at six something, so in a bit let's wake Phil and get moving. We can accompany her back to her place, then do a bit of sight-seeing and I can tell you how much money you're going to need to marry me.'

'Sounds good. Can't wait.'

Laura jumped on to him and put on a Marilyn Monroe voice; 'You betcha, fiancé.'

While still at James' flat, they said all their goodbyes. Philippa expressed her overwhelming gratitude for their friendship and support. She also insisted that she had to see James place the engagement ring on Laura's hand, then applauded extensively as he did it. She still had dark bags under her tiger eyes, but there were small creases of joy at their edges.

They parted from her at South Kensington tube station, then James and Laura changed lines and headed for Hyde Park Corner from where they walked right across the park, slowly unravelling thoughts and ideas about what they wanted their wedding day to be.

They agreed, unanimously, that there would be a service in Hampton Bishop church even though it could only be a blessing due to Laura's status as a divorcee. The official segment of the day would have to be at a registry office, and this caused neither of them any major level of distress. In James' eyes, especially, this meant there would be the right level of ritual, but only limited hypocrisy.

Laura made James discuss who he wanted as best man. She told him she didn't mind who he picked so long as it was someone that mattered to him. He confessed he had no idea and struggled a bit with the brass tacks of who might be his favourite; he didn't have favourite men. He said he'd think about it.

Laura was less tentative when he asked about bridesmaids. 'I don't want any.'

'Really? Why?'

'It's because I asked someone to be a bridesmaid before and I feel like I let her down. Anyway, it's a lot of hassle if we're moving between venues and I don't want your eyes to wander.'

James told her not to be ridiculous.

'So far, so good: we're talking registry office, then a church blessing at Hampton Bishop. How do you feel about the reception being at Mummy and Daddy's?'

'How many people are you thinking of?'

'Oh, no more than forty; but we need to sit down and make that list.'

'Well your house is big, but forty?'

'I'm thinking a marquee.'

James liked the idea but queried if it might be too cold in the spring. Laura looked defeated by that thought.

He said, 'It's a really brilliant suggestion so let's not dismiss it unless someone proves it's unrealistic. My dad almost certainly knows a solution, so leave it with me.'

'Ever since you proposed to me you've become so decisive and thrusting.'

James ignored her. 'What are you thinking about the reception; food, wine that sort of stuff?'

'A sit down meal but nothing heavy. Daddy will sort out some staggering wine and drinks, so we can leave that to him. We'll need to find a really good caterer. I'm thinking that has to be a *spare no expense* thing.'

James nodded. 'My mum will almost certainly insist on making a cake. Is that okay?'

'It would be lovely James. Do you think Carol would want to do photographs?'

'She would, but let's not ask her. I want her and Alex to be part of the event, not a supplier.'

Laura smiled at him, then dragged them to a halt by hugging his arm tightly. He looked playfully at her; 'Are you going to wear white?'

Laura giggled. 'That's a loaded question.'

'It's not. I would love it if you do. But I understand if you don't want to.'

'I need to think about that and talk to Mummy. She will have a view. I have no problem whatsoever about being in white, but not sure I want to be in something too crazy or puffed.'

They'd reached the Round Pond and turned north to head towards Queensway station. Once there, they'd outlined the basics about cars, flowers, decorations for the reception and some ideas about what James would wear. They also mapped out an evening event in the marquee at which maybe another couple of dozen guests would be invited. Both of them liked the idea of having a jazz band playing all night, but realised that most people would expect a disco playing pop.

'And for our honeymoon?'

'Well. Good question. Do you have anything in mind?'

'Not sure. I don't want anything too distant; and definitely no cruises.'

James was silent.

'What are you thinking?'

'I'm thinking I'd like us to go by train to Venice. A train with proper beds and a dining car. A couple of days there, and maybe in Verona. Then a week at Lake Garda; complete rest; just you and me.'

Laura blinked a few times. 'Is this something you've literally just thought of?'

'It is.'

'Can you afford it?'

James laughed; 'I don't have to.'

'How come?'

'Well, I think we should ask people not to buy gifts. No present list to torture people with. Let's just ask everyone to contribute to the cost of the honeymoon.'

'Neat. Some might not like that, but I think it's a great idea.'

'I have my uses. Tell me something: were you serious about moving to London, or environs?'

'I was. Aside from the fact that you have a home here, and that could be our starting point, I just think you're happy here and settled, and your career is here. I can move. My job is transferrable. What's up?'

James told her about his feelings the previous weekend and how he'd felt that their spiritual home was Hereford.

Laura was quick to reject this. 'It won't work. There's no job worth doing there. I honestly think you'd go mad within months of moving back. I can see it in you whenever you're there for more than a day or two; that sense that you find the place mediaeval and redundant. You have this need for closure on your past don't you? You think, perhaps, that by being with me in the scene of all those happy teenage times you will get that closure. But it won't work. Honestly, I think it would be a huge mistake.'

He was dumbfounded, not least because he thought his idea was romantic and nurturing.

'Please James, don't think about it anymore. We move forward, not back. Let's make Hereford the place we have as our favourite hidey hole. Somewhere to dash off to when we need it.'

At Queensway tube they bought tickets to different destinations but travelled together, once more to end up under Brunel's grime coated roof. The Hereford train was waiting to leave.

'Are you going to propose to me again?'

'Not sure. You might say no this time. Or ignore me again, and phone me later to tell me to piss off.'

'Never. But don't risk it. There's probably some old wives' tale about three proposals resulting in a plague of grasshoppers overwhelming Norfolk.'

'Then I must do it.'

Laura laughed at him. 'I want to hold your proposal yesterday as the most special thing you've done for me. Please: keep it that way.'

This time it was James who held on to Laura as if he wanted her to stay. But it didn't work; she soon boarded her train and took her rucksack from James. The last thing she said to him as they parted was; 'This is the start of something magical. I'm so utterly in love with you. I can't imagine how life could be without you. Always be mine.'

James nodded, and said he would. But his voice was thick with emotion, and soon all he could do was wave and watch the train disappear in to the gloom. She was gone.

Part 2
Pictures of You

22

One Friday evening in October, James was sitting quietly, scribbling and sketching, waiting for Laura. The telephone pulsed and made him jump, but then he smiled with relief that here she was, weary but patient, explaining another delayed arrival. She was on her way and the weekend could start to happen.

Then the entry phone buzzed. Suddenly he was in a dither. He looked down in to the car park, but Laura's VW wasn't there. As he pressed the intercom button next to his door, the telephone answering machine clicked on.

'Hello James? If you're there, pick up.' She sounded upset and James felt frustration with Philippa. Any other evening he'd be happy to talk with her about her slowly healing heart, or some dead-end man who'd seemed like a step onto the future's path. Right now, all James wanted was to see Laura walk through the door.

'Mr Clifton? I'm PC Davidson, and WPC Tanner is with me; we're Metropolitan police officers. Can we come in and speak to you please? It's urgent.'

James blinked several times, pressed the door release button then grabbed the phone. He could hear Philippa making a noise, like a sob and a deep breath.

'Hi Philippa, the police are here.'

'I know. There is terrible news.'

James frowned. 'About what?'

'It's Laura.'

'What do you mean?'

'I wanted to be the one to tell you. Not the police.'

'Tell me what?'

But as he asked the question, a ringing started in his ears. His eyes stopped focusing and his vision was enveloped in a border, like the white edges around an old photograph, confining his view to a single scene. There was a light tapping on his door.

'I'd better let the police in. Hold on.'

James opened the door and the two officers were there, headwear removed.

'Come in. I'm just on the phone. Can you wait please?'

They nodded, crossed the threshold, closed the door quietly and stood, patiently polite.

Philippa spoke slowly, painfully slowly; each phrase deliberate and strained. Her voice was weak and fearful.

'There's been an accident.'

She described the place. James knew it; pictured it; framed it.

'Laura's car went out of control and hit a wall.'

'When was this?'

Philippa hesitated. 'About five thirty I think.'

James heard himself ask, 'So this is... is this... the worst possible form of bad news?'

He heard one of the police officers cough.

Philippa seemed not to have heard his question. 'There was plenty of traffic and someone called an ambulance and it got there quickly. Laura was alive, but with terrible internal injuries needing surgery.'

James wondered how he could cope with seeing her in a wheelchair. He began a mental countdown. He vowed himself to her; to be a guardian; to be a nurse; nothing would be different; love would be all; he could get the flat renovated.

Philippa dashed his hopes. 'But she didn't make it. There was nothing anyone could do. James, I can't believe this has...'

She stopped talking so suddenly that James thought she'd been cut off. But she was still there, crying now, and he played back words of comfort that sounded distant and cold. He'd never done this before. Death, in his experience, had involved remote grandparents or barely known pupils from school. The starved and starving on television, or the famous and celebrated. James had never had to comfort someone in this situation, especially not himself.

Philippa started another sentence that remained unfinished. There was an awkward indecision, creating nothing more than a series of broken statements that said little and meant nothing.

'Are you in London?'

'No, I came up to Hereford yesterday to spend some time with mum and dad. We're at Angela's now. It's...'

'They must be...'

'I think Angela is going to call you but everything here is so difficult.'

Eventually James told Philippa to put down the phone and do her best for friends and family. He promised to call her soon.

A small noise reminded him that he had visitors.

'Come in please. I think I know why you're here.'

They declined the offer of tea or coffee and for ten minutes or so, broke the news to him about Laura's accident and death. It was business-like but sincere and he felt a genuine sympathy and condolence. As a precursor to their departure, they provided the number for the officer investigating the crash and a leaflet about bereavement counselling. It was all over in no time. They left his flat and James was alone.

He sat down.

His mind was almost completely blank.

Nothing.

No thoughts, no words, no tears, no pain.

Nothing.

No Laura.

Just nothing.

He sat staring at the wall opposite his sofa. His mind kept saying three words over and over again.

'Laura. Is. Dead.'

James slid into a trance and didn't hear the telephone ring on three occasions. It didn't register that Angela Drysdale's broken, shaking voice was talking in his flat. He didn't notice the video recorder turn itself on for a programme he always watched with Laura. All he did was breathe.

Then something clicked him back to reality. He frowned and looked around the room till his eyes found a clock. His head seemed to weigh a ton.

It was nearly eight thirty.

He double checked this on his watch and, as if released from chains, began bursts of activity. In the bathroom: cold water splashed on his face; teeth cleaned; hair brushed. In the bedroom: bedside light turned on; pair of old boots retrieved from wardrobe and thrust in to a bag with a fleece. In the kitchen: food put away; coffee cup rinsed and dried; torch retrieved from cupboard and packed alongside the boots and fleece. Finally he gathered together a pen, pencil, wallet, writing pad and keys and, after locking up, trotted out to his car.

The roads were still busy and the M4 was slow, painfully slow, until he was past Slough. Once he'd cut across to High Wycombe and the M40, the traffic was fluid and James sped along in silence, barely in control of the car. The actions of driving were almost instinctive, like a physical reflex in which all he had to do was aim the Alfa. He was completely devoid of thoughts or feelings. His face was set in a grim impassive frown. The stereo was silent. His progress was hampered when the M40 petered out and became the A40 to bypass central Oxford.

Shortly, James reached the stretch of road Philippa had described to him and he slowed to a crawl. In the light of oncoming traffic, he saw the damaged dry stone wall opposite. He accelerated and drove on to turn round at the next junction and was soon back at the scene. He steered his car on to the verge, turned off the engine then switched on the hazard lights and got out.

Twenty five paces and he reached the wall. What he found seemed wrong. There was broken glass; shards of coloured plastic scattered randomly. But no bollards and tape and flashing lights and coppers moving people along or diverting traffic. A pensive, opera-imbued inspector in a dodgy old Jaguar should have been in charge, patronising people. But all he found was a smashed up wall and some litter.

James felt that his physical actions were being controlled virtually. A dense tension had filtered through his neck to his arms and legs. Getting out of the car had felt like a fight with gravity. His torch seemed too heavy to hold.

He walked back to the road. It was a still, dry night and quite chilly with neither moon nor starlight. A faint orange glow tinged the eastern sky. When a break in the traffic allowed, he shone his torch on to the road and soon saw skid marks on the tarmac.

'Great jumbo jet sized skid marks.'

He sighed angrily and breathed in noisily through his nose. His clenched teeth ground together.

Where the skid reached the roadside there was a fractured kerbstone, then a series of gouges in the grass which he followed back to the wall. The damage to the stonework was pretty extensive. James found himself trying to repair some of the stones into a semblance of order. He lost his footing and crashed against the wall, grazing his hand as he reached out to break his fall. He sucked at the broken skin of his hand and wiped it on a trouser leg.

This made him stop his restoration effort.

Instead, he spent several moments in contemplation before heading back to his car which he manoeuvred so the headlights lit up the hole in the wall. He flicked on the main beam and sat staring at the scene, oblivious to the frenzied flashing from cars on the main road.

He eventually switched off the lights, but not before the dazzling emptiness in front of him had been filled with scenes from the last ten months: Laura's phone call and subsequent letter; their first meeting; her uncluttered loveliness; their arguments; their bodies together on the beach, in his bed, in all his dreams; her face as he knelt before her at Paddington.

Her voice filtered between his ears, but his mind couldn't process the words:

What would you say if I told you my name is Laura Drysdale?
Hello. I feel a proper arse not putting my number on that letter.
You, James Clifton, are a bloody thief.
Love meets Death on a train.
You can do pretty much whatever you like with me.
James you smell horrible.
Not even a quickie up against that gate?
Of course I'll marry you James Clifton.
He worships me.

He thought of every scene from their life together as if each was a photograph in an album. He heard her laughter, her voice, her sighs and moans. Giggles on a bad telephone line. Her impatience and anger with him. Soothing, whispered consolations for things gone wrong. He saw her parading every set of clothes he had ever seen her wear. He felt her tears on his face and neck. He brushed them away with his bloody hand. He smelt her hair and perfume and make up and sweat. He smelt the smell of their lovemaking. He heard the noise of smoking rubber, scraping bodywork, crunching steel, metal on stone, a scream, a siren, lowered voices, concerned shouts, machines coming to life with pips and bleeps; those same machines being switched off.

All this silent recollection made him doze and, when a knocking sound woke him, the dashboard clock read 23:07.

He looked out at a woman's face and a hand motioning him to wind down the window. Still drowsy from sleep, he said: 'Hello Phil.'

'My name's not Phil sir. Can I ask what you're doing here?'

James stared for several seconds at the police officer.

'I was thinking about my girlfriend.'

'I beg your pardon sir?'

James looked down at his lap.

'Have you been drinking sir? I remind you that you are in charge of this vehicle even though it's stationary.'

James stared at the wall ahead of him. 'Laura Drysdale was killed here earlier. We were engaged. She was five feet eight inches tall with long blonde hair and blue eyes. Birth mark on inside of left forearm. Age twenty five. Date of birth November 17th. Address, Westwick Lodge, Hampton Bishop, Herefordshire. The car was a Golf – F341 ARH. Red. No. I have not been drinking.'

She turned quickly away and spoke in to her walkie-talkie.

There was an exchange of words; pauses; noises. After several minutes of continuous crackling debate, she was ready for more from James.

'Could I have your name please sir?'

'James Clifton. Age 30. 15b Rosed...'

'Fine, thank you sir.'

'Can she call me sir?'

She walked around to the other side of his car and got into the passenger seat alongside James. She placed her hat on the dashboard. Her radio crackled continuously, broken occasionally by small beeps.

'Are you all right?'

'What do you think?'

'Are you going to sit here all night?'

'I might as well. It's as good a place to spend your time as an empty flat or a table for one or an empty bed.'

'Had you known her long?'

'About ten months. She'd known me for more than fifteen years.'

The officer frowned in the darkness. 'And she was travelling to see you?'

'Yes.'

'Can I call you James?'

'Call me whatever you want.'

'James. I think you should come back to the station with me and my colleague. Have a cup of tea or coffee or something; before you head back.'

James shook his head, then nodded.

'I'll go and tell my colleague what's happening.'

'Are you coming back?'

'Yes, don't worry. Two minutes.'

James sat peering hopelessly through the windscreen.

The officer was back and sitting alongside him. 'Right James. Let's go.'

They followed the police car back towards Oxford. The officer's radio was the only sound until they pulled up outside a small police station in a big village.

'Is it normal for you to help someone like this?'

'It isn't, so don't tell anyone or they'll all want it. But you're a long way from home, and kind hospitality costs nothing.'

He locked his car and followed the officers into the building. Strip lit glare confronted him and he had to shield his eyes.

'What have you done to your hand?'

'Oh; nothing. I fell, when I was looking at the wall.'

'We better get that cleaned up and put a bandage on it.'

'No. Well... clean it up. But it doesn't need a bandage.'

She led him to a small room. Elsewhere in the station a man's drunken voice kept tunelessly yelling the opening lines of Jerusalem. He would be told to shut up every few seconds and the singing would diminish momentarily, then slowly swell up again. After a while he must have either fallen asleep or been beaten unconscious, for the singing stopped.

'Apart from crimes against music, what has that man done to be locked up in here?'

'He was very drunk and driving. The doctor is here now but the guy is bang to rights.'

'Is in he in his Tardis?'

She giggled. 'No. I mean the police doctor; he needs to do tests on matey.'

James jerked his hand away as she applied some disinfected warm water.

'Sorry. But you need to have it cleaned up, then I can get the doctor to have a quick look.'

'Yes. Sorry. It was a shock. So what's a bad night for you then?'

'Oh, you know: affray; rioting; fruit machine fraud. It's all go here in the Cotswolds.' The humour was wasted on James.

'And do you have to deal with a lot of accidents?'

'Yes.'

'Serious ones?'

She continued to dab at his hand.

'Often. The A40 is a dangerous road, but we're also surrounded by boy racer heaven in the shape of country lanes. People drive too fast. But that's not always the cause.'

'What happened to Laura?'

She looked at him sadly. She didn't need this.

'No one knows the cause of the accident.'

'Where's the car now?'

'I don't know. You've got some blood on your face; have you hurt yourself anywhere else?'

'No. I wiped away some tears.'

'You need a bandage on this hand. The cut's deep and you'll need a tetanus jab.'

'No. Had one less than a year ago. No need.'

'Okay then. But a bandage. Let me see if the doc's free. Otherwise I think you might need to go to hospital.'

She left the room after giving James' forearm a reassuring squeeze. When she returned she said the doctor would be free in about five minutes. She sat down opposite him with a smile and James asked; 'What's your name?'

'WPC Atkins.'

'Do I call you WPC or d'you prefer W?'

She giggled. 'You can call me Jane. But maybe not in front of my colleagues.'

'Are you married Jane?'

'No. Single and carefree. You don't always have time for boyfriends in this line of work. And some men get put off by the job.'

'Surely you could find some sort of uniform fetishist?'

'They prefer nurses.'

'I suppose you deal with death and injuries on a more or less daily basis. This must wash all over you really.'

She made a small sighing sound. 'You get hardened to it, but not always to the reaction of people affected by it.'

'Was Laura badly injured?'

She looked at him sadly. 'Don't torture yourself like this.'

'I want to know. I need an image of her.'

Now she frowned, the realisation dawning that this was an unusual form of grief.

'It's difficult for me to answer your questions. I know she was badly injured but conscious when the medics got to her. She was still alive when they got her to hospital but died before surgery could start. It was incredible she survived the crash.'

'I suppose it's better to die instantly. No drawn out pain, like torture. Just an unconscious flash of it. Then nothing.'

She examined his face but he wasn't looking back at her. He stared down at the table top, his uncut hand scratching imaginary graffiti.

Tea arrived.

'At last. Here you go, drink this. I'm going to deal with a couple of things.'

'Will you be long?'

'Drink your tea and Doctor Edwards will be with you in a bit.'

'But you'll be back?'

'Yes.'

James sipped his tea. It tasted perfect; hot, sweet and strong.

'Good for people in shock. Like the ones I make. Wonder if they'll make me another. Or maybe it's time to go. Go home. Although... all this makes home a bit hard to define. It's wherever you lay your hat isn't it? Or where the heart is? The morgue.'

A yell burst from him. He fell forwards from his chair, crashed against the little table and down on to his knees. Within seconds, WPC Atkins appeared with a colleague.

'Leave him to me. He's all right. It's that RTA victim's boyfriend. Get some more tea in here.'

James looked up at them. 'That's right. There are only two people in the world now. The RTA victim and the RTA victim's victim. Two straightforward, unnamed things. No names, no pack drill.'

She came over to him, helped him up, set his chair on its legs then sat him on it.

'Do you want to talk? You seem to need someone with you all the time but you won't say anything other than to ask morbid questions.'

He shook his head like an admonished child.

'Why this outburst?'

'I got scared. There's nowhere to go.'

She put her arm around his shoulders. Fresh tea arrived.

'You should sleep James so I'm going to see if I can find somewhere near here for you to stay tonight. You can't drive back to Richmond.'

'Where can I stay?'

'I don't know. Wait here and just try to remain calm.'

Off she went.

When she came back, there was a man with her. 'James, this is Doctor Edwards. He's going to have a quick look at you.'

'My hand's fine. You made a good job of cleaning it up. I know about bandages and I know I don't need one.'

The doctor's bedside manner was calming and practiced. 'I'd like to talk to you James. Then we can have a look at this hand.'

'Where's WPC Jane?'

'I'm right here. Talk to the doctor.'

Ten minutes talking were enough. 'James, above all you must get some sleep. You're in shock so I'm going to give you a sedative. First we need to have this wound bandaged. It's nasty so I'll give you a tetanus booster just to be safe.'

As he set to work with bandages and tape he asked if there was somewhere James could stay. WPC Atkins answered the question; 'There's a small hotel just along the road and it's still open. They've a room you can have James. It isn't expensive. Your car will be safe here at the station.'

James kept watching the operation on his hand. 'Then it seems that I do have somewhere to stay.'

'Are you all right with syringes?'

'Just a little scratch?'

'That's the one. Can you handle it?'

James nodded and the accoutrements needed for inoculation were assembled. James didn't feel the injection. Doctor Edwards took out a small bottle of pills which he opened and dropped two into a tissue.

'How come you have all these things with you Doc?'

'When on call for the police, you need all kinds of things in your toolbox. Once you're settled in your room, take these two tablets with some water. It's called diazepam; you might know it as Valium. It will make sleep easy.'

'Thanks Doc. Side effects?'

'None to worry about although best not to drink any alcohol. Just let them do their job and you'll sleep well. And now I need to get going.' He reached out and touched James on the shoulder. 'I'm so sorry about your loss James.' The bedside manner was infinitely expansive.

Within thirty minutes, James had been escorted to a nearby building, had bypassed the processes for checking in, had taken his tablets and was asleep.

It was past eight the following morning when he woke. There was a tempting aroma of bacon but the less wholesome whiff of someone who had slept in clothes he'd been wearing for twenty four hours. James ventured downstairs to pay for his room and leave. The owner was harassed by the conflicting demands of breakfast and reception duties and James received no tea and sympathy, not even for his strapped up hand.

He chose to head across country instead of using the motorways and was soon racing hard along the road through Nuneham Courtenay, Benson and Wallingford, his good hand doing most of the work. He stopped outside Reading for breakfast and gulped down tea and a greasy cooked meal. At a petrol station he stocked up with fuel, chocolate and fizzy drinks. Stacked outside the shop, newspapers trumpeted headlines: about war; adultery in high places; economic Armageddon; tits out for the lads. No mention of a fatal accident on an A road in Oxfordshire. For a moment he thought about buying every single paper to see if the story was mentioned anywhere. He didn't do it. Didn't want to know.

The flat was cold because the storage radiators had failed. James swore in very precise terms at the electricity company. Ever since he had moved in, this magical system had regularly made up its own mind about when to come on. He started a letter in his head, complaining about the system to a series of organisations. It petered out after a couple of sentences.

The emptiness of his flat was oppressive. He looked around the living room and found very little connection with Laura. She had brought a few books and they were lined up on a shelf in the bookcase. James' eyes moved to a different shelf and rested on the old school book in which their names were listed close to each other.

He lit the gas fire.

The kitchen was neat and tidy, but this was his work. Laura had bought the wok that hung on a hook over the sink. The two crystal tumblers she'd brought for their mojitos sat on the window sill, each with one of those plastic stirrers in them.

He made a pot of coffee.

In his studio, nothing had changed. They had rarely been together in this room except, maybe, when she would bring him a drink, drape her arms over his shoulders and look at his latest piece on the easel.

No.

No.

That was Sally.

He never painted when Laura was staying.

There was too much else to do.

He drank his coffee.

Laura's bath towel hung neatly on a rail in the bathroom, its cartoon character's face half hidden by a fold. The bathroom cabinet was full and almost everything in it belonged to Laura. Bottles of mysterious liquids, some tampons, a toothbrush, a hairbrush, shampoo, soap, face pads, a cloth, shower gel, jars of oddly named creams and powders, deodorant, cotton buds.

He took every bottle and jar and packet and tube out of the cabinet and carried them to the living room. They were soon lined up neatly on the coffee table, like a cosmetic chess set.

His mind was bending out of shape and he mentally drafted a letter to Laura's parents, like a wartime military leader, informing them of her death and returning her personal effects.

He dabbed a finger into some of the jars and dabbed the contents onto his cheeks. He sniffed at some of the liquids and tubes.

Now he was in the bedroom. They'd bought extra storage here for a supply of clothes so Laura could travel light. He was making up scenes in his head again. A coroner deciding that, if Laura's car had been weighed down with a couple of hundred weight extra of clothes or make up, a terrible accident might have been averted.

In the wardrobe hung several dresses, skirts, blouses and jumpers. The drawers contained jeans, T shirts, knickers, bras, socks, tights, stockings, a sweat shirt and jogging trousers. Under the pillow he found her night shirt. On her bedside table sat a book, marked at page 114 with a postcard from Carol and Alex. He hadn't read the book. He hadn't heard of the author. In the bedside table drawer was a strip of her pills, enough to last several weeks. He concluded he should try one. It tasted of nothing.

There was also a neatly folded embroidered handkerchief in the drawer; an intricate scrolled pattern in one corner was barely recognisable as a letter *L*. On the floor in the gap between the bedside table and bed, and for a reason he couldn't figure out, he found Boris. Boris was a small, brown bear that Laura had sometimes cuddled. Under Boris was a piece of A5 paper, a list of names, some written in capital letters. The previous weekend they'd sat up in bed compiling this register of the people they would invite to their wedding. Capitals denoted a definite invitation.

Under the bed he found her small suitcase, empty save for a sachet of dried flowers. On the dressing table sat three bottles of perfume, another can of deodorant, hair mousse, hair gel, a brush, a comb and some trinkets. In the single drawer of this table were her hair dryer and a letter he'd written to her. He opened up the envelope.

Dear Laura,

Incredible news! I've just been watching a current affairs programme and it said that the Government is trying really hard to sort out the country. Whatever next?

Thanks for another wonderful weekend. I love being with you. But I also love being apart because I so much enjoy the delicious expectation of waiting for your arrival...'

James took this letter and envelope to the sitting room. He picked up an ashtray and placed it with the letter on the small hearth. From the kitchen, he brought a box of matches and was about to set his letter alight. Instead, he blew out the match. He rummaged in his box file, the one marked *Personal*, throwing out bills and statements and other detritus. Eventually, he found what he was looking for. Back at the ashtray he started to create small balls of paper out of the pages in his letter to Laura; he made a pyre from them, then lit it. As his words went up in smoke, he held Sally's letter in the flames; its single sheet was quickly incinerated. Finally, in the dying embers, he poked the letter Sarah Smith had given to him until it too blackened to carbon.

James stared at the ash, quivering silently in its resting place, and nodded approval for this ritual. He wanted to feel cleansed; freed from complication; absolved from memories.

'Maybe I should burn everything?'

The phone rang and the answering machine cut in as required. He turned up the volume, noticing that there were other messages. It was John Gold, wondering if James could be tempted out of retirement to play football the next day. James couldn't think of anything more pointless than football and hit delete. He turned the volume to zero and considered disconnecting his phone.

With a refilled mug he returned to the bedroom and sat on the bed sipping from it. When it was finished he put the mug on the floor, got up and rooted about in his wardrobe. He had always loved to see her in that dress; the silky, slinky black one. He touched it and it rustled. He took it off its hanger and clutched it to him. A faint smell of *Eternity* lingered on the material. He fell back on the bed and lay there caressing the dress, imprisoned by that pale perfume.

He lay there for hours.

The phone rang. This time, he decided to answer and it was Philippa.

'James, thank god. I've been worried sick about you. This is the fourth or fifth time I've called and got your machine. Where on earth have you been?'

'I went to see where it had happened.'

Silence. Then; 'I wish I could come and see you. I can't believe how sad I feel. It's simply awful.'

'That's one of many inadequate words that describe how I feel right now. But I suppose plenty of other people feel just as awful. Just as inadequate.'

He looked at the collection of bodily essentials ranked on the coffee table.

'I'm still in Hereford with mum and dad, otherwise I'd come over.'

'It's okay. I'm fine.'

'We should try to talk. Let's do that. Let's find time for a call every day.'

'Yes. I'm glad it was you that told me. I appreciate you putting yourself through that. How are you coping?'

'I just don't believe it's happened. Everyone here is numb with shock and sadness. There's still no news about what caused the accident. I'm not sure I can face travelling back, so I'm staying here until further notice.' These words were broken up by constant sniffing and vocal dropouts.

'Are you able to sleep?'

'Not really. How about you?'

'Time will tell. Let's talk tomorrow. I think I need to rest.'

'Me too. Goodbye James.'

Her voice had cracked on every one of those five syllables.

'Poor, poor Philippa. She must be in pieces, sifting through memories and mementoes. Call Bill and Angela. Come on. Do it.'

He had some lunch and a cold beer. Then another beer.

He watched the football results.

Hereford won 2-1.

He phoned his former football manager to confirm he was no longer available at any time.

Dinner came and went with more beer. He returned to the bedroom and lay with her dress. He fell asleep.

When he woke up the dress was tangled round him like a snake. He must have been struggling with it. He unwound it carefully and threw it aside. He was in the same clothes he had worn at work on Friday. He'd slept in them twice. After lying like this for several moments he grasped that he smelled vile and that a bath or shower was needed.

Twenty minutes later he pulled on jogging trousers and combed his hair. He put the badly creased dress back in the wardrobe on its hanger, put on a T shirt then re-combed his hair. He took the linen basket into the kitchen and loaded up the washing machine. He had breakfast and listened to the rumbling noise of the washer. There was so much food in the house. He couldn't see how it would all get used up. He hadn't lost his appetite but this was ridiculous. He hated the idea of throwing it all away and wondered about throwing a party to use it up.

James' mind was in tatters. He couldn't stay on track with any thought processes for more than a few moments.

He would have to call some people. What would he say? It was only six weeks since he had triumphantly phoned almost everyone he knew to boast about their engagement. But not now. He couldn't say those words twenty or thirty times. He could say them to himself. That was easy. But not to his whole family and all his old friends.

'Perhaps everyone knows. Perhaps it's in the papers now.'

When he got back from the newsagent's he scoured the first of the three papers he'd bought. Nothing. The big news involved the Middle East, like it had done since James was a small boy. The other papers were no more informative. He looked at teletext. Nothing.

He sat in the living room unscrewing and screwing tight the top of a bottle of nail varnish remover. Occasionally he sniffed the liquid. It was a nice smell.

He picked up the phone and pressed the single button that would dial his parents' number. As it reached the fifth digit he replaced the receiver. James couldn't create a coherent opening sentence for this call. Through his own feelings he had no idea and no way of knowing how this news would affect his parents. They knew Laura quite well; they had liked her, he thought.

Would they be sorry she was dead?

Or would they be sorry because he was upset that she was dead?

Or would they be hard about it?

Oh well.

Can't be helped.

Tishtish.

Plenty more fish.

He pressed the button again.

'Hello Dad.'

'James! Hello. Sorry old son but your mother and I are just eating our lunch. Can I call you back?'

'No Dad. This won't wait. Laura's been killed in a road accident.'

There was a pause then: 'Hang on a moment son.'

He heard muffled shouting by his father; instructions about the meal; something about bad news. When he came back on, his voice was lowered, soothing and collected.

'What happened?'

'She was coming here. The car went out of control.' His voice gave up.

'Steady son. Take your time.'

'All I know is that the car hit a wall. She died in hospital.'

'Where was this?'

He told his father the spot.

'I don't know what to say James. This is awful.'

'Can I ask you to pass on the news please Dad? Carol, David and Annie.'

'Of course James. If that's what you want.'

'I don't think I can face it.'

'Of course. Do you want to speak to your mother?'

'No. I'd like to go now. I'll call you later in the week.'

'All right then.'

'Bye Dad.'

'Why don't you come up and stay with us?'

'Not sure I could get the time off work.'

'Oh. I see. Well, we'll speak to you later on. Do you know the funeral arrangements?'

'No. I will find out.'

'All right James. Let us know.'

'Goodbye then.'

'Yes. Keep your chin up. Your mother sends her love.'

'Right. Bye.'

'Yes. Bye.'

He reset the answering machine so it would shield him from calls. The two minutes talking with his father had made James certain he couldn't handle sympathy and pity and conversation. He'd said he would call Philippa daily, but now knew he wouldn't.

He switched on the telly then turned it off when all he could find were either politicians stating the bleeding obvious or people bleating about their gods. He went to the bedroom and looked around. He picked up the book he'd found earlier and started to read it from page 114. Someone needed to finish it.

Several hours later, he closed the book. It was about a butler; immensely moving, undoubtedly. But none of it sunk in; none of it meant a thing to him. He put it back on Laura's shelf then went off to bed and, cuddling Boris, he fell asleep.

23

He went to the office and pretended he was fine. Maxine asked him why he was at work when he looked so ill, which he fielded by saying he needed to be in a critically important meeting. She wasn't convinced but didn't press the point; James was her boss, not her concern.

So they sat down to prepare for the meeting. He could hear Maxine talking, but he wasn't really able to listen and was relieved she was taking notes. James' mind was stuck between a hole in a wall and an empty flat and times with Laura. He could hear Maxine talking, but he wasn't able to listen.

The session was not a triumph for James. With limited involvement from the start, he disengaged and dived in to an appraisal of the brief part he had played in Laura's life. He drifted between big things (their initial meetings; that holiday; those wedding plans) and the mundane (eating together; drinking to get drunk; meeting people; supermarket shopping; bickering in the car). It was like being in a cinema where the reels changed every few seconds.

Around him, negotiations, discussions and battles rumbled on while James was losing control. He saw no reason to be in this room. The corporate irrelevance spewed around him, offending his nostrils – its stench drowning him. The jumble of words, spoken or displayed, was like a complex puzzle with no solution. They trapped him tight. He was suddenly hot and faint.

Tears prickled behind his eyelids.

He fought them and squirmed in his chair but the prickles became thorns and now a droplet leaked from his eye. He pulled out a tissue and made a hash of trying to conceal his tears as a nose-blowing necessity.

Miles spotted James' lack of composure and engaged him in a lingering, challenging stare. It made James nervous and he suspected he couldn't speak if spoken to. Under Miles' impatient gaze, he sat up straight to pay attention and halt his distracted indifference. He became calm and felt like he had caught up with the ebb and flow of the agenda. He was wrong.

'James; any thoughts on that?'

He stared around the table in panic. 'I'm sorry everyone. I was distracted briefly.' His voice was an adolescent croak and, once more, he smothered his face with a tissue.

'Are you feeling all right?'

'Sorry Miles; no, I'm not.'

A brief recess was called and refreshments served. Miles motioned James to join him outside. 'What the hell's wrong with you? If you weren't up to the meeting Maxine should have attended. You made a complete cunt of yourself in there.'

James was shocked to hear Miles swear. It had never happened before.

'Sorry. I'll get Max now.'

He rushed to their desks where Maxine was on the phone. James gestured that she needed to hang up.

'What's wrong?'

'You need to take over. Miles is pissed off with me.'

'Of course. I think you should go home; you look terrible.'

He ignored her. 'Go on. They're waiting. I left your notes on the table; I didn't add much but nothing's happened. Speak to Miles if you can. They're taking coffee and biccies.'

James felt relieved of a burden and occupied himself with a pile of mail whose mundane neutrality proved comforting.

At the end of the meeting, Maxine and Miles were last to emerge. They were deep in an animated discussion. As they looked at James their mood subsided and something quiet passed between them; nodding ensued.

Maxine passed some paperwork to James. It had gone well.

'Miles wants me for another half an hour to agree next steps. Do you want to come along?'

'If you can handle it, I'll stay here.'

'That's fine. But really, if you feel as bad as you look, please just go home.' She emphasised this plea with a squeeze of his shoulder. It felt nice.

'I'll be all right. I need to finish this letter.'

When Maxine finally returned, she tutted and said, 'Still here? In which case, how about coming and having some lunch? My treat. I can update on you on the meeting and what I've been discussing with Miles, and you can tell me about that bandaged hand.'

James was off guard and no ready excuse came to him. 'I don't want to go to the canteen.'

'I was thinking of popping over to the Redwood Arms. It's good food in there and should be quiet on a Monday.'

Maxine walked quickly and he struggled to keep up. When she stopped at a pedestrian crossing, James caught her and Maxine linked her arm with his. 'I wish you'd talk to me. I can tell you're not ill because you're not making enough fuss about it.'

He chuckled.

'Come on; what's up? Has something happened between you and Laura?'

He looked at her briefly then faced forward again. She saw the distress in his eyes. 'What is it James?'

The crossing signal bleeped its approval and James marched on to the road. Maxine followed and, when they reached the far pavement, grabbed an arm to restrain him. 'Is this a relationship thing? Have you and Laura split up?'

'In a sense.' He withdrew from her grasp and set off again, pumping out words in time with his footsteps. Maxine fell in line with him.

'Laura was on her way here on Friday, like she always did. She was driving her car and lost control. There was a crash. No other vehicles involved. She's dead.'

They arrived at the pub and James held open the door for Maxine who had stopped to stare at him. Someone else went through the door, with a brief word of thanks. They stood on the threshold.

Maxine reached out to him and guided him through the door and on towards a table. She went to the bar for drinks and returned with a glass of scotch for him and water for her.

'I can't believe you came to work today. What did you think would happen?'

'I don't know.'

'Why didn't you tell someone?'

'Couldn't. I told my folks yesterday and it was torture.'

'I'm not saying it would have been easy but to try and pretend everything is all right is just stupid. And a little insulting.'

He was staring at his glass. 'I didn't know who to tell or how to tell them so I said nothing. It really was easier to pretend. To avoid it. There's no insult involved.'

'Shit James; that is madness. What did you think would happen? That you could just get away with telling no one, ever? Don't you respect me enough to open up and tell the truth?'

James liked this. Maxine wasn't cluttering up the conversation with platitudes and sympathy. In turn it meant he could cope and didn't need or want to tumble over in to being a wreck.

'Where did it happen?'

'Near Burford in Oxfordshire. She smashed in to a dry stone wall. I don't know why. I suppose it might have been her fault, but she was a good driver.' He stopped. Maxine was watching him too intently and he felt himself shrinking and curling up.

'Shall we get some lunch?'

He looked at her and sat up straight. 'I ought to eat.'

'Yes. What do you want?'

James felt overwhelmed by the need for her to hug him, but he scanned the menu instead. It was another jungle of words he couldn't penetrate. 'Can you just pick something for me?'

'Hot or cold?'

'You choose. Please.'

She softened her gaze and reached out to squeeze his hand. 'I'll be back soon. I need to make a quick phone call after I've ordered.'

James nodded glumly. He watched her exchanges at the bar and how she pointed to where they were sitting before handing over some cash. Then she left the bar area and he sat sipping his scotch.

Maxine was back in less than ten minutes. 'I've been speaking to Miles. I told him about Laura.'

'That was kind. But I would have done it.'

'I don't think you would. Miles wants to see you when we get back.'

This was what James wanted: other people taking control; making decisions; directing him out of harm's way.

'Will you be all right on your own at home? Is there somewhere you can stay? Someone you can be with?'

'Yes I'll be fine. Don't worry.'

'Someone needs to worry. I don't think you can cope. You seem lost. Incapable.'

James said he wasn't lost and could cope. He thanked Maxine for caring, but he couldn't look at her while he said it. She handed him a scrap of paper.

'This is my home number. Don't hesitate to call me, at any time, if you need to talk or just to hear a voice. I'm usually at home and rarely occupied by much more than chores.'

He blinked with astonishment. In the months they had worked together, James had seen Maxine repel any attempt, by anyone, to gain access to her private life. He took the note with whispered gratitude.

Back at the office Miles talked to James. His empathy was smoothly efficient but detached enough for James to understand that this was a dutiful process of design with neither link nor bond. Above all, the message Miles seemed most eager to convey was that he wanted James out of the office.

'You need to take a break and I'm happy to authorise a couple of days' compassionate leave. I can't let you place a strain on yourself and maybe your colleagues by being here. This morning's meeting was, with hindsight, understandable. But it can't happen again.'

James said he didn't want to be absent and needed the distraction of work. Miles rejected that with a gesture and repeated his concerns. An impasse loomed so James broke out of it by agreeing to go.

He had rarely travelled home outside of the rush hour and found the experience unnerving, as if he was an outcast. His flat, in the grey mid-afternoon dreariness, also felt unwelcoming and cold. James had no idea what to do with himself.

So he just sat and did nothing until darkness fell and only the tiny lights from various machines lit his living room.

The telephone shattered this vigil.

It was Bridget. 'We heard about what's happened. Are you all right?'

'I'm alive. I wish I wasn't.'

'That is silly talk. It solves nothing.'

'I don't wish I was dead half as much as I wish she was alive.'

'Do you want some company?'

'No. I think I'd rather be alone this evening.'

'What about tomorrow? Why don't we come round and we'll eat?'

'Yes, okay. I've got plenty of things to eat here. Is Gary there?'

'He's out rehearsing. He's very upset.'

'Because I didn't tell him?'

'Heavens no. He understands that. He's just stunned; we both are. You end up feeling so useless.'

'I know.'

'But you must try to be positive and above all you must look after yourself.'

'Mmmm.'

'What are you doing over the next few days? I hope you're not working.'

'I went in today but got sent home.'

'That's best. When is the funeral?'

'I have no idea.'

'Don't you need to know? Have you been in touch with Laura's family?'

This made James tremble with ineptitude; Bridget was asking questions he should be able to answer. But in the absence of a reply to her question, she continued; 'You should make some calls. Don't sit around being pale and windswept. What time shall we come tomorrow and what shall we bring?'

'Any time after six is fine. Just bring yourselves.'

'Fine; we'll be there around seven.'

'Good. See you then.'

So everyone is really sorry. And they know how I feel. And they understand. Marvellous. I should just leave them to it and move on. Ungrateful to the last. But there's just too much bloody sympathy. Too much.'

The telephone rang again, inevitable and irresistible. When he picked up and heard her voice, he nearly fainted. It had all been a mistake. They'd got the wrong car and the wrong body and the wrong boyfriend.

But it wasn't her and the minute hope sank back down.

'Hello James. I've been trying to call you so it's such a relief to finally speak.'

'Hello Angela.'

'There's been so much to do. We're both rather bewildered. I left a message for you. But maybe you couldn't respond?'

The telephone receiver made the voice sound so much like Laura's. It was bewitching. If he could only hold on to this voice forever. Perhaps he could tape it and play it back to himself? Lie in bed looking at Boris and listening to *Hello James.*

But the voice was bleak; sad; doomed. Angela spoke as if these events were an abstract. 'We had to go to Oxford and identify Laura. That took up most of Saturday and Sunday; and Bill wouldn't drive past where it had happened. Then yesterday we seemed to do nothing else but talk about funerals; getting her body back here and sorting out the church. Everyone's been very kind.'

She ran out of steam.

James filled the silence. 'Is there anything I can do?'

'I don't think so, but thank you. Obviously you'll come to the funeral. It's on Thursday at the village church; you know. Half past two. You must join Bill and me. That would right.'

'Thank you. I will.'

'It's very much what Bill and I want. Perhaps you could read something appropriate. Something Laura liked.'

'I'll try to think of something.'

'But James, you mustn't do it if it would upset you too much.'

'No, it's the right thing to do and I will do it.'

'Come up to the house at about one. And please ask your mother and father to come. Ask the rest of your family too.'

'Thank you, I will.'

'When will you be travelling?'

He said he didn't know.

'I see. I understand. Do whatever is easiest for you but it would be right for you to join Bill and me in the church.'

'I'll be there.'

'There's no pressure to come to the house. It will probably be rather busy I suppose. So make your own way to the church if you prefer. Bill and I won't be offended. Just sit with us in the church. Please.'

'All right.'

'And if you want to see Laura, the chapel of rest is in the city; near the General Hospital. Pearson's.'

'Pearson's. Persons. Persons at Pearson's passing plaintively past.'

James said nothing.

'You should go. It might seem a little scary. It *is* a little scary. But if you don't do it you might always regret missing the opportunity to see her one last time.'

Angela's voice faltered. James had been confronted with something that terrified him.

'Yes; I know I should go.' His voice was tiny and scared.

'Try to. And...' This pause sounded deeply ominous. '...be prepared for her... for Laura's face. They've done their best but....'

She ground to a halt again. James suppressed a shiver before continuing.

'There are a lot of things here. Clothes and books; some jewellery. Shall I bring them back?'

'I hadn't thought of that. No. Obviously keep anything you want but otherwise give them to charity or something. We'll see you on Thursday. And you'll definitely come to the house afterwards. You and your family. There'll be some food and so on.'

'Yes okay. I'll see you then.'

'Take care of yourself James. Goodbye.'

'Bye Angela.'

James looked at the collection of bottles and jars and packets and tubes. They were untouched since his tidying out session. He didn't want to throw them away and wondered if he could use the pastes and powders like paint for a picture.

Bridget left a message saying they wouldn't be joining him after all; she didn't give a reason. James was using the answering machine to sift out calls he didn't want to take. The news pleased him; he breathed a sigh of relief that he would be alone for another evening.

Philippa also left a message wondering why they hadn't spoken as planned. She sounded sad and lonely and he almost broke his silence to call her. But instead he called Carol. They didn't talk for long, just enough for him to confirm that she would be attending Laura's funeral. She was warm with him. He could imagine her face and her embrace as they spoke. She told him to have a good cry and stop being a brave and manly. Those words hung in the air after he replaced the receiver.

That night, for the first time since the accident, he had difficulty sleeping. A booming, echoing voice seemed to be repeating everything anyone had said to him during the last few days. Boris and Laura's T shirt provided no therapy and James tossed and turned. His thoughts bounced around; about the journey home and the funeral; about how he couldn't face Bill and Angela; about how it was his fault that their daughter was dead; about how he couldn't face his own mother and father. He didn't know what he could face.

James must have dreamed he was constantly awake because he woke with a start to find the red digits of his clock showing 06:10. The storage radiator outside the bedroom door clicked and creaked. There was no reason for him to be up this early but he was wide awake so he got up to make tea. With a resigned sense of duty, he started to pack a suitcase with casual essentials and a suit carrier with a neatly ironed white shirt and his darkest sombre suit. Then he showered and dressed, grabbed two anthologies of poetry and a novel from Laura's bookshelf, and set off once again for Hereford.

24

His parents weren't at home when James arrived so he decided to take Angela's advice and go to the undertaker's. But, as he reversed from the drive, it felt like he was being compelled by an alien force; like a character in one of those dire fifties television shows about intruders. His mind started playing the dire, spaceman music and it swelled up as he drove. He could almost sense the dire, thinly veiled anti-Soviet propaganda gripping his senses.

At a red traffic light, he sat and let these crazy notions grip him.

He hit the steering wheel.

He hit it again when he pulled into the small car park outside the funeral parlour.

The place seemed deserted but that was probably the idea. No *Open/Closed* sign swung jauntily inside the glass door. This place spoke of *The End*.

The books from his flat lay on the passenger seat and he looked at them, then picked one up – *The Metaphysical Poets*. He opened it at random but it seemed terribly complicated. He closed the book, then threw it over his shoulder.

Of the other two volumes, it seemed to James that the one by T.S.Eliot had been read more, used more, and maybe loved more. He opened it to the contents page, which indicated that many of the poems inside were all epics of thirty or more pages. As he scanned the list, his eyes kept being drawn back to one title and he turned to that page. He read the poem, feeling defeated by the meter and form. But the words said something perfect; there could have been a hundred or a thousand poems in anthologies all over the world. This was the only one he needed.

The door ahead of him struck him down with uncertainty. That dire alien music restarted as he opened the car door and walked to the entrance. Inside it was warm and still. A thick carpet muffled the noise of his foot fall. The place seemed unattended. James searched for a bell-button to push or a ticket machine. He coughed quietly.

A man appeared from a door to his left and smiled beatifically at James.

'Good morning sir. I'm Leonard Pearson. How may I help you?'

'Good morning Leonard.'

The man waited patiently with his head cocked slightly to one side. It was an encouraging, gentle gesture.

'I'm here to see Laura. Laura Drysdale.'

'Ah yes sir. Are you a relative?'

'We were engaged.'

'My deepest condolences Mr...?'

'James. No, it's Mr Clifton. James Clifton.'

'Mr Clifton, yes of course. Mrs Drysdale said you might attend. Would you come this way?'

He turned back to the doorway from which he'd emerged. James followed, bewitched by the man's calm air.

'Miss Drysdale is resting in room three. Have you ever visited a chapel of rest before sir?'

'No.'

'It's very private and, should you wish to speak aloud, you won't be overheard. Ah, here we are.'

He flicked some light switches, then pushed open the door. James paused and stared around him in panic: at the man; at the door; at the segment of coffin he could now see. Leonard gazed evenly back at him with the same patient stance.

'Please take your time James.'

He was shocked by the sudden use of his forename.

'No. Right. Yes. Thank you.'

James walked past the man and into the room. It was dimly lit by four wall-mounted lamps. A single brighter light shone down on the coffin. And it was cold. The door shut with a gentle swish.

James stood, motionless with terror, just inside the door. He was scared, helpless and lost, like a small child separated from mum in a department store. He had never been close to a dead body and was easily frightened by ghost stories, vampire films and satanic rites. Despite his rational atheism, he had a wholly irrational sense of the power of evil and, in his mind, a dead body was bound to suddenly leap forth and kill him with a chill blast. He couldn't think beyond that. His mind was gibbering.

He finally took a step forward and could make out clothing in the box. He stared resolutely at the middle of the figure, not daring to see the face.

And then he did dare. He moved his eyes so they rested on Laura's face. Despite the barely concealed injuries, she still looked beautiful. He felt anaesthetised by the silence, the subdued lighting and the presence of a corpse. He couldn't think or talk. He could hardly breathe.

He moved closer still to look again at Laura. He stood staring at the body.

'Say something. Like what? Don't know; but just say something.'

'Hello.' The belief that she might leap up and chill his bones had flowed away.

'Hello. And goodbye.'

His sensory impotence returned.

'I don't know what to say. I always found I could talk to you but here...'

The soundproofed room made the words flat and dissonant.

'I hate the knowledge that you suffered and were in pain. I can't bear to think of you in pain.'

He took out the book.

'I'm going to read something tomorrow. Angela. Your Mum. She asked me. But I don't know what to read. I think this could be the right book. I know you liked his plays and this seems well-thumbed. I've found a poem that seems appropriate; one you would like. But I don't know. You see?'

He opened the book and flicked through to the poem.

'This one here: *Eyes that last I saw in tears*. What do you think?'

He looked enquiringly at her face.

He frowned, then nodded. 'Yes. I'll do this one then. I thought it would be right.' He turned over the corner of the page, closed the book and slipped it into his pocket.

'I've no flowers. Sorry. I should have brought flowers. Or a drink maybe. Who will I drink with now? Yes. I know I drink with anyone who'll pay; but who will share those quiet evenings with me? The ones when we just sit and talk about whatever comes up, or watch television and drink too much. Will I do that alone now? Because I don't think I want to.'

James looked down at his feet. His knees were shaking. He looked at his hands. They quivered like leaves on the wind.

'I've got to go. This is beyond me Laura. I can't do it.'

He turned away from her and stumbled to the door then rushed through the reception area and out of the building. He fumbled for his car key and took several attempts to get it into the lock. He grabbed the wheel and stared at the dashboard, not knowing what to do to make the car work. When he put the key in the ignition and fired the engine it seemed like a surprise.

You didn't tell her you love her. You didn't say goodbye properly and finally. You didn't try to find out if she is still wearing your ring. You did it all wrong. You didn't even cry. Fool.'

His parents were still out, so he sat in the car and started reading the novel from his bookshelf. Laura's youthful handwriting had scribbled her name and class number on the inside cover and, as he began the story, her notes guided him through it.

He'd read about thirty pages when he heard a car pull up behind his. Soon, with the dogs milling around them, parents and a son stood together in the drive.

'Hello. This is a surprise.'

'Hello Dad. I know. Sorry, I should have called but it slipped my mind.'

'Well that's perfectly understandable. And there's nothing spoiled. I'm sure we can rustle up some lunch and dinner for you, eh Rosanna?'

'Of course we can.'

Both parents were looking at him with a combination of uncertainty and sorrow. There was a touchable indecision.

'Let's get inside and I'll make some tea.'

James' mother moved towards him and smiled, taking him in her arms then guiding him to the front door and in to the house. His father tried to break the ice with small talk: football results; trouble in Commercial Street; some excellent wine he'd found at a new shop in town. James responded with a grunted feigned interest.

A tray arrived, laden with drinks and food: tea; sandwiches; cake; comfort. James learned that Annie and Andrew would join them soon, and David later in the afternoon. So they would all have dinner together.

As if broken by James' indifference and lack of grief, his parents soon announced they needed to get on with things. He was told to rest and make himself comfortable with his book. He was grateful for the escape.

When she arrived with Andrew, Annie's surprise and pleasure at seeing James were stated in a long, loving embrace. 'It's lovely to see you. I tried to call; I really wanted to call; but I kept putting the phone down because, really, what I want to say needs to be said in person. Once I've got Andrew settled down and given Rosanna a few things, come with me for a walk.'

He was tingling from the therapy of a warm, loving hug.

Annie handed Andrew to him and went off to see Mrs Clifton. James concentrated on the child, who sat on his knee gurgling and smiling amiably at his uncle. Andrew made a variety of noises, one of which was probably *mama*. Another could well have been *bugger off*.

When she rejoined them, Andrew looked expectantly at his mother, but she told him to stay with grandma and granddad, and to be good. He kept smiling.

'He's always good, always smiling; a really lovely kid. He's bright as a button too. I'm so proud of him; so in love with him.'

'He's like you. Physically. Facially.'

'Yes, that's what people say. But he's going to be big, like David; strong; handsome.'

'How's David taking to fatherhood?'

'He's okay. He does what he has to but I don't think he's quite got used to the fact that we have a child now; another person living with us. David was accustomed to having the house to himself, perhaps three or four evenings a week. Now, I'm in all the time and Andrew is already quite mobile and consequently, quite demanding. And the thing that really pisses David off, I'm afraid, is what you just said. Everyone says that Andrew's like me. I think David would like someone to acknowledge that it's his child too.'

'David always did like space; and silence.'

'I know. But we'll be fine. What about you? How are you handling Laura's death?'

It shocked him to hear someone confront the subject and use Laura's name. He was used to saying nothing in response to nothing.

'It's grim; horrible. My grief feels lonely because I'm on my own and everyone else who's grieving is miles away. So, perversely, I've found it a bit unemotional, like I can't grieve. Maybe if I was up here with Bill and Angela, and mutual friends, it would have been easier to feel something deeper. This detachment means I focus just on me. And I don't really know how or what I feel.'

'Have you been in touch with Bill and Angela?'

James felt panic rising through his stomach. He hadn't made a conscious decision to avoid Laura's parents, but aside from his phone call with Angela, had done nothing to show them his support.

'Please tell me you've been in touch with them.'

'I spoke with Angela yesterday. It was so difficult.'

'For her too.'

'I know. But I just feel so guilty; that Laura died because of me.'

'No. Stop thinking that. I would be astonished if her parents feel that way and if they do, it's their problem not yours.'

'I'm going to sit with them in church.'

'That's excellent. Good. But promise me you will keep a dialogue open with them. They almost certainly need you to do that.'

James nodded, and Annie continued her questions. 'So go on, tell me how it's been for you.'

He was back on safer ground. 'The hard part is how everyone handles you worse than you're handling yourself. It's innocent; meant well, full of concern and sorrow. But it all seems to distil down to *I don't know what to say*.'

Annie picked up on this thread. 'And that sanitises your own feelings, doesn't it? Because you start to feel for the people who are making such a mess of trying to console you.'

James nodded slowly. Annie went on: 'And there's this thing

that's supposed to lift you up: *You'll get over it; it hurts now, but time is a healer.* Bollocks. It isn't true. They say you'll forget but what they mean is that it's *them* who'll forget. You never forget someone you love. And for you James, it's still very early days; sorry.'

'You're talking of your mother. We've never...'

'No. But it's okay. What matters here and now are your grief and how you feel. You seem to be keeping a lot inside.'

'I feel like tomorrow will be the worst part.'

'No; it won't. It will be tough. But what feels bad can't be tied down to one specific period or event after someone's death. It isn't now or next week or next month. The hardest part is yesterday; your memories; because every anniversary will scream at you; everything you and Laura enjoyed together will kill you when you remember them.'

'But won't it be different for me? I only met her nine months ago; nine incredibly special months.'

'Maybe. Maybe not. But big or small, long or short, your memories will hurt forever.'

'Thanks.'

'Sorry but it's better than hiding behind *I don't know what to say.* Tell me how you really feel. What's in your head and your heart?'

'Both are empty. Everything seems irrelevant and pointless. I can't see a time or place when I will ever be happy again. Occasionally, I want to scream it all out and punch the ground and the walls, hoping it will stop this lack of suffering. I can't see the point of living without Laura. She was so special and there's no one to take her place and I'll never find someone new and build on that and fall in love. Laura was my last chance. I sound like a selfish twat don't I?'

'No. You sound like someone with things to say about how you feel; like someone whose been given a chance to say them. But be completely clear: you're a good man, with a good mind and soul and heart. You're not alone and you won't be alone. Laura's death isn't the end.'

James had stopped walking and was gazing up at the dusk-filled sky. Annie had walked on and became puzzled that he was unresponsive. Looking back at him, Annie saw his body trembling with sobbed exhalations. There were tears streaming down his face.

She went to hold him, to wring out his pain, and kept saying; 'Don't stop.'

They stood like this, alone and unnoticed. Dusk had become

night and they set off back to the house in silence, Annie guiding James as if he was blind.

Back home, Andrew was asleep upstairs and Mr Clifton was dozing in front of the television. There were noises from the kitchen; chopping and faint music. James was snuffling and hiccoughing. Mrs Clifton looked out from the kitchen, then joined them in the hall. James was only vaguely aware of a brief conversation.

'It just seemed to come flooding out.'

James felt his mother stroke his hair. 'Bed for you; come on.'

'She's right. Have a lie down.'

They led him upstairs to a spare room where he lay on the bed. His mother pulled a duvet over him and kissed his forehead. Annie squeezed his hand.

He heard his mother say: 'He hasn't changed. Always had to sort out his own...' and the voices faded away.

He didn't sleep for long and, when he woke, felt no better. He lay still in the dark, drained like a collapsible tank. Someone had turned the valve open and let all the contents flow away. He was flat and flimsy; ready to be refilled.

But he got up and walked onto the landing. From downstairs he could hear David and Mr Clifton talking about wine from the new shop in town. The inevitable noises of food preparation were accompanied by music: someone was playing the piano.

A small noise from one of the bedrooms distracted him. He found his nephew lying peacefully in a travel cot. James sat on a stool and, with his chin resting on folded hands, examined the sleeping figure and whispered; 'Laura looked wonderful when she had you in her arms. She would have been the best mother. And apparently you're the best boy. But be that for both your parents. Your mum and dad love you equally.'

Andrew woke up and smiled, held out a hand and made one of his noises. James couldn't resist that smile and picked up his nephew. They went downstairs, baby noises gathering impetus, to be greeted by a clarion of welcome in the living room.

James announced; 'It was all Cliftons together up there, doing what we do best; sleeping and messing our pants.'

David burst out laughing and stood to hug his brother with Andrew sandwiched between them. Annie stopped playing the piano and Mrs Clifton joined them all, smiling encouragement at James. David took Andrew away to change him and Mr Clifton handed James a glass of malt, then stood by in case water was needed. James drank it neat.

Annie joined him on the sofa. Normal family service was in play.

Later, as they started their main course, Mr Clifton poured the wine he had bought at the new shop in town. Everyone was politely waiting for Mrs Clifton, who was pottering in the kitchen. They had always ignored her exhortations to *get on with it while it's hot*. When she finally sat down Mr Clifton raised his glass. Puzzled, askance, David and James followed suit unsure what the toast would be. Their father looked at his sons, panic gripping his features.

James cleared his throat.

'Absent Friends.'

Mr Clifton looked gratefully at him and nodded. Then led the chorus, firmly and proudly; 'Absent Friends.'

The wine from that new shop in town tasted good. There were sniffs and snuffles around the table, then the clinking clatter of cutlery on china filled the room and conversation was crank-started.

Later, David and their parents cleared things away, and Annie sat at the table with James. 'Well done.'

'Someone had to say it. We could have been here all night.'

'I think it might be the first time your father has ever been lost for words. He looked so sweet, didn't he? He's such a dear, dear man: the perfect father-in-law.'

When James said nothing, Annie said, 'Are you all set for tomorrow?'

'No. But I will be. Soon.'

'If you want to talk, any time, you know where I am. David too.'

'The talking is over now. And the listening. It's all said and done. Forever.'

25

In Die Illa Tremenda

Mr Clifton's Saab pulled in to the pub car park and, within a few moments, a second car drew alongside it. Carol looked out from the back seat of David's Volkswagen and waved at James.

They stood in a long embrace after the rest of the family had gone into the pub. James felt love from his sister's touch and whispered words, but neither gave him strength.

When Carol and James joined everyone inside, Mr Clifton was at the bar but soon brought a tray of drinks to their table. There were twelve glasses of scotch – each with what looked like a double measure – a bottle of sparkling mineral water and six empty glasses. Without waiting for anyone else, James took one of the whiskies and downed it. His father did the same. David and Mrs Clifton helped themselves to water.

There was a round of fractured small talk but, after throwing back a second scotch, James excused himself and said he was going to walk to the church. His father began an objection, but his mother stopped her husband with a waved hand, and told James he should go.

He left the pub, crossed the main road and decided to walk the long way round to the church. Across the fields, he could just make out its squat spire on a half-timbered tower. All around were partially leafless trees and a chilly autumnal greyness. It all seemed suitably forbidding.

James had called the Drysdales to say he would prefer to meet at the church. He told the truth: that he didn't feel he could handle being at their house. Bill said it was fine, that he understood and told him not to worry. But James had been worrying ever since.

A hundred yards or so from the church James heard a low, powerful engine approaching and instinctively looked round. The hearse growled past him followed by two limousines. Bill and Angela didn't see him. They were staring straight ahead at the car in front.

And it was her in the box.

No smile, tears, hopes, fears, love or hate.

No life.

As he approached the church, James heard then saw a commotion of traffic in the small lane. He had a mounting desire to run off and sit in a field until it was all over, but the proximity of the church and the sights and sounds of a funeral party being organised hit home to him that he had a responsibility to fulfil. Standing at the church gate, Angela and Bill saw him and held out their arms.

James crunched together with Laura's parents in a hug, holding each other in silence. Angela broke this with a whisper that everyone was waiting.

Dazed by the over-flowing of affection, James wondered if the scene that greeted him was a mirage. Over by the west end stood his father and David. Then behind David was Simon, who he had not seen since Andrew's christening. Someone took his hand and squeezed it; Gerry whispered something in his ear and he turned to find her with Wendy, his mother, Annie and Carol.

And Philippa.

'Women look so beautiful in black. It accentuates all the other colours: eyes; makeup; hair; Mum's brooch; Annie's scarf; it's like someone is colouring in the gaps in the darkness.'

It was time for action and this was reinforced by the Vicar who was relaying instructions from the funeral director. The curtain was about to go up.

'How has all this been done? What part did you play in making it happen? Who made everyone part of this without telling me?'

Philippa took his hand, then took him in her arms and kissed him on the cheek. She kept her face close and whispered; 'It's so good to see you James, and looking fucking brilliant actually.'

In spite of himself and the occasion, James giggled at this memory.

'Seriously; you look more handsome than I ever remember you looking. Be brave and strong. Imagine I'm holding your hand, even though I won't be.'

Over her shoulder he saw his brothers with Paul, Leo and Graham, so he joined this group of men and, wordlessly, they followed the funeral director's instructions as Laura's coffin was taken from the hearse. Bill and James led the pallbearers; Bill grabbing his shoulder as if they were a second row, scrumming down for England. David and one of Laura's cousins were next, followed by another cousin and Simon.

'I am the resurrection and the life, saith the Lord; he that believeth in me, though he were dead, yet shall he live; and whosoever liveth and believeth in me, shall never die.'

They moved slowly around the outside of the church.

'...and the Lord hath taken away: blessed be the Name of the Lord.'

During this prayer, Bill made a noise; a snuffling sob. James turned to look at him and saw tears streaming down his face. He gripped Bill's shoulder tighter, but this moment was lost as they negotiated the few yards in to the small porch and through the tiny door.

The interior had a few flowers and was over lit. James was gripped by the need to switch off the lights. The organ was playing something, but it was piped discord with no discernible tune. There was a table draped in a deep purple cloth and the Vicar stopped beyond this stand then turned to face the oncoming procession. He nodded, somewhat superfluously, at the table and, with whispered directions from the funeral conductor to guide them, six men manoeuvred the coffin slowly in to place.

James turned and walked with Bill to the front pew. During the short walk, he registered the location of his friends in the congregation. They were all sitting close together. Philippa was near the front of the nave with her parents; they were all crying and Philippa looked like she'd never stop. His own parents and siblings were sitting with Laura's aunts and uncles in the second and third rows.

The organist droned out his or her last and a hush descended. A door closed noisily. Sniffing and occasional weeping increased as the Vicar began to recite Psalm 39.

'I said, I will take heed to my ways: that I offend not in my tongue...'

James frowned at the realisation that the service was traditional and very formal. He wondered why; and who made that decision. He glanced to his right at Angela; she was ashen faced, a hanky pressed to her nose and eyes in turn. To his left stood the still weeping Bill. Now, relieved from the burden of carrying his daughter on her last but one journey, his shoulders shuddered with heartache.

'...and cannot tell who shall gather them. And now, Lord what is my hope: truly my hope is even in thee...'

James looked round again. Carol, behind and to his left, smiled at him. Annie was staring at Laura's coffin and clasping David's hand. Mr Clifton stood to attention.

'...and a sojourner, as all my fathers were. O spare me a little, that I may recover my strength: before I go hence, and be no more seen...'

He turned to face forwards again.

'...world without end. Amen.'

James' thoughts flashed back to Hereford Cathedral; morning prayers; a hymn or two; school announcements and the sometimes overwhelmingly powerful torrent of seriously good organ playing. And reverse races, in which the aim was to say *Amen* as late as possible. It sounded like a small springboard vibrating down the nave. James turned to see if Leo or Paul had the same recall. They just stared back at him.

'Please be seated. We are here today for the saddest of reasons: the death of Laura – our beloved daughter and friend. If you find during the service that you are crying, please don't be ashamed or try to suppress your feelings. There will be others crying just the same. Let us all express our emotions together in God's sight.'

James looked at the Vicar. He was bearded and sincere with no notes; just a book, presumably of prayers. James' attention shifted to the coffin. Laura's lovely face drifted through his mind. The smells of her hair and her body filled his nostrils. He shook away these torments and swallowed hard.

'There will be a single hymn, number 329, *O thou who camest from above.'*

It was one of the very few hymns that James could stand but a grand tune called *Hereford,* composed by a great organist of his age, was soon being massacred by one of his less noble progeny. The congregation made disjointed, half-hearted efforts to sing along, led by the Vicar who intoned the hymn with the prerequisite gusto of his calling. James was unable to sing. He listened to the tune and, despite the way it was being performed, its grandeur started to close in on him. He breathed in and fought hard with his despair.

He was not going to cry.

He didn't care what the bloody man in black said, this was not going to happen; he was not going to cry. He looked up at the ceiling and wished he had a handkerchief. He looked at the memorial stones lining the walls and wished they were co-ordinated and rectangular. He looked at Angela. She wasn't singing. Neither was Bill. They were both just staring at the coffin.

> *Still let me prove thy perfect will,*
> *My acts of faith and love repeat;*
> *Till death thy endless mercies seal,*
> *And make the sacrifice complete.*

James shivered with stifled emotion. He continued an internal fight with his feelings and couldn't find the space for any thoughts. As the Vicar began to read more verses James lapsed in to a kind of neural paralysis. He couldn't hear the spoken words in any detail. He felt Angela shake and it moved him back to reality; a reality in which he was between Bill and his wife. He'd got that wrong. He had no business to be between them. It signified something that he preferred not to think about.

Then, as if from the end of a long and very thin tunnel, James heard the words that signalled the moment he had been dreading.

The Vicar ended his short introduction to James, in which he seemed to excuse himself for allowing a new-fangled intrusion. James stood and there was a moment's confusion while Bill worked out that he needed to let him pass. He moved out into the aisle, footsteps slow and measured and he sensed many eyes on him.

'Do this right. Do not fail. It's a last chance to do and be all the things Laura needed. Be brave and strong and lucid. For once in your useless life, do what needs to be done effectively and decisively. No fuck ups.'

He reached the coffin and shivered. Now he wished it was open again so he could see her and say all the things he had forgotten to say.

He took the book from his jacket pocket and opened it at the marked page. He looked up at the congregation. Most were looking back at him. Bill and Angela were still staring at the coffin. His face tightened near his temples and he coughed. He had the sickening sense that he might faint.

When he spoke, finally, his voice boomed out.

'Laura loved T.S.Eliot, mainly because of his poetry and plays but also because – as every first former knows – his name is an anagram of Toilets.'

A couple of small, sad laughs broke the silence. Someone laughed loudly; an over-compensation.

'I have no idea whether or not this particular poem was Laura's favourite but in the absence of any contrary view, I'm going to say that it was. And anyway, it sort of makes sense at a time when we feel nothing.'

He coughed and sniffed. As he looked at the poem, his mind collapsed. The words were just a mass of symbols and smudges. When they returned to focus, he still couldn't say anything. He looked across at Angela. She raised an eyebrow and gave him a crooked smile.

And without looking down at the book, James began to speak slowly and clearly. The rhyme and meter of the poem flowed out. James never faltered and his voice never cracked. When he finished, he looked down at the book as if noticing it for the first time. Someone in the congregation was crying quite powerfully now. The Vicar walked to him and clasped his arm. He whispered something comforting, thanked James and asked him to return to his seat.

As he passed the coffin James stopped and placed the book on it, just under the name plate. Then he placed his hand flat on the lid of the box and tried to whisper something. But words, even whispered words, would not come. He walked on and sat down as if he was made of lead. He felt a hand touch him gently on the shoulder and his father's voice saying: 'Well done. Well read.'

Shortly afterwards, the service ended with a brief announcement from the Vicar that anyone wishing to spend time in private prayer or reflection was welcome to stay in the church for this purpose. Evensong was some way off.

The same six men lifted Laura to their shoulders and trooped from the church to find her grave.

James thought he was going to scream.

At the graveside, experts took over and the elaborate business of lowering the coffin in to the ground was left to them.

'Man that is born of a woman hath but a short time to live, and is full of misery. He cometh up and is cut down like a flower...'

James was staring at the slowly descending wooden box. The book of poems was still there. Who had done this to him? By what authority did that person or persons act? It was unacceptable; no one had the right to take her away. To put her in the ground. In a box. With a silvery name plate. That name plate was an appalling affront to his sensibilities.

Angela linked her arm through his. Her other arm was around Bill. The three of them stood alone on one side of the grave.

'...to take unto himself our dear sister here departed, we therefore commit her body to the ground; earth to earth, ashes to ashes, dust to dust...'

James couldn't stop David Bowie's song slipping in to his head. *You better not mess with...*

'Lord have mercy upon us.'

Only a small number of people gave the response. But the Vicar persevered and whirred on in to the Lord's Prayer.

Angela stepped forward and threw something in to the grave. She stood there for a moment as if contemplating a leap to join her daughter. Bill stepped up to her and guided her back a few paces. It was a touching scene and James wept uncontrolled tears as he watched it.

Ten minutes later the formalities were done and people drifted away. Angela was still clinging to Bill and her voice implored James, 'Come now; we need to be together a little longer.'

James looked from her tear-stained face in to Laura's grave. 'I need a few moments here. Please; just Laura and me.'

Angela's attempt at a protest was cut off by Bill. 'Of course. But don't linger. Join us soon.'

There was a pained pleading in his voice and James was still looking at the grave when he replied: 'I won't. I'll be along shortly.'

His brain was locked on another old song about waving Brenda and Eddie goodbye.

James turned away from the graveside and saw he wasn't alone. Philippa stood a few feet away, helpless and hopeless; she walked forward to stand with him. They touched hands then James put an arm round her waist and she rested her head on his shoulder.

A conversation began; small speeches of sadness; soliloquys of sympathy.

He said, 'So here we are then; tied together, trying to fix something broken.'

'I know. I wonder how you're always in the right place when I need you.'

'When you need me?'

'Yes James. When I need you.'

He pulled her closer and handed her some tissues. 'Bloody hell. Bloody churches, bloody coffins and bloody...hell.'

'Your eloquence knows no bounds. And this foul-mouthed tirade is for?'

'For Laura. And for me a bit too. We planned, she and I, that the next and possibly only time we would be in a church together would be our wedding day.'

'That was her dream. Once upon a time she was certain you'd be together some day. Her little crush, she called it, but it was nothing of the sort.'

'Why wasn't it?'

'It was too real and permanent and certain. That's not a crush; it was more an ambition or a strategy; something that could be dormant if it needed to be. Laura loved mystery and some things never came out in the open. She lived inside many secrets, so her feelings for you ebbed and flowed. I think deep down she was terribly scared of being open and sometimes it made her lash out. Like that time you spent an evening with your work colleague.'

'She told you about that?'

'She did. Her reaction was appalling and I had a real go at her about it. I knew her all these years, yet some things I just never understood.'

The silence of the churchyard was almost physical; almost painful. A cold, grey, murky afternoon made it feel like night was closing. Tiny slivers of light were twinkling through the church windows.

James talked in to the top of Philippa's head. 'That's a strange thing to say, today of all days.'

She shook her head. 'It's simply the truth. Our friendship was strong and real, but Laura could be difficult to know. Sometimes she was quite superficial. Bloody hell: this sounds awful.'

'Superficial in what way?'

Philippa sounded strained and a bit anxious. 'Let's stop speaking ill of her.'

'No. This is the place to talk of her, and to listen to each other. Finish what you've started.'

Philippa breathed in slowly, then out with more force. It wasn't a sigh. 'She could be very unpredictable and inconstant. I saw her in many situations, and she was a different person depending on the time, place and people.'

'Are you saying she was a hypocrite? Two faced?'

'No; I'm saying she could be superficial and insecure. She managed her image very carefully indeed.'

James shook his head. 'She was always the same with me. Always very precise, assertive and detailed.'

'Laura had to be that way with you. It's why you were such a great match.'

'I thought that was because we loved each other, and were....'

Philippa's small chuckle cut him short. 'Of course it was. But a big part of your bond was the whole being superficial thing, because you both were; are. What she had with you was perfect for her by any number of measures. She'd got her man, the one she'd always wanted. She'd found you ready and willing to be with her. She'd taken a huge gamble and it paid out: big time. She didn't want anyone to get too close, or peel away the veneer. So when Laura found that you are also self-centred, and capable of being pretty shallow, she knew you would never dig too deep into her thoughts or feelings. You didn't represent a risk or a threat because you weren't curious about anything. You take things at face value. So when a beautiful young woman parachutes in to your life, saying the magic words *we were at school together, and I always really fancied you*, you just let it happen. It was as if all your dreams collided. You were smitten and she knew she'd got you. And it was for the whole of eternity.'

'Or not, as it turned out.'

Philippa made another small noise; half laugh, half exhalation. 'Yet, despite all the history and chemistry it was a completely random encounter in the Lich that brought you together. She called me that evening, breathless and demanding. I gave her your parents' number.'

'So you're to blame.'

'Only for the call. Everything else, the letter, how you grew together, all you had; that was just you and her.'

'Just Laura and James. But there was someone else wasn't there?'

She looked up at him. 'Who? What do you mean?'

'Her husband. That was just so bizarre.'

'In every sense.'

'Really?'

'Telling you about him was causing Laura really serious anxiety. She was certain you'd jack her in once you knew. You're very moralistic, aren't you?'

There was a pause. James asked, 'Why do you say that?'

'It's true. You have this rectitude about things. You don't mess with anything that's not yours to mess with.'

'I never knew that.'

Philippa chortled softly. 'Of course you know it. It's one of your little games. Laura and Steve was a colossal mistake from start to finish. I knew it; Angela knew it; everyone knew it; even Laura knew it. But it gathered this momentum and no one could really tell what caused that. Getting pregnant was a convenient excuse.'

'There's little point unravelling that now, is there?'

'No: true. Sorry. Tell me how you feel.'

'If I wasn't holding you, touching you, I'd say I was devoid of any sense of anything.'

She moved her hand across and ran her forefinger from the edge of his eye to his chin, as if tracking a tear. 'Can you feel that?'

'Yes. Thank you. But you won't be around to touch me, will you? The loss of feelings is permanent.'

She shook her head. 'It won't be. I know it's not the same – not even remotely the same – but don't forget what you kept saying to me about Ade. It's over. There's no hiding place and nowhere to run to. So just stay in the open and learn to cope with the incoming.'

James stared at the gravestones surrounding them. 'I wish she was here. I know she can't come back but I want to say some things that'll never get said. To say I love you.'

'She knew you loved her and it made her ridiculously happy. Forget what I said just now. You were perfect together and Laura wanted all of you: your insecurity; your sulks; the moods; the awful jokes; that smile; all those works of art; the whole perfectly imperfect James. And she adored the feeling that you told her stuff and were becoming less closed.'

'I found it easy to tell her things. Laura made me want everything to be crystal clear. Whenever she told me I needed to change, and she did it a lot, it never felt like an imposition. It was for both our benefits. She said I should never change just because she demanded it.'

'Of course she did. But she did need you to change a lot of things, especially to stop you being the old man you'd become.'

Their eyes met. James was frowning. 'She never told me that.'

'I'm prepared to bet that she did, even if it wasn't explicit. When you and I met, at Gerry's place last Christmas, the time we spent chatting was wonderful. But I was really troubled by something about you and I couldn't get my head round what it was. Once you and Laura had been an item for a few weeks, we met in Hereford and pretty much the first thing she said was: *James sometimes behaves and talks like a fifty year old; like he's never been young; he's like a lifeless shadow.* And that was what had been bugging me too. I even said you were a silhouette; remember?'

'Well this is cheery news.'

Neither of them wanted to laugh, but Philippa was quivering with amusement at his comment and James had to join in. But soon he was deadly serious: 'I suppose I will have to change now, because something nobody wanted has changed everything: permanently.'

Philippa stretched her hand out and once again traced something on his face. 'Not everything. Some things are constant.'

'But what about you? All we've done is talk of Laura and me. Tell me how you feel.'

James pulled her round so their embrace became frontal; face to face; eyes locked.

'I still can't believe it's happened; that she's gone. I've known her since she was four; more than twenty years. When my mother told me about the accident it was like being told I'd been given a life sentence in a prison where Laura was just a memory, interred in a cell no one could open. After I called you, I spent the whole evening and night crying my eyes out. It doesn't seem possible for a human to have so many tears. Above all I simply can't rationalise it. Since her death I must have said her name out loud four or five times a day. I wanted to hear her say something back to me; *Hey Mrs Pippatruck – sing me a song.* But there was nothing in the room but my voice; and it hurt so much.'

'Mrs Pippatruck??'

Her eyes creased at the edges. 'When I was little everyone called me Pippa, and young Laura thought it was Tipper. When she realised there was something called a tipper truck, she did the rest. She could be so lively like that; inventive and funny. I will miss that forever.'

Now James couldn't look in to her eyes. 'We should head back to Bill and Angela's.'

'I know. Time to say goodbye.'

'To Laura, and plenty more besides.'

'What do you mean James?'

'Somehow it feels like my past is gone; finally and irretrievably. It's buried right there in that hole. It might be that that's a good thing; but it's so frightening. I need that past. Without it I don't exist.'

Philippa and James arrived together at the Drysdale's unhappy home where they found people standing in groups, holding pianissimo conversations.

They headed together to the buffet. Philippa loaded some snacks on to a plate and said she needed to find her parents. James nodded and stayed where he was, watching the gathered mourners and their various coping strategies. Increasingly there were small swellings of laughter. Some spoke more openly about their memories. People were either comfortably in fixed groups, or restless and nomadic; joining in wherever they knew a face. Others were linking the dotted lines to explain how they knew Laura and what she had meant to their respective histories. There seemed no end to the constant need for food and drink, as if eating and drinking were a sanctuary from the occasion.

The small team of caterers busied themselves with fresh plates of food and refilled the urns of tea and coffee. They wore sympathetic, professional smiles.

Across the room James could see Philippa with her parents. Their eyes met as another restrained fragment of laughter rent the air. They shook their heads in despair that anyone could be having fun. And then they gave each other tiny smiles.

James grabbed a plate and some food then went in search of his family. It didn't take long and he was absorbed in to the group with words; sounds of comfort and support. Leo and Gerry and Graham joined them; then Paul and Wendy. All together now.

Bill and Angela, with their brothers and sisters, drifted among their guests like clouds. James watched them closely. He wondered at the feelings of parents when a child dies. Someone you've created, suckled, sent off to school, punished, developed, and loved even when they come home pissed, or fail exams, or start smoking. Someone you've seen as a baby, child, youth and adult. Someone you expected to be around long after you're a pile of ash or a box of bones. And suddenly they're gone. James kept monitoring them. Bill was the only person in the whole house who was smiling with sincerity. Why? If he had known, when he and Angela laid down to make love – to make Laura – that this day would come, could he possibly have got through it all?

Angela beckoned to James. When he reached her, she hugged him and brushed his face with her hand.

'Hello James.'

'Hello Angela.'

'Have you eaten? You must be hungry.'

'Yes. Thanks.'

'Please stay behind a while after people have gone; will you? Bill and I would like that.'

'Of course.'

'Philippa will join us too.'

'Is there anything I can do?'

'No. Nothing.'

She left him to rejoin Bill and they positioned themselves near the front door. People were starting to leave and over the next three quarters of an hour everyone left with closing, mumbled sympathies.

Aside from the caterers, who busied themselves with the removal and disposal of all they had created, James, Philippa, Angela and Bill were soon alone in the house.

Bill's smile looked fixed now, as if drawn on his face. There were long lines and bags under his eyes. He seemed to have aged, even since earlier in the afternoon. But he was business-like.

'Thanks for hanging on you two. It won't take long to say what we want to say.' He looked almost constantly at Angela who smiled sadly back at him.

'And what we wanted to say is thank you; our private thanks to you both. To you Philippa for all you've ever done as Laura's friend and confidante. We know how much she cherished your friendship and respected your views and values. She looked up to you from the moment she knew you. I'm sure your influence wasn't always wholly benign, but we felt... we knew you were good for Laura. And maybe she was good for you too.'

This was killing him. It was killing Philippa. Death was killing them.

'And James; in a remarkably short amount of time we've come to know and love you, almost as a son. You made Laura happy; happier than she had ever been. Through our own loss, perhaps we can't really know what you feel – what either of you feels – but please don't be alone in your grief. I'm sure it was difficult for you these last few days, but come to us James whenever you want or need to. Don't ever be a stranger to us. Please.'

James returned Bill's gaze and said, 'I won't.'

'The way you read in church was simply outstanding. I don't know how you did it. Thank you. It was very moving. Laura did love Eliot and adored that poem.'

Angela muttered her assent.

'And one last thing James; this is crucial. You must never think or believe that Angela and I blame you in any way for Laura's death. We don't; and we never will.'

James blinked back tears and inhaled, with tiny shudders of relief and gratitude. He felt Philippa take hold of his hand.

'And to both of you, this is likely to be goodbye for a bit. Angela and I had been planning to go away so we've made additional arrangements; a cruise and some extended time overseas; to get all this behind us. You understand.'

Angela took over.

'There are some things here we'd like you to have. She hadn't made a will or anything. Philippa, this bracelet was special to Laura and we think she would want you to have it rather than it go to charity. And James, this was given to Laura as a bracelet charm for her christening. It was my grandmother's. It's yours now.'

It was a small silver teddy bear.

They muttered thank you and examined these gifts without much pleasure.

It was Philippa who broke in to the ensuing silence. 'I think I should be making tracks. It's late and I have an early start. James? Can I give you a lift?'

He made a distracted, grateful reply that she could.

Bill shook James' hand with both of his. James looked one last time into Bill's eyes and saw hopeless, eternal defeat. Then Bill moved away to hug Philippa. Angela took James' hand to shake it, then pulled him in to a hug. 'Come on now darling James. We all have to be fine; starting now.'

They drove off down the lane and back to the city, not talking much until Philippa brought her car to a halt near the Clifton's house.

'I'll come over to Richmond and see you, maybe next weekend.

We can have lunch.'

'Yes; let's. And we could meet over Christmas? It's not far off now. Will you be up here or are you stuck in London?'

'I'll be here at some point, but we can meet wherever and whenever.'

'Will you be all right? On top of everything with Adrian?'

'That's a speck of dust alongside this.'

'I suppose it is. But call me, any time. I'm sorry I didn't call you much this last few days like we agreed. I'll make up for it.'

They embraced and then brushed each other's cheeks with kisses.

'Make sure you do. We're all alone now. Talking will keep us afloat.'

'Yes.'

James watched as Philippa drove off, then rang the doorbell and prepared to face whatever was left of this day.

26

Exhaustion overwhelmed him and James went to bed early. When he turned off the bedside lamp his tiredness didn't turn to sleep. His head was full of reminders with flashes back to the grey, muted atmosphere at church. That hymn tune swelled symphonically in his ears. Then he was led back through recent events: the chapel of rest; a phone call with Angela; leaving work early to sit on an empty train; lunch with Maxine; Miles' reaction at that meeting; his father's disbelief; the inventory of Laura's possessions; police station tea; a smashed up wall; Philippa's call.

It was like being on a ghost train with these memories thrust at him randomly from hidden traps. He couldn't control what he was being shown and, when he tried to overcome this by evoking something different, he found his recall of anything else was blocked. He lay there on his back, wide awake, frantic with misery.

So he conceded, allowed the storyline to rule and slowly the looped repetition made his fatigue return and his eyes flutter between sleep and wakefulness. The mind games he was playing with himself channelled in to a dream; and he never had dreams.

James was in a room; it was dark and noiseless until the silence was broken by a rapping of wood on wood and then a voice. The obscurity turned to light and he saw this was a courtroom. A solitary spot-lit chair gleamed to his left, unlit chairs lined up alongside it.

Women began to fill the chairs.

The first, dressed in green, was Sarah Smith and when she sat down the light above her head dimmed, superseded by the one to her left. A row of six seats was soon occupied by women dressed, alternately, in green and red: Sarah; Mrs Clifton; Sally; Tracy; Carol; and Philippa. Then the whole process repeated so a second row of six chairs was lit, then occupied.

The sequence ended when there were two of each woman; one in green, one in red.

The voice made another noise, words James couldn't define. Laura walked into view and sat directly opposite him. She wore black, highlighting her spectral white face. Her mouth was a faint crack of pale pink, her eyes like drops of ocean in an arctic landscape. She motioned to her right and the voice intoned again.

The women stood in turn, giving testimonies summarising their relationship with and feelings for James. The red women were angry with or bitter about or frustrated by James. Those in green were loving, accepting, warm and embracing.

James squirmed in the chair and looked, with pleading eyes, at Laura. None of the women looked at him as they spoke. Each invocation was projected across the space between James and Laura, guilt and innocence in equal measure.

Trial.

And error.

At the end there was silence. All the lights went out except the ones illuminating Laura. She spoke.

'None of this matters. Case dismissed.'

27
Revelations

The Drysdale's villa had a south-facing terrace and was drenched in sunlight from mid-morning until late afternoon. James sat in the warm, soporific sunshine as he had for several weeks combining work and relaxation. At his side an easel held a near complete image and he was gazing into the surrounding trees for whatever inspirational threads might tie up this work.

He felt reassured by the remoteness of a perfect place. Any sounds – wildlife, vehicles, voices in the distance – seemed to amplify the silence. James revelled in the detachment and solitude he had found.

Every couple of days, he walked to nearby Sorges for food and a quick stop at a café. He bought bread and croissants from a mobile baker and occasionally took a trip on the bus to Thiviers if he needed more extravagant food and drink. But otherwise, he was a benign outsider.

Generally he ate good, simple food. Early every morning, he cycled to the local outdoor pool and swam sixty lengths. He drank water, coffee and, at weekends, a little wine and maybe a brandy. He'd stopped drinking beer. This regime had combined to make James look and feel excellent. He had grown his hair long and tied it into a ponytail when out and about. His complexion was a light chocolate colour. For the first time ever, things were how he needed them to be. Yet this beautiful calm and seclusion had not been part of the plan.

Around two months after Laura's death the pain of loss was slowly receding. He didn't want to let go but something loosened his grip every day. A kind of normality had descended. Christmas was coming and, to help him on his road to recovery, someone bought one of his paintings.

Roger Whitham's call took James completely by surprise because he'd pretty much forgotten about the three pieces on display at the gallery. His delight at the news was tempered by nagging doubts that, maybe, this wasn't a real transaction. That, maybe, a well-meaning soul had decided to pay something for James to be happy.

But this was misplaced; the buyers were real. They were enthusiastically in love with *Simple Cell* and with the notion of owning something by an unknown artist. This naivety led to an inflated price: £1,175.

He'd done it.

What a feeling!

The elation and highs carried him through a week. James felt occasional pangs of sadness that Laura had gone without sharing this; it should have been her deal too. But James remained buoyant and decided to muster some friends for a celebratory night out.

Roger couldn't be there, with regret. Gary and Bridget said yes, of course. Philippa was away on a work assignment. Sue from Finance agreed to come along, even though she wouldn't be drinking or staying long. Carol, David and Annie said it was too far to travel. Gaggi and Big Phil said no, but good luck. Maxine and Petra said they would love to join the party.

After a rushed early meal, they piled into two cars and drove off towards Epsom and a club recommended by Gary. James' support group was delighted to be part of something that had cheered and uplifted him, more so since he insisted on paying for all the champagne. None of them was particularly sure how significant the sale of a painting could possibly be. But they sensed this event was good for James and, with the social and commercial imperatives of Christmas approaching, there was a glimpse of an environment in which James might be back to normal.

Before her departure at ten thirty, Sue offered a lift to anyone who wanted one but there were no takers. James kept the champagne coming and the remaining five people danced, chatted and drank. When the smoochy songs started, James had a slow dance with Maxine and then with Petra. It was all great fun; exhilarating; it felt like a release.

Petra and Maxine had to go, reluctantly they said, just after midnight. James walked with them to the front of house and, when their taxi showed up, watched them leave with a possessive jealousy. He'd enjoyed the slow dancing; not because he wanted it to lead anywhere; he'd just needed some comfort.

Gary and Bridget were on the dance floor, kissing passionately and grinding in time with *True* as it oozed from the sound system. It made James resentful and upset that his decoys had left.

It was time for him to get out and he downed one last glass of champagne before heading to retrieve his coat from check-in. At the free-phone for taxis he booked two fares; one for Greig; one for Clifton. When they told him there was a forty-five minutes wait, he cancelled the booking for Clifton, took out his keys, lurched to his car and got in.

Needless to say in this story of clichés, James didn't make it. He was drunk, although the heady atmosphere of the club had masked the full extent of that condition. The frosty December night air hit him hard and, cocooned in his car, he set off in the wrong direction.

He vaguely recalled a loud skidding noise and the smell of hot rubber. Then there was something else: that noise a car's bodywork makes when it hits something large and immovable. Petrol fumes mingled with the rubber.

Then there were blue flashing lights that made concerned faces phase in and out of his vision. Pain, searing pain, in his arm and side and shoulder. He rolled and rocked in a cabin of some sort, now with just one concerned face watching over him.

James came round in great pain, which he projected with a loud moan from his hospital bed. A nurse arrived quickly and asked about the pain. He was not coherent but indicated his right side by pointing with his head. The nurse asked him questions repeatedly: about his breathing; about his ability to cough; about his vision; about pains in his head and chest. He mumbled an approximation of either no or yes in response, but the nurse seemed dissatisfied. He could feel that a line had been put in his left hand and saw that his right arm was strapped. The nurse finished this interview by saying she was going to take a blood sample.

Reality dispersed. James lapsed back in to semi-consciousness, waking occasionally to find nothing registered beyond a general throbbing soreness and pains in too many places.

It could have been hours or days but he eventually became lucid enough to interact and be told some details. His right forearm was fractured, he had broken ribs and a dislocated right shoulder. There were superficial wounds peppered around his face and throat. His stiff, painful neck was attributed to whiplash. The nurses continued to ask him about his chest and head and, now he was able to answer more clearly, concerns receded about punctured lungs or brain damage. The clinical view was that, in spite of serious injury, he was not in danger; he would mend and survive.

He was moved from observation to a general ward and told to expect to be in hospital for weeks rather than days. There were tutting and sighing about this avoidable, negligent situation. He could have killed himself. He could have killed others. There was not much sympathy. It seemed the police were eager to speak to him but, meanwhile, he was encouraged to rest and sleep.

James lay there, turmoil flooding his system. He didn't think he'd done this in order to kill himself. He didn't want to die, because – yes – he'd sold a picture and that was cause for optimism and courage. But his anguished soul kept reaching a conclusion that he hated: if he had died, it would have been no loss.

The police eventually dropped by to interview and charge him with drink-driving. Samples had revealed more than four times the legal alcohol limit in his blood, so he was bang to rights and could expect a ban and hefty fine. The officer clearly shared the medical staff's contempt for what James had done, but remained business-like. It was explained that as soon as possible after his discharge from hospital James would have to see the police again to sign formal papers. He also learned that his car had been impounded and he would face a bill for that. The officer explained the evidence that James had lost control when turning left and doing about fifty five to sixty miles per hour. The car had skidded sideways and hit a large tree about five yards from the roadside. The impact had been directly on the driver's door, forcing most of it into his side. His right arm, shoulder and ribs had borne most of the impact. The officer exuded a grudging admiration that James had retained enough control to stop the car flipping over. Any scintilla of respect was washed away by a threatening final remark that, thankfully, no other vehicle or party were involved.

Mr and Mrs Clifton were with James daily, and once he was rational made it clear how unhappy they were about being dragged away from home with Christmas so close. He was given a full volume lecture by his mother about responsibility, breaking the law, considering others and moderation. She soon stormed off leaving James' father to probe and test the possibility that this accident had been deliberate.

His parents stayed several days, returning home only when it was clear James was not at risk and Carol, David and Annie were carrying the family baton. Meanwhile he had a steady stream of callers who shook their heads, smiled wanly and didn't stay for long. There were cards from more distant family and colleagues. A message arrived from Bill and Angela, grateful for James' safety.

He soon amassed a small stockpile of fruit and chocolate.

From the start, Philippa was constantly at his side during visiting hours. When he became capable of noticing, he saw that she looked shattered and wept as she told him her fear that someone else dear to her had been killed.

She told him it would have left her with no reason to live.

Philippa came every day, sometimes twice in a day, and was the only person James wanted to see.

He spent Christmas in hospital, which was made special by

staff who tried hard to make it a festive home from home. James had become more mobile and enjoyed Christmas Day. The following day, the anniversary of his first ever phone call with Laura, James withdrew to his bed and stayed there. Towards the end of that afternoon, he had converted a series of ideas and thoughts into a decision.

It was simple.

Couldn't be simpler.

Why hadn't he thought of it before?

He couldn't write so he made lengthy mental notes about what to do. The notes became a plan about finances, property, destinations and people. Every morning he rewound and replayed the script. It was soon thought perfect and stored.

His stay was prolonged in to the New Year because he fell victim to a chest infection requiring a course of antibiotics. But his bones were strong, mending well and during the second week of January 1991, he was deemed able to care for himself at home and was discharged. Laden with pain relief, his convalescence was short so he set his plan in motion.

James resigned from his job, giving his contracted notice period. He put his flat up for sale and soon accepted an offer. He paid the costs needed to release his car and found it could be repaired cheaply enough to make it worth selling; so he did both. He cashed in as many policies and investments as he was able.

At the Magistrate's Court, he pleaded guilty to the charge of driving while under the influence of alcohol. His own defence made much of his mental mayhem after the death of a loved one but this cut no ice with The Beak. A two year ban and a massive fine were generally agreed to be pretty much what he deserved.

He had a series of sessions with Roger to discuss his plans and ambitions. These discussions resulted in an agreement in which Roger would store James' work and make his own judgement about what to display and sell. He heartily approved of James' ideas and they spent a weekend preparing a detailed inventory of all James' pieces which they copied and signed. James deposited his copy with a solicitor.

The only other person to learn of James' plan was Philippa who he swore to secrecy. She wanted James to be close but he played and replayed the message that this was what he had to do. Her support was conditional, but she didn't withhold it.

He called Jon Morgan, his neighbour at the dinner table during that evening at the Drysdale's. From this conversation James learned that Jon was able to contact Bill in the Caribbean so he explained what he wanted to achieve. Within twenty four hours, James had confirmation that he could stay at the Drysdale's villa in France – within reason for as long as he chose. Jon relayed that Bill refused to accept payment for this, but that James would have to cover any running costs while there.

James also sought Jon's help to arrange the delivery of a bike, some luggage and chests containing his artist's accessories. Several days later, a registered letter arrived containing a copy of the letter Jon had sent to the villa's manager telling him to expect delivery of James' belongings. In a separate note, James was instructed to contact the manager with two weeks' notice of his planned arrival date and time.

His flat was sold quickly to a first time buyer and they completed in the middle of March. His furniture and personal effects were either sold, stored or scrapped and he'd amassed a large amount of cash in the bank. James moved out and stayed in a hotel for a few days where he made phone calls to his family and friends explaining that he was taking an extended holiday to get over all that had happened. He only outlined the full extent of his plans in a letter to his parents.

And he was all set. There was nothing to keep him in England, so very early on a grey morning at Charing Cross station, he posted his letter and carried his small rucksack on to a train for Dover.

He was on his way.

The ferry was quiet and the crossing calmly unexceptional. He ambled round the decks and, as the ship approached Calais, watched the activity on and off shore. Around an hour after docking, James found a seat on a train to Paris and spent the journey reading and sketching, occasionally gazing at the countryside that flashed by. The sun was out and Picardy looked inviting and warm.

The train pulled into the Gare du Nord shortly before three o'clock and James strolled with confidence through the concourse. He grabbed a hotels guide from an information desk and selected one on the Rue de Rivoli. A taxi ride ensued, and after checking in and leaving his baggage with reception, James walked through the gardens that led him to Le Louvre.

He didn't sleep well that night, but was revived by croissants and coffee before settling his bill. He took the Metro to the Gare d'Austerlitz and, soon, another train sped him south from the city. James dozed for most of the next couple of hours, oblivious to any sights. At Limoges, he changed trains and soon did so again at Thiviers where he joined a rickety old diesel train that rattled and shook. This was much more like the ones in England, and the piles of general litter, discarded bottles and a less than satisfactory smell from the bog completed that entente. Progress was slow. The train stopped frequently revealing place names he couldn't pronounce. Announcements during the approach to stations were a meaningless burst of noise but eventually James thought he heard the word *Agonac* in one of them and he became alert to the scenes outside. When it stopped, the train had apparently arrived in the middle of nowhere because he could see no obvious buildings, platform or life. But there was an old wooden sign with *Agonac* on it and, gathering his rucksack, James stumbled from the train.

A pleasantly warm spring day had become a chilly evening. The train farted off into the distance and after getting his bearings James set off towards a road bearing the sign; *Sorges 10*.

He looked around, despairing, for signs of life. In his letter to the villa's manager, James had provided quite precise details of his arrival time but this had never been acknowledged. There was no car parked nearby and James began to fear he might have to walk. He worked out, after some clumsy mental arithmetic, that ten kilometres was about six miles and he swore aloud; it could take him up to two hours to walk that far.

As he stood in the gathering dusk a car drove by, its occupants looking warily at a rough looking stranger. James set off on his hike but he'd walked less than two hundred metres when another car approached, passed him then drew to a halt. A man got out; he had a face the colour and texture of a walnut shell. He spoke slowly.

'Ça va chef?'

James replied equally slowly; 'Oui. Ça va bien merci.'

'Vous allez loin?'

'Vers Sorges.'

'Vous êtes James Clifton?' It sounded like he said gems.

'Oui, c'est moi.'

'Hello Gems. I am Jean Pannet. I'm sorry I missed you at the station.'

'It's fine. Thank you for collecting me.'

'Let me take your bag. Get in.'

As they drove, James discovered that his effects had arrived safely and were secure in the villa. Ten minutes later they passed through some gates and stopped outside a single storey building with long sloping roofs. It looked rather sinister in the gloom but inside it was modern, homely and bright. Jean showed James around, explaining where things were stored and how to operate the alarm and other equipment. Then he took out a map to describe the locale and where to find various shops and other nearby facilities. James felt thoroughly welcome but declined Jean's invitation to meet his wife and have supper, citing fatigue from his journey. Jean said he understood and after a final check that James was clear about everything, bade him farewell.

Once alone, James realised that the villa was disconcertingly quiet. He loaded Soul II Soul's *Vol.II: 1990 – A New Decade* to a stereo, turned it up loud and roamed the building. He tried all the chairs and sofas in the living room and sat for a while at one end of the long dining table. A rumble from his stomach reminded him that he hadn't eaten anything meaningful since breakfast.

Back in the kitchen, he found cheese, bread, red wine, more cheese, ham, some sausage, apples, fromage frais, bottled water, coffee, some tea bags, croissants, eggs, jam, potatoes, walnut oil and onions.

He stuffed himself with bits of anything that didn't need to be cooked, gulping down the Bergerac wine in between mouthfuls. After an initial binge lasting several minutes, he loaded some morsels on a plate and took it to the dining room.

James ate, looking constantly at the framed photographs of Laura perched on unit tops and hanging on walls.

The music had stopped.

28

The sound of an approaching car made James stand and walk to the front of the villa, where he greeted his sister with a hug and a weary, wary smile.

'Hello sis.'

Carol was oblivious to his reticence. 'You look fantastic, long-lost brother of mine.' She tugged at his ponytail. 'This really suits you.'

James looked at his sister and felt some of his worry drain away. She seemed relaxed in spite of a long drive.

'Are you ok? How was the trip? And have you brought the gin?'

Carol looked at her brother. 'I'm ok, but need a shower and some coffee. Journey was brilliant despite occasional moments of abject terror around Paris. But today's leg was wonderful, and slightly surreal; aren't the roads quiet? It's like no one travels.'

'Today was a very good day to be driving in France. It's Bastille Day.'

'Right. That explains a lot of things.'

They were still standing next to her car reviewing her itinerary. The hotel James had arranged for her to stay at near Tours was given a big thumbs up. As his sister reeled off details of the hospitality she'd enjoyed there, James retrieved her bag from the car then, when Carol paused for breath, repeated his question about gin.

She reached in to her car and pulled out a pack of tonic water cans which she threw to James. Then, with a cheery *ta-da* two bottles of gin were held up like trophies. James smiled broadly.

'If I didn't know better, James Clifton, I'd say you are happier to see Mr and Mrs Gordon than you are to see me. In which case I'm going to make you wait while I have a shower, unpack my bag and change in to something cool and comfy.'

An hour later they were sitting together in the now shaded terrace making small talk. James hadn't drunk gin since before he left England and was guzzling it. Their discussion was uncomplicated and drifted from a review of the weather back home to the benefits of toll motorways, the horrors of sea-sickness and how duty free fags and gin must be cherished. The combination of this amiable repartee with several drinks lured James into a falsely secure place. The mood dipped, then frosted, when he asked, 'How is everyone?'

Carol looked at him steadily and began to deliver a lecture that turned over many stones. He had nowhere to hide so he just sat there as a tide of frustration and anger cut him off from the shoreline. Unfortunately, he made things much worse about ten minutes into Carol's deliberations. She started to sound so much like their mother that James gave a snort of laughter. She bristled at him and her voice went up a notch or two.

'So you think this is funny? Let me assure you that no one in our family is laughing.'

The accusations of irresponsibility and stupidity were supplemented by disbelief about James' financial recklessness and poor family values. How could he just sell everything he'd worked for? What security did he have now? What possible justification was there for his cowardly lack of communication?

But he had switched off, these words ricocheting harmlessly in to the surrounding woods.

Carol reloaded, and kept shooting. Mother had washed her hands of him, and had even said she never wanted to see him again. Father was tight lipped and, at various times, had been more livid than Carol had ever seen him. Mr Clifton refused to discuss the subject which was an unbelievably bad sign. As was the divide that had opened in the family. Annie's suggestion, that James' actions were understandable, had caused a huge row.

David and Annie had not returned to their parents' house since that debate.

Her final tirade was about how he'd made her feel; how he'd made things bad for her; how she couldn't defend what he'd done. James had made his sister angry many times before. But not like this; Carol was emphatically different and detached.

Her tirade lasted several more minutes and ended with a flourish: '...and you better have some bloody good answers to all this James, because I'm really not going to take any bollocks from you about needing to *find myself* or *have an outlet*.'

'Well thank you for being so caring.'

She glared at him and started all over again, this time about the worry and anxiety he'd caused. James just stopped listening and gazed at his sister and then through her at the easel with its unfinished work. He started to wonder why he'd asked her to join him in France.

'Well?'

'Well what?'

'When are you coming home?'

'Home?'

'To England.'

'Not sure.'

This was a show-stopper. 'You mean you might stay?' Her voice was lowered and uncertain.

'Why not?'

'James; please stop arsing about. Come on. Talk to me.'

'Why? I don't think you want to talk; you just want to preach. So while you're in your pulpit, forget it. I've got nothing to say.'

She glowered.

'And stop looking at me like Mother. It's bad enough that you sound like her.'

Carol fought hard, but couldn't prevent a smile.

'The words adult, responsible and unfeeling have never applied to me. I demand a retraction.'

Now she giggled. 'All right. But I'm not going to apologise or retract. I've soaked up all that stuff from Mum and Dad and swore that you would have to hear it too.'

'Yes. I'm sorry about that, but I didn't do all this to get you in trouble. I get the message; you're pissed off with me and so is everyone else. Can we perhaps draw that to a close now? I've booked a table for dinner tonight at the hotel down in Sorges. You will not believe what you can get for two hundred and fifty francs each in there. We can walk – in fact we probably have no choice after all this gin. I do have answers, and I will give them; but let's leave all that till we're eating. Okay?'

Carol agreed and their conversation reverted to the banal and trite, neither of which James had missed since his semi-emigration. It was a relief after the extended lecture and it continued during the walk to Sorges and the preamble of their meal. As their first course plates were cleared away, Carol ventured the question James had been waiting to be asked. 'Let's have it then James: what's the script?'

James frowned, wiped his mouth with his napkin and sipped at his wine.

'Cut out the performance. Just start talking.'

'Well that's the problem. I'm not sure where to start.'

Carol made a gesture that said *go on*.

'Laura's death made me realise I needed to do what I've done. And when she was still alive, it was her perceptions of me as a person that created this impetus to be something new.'

He seemed to be constantly searching for lines and spoke without conviction. He only looked at Carol at the end of sentences, either to seek affirmation of her understanding or to make sure she wasn't about to jab a fork in his hand.

'When I first met Laura, I was convinced I was no different to what I'd always been. Some things had changed – material things. I had an income and owned a home. I had a well-paid job. I'd been in one mainly successful relationship. I had friends, near and far. But nothing had changed me. I thought and behaved like I always had. The same things still made me laugh, or moved me. I felt all those links to school and Hereford meant that I was preserved.'

He drank some wine and chewed a piece of bread.

'But I was wrong; really, really wrong. And without Laura I'd have gone on duping myself that I was in some way a thirty year old version of the James who once pinned up a cartoon depicting the Headmaster as the wind being farted from Bismarck's arse.'

He drank again hoping Carol would make an observation. She said nothing and made the same gesture for him to continue.

'More or less from our first meeting Laura told me, subtly and directly, that change had almost overwhelmed me. She said I was delusional if I believed otherwise. She used all kinds of words to describe me: complacent; uncaring; insular; cynical. She called me an unexceptional nobody with a mixed up and inconsistent attitude to all sorts of things.'

'Such as?'

'Being negatively self-critical; being easily defeated; having no real interest in the rights and wrongs in the world outside a very narrow band of vision. Such as seeing a mortgage and property as life-affirming. Such as how I was satisfied with being ordinary.'

'What gave her the right to say or think those things? I mean how could she possibly link the man she met last year to whatever reference points she had from your adolescence? You were, what... three years above her at school?'

'Four; and she had the right because she'd held on to something important for twelve years. She just knew. She had ways to know.'

Carol seemed sceptical. 'I see. Go on.'

'I always got backed up by the criticism and my defence was that I did see myself as out of the ordinary. I was better than the crowd; something set me apart. Laura just rejected all that. She said being superior was the whole problem; I hadn't been raised and educated to put myself above and beyond people. She said I should have been showing the world my skills and cherishing any reaction. Instead, I dismissed even the possibility of being good at something yet still claimed I was better than everyone. She said that, at school, I didn't compete and wasn't insecure. I had a unique talent none of the others had and I made that work for me instead of treating it as a defensive shield. I'd been kind-hearted, loving, laughing and gifted. Essentially a humble young man who stood up alongside other quite brilliant young men as an equal because they knew I was special. It was a nurturing environment.

She told me I'd lost the ability to be gifted and was just another salaried office boy. I was satisfied with second best.

All the time we were getting to know each other, I kicked against Laura when she said this stuff. I didn't see how it could be true if Leo or Paul hadn't mentioned it to me. If they had never seen or revealed these changes in me, how could Laura be so clear about them? Yet she wore me down and I think, by the time we went on holiday, I believed her and distrusted them.'

'Why? That's a very strange reaction.'

James took a break to eat. 'I know it is and I think I felt like that because, in fact, those school day memories were always too skewed in our favour. We were all horribly arrogant, and what Laura did was to slap down some of that history. I'd never had a second opinion before; I just agreed with the consensus about all the girls, parties and classroom outrage.'

'I think you might have worked all that out for yourself.'

'Maybe, but I hadn't. Then there was the under-achievement. Jumping in to any old job. Living somewhere a bit basic. Not going to university or an Art College. These weren't bad per se, and she wouldn't let me regret them. She just didn't understand my lack of curiosity about how things might have been shaded differently if missed opportunities had been taken.'

'So, all that meant you had to run away from everything you've ever worked for?'

'Ultimately, yes; it did. Because all those things were shite. A house. A car. A job with prospects and money. Briefly, a loving partner. And what else?'

'The respect and love of a family?'

James reflected on that while he cut into his omelette. 'Well if that only comes from having shit aspirations and achievements then I'm not sure I'm all that bothered.'

'That's very, very unfair and ungrateful.'

'No it's not. By and large, whatever I have or had was my own work. It may have been poorly planned, badly executed and limping along on the hard shoulder but it was all mine. No one, not you, not our parents, not our siblings – not anyone – ever took time to correct any of it. I've got to here with nothing more than my own guidance; so it's pretty fucking hard to accept all this scorn now, when I've done something worthwhile and new.'

Carol was chewing and looking down at her plate.

James lightened his tone. 'If everyone at home is shocked by this, is it because it's about improvement and stepping up?'

Eventually Carol muttered, 'Maybe it is. Maybe it's precisely because of your general lack of ambition until now.'

James nodded ruefully. 'I've never had dreams. I've never known what I should be. Lying in a hospital bed after nearly killing myself I realised that couldn't go on. And that's why I'm here. Making something from whatever talent I have.'

'But couldn't you have done all this in England? A cottage in the Cotswolds or something?'

'Not really. I had to get away from the machinery; from the temptation to be nothing. I had to become a stranger so I could have no distractions. You're only the second person I've seen from home.'

'Who was the other?'

'Laura's father dropped by to say hello. It was the first time we'd seen each other since Laura's funeral.'

'How come Angela didn't travel?'

'She hasn't been well. She has suffered so much pain.'

'It must have been awful for both of them.'

'Bill was very subdued when he was here. He was confronted by memories of Laura; tangible ones, like photos. And the intangible; her presence and his recollections. Bill told me it was a huge shock to be reminded that there was another place where Laura had lived.'

'How were things between you and Bill?'

'It was like we've formed a bond; it's so strange. I kind of assumed any links between us would slowly dissolve. That we would move on and apart. But it's like I'm all he has. I simply don't understand how that is possible when we only met about a year ago.'

Another round of plates was cleared away. Carol wanted to keep digging. 'Let's get back to you and what you've been up to. I don't understand what's changed. We both know you've never worked hard.'

'Exactly. I never have, except at the things I don't want to do.'

'What do you mean?'

'I mean my day job. I was so busy with business, and so consumed by the need to be in some sort of race, that I wasn't being me. I was only ambitious for the pointless; for baubles; for wants, not needs.'

From nowhere, a snatch of Gary's song about ambition fizzed through James' mind:

'I've got a story to tell, I'm gonna give them hell...'

It distracted him, but Carol's quizzical face brought him back.

'Now, all that has gone and I have a vision and objective. It's why I'm here and what the last few months have stood for. Away from the futile limelight of work, mortgage, commuting, owning, existing and all that over-consumption, I've been able to complete things instead of just imagining them as such.'

'Art you mean?'

'Of course I mean art. What did you think it would be?' James' suddenly curt manner made Carol look startled. She didn't respond.

'Just before Christmas and before the accident – my accident – I sold a painting via Roger's gallery.'

'Yes. I know.'

'He'd had three of my paintings for several months and deep down we'd both begun to give up on them. But *Simple Cell* hit the spot and when I got out of hospital I started talking to Roger about four other pieces. When I showed him he was really, really impressed, and had a go at me for holding them back. Then, over time, he came round to my place and we went through everything. He was – well it was so flattering – he was stunned by much of it. It all ended up with him agreeing to store and try to sell all my works.'

'Was that wise?'

'I trust him and there's a list of all he is holding for me. And we've a written agreement.'

'Even so: if they're valuable? '

'Then they will sell. That's what I want. And what he wants for me.'

'So where are you going with this?'

'He's sold seven more of my pieces. He got over two grand for one of them.'

Carol whistled softly.

'Yes. During the time we were looking together at what I'd done, Roger kept saying he thought I developed my ideas best in a sequence where themes could be developed. We discussed the possibility of me doing some work about Laura. I built on those thoughts and that's what I brought here. I wanted to create twenty, maybe twenty five pieces showing a life with, and without Laura. Works that show what the relationship was. How it started. How it finished. I've done a few other things, unconnected with the series, in case we need padding for the exhibition.'

'Exhibition?'

'Yes at Roger's gallery. He's already doing some initial hype about it.'

Carol was suddenly alert, sitting upright and focused. 'Right. So twenty-five paintings.'

'Twenty definite, five possible.'

'Okay. And one from the sequence gets sold; let's say I buy one; how do I see it as part of the set?'

'That's where you come in.'

Carol was puzzled; 'I don't see how.'

James explained that each painting in the series will be up for sale at a minimum price, as yet unspecified.

'Part of that deal, for anyone who buys a painting or drawing, is a glossy photo pack of the whole set of pictures.

'What do you mean by a glossy photo pack?'

'Like a calendar.' He looked excitedly at his sister. She swilled some wine around her mouth and returned his gaze.

'So I do the photos?'

'Yes please.'

She drank some more and narrowed her eyes. 'It seems to have merit. I just wonder...'

'Yes?'

'...isn't it a bit pretentious?'

He put his fork down noisily. 'Pretentious? Oh come on, not you too? That's the sort of thing I'd expect from the fools I worked with. Don't understand; won't ask questions; have to give a label to everything they encounter; better call it pretentious. I never thought you would be in that bucket.'

'I'm sorry. Maybe ambitious was the right word.'

'Well we covered ambition just now. Nothing in this is pretentious Carol. It is most certainly ambitious. I really thought you'd try a bit harder.'

There was something close to anger in James and it halted the exchange. They were quiet and troubled; neither seemed willing to break the ice.

It was a calmer James that took the plunge. 'Anyway, if you're still interested, that's why I asked you to come over here. To have a look at the paintings and drawings, talk the thing over and give me some idea about what it might cost to do the glossy prints. I also want you to take a good quality photo of each to deliver to Roger. To give him an idea of the flow. Despite my desire to be away from things, I still value your feedback and crave your endorsement.'

The chef and patron was ambling amiably amongst his guests and soon arrived at their table. 'Aaaah, Monsieur James l'artiste anglais.'

'Bonsoir Chef. Félicitations, le canard était superbe ce soir.'

'Merci, merci. Tu es gentil. Mais tu as apporté une autre belle femme.'

'C'est ma soeur Chef. Puis-je introduire Carol Clifton?'

Carol smiled and mumbled something to the man.

'Enchanté Mademoiselle. Mais, veuillez m'excuser. Il y'a des autres invités.' He sauntered off, stopping to talk to every diner in the room.

'What was that about another woman?'

'I dunno. He must be pissed or something.'

They ate and drank, still enveloped in a morose atmosphere. When the silence became too much to bear, they both started to speak and in the melée of words neither noticed that the other had apologised.

James picked up the storyline. 'Roger has taken on the role of a kind of agent for me. He gets a cut from the sales. In fact, agent is the wrong word. Mentor might be better. Yes. Mentor.'

'You seem to have faith and trust in this man. How much is his cut?'

'Thirty per cent.'

'Did you ask around about that? It sounds a lot.'

'I'm comfortable with it. For now it's not about the money. It's more about his efforts and input. He understands and doesn't need to have things explained to him. I see someone who works hard on my behalf.'

'All right then. So how exactly do I come in to all this?'

'First, will you do the photos? You'll know the right lighting conditions, format, and weight of paper – that sort of stuff. Then, will you help out with packs, in particular what they will cost.'

'Photographing the works will be easy in my studio.'

'So you'll do it?'

'Wait. Some physical attributes will make things harder; for example, anything with a glossy finish or any fine drawing. The printing is a pretty small job but that won't make it cheap. You're asking someone to set up equipment for around thirty copies containing about two dozen pages. That's less than a thousand sheets. The quality of the paper is crucial and you'll have to spend more to get the right effect. Your calendar allusion is about right. Heavy-ish paper, not too glossy. I have a contact in Bath who does that stuff well, but we should shop around.'

'So how much then?'

Carol looked squarely at him. 'I'll do my bit for one of the paintings.'

'Oh.'

'The printing will cost quite a bit and I don't want to guess.'

'You want one of the paintings?'

'Why not? I'm sure they'll be good.'

'Well yes. They are. But why?'

'Because you're my brother and I'm proud of you. Because I want to be able to say I have the reminder of something special to you. I liked Laura. She was good for you and we always had fun together. Her death is a terrible tragedy and loss. And above all, because I love you.'

After their tetchy reunion and combative discussion, this made James feel renewed warmth and love for his sister. He reached out and took her hand as she carried on.

'It also has the benefit of meaning you can slap a sold sticker on one of the paintings. That can only be encouraging. Also I believe the work you're asking me to do will take up time, effort and expenditure equivalent to what you might be asking for the paintings. I'm not cheap.'

James decided her case was a good one. 'Fine. You can take your pick later on.'

Carol wanted to know more about presentation and location so James talked about how Roger's gallery would be configured. 'His gallery looks small at the front, but there's space at the rear so by using partitioning it's possible to create a lot of discreet areas.'

'So you mean each painting has its own space?'

'No. Some of the works go together and those subsets will need to be closely positioned.'

'Does Roger know the right way to use lighting, ambience and décor?'

'He does. We are aiming for plain, quite rudimentary surroundings.'

'And what about timing? Tell me more.'

He outlined the plan for two private viewings with invited guests. Champagne and canapés for all, plus a brochure containing a condensed version of the packs available to buyers.

'That audience won't see any of the pictures until the scene has been set. During the drinks and nibbles, Roger will deliver an introduction and I'll say a few words about myself. We hope to get someone from the national press to do a more formal overview of the pieces.

Once those sessions are complete, the exhibition will be open to the public and will run for a week; all day, every day. We're targeting press coverage, local and national, as well as leaflet drops locally and if it's not a crazy amount of money, one or two radio adverts. After the initial activity, we will decide how to follow it up, and where, but we plan to run the whole thing again.'

Carol stood, and walked round the table to kiss James on top of his head, cradling it in her arms as she did so.

'Let's get out of here so I can see these paintings. I can't wait any longer.'

29

James handed her a small notebook. 'This is the kind of stuff I want in the brochures. Some of it is sketchy, and I still need to work on several titles.'

'I will help you with that while I'm here. Where are the pictures?'

He pointed at the dining room door. 'Through there; in sequence and ready to go. I think you should look at the picture first, then read the notes.'

'Oh god, stop being so bossy.' Her friendly poke in his side was accompanied by an exchange of smiles.

'Okay, but I'm bossy because I'm really excited; come on.'

They moved to the other room. When she opened the first page of notes Carol saw *Unknown* at the top of the page with a small rectangle below it, filled with scribbled lines. The remainder of the page comprised James' handwritten summary of his picture. When she'd finished reading, Carol looked up to see a large canvas.

A cloudy day and a school playground. The background has vague two and three storey buildings full of windows. Ill-defined crowds of children smeared by green and black clothing fill the canvas. They are running, playing football, reading books, fighting. They mill about in a blur, like speeded up film. A figure, the impression of 'James' rather than a portrait, is sitting at a desk in the middle of this crush. His hands are up to the sides of his face like blinkers on a race horse. He looks straight out of the canvas. A young girl, also an impression of 'Laura', stands close by his left side, pulling at his hand which has a bandage across the knuckles. His face has an expression of grim resignation. He seems older than a schoolboy should be.

'Another bandaged hand.'

'I know.'

'Does it work? Isn't it becoming a predictable motif?'

'Yes, and no.'

'Right. I like the way you show all this activity and the way this character – you I presume – seems to be stuck in time. I find it very grim and forbidding, but it's good.'

'Not too grim?'

'No. The grimness is good. It works.'

They moved together to the next frame, titled *Missed Call*. Carol stared at it intently.

A large, framed mirror set on a plain tiled wall in a well-lit room. The viewer sees 'James' from behind, seated in a large chair as if in a barber's shop. Over one shoulder, the viewer can see 'James' reflection staring back. 'James' holds an old cut-throat razor slightly away from his face. Traces of white foam are streaked around his face and neck, but most of it has gone leaving a lot of tiny cuts and a single quite large wound on his left cheek. Blood trickles from it. Also reflected in the mirror is 'Laura'; slim and elegantly dressed. She is walking away but gazing back towards 'James'.

'You are overdoing the wounds. Seriously. And the character's expression? Will you always look the same? Haven't you grown up yet?'

'I think the wounds are valid. I always have and probably always will. I think the constant use of that imagery really works. And anyway, the end of a relationship feels like a wound or wounds, like a knife slicing you to pieces. I take your point about the face. No, I haven't grown up but this face should look older than the first, in which I wanted to show a prematurely aged young man. Maybe that takes something away from this one. Might need to re-work the first one.'

'I think you should. If they were further apart in the chronology, maybe it wouldn't be so obvious. I also don't fully understand the story here. This is Laura walking away from you. Why?'

'Because I nearly made her. She phoned me that Boxing Day about ten minutes before Sal called. I didn't know what was going on and then her money ran out. But I never tried to find out who she was.'

The viewer sees a seated 'James'. His eyes are lowered and his face appears almost grey from being partially hidden by a hood; but it's possible to see a vivid scar along his left cheek. To his left sits 'Laura', blonde, serene and naked. Her arms are clasped around his shoulders and her left leg is stretched across his torso. All of this is shown against a smoky, charcoal coloured background.

'I like this one, and love the title, *A Wakening*. Really evocative, and in my head creates the sense that, until now, it was just a dream. There's a calmness missing from the first couple but this shows how Laura created that for you and kept you both safe from harm.'

'I wanted to portray her intimacy and my ignorance. But also that I never knew she was there; that everything we had was much more than our nine months together; it was about fifteen years of her wanting me.'

'Yes, I see that. She is making it possible for him to share the intimacy.'

'Yes, exactly.'

They moved along to *That Now Girl*.

A bar scene. Sitting at a table to one side of the room is 'James'. He is clutching a glass and has his head down. Next to him is a telephone. 'Laura' is at the other side of the room, also with a telephone but she is holding the handset and looking beseechingly in his direction. In between them is a shock of colour and movement and crushed up people.

'The way you create the sense of movement and colour is very similar to the one in the school yard. It's clever the way you've achieved that idea that all around is a massive hive of activity but the world stands still for these lovers.'

'I'm actually a bit worried about the similarity to the first one but I like both pictures a lot. When we first met I was still really unsure about what was going on.'

'So this is the first meeting with Laura?'

'The first call, drink together, meeting. If I could have shown a letter somehow, I would have. Beginnings; with doubts; and with no one noticing.'

On the next page of notes, James had scribbled through the word *Entangled*. Instead, the painting had been named *Entwined*.

A stark, black and white painting. No greys, just jet black and snow-white. A series of lines and circles covers the canvas. The lines are either tipped with an arrow or form a cross. The circles are always interlinked.

'Sorry. Nothing in the image conveys what you're saying in the notes. I simply don't see how this projects sex, or sexual happiness.'

James pursed his lips and stammered during his response. 'I wanted to show that our sex life had so much equality. When things went wrong there were no hang-ups or sulks. I really wanted an image for all that and spent hours and hours thinking up this idea. I thought the female/male symbols made sense, especially overlaid. Then I thought it would be better still if they were shown all broken up with no set agenda or form.'

James paused and looked long and hard at his painting. 'It's not very good is it?'

'It's a great painting, technically and in its execution. I just don't think the message is delivered. You've done an amazing piece of work. But it doesn't work.'

James became troubled when the next image, *Look, Listen and Learn* also brought a circumspect response from his sister.

> Two transparent figures, outlines of the images seen in the first four pictures, stand back to back and holding hands on top of a large white cylinder. Entwined around the cylinder are staircases, each with a solid version of the figures climbing to the top. They are taking different routes which occasionally cross or take the same path. Below the point reached by the figures, the stairs are green and have shoots like a beanstalk. Above them, the stairs are black and occasionally blurred.

'This is too clinical and stark, and again it doesn't show what you're saying in your notes. I don't see two people getting to know each other. I see just chaos.'

'The idea is that the bits they've learned about one another have blossomed but there's still plenty to find out. The outstanding stuff is blank; unknown; uncertain. Chaotic.'

'Well my experience of getting to know someone is that it is exciting, warm, and full of potential. That the uncertainty is a nice thing. Positive.'

'Mine isn't. I always dread that there's something terrible round the corner. Until you know the truth and facts the future can only be either blurred, or cause for speculation. Guessing is stupid because you end up building images and notions that can't deliver your dreams.'

Carol shook her head. 'I feel like this one lacks the warmth in some of the others. Those have something like hope in them, even if they are cold. This one is more like a process. And I don't really like the title.'

'Let's call it a working title.' But James was looking at the painting, and the two transparent figures. He felt it was so strong.

They shuffled on to *Eyes Open*.

Similar style and effect as *A Wakening*, except that 'James' is now naked and 'Laura' has more a certain, confident aura. He has his arm around her and is kissing her head. She is snuggled into his side and has her arms around his chest. Both have wry, almost inward facing smiles.

'I like how you've established some balance with the earlier pictures where you use similar characters. It's nicely done; more mature.'

James was less positive. 'Sometimes, I wonder if it's different enough to *A Wakening*. They must show two distinct stages. Every stage needs to be different.'

'Yes; I think it's there. They seem content and together on this. *A Wakening* has more anxiety.'

Carol was constantly reading James' notebook and nodding. Occasionally, she would walk back to a painting earlier in the sequence. They walked together in silence past *Raged Ragged*, *Over-Exposure* and *Free Focus*.

She breathed in as she returned to *Raged Ragged*.

In the top left hand corner, a large square about six inches across. It is a bright crimson colour. In a diagonal line across the canvas, more squares gradually reduce in size until they reach a box about one inch across. Through the course of the graduation, they also become less and less red so that the lower right hand box is orange. This is set against a deep, ochre yellow background.

'Whenever you step off the routine of using those characters, I get lost. Why the need to step in to surrealism.'

James bit his lip. 'It's not surrealism; it's symbolism. It's supposed to show how arguments don't matter in a good relationship. The big box is the anger or indignation of a dogmatic point of view which gets eaten away by the need not to fight; to realise that an argument can be a good thing so long as it eventually fades into the background.'

Carol read the notes and looked again at the painting. 'The idea is too obtuse and the painting too abstract. Will the colours possibly suggest a political leaning?'

'I considered that and just felt any colour could cause a misunderstanding. I simply feel red shows anger and orange is neutral.'

'It's just a splash of colour.'

'Like a lot of arguments.'

'Maybe. Although that's not going to convince me. Ever.' She set off towards the next painting. 'But the good news is that this one, *Over Exposure*, is simply stunning and you've won me back with it.'

James laughed and thanked his sister with a hug.

> The image is of an old style family portrait, like a photograph. This effect is reinforced by monochrome and shades of grey. The group is posed in front of a bookcase that stretches above them and to either side. The faces are anonymous and slightly bland – a mix of age and gender. At either end of the back row two figures are not posing for the photo and, instead, are looking along the line of figures at each other.

'I don't know how you did it, but I could mistake this for an old photo. There's all the subtlety of a good black and white shot.'

'It's a very pleasing piece, but I'm worried it's too bland.'

'The opposite James. You've got it spot on. It's a powerful image of how a family is potentially rigid and unwelcoming; the pose is more important than the reality.'

Again, she moved on to the next picture while she spoke. 'And the pose here, in *Free Focus*, is also brilliantly real although you need a different title because it doesn't do justice to the piece.'

> An aerial view of four people sitting in large armchairs at the four points of an imaginary square. They look in on each other, laughing and openly relaxed. There are two men and two women, and they seem to be of an age despite one of the pairs being wiser looking and more sombrely dressed. The older man is holding a champagne flute.

'Will this and the last one be displayed close together?'

'I think so.'

'Good. They are definitely complimentary. But I think a circle drawn round this scene would work.'

James looked at Carol. 'Why?'

'To show that this was very tight knit. Bill, Angela, Laura and you.'

'Yeah. Maybe.'

'No; really.'

The viewer is presented with another scene of activity and colour. It is a party, or rather, a glimpse in to a single room at a party. There is a table with food and multiple groups of people stand in animated social discourse. 'Laura and James' form part of each group, their figures dressed differently in each case. 'Laura and James' are also leaving and entering the room, also in different clothes.

'You've caught a great mood here. The people all seem so lively. It's also the first time you've shown your characters sharing their joy with others.'

'That's how we felt at your party last year. Whatever was happening, whatever the context, I always felt as if she was next to me.'

'You need a different title though. *True and Deep* is just too Hollywood. Tell me why this next one has no title. And, by the way, the blurring effect is stunning.'

'Laura' is holding a baby in its christening gown, like a Madonna and Child, but with none of the glowing, radiant light from either figure. It is simple and plainly coloured but blurred and hazy, like an unfocused photograph.

'I simply don't know what to call it, maybe because it's so utterly, profoundly personal. When I saw Laura holding Andrew at the christening, she looked perfect. I don't think I ever saw her look more serene and natural. I would have liked for us to be parents. And there was the awful tragedy of her stillborn baby; you could sense that loss in her whenever she was with Andrew, like she had someone to hold at last.'

Carol gave him a sad little smile and held his hand. She looked back at the picture. 'Why don't you call it *The Mother is Born*?'

'Maybe. Yes. Let me have a think. Better still, let me make a note of that in the text.'

'This next one, *Gran Turismo* is funny. I love how you've portrayed tourists as sheep.'

An aeroplane stands on tarmac. In the background an arid, barren, brown landscape with a single squat building nearby. The sky is white with heat. A line of sheep, walking in twos, has descended from the plane. Sheep dogs with guns and sunglasses guard their way. On the steps, at the end of the line, are two black sheep.

She laughed; 'I truly don't know whether to admire the modesty or the arrogance but it is a terribly funny idea.'

'This was the first one I did. It was Laura's idea.'

'Really?'

'Yes. She mentioned it to me as we left the plane at Chania. At one point, she bleated so loudly and authentically it caused mild panic.'

Carol spent some time looking at *As Long As*.

A vague, dreamy view of a seaside: cliffs; an arc of golden white sand; azure water. In the centre of the beach, a couple lie on towels. It seems very ordinary but the effect of the colouring, the figures and the graduation of sands into water also creates the impression of an enormous circle. A huge ring, half in water, half on earth. At its head, amethysts.

'Why isn't there any description in the notes? I don't understand. There's a couple lying on a beach, but so what?'

'You can't see that it's a huge ring, with jewels?'

'No. What do you mean?'

'The arc of the sand is supposed to be a sweep of white gold and the couple lying there the amethysts of our engagement ring.'

She drew her breath in so sharply that James thought she was going to cry. 'Oh no; I'm so sorry; it's obvious now. I feel bad.'

He told his sister not to feel she was wrong or mistaken. But James felt discomfort that, not for the first time, Carol simply didn't get what he meant. As he reviewed these feelings, she started talking about the next painting.

'What's important is that this next one, *...we both* is located right next to *As Long As....* – they complement each other.'

Two hands are shown clasped tightly. The hands are drawn in minute detail. One has glossed nails and smooth, slender fingers. This smaller hand has a large, bejewelled ring on it. The other hand is rougher, small hairs are tufted along the fingers and back of the hand. Its nails are chipped and chewed. The hands are bound at the wrists with a bloody bandage. Surrounding this central image are dozens of pairs of other hands clapping.

Carol stood and gazed at the picture. 'It's like a cartoon or a poster.'

'Yes, but that's entirely accidental.'

'I was surprised when you two got engaged. You always seemed so equivocal about marriage. And it seemed to be so soon after you'd met.'

'In the end it was impossible not to propose. It made our last few weeks together perfect. But that was inward. Externally, all that seemed to happen was a stream of congratulations. It all became incredibly public; incredibly owned. The removal of our privacy.'

'So this isn't a celebration of the decision?'

'Not really. It's more a portrayal of its lack of meaning to anyone but us.'

Over the course of the next few paintings, Carol become sombre, then quiet. In *Newsflash*, a series of clocks revealed time moving forward with other details slowly disappearing. An untitled piece presented a road stretching away into the distance towards a fork; the right hand road continued off into the sunset, but the left ended abruptly shortly after the fork.

'This is becoming sad and I think I need a drink.

'We can leave till the morning if you like?'

'No, I want to see them all now – this evening. But maybe a drink and smoke will settle me.'

They returned to the kitchen and James made a couple of gins. As he sliced up some lemon he said, 'Can I ask you something?'

'Yes, of course.'

'It might not be easy to answer. But I want you to be truthful.'

'I will. Go on.'

'If you're unsettled, is it because of the content and storyline? Or simply because of your intimacy with the subject?'

They moved outside for a cigarette and Carol stood silent for a moment or two, inhaling smoke.

'Can't say. Can't divorce myself from knowing it all. Can't think like someone who is simply viewing the pieces. I know the facts which makes it difficult not to be moved. But I'd be moved without the paintings. And vice versa. I think.'

'Very articulate.'

Carol smiled at him and stubbed out her cigarette. 'I'm going back inside to start again from the beginning. Finish your drink out here. I want my own space to look at everything up to *Newflash*.'

James watched her walk away and lit another cigarette. He remained alone for so long that he decided to see whether Carol had fallen asleep somewhere.

He found her standing looking at *Newsflash*.

She seemed not to notice James' reappearance and moved, in a sideways shuffle, to the next painting and its fork in the road.

'Oh hello. You know, *Newsflash* is another brilliant piece. There's so much depth in the light and shade. And now I've walked through from start to here, it's tough because I know it's leading to the accident. James, this is beginning to make me feel so sad.'

'Art does that to people. It always has to me.'

'Don't make fun of me. I'm really not happy with seeing all this: being reminded how horrible it all was. I think I'd like to look at the rest on my own. Do you mind?'

'I don't mind.'

'There are three more pictures. Come back in twenty minutes with another drink.'

He left her gazing at *Smashed*.

A bed floats in a pool of blood red. On it, shattered body parts lie in a random assortment. It is macabre, like something from a horror film. Around the bed float tyres and lumps of wreckage with doctors and nurses clinging to them. There is machinery and equipment high up on the walls, out of reach and untouchable.

When he returned, Carol had been crying and seemed to be shaken. James set down the small tray of drinks and sweets he'd prepared and stroked her arm. She took his hand and led him back to *Smashed*.

'This is a shocking image. Brutal; macabre, like something from a horror film and it really troubled me.'

'Because of its horror?'

'Partially. But also because it's the first picture in which there is a quite profound sense that this is about death.'

'Is it too shocking?'

'No. Not at all. But it needs to be carefully staged and managed when you exhibit it.'

'Why?'

'As well as the bloody mess and wreckage it portrays, all those doctors and nurses clinging onto life rafts, unable to get to the machinery and equipment that is up on the walls, out of reach and untouchable – it's quite overtly political.'

'Really?'

'I think so. It looks like you're having a real pop at the state of the NHS.'

'Well it's not meant to, but I'm happy for that to be a subplot.'

Carol had a very doubting expression. 'It's fine if you understand, on a personal basis, the horror of what Laura went through as a shattered victim, irreparable and smashed – which, by the way, is another brilliant title. But I think the first thing people are going to think is that you've taken a step out of the story line to have a go at the Tories.'

'No bad thing.'

'It might be for the credibility of your exhibition. There's nothing in it that offends politically until now. You could get some backs up.'

'But I think it's so strong. The idea that they were powerless to stop her death. That no technology or treatment in the world could save her. That they were drowning in her blood.'

'There must be a way of saying that but making it less like a protest.'

James doubted it and decided to stand up for what he'd done.

'You know something? I don't care. If it winds people up, then maybe it should. I can't spend my life worrying about causing offence. Otherwise I'd never do anything.'

Carol giggled. 'Bravo. Excellent defence. And this next piece, *Line Out* is magnificent. It's the best of the set. It's left me feeling that you've tied everything up so brilliantly. You're no longer a transparency. These pictures, even the ones where I don't necessarily get it, have completed you. Haven't they?'

James nodded and looked at *Line Out*. It was his favourite too.

Garish in black and white. A line of coffins on a conveyor belt. At one end a coffin is dropping into a pit. At the opposite end a priest stands next to a huge lever shaped like a cross and on which his hand is resting. In front of him the conveyor belt is on the verge of producing another coffin. On the belt, immediately in front of the cleric, is a coffin with a small silvery plaque on top. Wispy images of mourners, holding books and looking downwards, stand all around like sentries.

Carol was flipping pages to and fro in the notebook, then read for a moment. 'So where's the last one, *Judge Mental* according to your notes? Where's the actual picture?'

James went to another room and returned with a canvas.

'James' lies naked on the floor of a court room. He is chained to the chair wherein 'Laura' sits in pale and ghostly judgement. In the background, a jury of women dressed alternately in green and red sits pointing at 'James'. They are lit by powerful beams emanating from undefined sources. All around are panelled walls and barred windows but these can only really be made out if the viewer actually looks for them.

'Is this supposed to be heaven or something?'

James breathed in deeply. 'No. The night of Laura's funeral, I had this dream. It was creepy. I heard various women in my life – Mum, you, Sally and others – give their views about me: one positive; the other negative. It was not comforting but it ended with Laura, perhaps Laura's ghost, saying it didn't matter. None of it... fucking... mattered.'

Carol looked from the painting to her brother repeatedly as he said all this. 'What did I say?'

'That we were and are such good friends.'

'And?'

'That you control me.'

Now she stared at him. 'And which is true? Which is the one that matters?'

He looked at the still unfinished painting. 'I don't know.'

30

By mid-August James had been in France for five months. He had worked incredibly hard but the lack of intrusion had made it seem easy. Ideas flowed quickly and were soon either converted to finished product or rejected. He'd been focused on completion rather than contemplation and, with no external framework, he quickly knew what was good and what was not.

James had no concept of whether it was right or proper for someone to create so much so quickly. He'd always worked with haste but in this recent process he'd felt more certain about his decision making. He adopted a freedom to abandon anything that didn't fit and had no guilt when he did. He also never looked back with regret on any rejection. There was so much to do and he just got on with it.

It never once occurred to him that this was now his day job.

After Carol's visit James undertook a lot of rework. Several changes were basic, others more significant, but nothing was removed. He used his sister's observations and what he had seen in her unspoken reactions as the motivation for change and it left him with what felt like a finished body of work. All that remained was tinkering, a phase that was now complete.

There was a deadline for him to leave the villa – Friday, September 13th – for Bill and Angela were scheduled to arrive that weekend with numerous guests. Regrettably, James had agreed with Bill and Jean that it was not possible for him to have even a brief overlap with the Drysdales. He had too much clutter that needed to be removed so the villa could be given a thorough clean and tidy.

Now he was finished, several switches flicked off causing James to grow tired, anxious and lonely. The work he'd done was supposed to have purged not only his grief but also his chronic underachievement. Yet now he prowled around the villa hissing a frustrated commentary to himself. One-sided conversations in which he berated himself for being pretentious, talentless and a charlatan.

He knew what was wrong and he knew that the solution was more work; a different subject; a new direction. But instead of putting money in the meter to renew his energy and self-esteem, he chose a different route.

James lapsed in to a lamentable mode of behaviour: drinking and smoking hard; staying up past midnight listening to music or watching videos; the cessation of any physical activity; and eating large portions of bad things. His release from all the exertion and creativity was probably a good thing. His reaction to that freedom was a massive backward step.

This wasn't helped by a disquiet about money. His travellers' cheques had run out and his supply of cash was dwindling. He had money in the bank and money owed to him from sales, but he had no access to it. His plan should have covered some sort of financial back-up, but that was a gaping hole in what he'd set out to do.

One night he lay awake fretting about all this and how, with no money, he would get his pictures out of France. He couldn't carry them by train, even if he could afford to buy a ticket. If he got them to a port, he didn't know what he would need to prove he was the artist and owner. He'd heard horror stories about French bureaucracy and soon fashioned a crisis in which customs officials, police and secret service agents were chasing him from Calais across countries and continents. This pursuit was joined by an increasingly large number of executives.

James was a fugitive, above all from reason.

In a paranoid blind panic he phoned Roger, who didn't welcome a call at two in the morning. Despite this frustration, Roger managed to soothe James' fears and instructed him to go back to bed and sleep. As the conversation ended, James felt marginally reassured that someone was in control. That comfort became real when, several days later, a letter arrived from England containing ten 200-franc banknotes between a neatly folded sheet of writing paper. Roger's handwriting covered both sides of the paper.

The sight of the money caused a whoop of approval and James fanned it in front of him before he read the letter. Roger was bringing a van and some paperwork to facilitate the return trip with James' pictures. He asked James to call him with directions and to confirm he could stay one night at the villa. Roger finished off with news that four more works had been sold; that fact made the exhibition an essential event. He'd been hugely impressed by Carol's photos and was excited about James' future.

With money in his pocket, James took the opportunity to redouble his poor lifestyle choices, lost dignity and gained weight.

Roger arrived on the Wednesday before James' scheduled departure. He bore goodies: cigarettes and alcohol; chocolates; a loving note from Carol; and a lot more cash. Without preamble he told James he was desperate to see the pictures and they spent the next three hours reviewing them together.

During this inspection Roger didn't say much. Occasionally he asked a question about technique, or how James had achieved something. After walking around the pieces several times, and reading the now complete notes in James' book, Roger held out his hand to James in congratulation and praise.

This boost to his morale was temporary and, by the time they sat down to enjoy some food and wine, James revealed the almost total loss of confidence in all he'd created and with the whole idea of an exhibition. At last James had an audience so he trawled up a backlog of dismay: he could see nothing in his work that could be of interest to anyone; it was small, self-indulgent, charmless and dark; it lacked inspiration because it was contrived.

They sat up in to the early hours; James drinking and rambling; Roger patiently and skilfully countering each complication. James ended up drunk and embittered, eventually falling asleep in his armchair but not before a closing proclamation that he wanted no exhibition.

The following morning, before James could dredge up more

gloom, Roger hit him with an unexpected change of plan. 'You've obviously worked hard and you need to recharge. You look and sound flattened by emotional, physical and spiritual effort. You also look terrible, you're obviously drinking too much and smoking as if you want it to kill you. I don't like this air of defeat and silly notions of worth.'

James started to summon an objection, but Roger sustained his rallying cry.

'Since I got here, you've been a pain in the arse James. I've not heard a single good thing from you. No original thought or witty remark. No small thing that might be a grand idea. I've come to expect that of you and I can't believe it isn't still within you. The negative, destructive shadow I'm looking at could not possibly have devised, planned and executed that extraordinary set of pictures.'

Again, James tried to interject with a barrier; Roger was relentless.

'So I want you to take a holiday. Don't come back with me. Instead, pack up some essentials and absolutely no brushes or pencils or paper. I'll take everything else home for you. I'm going to take you to Lyon and you can be necking Kronenbourg on the Cote d'Azur by tea time.'

James still fought this. He wriggled and squirmed and whinged like a small boy trying to escape a haircut or trip to the dentist. Roger wore him down with evocations of the Med and Provence; the legendary light that had inspired artists since time immemorial; long warm days with dreamy sunsets; beautiful women; bouillabaisse on the seafront at Villefranche; nothing to do except soak it all in.

And he had a trump card. 'I phoned my friends Penny and Yves this morning while you were still snoring and farting in that chair. They live in Fréjus on the Cote d'Azur and have a small apartment in the town. It's free now, and for the whole of the next three weeks, and they'd be delighted to meet you. It's a wonderful opportunity.'

'I can't possibly go.'

'You absolutely can. And you will.'

James didn't seem convinced but his excuses were feeble and vapid. By the time they were carefully packing his pictures to load in to the van, James had lost the argument.

When everything was cleared, and James knew he was ready to leave, he called Jean. The Pannets soon arrived at the villa to say *au revoir* and to hug *Crazy Gems*.

And that was it: all over; all done; James was moving on again. Roger drove them away to the east, with several hours to review what was to come.

The outline for the exhibition that James had revealed to Carol was unchanged and Roger confirmed that he had already lined up a lot of guests for the private viewings.

James wanted to know some details. 'Tell me what Carol has been helping you with.'

'When she brought me the photos, she mentioned that she could help out: with lighting; moods; layout. So that's been good. She's very enthusiastic; she loves what you've done. Is it true you've sold her one?'

'She said she wants one as payment for her work on the brochures.'

'I'd give her cash.'

Roger looked across at James and saw something in his expression. 'Is there a problem with Carol?'

'No. Maybe. You surprised me there. I wasn't sure how much she would help. There was some friction when she was here. I'm not sure what I want from her.'

'Well you need to tell her. Don't make that my problem.'

Many miles passed in silence. James watched the scenery rolling by. 'Did you follow the flow in the sequence?'

'Absolutely. I thought I did from the photos but the real thing proved it. And the order is important to the set up in the gallery. What I want to achieve is that when people arrive at the opening events they won't be able to see anything. The food and drink can be there and, once we're ready, I'll welcome everyone and do an introduction. Can't make my mind up about whether you should say something at the start. I'm confident I've got an important guest lined up to give an appraisal, not of the exhibited pieces, but of other things you've done.

So two, perhaps three speeches, taking up no more than ten minutes, and then we let them set off in twos and threes. We don't want them all cluttering round each painting in turn and we can't have them marching round out of sequence. You'll have to be available to talk to anyone who wants a word.'

James signalled a service station ahead. He needed a piss and a smoke, neither of which Roger would allow in the van. They grabbed a coffee too.

'Once that first weekend is done, I'm expecting two things: a sale, because a sold sticker will be a huge temptation; and some positive words in the press, possibly on local radio. This depends on how much PR we can generate between now and D-Day. I'm selling your existing stuff, mostly to punters but a couple have gone to good homes. That's not enough though and Carol suggested we need some sort of campaign to advertise what we're doing.'

'I'm confused. When Carol and I spoke about her buying one of the pictures in lieu of fees, she pointed out that it would mean a sold sticker on something right from the start. Isn't that the same as you're saying?'

Roger became silent. James repeated his question.

'I'm thinking about it James. I suppose she's right. I was just thinking I'd like the buyer to be someone who attends one of the opening events.'

'Seems to me it's the same impact, except it exists from day one instead of day three.'

'Agreed. In which case, sold to the lady from Bath.'

James sensed Roger still wasn't persuaded by the idea, but now he had other worries. 'And what about me? What am I doing? What's my role between now and the exhibition?'

'I think that is what we need to work on, and it's what Carol meant about having a campaign. I believe we need posters advertising you, the gallery and the exhibition. I'd like to get you doing an interview in the local rag. If I can swing it that might get passed on to a national.'

'Is it real? Or a wish list? I know I'm not happy or easy right now, but this all seems too difficult.'

'Yes it's difficult and yes there is a lot to do. But you have no *do nothing* option.'

'Okay, but how will you swing it for something to be in the national press?'

'I've got contacts in the critic community. One says he's definitely coming.'

'Right.'

Roger resumed his dialogue about logistics and expectations but his enthusiasm wasn't contagious. James dozed off and slept which made him marginally grumpier when he woke up.

'I don't understand what you want me to do during the two events. Nor once it's all public.'

'I want you to be there. You're the artist; talk to people; confront them with the reality of your work.'

'To justify it?'

'If necessary.'

'And what if people want to criticise or nit-pick?'

'You're scared.'

'I lack confidence and conviction. Perhaps if I'd had formal training, at Art College or something, I might have some certainty to fall back on. So yes, I'm scared.'

'Don't be. You're the one with the answers. If someone wants to question things, or impose meanings, it's really simple: you know the truth. All you have to do is stand by it.'

As they slowed to navigate in to the centre of Lyon Roger took the time to restate all he believed about James' work and how it would be exhibited. As they pulled up outside the railway station, he concluded: 'This is where we say goodbye for now. Get out of this van, get on the first train south, have a break, have a rest and stop thinking. Be a tourist and be happy. And give my love to Penny and Yves. You've got everything? The address and phone number, money, passport?'

James patted pockets and nodded before hauling his rucksack from the cab. 'Look, Roger, I don't want to be like this. It's just how I am. You understand.'

'Of course I do. I honestly haven't taken any notice of anything you've said. So just get your head around the fact that this is worth doing. It's a small, modest beginning, but you're worth it.'

'When do you want me back in England?'

'I'll call you. For now, just leave everything with me. Carol is helping. You can relax and forget about all you've done and what will happen to it. And cut down on the cigarettes and drinking okay?'

'I'll try. See you whenever.'

He climbed out of the van, slammed the door then thumped the side and headed in to the station. There wasn't long to wait, but enough time to make a call. He found a public telephone, dialled the United Kingdom country code and then a London number.

'Hello?'

'Hello Philippa.'

'James. Where are you?'

'I'm in transit. Listen; how do you fancy a holiday?'

He slept throughout the journey south, arrived in Marseille St. Charles feeling refreshed and was soon on another train bound for Fréjus. It was virtually deserted and, when he arrived there, so was Fréjus station. He walked along the route Roger had explained to him and arrived at the designated building to be confronted by six bell buttons each with a scribbled word alongside it; the occupiers' names, he assumed. None said *Penny et Yves*.

James was almost defeated by this, as if it left him shipwrecked. He looked around the street and its parked cars. Why hadn't Roger told him a surname? Or a flat number? Tutting and sighing, he scanned the list of names again; one said *Desmargues, Y.*

It wasn't long before a woman opened the main door and greeted him with a kiss on the cheek. 'Hello, you must be James. I'm Penny Desmargues, Roger's friend. It's wonderful to meet you.'

She was English, blonde, tanned; older than James; the opposite of chic, yet immensely beautiful. She spoke with minute inflections of a French accent.

'Yes, I'm James. Good to meet you too, and thanks for having me. How are you?'

Penny invited him in to the foyer then led him up two flights of stairs. She explained that Yves had been unable to be with them due to a work commitment, but hoped to meet James the following evening when he was invited to dinner.

James accepted as they stepped in to Flat 4.

He was shown round the apartment: a living room; a kitchen/dining room; two bedrooms; and a bathroom. After the luxury of the Drysdale's villa there was a perfect simplicity in this place. Penny also indicated food in the fridge; enough for a meal that evening and the next day's breakfast. There were also a four pack of beer cans and bottle of wine. She used a street map to give directions to shops, banks and other facilities, then pointed to the best beaches and warned against certain bars in the town. James was free to stay as long as he chose and there was no question of him making any form of payment. A friend of Roger's is a guest, not a customer.

'It really is wonderful to meet you James, and we're both looking forward to hearing all about your paintings. Yves and I are very excited about having such talent in our home.' She smiled gorgeously at him.

'Well I hope I don't disappoint. May I ask something?'

'Of course. What is it?'

'Is there a problem if someone joins me here?'

'No problem whatsoever. The flat is at your disposal.'

'My friend, Philippa, will be here tomorrow; if flights work out okay.'

'From where? London?'

'Yes. I'm not sure which airport.'

'From Heathrow or Gatwick she will come to either Nice or Marseille. Nice is closer, but both are easy to reach from here.

Call me when you know and I will explain how to get there. Then you must bring Philippa with you tomorrow evening. That will be lovely. Oh, but please don't dress up; either of you. We will be informal, and so must you.'

This hospitality continued to ring in his ears for several moments after Penny handed him the keys and let herself out.

After choosing the smaller of the two bedrooms, he showered and changed in to a T shirt and shorts. From the fridge he took a ready meal and followed the instructions for cooking it in the oven, then opened a bottle of beer and sat to read a tourist guide. After eating the lasagne, and washing it down with a couple of glasses of Provençal rosé, James felt tired and soon went to bed where, away from his dreams, he slept deeply and didn't wake until a phone rang somewhere.

31
In the Beginning

It was Roger. 'Settled in?'

'Yes. Just had the best night's sleep since I don't know when. I can't thank you enough for making this possible.'

'How are Penny and Yves?'

'Haven't met Yves. Penny got me settled in here. She's lovely and we're having dinner this evening. With Yves, obviously. How was your trip?'

'Sundays on French motorways are a doddle; caught an earlier ferry than expected. It's good to hear you sounding relaxed. Keep being like that and don't worry about things here. Will you be all right on your own?'

'Well a friend, Philippa, is coming to join me. You haven't met her.'

'Excellent. It'll keep your mind off the exhibition.'

'It might. No, it will. We'll have fun. But Roger, please keep that to yourself. Please don't mention Philippa to Carol, okay?'

'Sure. No problem. I must go. I've lots to do.'

'Right. Roger?'

'Yes James?'

'Thanks.'

'No problem.'

'No, listen. Everything you've done has been brilliant. I've never had this kind of support before. I won't forget it.'

'Right.'

'And forgive all my whining the other day.'

'You just look after yourself, lie in the sun, dance and laugh, do naughty things with your woman and come back here to win some hearts and minds. It's not hard. You have the ability.'

James' face darkened to a frown. Thoughts of his pictures made him want to see them. After just twenty four hours without them he sensed loss. He was sure they were poor and worthless, but without them to hand he couldn't confirm it.

He concluded he wanted them close as a reminder of how much he hated them.

James prowled the flat looking for a pencil and some paper. He found a small notepad and one of those pens with four different coloured inks. A few seconds of clicking and scratching indicated that only the blue one worked.

In around twenty minutes he'd sketched a version of one of his paintings: the two people climbing a cylinder of life. The blue lines made it stark but he set it in front of him and stared at the drawing. Small, inky stick versions of Laura and James were moving up the tower.

James realised this was not a good copy of the original.

For several moments he tried, in his mind's eye, to transform it to the full painting. When he failed to conjure it, he snatched the sketch from the table. With the paper held in both hands he spat into the centre, folded it in half and smeared his saliva till it covered as much of the sheet as possible. Then he unfolded it and put it back on the table. It lay soggily glum in front of him. The lines were blurred, the overall image ill-defined.

In this state, James felt it looked right.

He got more paper and set about penning another facsimile picture, upon which he fully intended to spit. As he put pen to paper, the phone rang again.

It was Philippa, in a rush: she was at Gatwick; she was booked on a flight to Nice, landing at quarter to four; would he collect her as she had no idea where Fréjus is?

He said he'd meet her at the airport and couldn't wait to see her. She laughed and said she was missing him like crazy.

He called Penny to learn how to get to Nice airport and how long it would take. When he returned to the living room, his defaced drawing was no longer on the table. Breeze from an open window had wafted it to the floor, where it flapped like a giant dying butterfly.

There was plenty of time, but James set off. It was a hot day and fifteen minutes of walking made him sweaty. When he reached Fréjus station, he bought two return tickets then a cold beer at the café. He downed it in two gulps and ordered a second which he carried on to the train when it arrived.

He had lied to Carol about visitors to the villa. It was true that Bill had been one, but Philippa had travelled to be with him about two months after his arrival. During her visit they became lovers. Something clicked in to place and, for the week she was with him, James felt they had always been a couple; always been in love; always been one.

The last he had seen of her was an arm waving forlornly from her hire car window as she left for the airport. It made him more upset than he had been at any time since Laura's death. He was so distracted that he seriously thought of packing up and following Philippa home. But there was work to do and James had impetus to complete it. Philippa's comments, feedback and thoughts about the pictures he'd done to that point made James work even harder. New ideas consumed him. He was possessed and felt driven.

Another train blasted past in the opposite direction, making him start but the train's lurching and rolling soon lulled him to sleep. When he woke up the train was stationary in the wrong place; James was at the Nice-Ville station, miles from the airport. After a minor bout of dread-induced indecision, he rushed to the taxi rank and was soon in a car driven by a villainous man who shouted constantly at his surroundings, at other drivers and at pedestrians. He also called James *chef*, which he absolutely loved.

At the airport, James stood in the oppressive warmth of the arrivals area wondering what he would say to Philippa and how to eradicate his horrible body odour. Her plane was on time but he was early, so James was able to calm down and get cool. Several weeks of poor care and attention had made him overweight and unfit. Relatively minor exertion was a struggle and made him sweaty and breathless, the inevitable consequence of consuming the wrong things and taking no exercise.

With change in mind, he bought a bottle of Évian from a machine and drank it sitting on the floor in the lotus position.

When the arrivals screen showed the Gatwick flight had landed, he moved near to the door where passengers would emerge. James sipped at his water, making a mental countdown of the processes she'd be going through: the futile rush to leave the plane; mistrust and contempt at passport control; the confused search for baggage collection and a trolley; standing helpless by a static conveyor belt; the lurch of joy as the belt starts moving and bags appear; the rising terror that your bags are in Tristan da Cunha. He clicked and ticked through this conceptual timer and, at the precise moment he expected her to appear, flicked his fingers and pointed at the doors. They remained shut.

Ten minutes later, the doors parted. Among a crowd of people, he saw Philippa pushing a trolley laden with a sports bag, a large suitcase, a handbag and a carrier. She smiled when she saw him, almost to herself.

James rushed to greet her and take the trolley, but she stopped and grabbed him in an enormous, breath-stealing squeeze.

'James, my love. You look awful and smell worse. What have you been doing?'

'I've missed you so much Philippa.'

'I've missed you too babe.' She looked him up and down. 'You're fat; and not just a little. Have you been washing?'

311

He shook his head sheepishly. Philippa hugged him some more then gave him a deep, passionate kiss.

'I didn't expect you to kiss me.'

'Why?'

'Because I stink.'

'You do. And when I kiss you, I can't smell you.'

James chortled. 'You better kiss me again then.'

They stood welded to each other for several minutes.

'Why on earth are we here?'

'I'll tell you later. Your journey isn't over yet.' James explained that there was a train to catch.

'No, I'll hire a car. I've brought wealth beyond your feverish imagination and intend to spend it all as this is my last chance for a holiday this year. I'm happy to spend it on you too, if you can get clean.'

James laughed; 'Great, then let's hire a Ferrari. I'll drive'

'You're banned, from recollection, and anyway I want a car not a fanny magnet. A nice little Renault or Citroen will do. Something French; something with joie de vivre.'

Once they were on the autoroute back to Fréjus, with the rear windows wide open to counteract the heat and malodourous James, Philippa put her hand on his leg and started asking questions. They were shouting to offset the wind and traffic noise.

'Come on then; why are we meeting again in another strange place?'

'Roger came over to take the pictures back to England. He arranged for me to have a break here.'

'I see. Do you trust Roger with your paintings?'

'That's a strange question. Of course I do; he's doing good for me.'

'And why did you stop calling me?'

'I don't know.'

'That won't do James.'

'I know I should have. I know I wanted to; I really wanted to. I nearly came back after you left. I was so miserable. But the work kind of took hold of me.'

'That's a much better answer. Thank you.'

'You're welcome.'

He glanced across at her. 'And why did you stop calling me?'

'Mainly because you didn't call me.'

'Childish.'

'Yes. But also, and more to the point, because I knew that I would be disturbing something that I had no business to interrupt.'

They had been speaking a great deal, three or four times a week, in the immediate aftermath of James' move to France. It became something they both relied upon and formed a bond that ended with Philippa's visit to Sorges.

'While we were together, I realised how important it was for you to be alone. After I got back, I wanted to talk, and see you – god I wanted to see you and hold you – but it felt like I had to leave you to do what you needed to do. I was miserable too. I never thought you'd do this to me again.'

'Again?'

'Yes again. Of course again.'

She looked across at him with an expression that catapulted James back to the time they'd met on her first day at his school. But now she didn't have to smile coyly and rush away to a lesson; and now he didn't have to regret that she was someone else's girlfriend and walk away, kicking stones.

It didn't take long to get back to Fréjus and, once inside the apartment, it also didn't take long for Philippa to grasp him and start pulling off his clothes, which he reciprocated. As that situation escalated, they whispered how much they'd missed each other, how much they wanted each other, how much they loved each other. They asked why they had to be apart, whether they could ever again go so long without each other. Questions without answers, and this minor orgy moved crab-like along the hallway to the sitting room and soon ended in a sweaty mess on an inadequate armchair.

Later, sated and washed clean, they lay together. Philippa was still asking questions; 'Where are you taking me for dinner tonight?'

'Well, we are invited to dinner with our hosts, Penny and Yves.'

'Where do they live?'

'I'm not sure but not far. Penny will be picking us up at eight thirty.'

'Why did you ask me to join you here?'

'I can't believe you're asking that.'

'Let me say it another way: I meant that I'm surprised you asked me. Don't you need a complete break; alone; to re-charge?'

'No, the exact opposite. I had to see you. Had to put our lack of communications and togetherness right.'

Philippa leaned over so her head was resting on the left side of his chest. With an index finger she traced lines on his stomach, sometimes pushing it to make it wobble. 'So we're here all alone for two weeks?'

'Yes we are. Is that a problem?'

'I'm asking the questions.'

'That's what you said that night at Gerry and Gra's.'

'It's still true. It will always be true. And after we're finished here: what then?'

'I want to travel back with you. Don't want to wave goodbye again.'

'No, me neither.' She bit him on the pectoral.

'Owww; that really fucking hurt.'

'So did not knowing what I'd done wrong for you to make no effort to contact me after I was with you in May. Everything fell in to place, and I finally and utterly fell in love with you that week. The complete works, and when I got home it was awful being without you, despite what I said in the car. Shivering through mornings and evenings waiting for the phone to ring or the letter box to rattle. Yearning for long, long conversations at night when I got home from work but just having silence. Silence I had to fill with songs – an endless list. There were no happy, hopeful songs.'

She stopped, as if wondering whether to continue.

'You know something? I've never told you this. I always had an our song: Thin Lizzy's *Still in Love with You*, from *Live and Dangerous*. It wasn't because you and I had found and lost each other back then, but because even though we were never boy and girlfriend, I always thought we should be, one day. So I listened to it then, and I have listened to it constantly since May. It was always about you but I was just never sure how or when to show it. I think I was too proud and somehow I'd got it into my head that you were so insufferably arrogant that the last thing you needed was extra help from another adoring woman. To make you god's biggest gift.'

She dug her finger nail in to his side, but it was a half-hearted assault.

'When I wasn't listening to music, I was writing it; songs and piano pieces; things to develop and sell. I tried to avoid making you the subject matter, but couldn't stop myself and I wrote this song called *Here and There*. The first lines go:

There you are on your own,
Here am I all alone,
Both gazing back on a lost appeal,
Finding something false is real.

I've never, ever written crap like that before and the music was dreary. My music has always been about having purpose, not about emotional outpourings.

Our time in Sorges utterly transformed me. I felt you had validated me in every way and that literally nothing was the same as it was before I arrived. I felt surrendered; sexually; emotionally; every way. After all this time, I was yours and you can't begin to understand how much that scared me. I think I'm strong and a woman who doesn't need that stereotypical moon-in-June bullshit about being in love. I was never willing to be someone's little woman or safe bet. But how I felt about you smashed the rules. I was totally derailed. I couldn't concentrate on anything and was constantly, irretrievably preoccupied. Kept feeling sick; lost my appetite; lost ten pounds. My whole system was on overdrive, with masses of energy being burned; but on nothing.

Being together, being part of a couple with you feels amazing. I want to care for you and be there for you – all the things my independent upbringing warned against. It's completely wrong, but when we're together I really don't need anything or anyone else. Can a wrong be right? In Sorges, it seemed like we were really one person, or maybe two halves of the same person. Our lovemaking was almost sacred, as if it could only ever have been what we were made for. That week left me feeling that no matter how much love I give to you, I know I'm not losing any of myself. That it's perfect. That we're perfect.

It was never like this with Adrian, and that lasted five years and nearly killed me when it ended. Nor with anyone else. And now you've done it again, James Clifton, and made me cry.'

She turned her face further in to his chest and he could feel her eyelashes brushing tears on his skin.

'When have I made you cry before now?'

Her reply was a muffled noise; 'I'm asking the questions.'

He sighed. 'I know. Yes. Let's try it another way then. You're being ridiculous; I've never made you cry.'

She lifted her head to look at him with bleary, fiery eyes. 'Five times, James Clifton. Five times.'

'I don't believe you.'

'Late 1977, when I finished with Leo; I felt like shit, and all I wanted was someone to hug me and justify what I'd done. But all you could say was I was a bitch for destroying your friend. I'd been there for you, when Sarah left you. But you weren't there for me.'

'I see.'

'Don't speak. February 1978: I went to a party; somewhere

in the country – one of those desperate village-hall-hoedown ones. I fully intended to let you get off with me because your constant chipping away had started to work. I wore new clothes and especially alluring make up. When I got there, you were already drunk and upside down in the back seat of someone's car. Useless.'

'What a twat I was.'

'Shut up. I mean it. I can start biting again.'

James' face signalled compliance.

'1990, when Laura told me about how you'd proposed to her. We were all in your flat and I'd been split up from Adrian for a matter of days. I ended up having to put such a brave face on it. I cried a bit while we were there together, and it honestly was because I was genuinely happy for you and Laura. The tears were for both of you. It was the best possible news and a tonic for me after what had happened. But there was this little voice in my head saying that I had lost you for ever. And I couldn't stand that I felt that way. You and Laura left me at the tube, and I watched you go and I just thought *there goes my oldest friend with my oldest friend and one of them is the man I want.* When I got home, I just broke down; crying because I was such a bastard.'

'Please let me say something.'

'No. 1991: about four months ago. We had that sublime week and finally we'd connected and I knew we'd be together. After I'd been home a week, you'd neither called, nor written, nor shown up. I spent time every day convincing myself the whole thing was fine; you needed space to do your pictures; you'd find time to call. But you didn't. One evening I got in from work and just wept, like a broken-hearted teen.'

'Shall I bite myself now?'

Philippa laughed. 'No, wait. 1991, about ten minutes ago; because I tell you I'm crazy in love with you even though you look and smell like shit and couldn't get a hard-on in the shower.'

James made to speak.

'I haven't said you can say anything yet James. It will never happen again. Ever. For these two weeks we are going to put right everything that is wrong in your head so I can return to some sort of normality and be in love with someone who completely understands the implications of what my love means.'

James waited a moment, wondering if there was more. He made a small noise, like the start of a word, and wasn't told to be quiet.

'I've got something to say now.'

'Go on.'

'I was in love with Laura and wanted to spend the rest of my life with her. But I was a bastard too: when I heard you and Adrian had split up, I was glad.'

'What?'

'I was. Aside from the fact I thought he sounded like a wanker, and completely beneath you, I just still felt this draw towards you; like I've always felt. I shouldn't have, because of Laura, but I did.'

Philippa chewed on the inside of her cheek. 'Bloody hell James; this is dreadful. We're both twisted as fuck.'

'No, we're not. Because despite those thoughts and feelings, nothing changed. No action was taken.'

'Even so, it's shocking. I can't even take the moral high ground.'

She bit him again, hard, on the top of his shoulder then lay back. He didn't react despite the pain she'd caused.

'Tell me about the exhibition. No; first tell me about the stuff you've done since I was with you in Sorges.'

James retrieved his notebook from another room. 'It's all in here. These are the notes I've made to accompany the pictures.'

Philippa sat up to read the book, flicking slowly through the pages, sometimes going back to a previous page.

'Why didn't you take photos of them before packing them away?'

'Good question.'

'Yes. That's why I asked it.'

'Carol took photos back with her when she came over. It never occurred to me to ask for copies. But in truth I've become so ambivalent about everything I've done.'

James sighed and looked hopelessly at Philippa. Here she was, beautiful and naked. She'd just opened up her heart to him and he couldn't find any mechanism for explaining his feelings about what he'd been working on and why he felt so negative about the outputs.

She was staring impassively at him. 'Are you scared?'

'Yes I'm scared.'

'How? Why? Of what and whom?'

'Right now, of you. Of the possibility that what you've always said about me is true; that I can't do this.'

'I've never said that, and please look at me when you're talking.'

He dragged his eyes away from the wall and looked in to

317

Philippa's eyes. She continued, 'In fact I've always said the opposite. That you can do it, and must do it.'

'I feel like whatever I'm doing as an artist is a threat to us being together. After you left me in Sorges I was in pieces. But what I had to do on the pictures became more important than you; than us.'

'That's stupid; really stupid.'

'Is it? Why?'

'The things I love about you and the reasons I'm with you aren't because of what you might achieve or what you're working on.'

'It worries me you'll think I'm not yours, completely yours, if I'm immersed in some project or other.'

Philippa shook her head and smiled. 'You know that can't ever be the case. If there's work to do and if you are taken away to places and situations, it won't change anything we have unless you let it. But I will be happy that you're doing something you're very, very good at. What else are you scared of?'

'The idea of all this attention. Of standing in that gallery, listening to people getting it hopelessly wrong and wondering if what's hopelessly wrong is, in fact, the shite they're looking at.'

Philippa closed the notebook and slapped it against his stomach. 'I haven't spent time and money travelling here to listen to you being small minded, self-indulgent and destructive. The pieces you've created are not shite; but your thought processes are.'

'I feel like I have to do something I have no faith in to make you believe in me. And if I can't go through with it, if that's really true, then you won't want me. That's what you said at Gra and Gerry's party.'

'Also not what I said. Let me recap: I told you that night that I find it sad that someone with talent has no outlet for it. That you have abundant creativity and you should use it. Stop twisting things round to your negative way of thinking. What I want from you, and what I believe you can achieve, are completely separate. I have absolutely no doubts that I love you and I want to be with you; always. But I'm not giving you any escape routes from your goals. I will not say that you can stop painting and drawing just because you're scared it's a barrier between us. You have got to go on. Not for me, not for Laura, not for anyone. Do it for you James.'

'So there is pressure. The James you want is the artist.'

'No. Wrong. The James I want is you: good and bad. I don't need to be convinced of your abilities. I know you're good; you've always been good and it's what you should be doing. Realise it. Grab everything you can. Stop thinking of yourself as just another untapped talent. What you showed me at Bill and Angela's villa, and what I've just read in your notes today, is strong and evocative. It makes me proud to know you and that you've finally taken a step forwards.'

'And what if it all goes wrong and I get nowhere.'

'Then you'll have tried and made yourself into a better person by trying. And as a better person you won't want to stop, even if you don't succeed. You'll want to improve and grow.'

'I love you.'

'Well show me. You smelled too much last time.'

'Wait. I can't express this as eloquently or passionately as you just did. Maybe you need to teach me. But I don't want, ever, to be without you.'

Philippa looked up at him, searching deeply in his eyes. 'We will be together. But we have got to sort out what that means. And this isn't about me demanding that you're different, or imposing a personality mode, or making you wear the right clothes, or controlling how you think. It's about getting us to talk, listen and evolve; to agree how we find time for love alongside the creative things we both need to do. And it starts now, here, in the sunshine. So like I said, show me you love me.'

They had an amazing evening. From the moment they arrived, everyone seemed to be laughing. Conversation was free and open. The food was simple and delicious. Penny and Yves were generous, easy people who made a meal with strangers seem as if they'd always been friends. After dinner they sat round the piano and Philippa played a Chopin prelude that moved Yves to tears. She kept the music coming, increasingly accompanied by everyone singing along with old favourites. When Philippa began to sing Carole King's *You've Got a Friend*, James sat transfixed by the words and couldn't join in when everyone else sang the chorus.

It was past three when they finally left. As they lay together later that morning, still occasionally singing tipsy snatches of old tunes, Philippa said; 'Something's still troubling you isn't it?'

'How do you know?'

'You go very quiet when you're discontented; even your breathing's quiet. So come on. What is it? Still scared?'

'Yes.'

'Talk to me.'

'Well think about our time at school. What was I?'

'Young James: trousers too long; shirt buttons missing; ridiculous platform-soled shoes; messy hair; nice smile; disarming eyes.' She grabbed his penis. 'Might have had one of these in there somewhere too.'

'But what about art; what was I up to?'

'Well I never saw that much, just the stuff the school displayed, or whatever was hanging in the Art Room. But what I remember is that it was good; it all had a kind of grace. I liked it. But maybe that's because it was yours and not necessarily because I knew what I was talking about.'

'Did you realise that when I was with Sarah I more or less stopped doing any kind of creative work?'

'No, but how would I?'

'I suppose you wouldn't. But that situation has been a constant. Something seems to stop me being creative when I'm in a relationship.'

'Do you feel creative now?'

'Not especially. But then I've had months of doing nothing else.'

'True. Keep talking.'

'It just seems that whenever I'm alone there is more drive and compulsion for me to create and work on my art. As soon as Sarah chucked me I was quickly working on endless new ideas. Some were conceptually very strong. And that situation just seemed to go on and on, all through a period when I was in a kind of prison. But no one saw whatever I did; it just got filed away.'

'You're saying you can't create if you're happy?'

'I'm saying I don't know. Can you? You're creative too.'

'Well my mood or frame of mind can affect what I do. But I don't think it's ever made me stop working. Don't forget, almost everything I create is work, and part of a process. What I do is a means to an end; an output; things aren't wrenched from me by some romantic force.'

'In the time before I met Sally, there was a spell when I didn't do much. But I was off the rails; work during the day; drink and/or drugs in the evenings and at weekends. I created sporadically, in fits and starts. I suppose some of what I did was all right. Then Sally was helpful and encouraging; she wanted me to do stuff but it stopped being any good.'

'Who told you it was no good?'

'I did.'

'So you were still creating things when you were with Sally, but you didn't think it was good enough.'

'It just all seemed to lack a spark.'

'Right. Did you try to fix that?'

'No. I just felt disinclined to work hard at it. The combination of loving her, living with her, needing to be responsible about life and work and play – about everything; it just stopped me being an artist.'

Philippa reached to him and held his hand. 'And what about Laura.'

'With Laura we were apart more than we were together. In a way, that felt like the right arrangement. Weekdays, art. Weekends, Laura.'

'And now there's me.'

'Yes. Like I said before, I'm so scared that with my exhibition to work on I more or less forgot about you. After our stunning week together and all the certainty that at last we are lovers and friends and a couple, you were gone and it was like it never happened. And I'm scared – terrified – that I can't be madly in love with you and still be an artist. If I can't feel alone – a victim, discarded – I won't create.'

'You didn't forget about me, did you? That wasn't a case of it being an ending: it was a case of you being single-minded, and having a plan and a goal. If I'd been with you during that time, I'd have made you do the work.'

'How?'

'By doing what we're doing now. Talking, deliberating, and driving out the demons, knocking down the doors. Really James, I just can't believe that you want and need me more than you want and need to be creative. Is this you saying you don't want us to be together?'

James sat up, alarmed; 'No. Don't ever think that.'

'Then I don't understand all this. You're being really weak and deferential and that doesn't sit alongside who you are. You're capable of being selfish and ruthless, logical and calculating. Yet in this situation, you're basically saying you won't work out the answers. You're just accepting defeat. Sort this out and stop making things complicated by jumping to the easy way out. You have everything it takes to succeed and I know you can love and create simultaneously.'

'I can't.'

'You can, and you've done it before.'

'I haven't.'

'You have; at home and at school. Your work thrived while you juggled with four or five complicated, growing, loving relationships; perhaps more.'

'But that was just growing up, being part of the gang. It wasn't love.'

'It was love James. It might not have been physical or sexual, but your relationships with the guys in the gang were loving, committed friendships. And it's the same with your parents, your brothers and your sister. And with me too. So get your head around it; it really is not the lack of a woman's love and affection that fires your abilities.'

'It's been my experience. And like I said, I don't want to lose you because I can't be an artist.'

Philippa sighed deeply and stopped holding his hand.

'Listen. You're gifted, really gifted; but you have to kick this starry-eyed notion of creativity being about suffering and sadness. There might have been some driving, tortured force behind the outputs of the great and mighty. But that's not ordinary people like us. I really don't think this is about being in love or in isolation. I think it's more about your insecurities and your arrogance.'

'Thanks.'

Philippa made a loud buzzing noise, like on a game show. 'Rule number one: no sulking and being huffy when we talk about each other's faults.'

James giggled. 'I'll remember that.'

'Rule number two: Philippa determines the application of rules.'

He laughed aloud. 'I feel better already. So, I'm insecure and arrogant. What else?'

Philippa lifted herself up so she was resting on her right arm and facing him.

'First, I think it's bullshit that anyone needs to be emotionally scarred or in mental turmoil to be creative. Lucid, rational, happy, contented people actually do write novels, paint things, compose operas and sculpt statues. You're not stopped by any of those things. What's stopped you is the lack of real happiness.'

'You're saying I've never been happy?'

'Yes. I am.'

'I'm really very happy indeed to be lying here in bed with you.'

'I know. But your happiness isn't defined by looking at my tits, or stroking my hair or feeling content because you finally got me. And our happiness isn't about today's fixed point in time, snogging, walking hand in hand on a beach at sunset or gazing soppily at each other. It's about where we go and how we get there, what we think and how we resolve conflicts. It's about being one, together, forever and knowing there's nothing else. So I mean it: you've never really been happy, because you can't define what makes you happy. I humbly submit, m'learned friend, that whatever switches your creativity off, being happy is not it.'

'I wasn't looking at your tits.'

She made the buzzer noise again. 'Rule... what rule are we up to?'

'Mmmm, five?'

'Rule five: James, look at my tits always; they are fabulous.'

He laughed loudly and did as he was told.

'I'm no expert in this, but what I see when I work among creative people is that they aren't talented because of depression and anxiety. It's because they have skills and know how to use them. I'd go further and say that, give those people a bad day and a bad mood, it might inhibit their capacity to work but might just as easily improve it. There isn't a formula. But I think what you do is to paint yourself in to a corner – badly phrased, no pun intended – where you assume the mantle of being a genius. You throw out this challenge to people that says *look at me, and if you don't get it then you're not worthy*. But that's not how it works. You can't be perfect, and you'll never please everyone. By all means soak up all the great things that are out there and try to emulate them. What you mustn't do is assume that having a gift means you have to have a problem.'

'How come you know all this about me?'

'Because I listen when you talk, and I watch when you're silent. And I remember how you used to project yourself whenever you had an audience. You did it a bit last night with Penny and Yves. You're such a show-off; you crave attention, and love the limelight and that isn't the behaviour of someone who can only work in a darkened room with a tiny cloud over his head dripping constant rain. You're too controlling and intentional to be a genuinely tortured genius. You're not sensitive to other dimensions like a depressive. You have mood swings, and not very wide ones. All that proves is you do have some adaptive traits, like intelligence and proficiency. But it doesn't make you van Gogh.'

'You make me sound like a compulsive liar. And a cynical one.'

'Well you can't be a very good liar or I wouldn't be able to see all this. But, yes, I think some of your behaviour is cynical. It's certainly manipulative.'

'Now I'm really scared.'

'Good. I like to frighten people.'

'But what do you want from me? I'm still worried that you will hate me if Mr Angry the Artist becomes Mr Happy the Homely Husband.'

'Oh for fuck's sake James. Have you been listening? What I want from you is you. And you are both of those characters, and plenty of others beside. I want to be with all of them.'

'And what about the exhibition? Do you think it's important?'

'For us, no. For you, yes. It has to be.'

'And if I can't face it and don't go?'

'I'll still love you and try to understand. But I'll do everything in my power to persuade you to go; because if you don't go, and it fails, you'll never forgive yourself for not being there to convince people.'

'And if I don't go, and it succeeds?'

'Then you'll never forgive yourself for missing all the adulation and champagne.'

32

All the Things that make up a Life

May 1997

All that history flashed through his mind. It seemed to have taken no more than a few moments and James snapped from the reverie. He was sitting at a desk holding an open photograph album. Four 5 x 7 prints were in front of him, all with Laura and James as the subject; together in these images for eternity.

James had found the album in a drawer next to his desk, one of five folders containing many memories. He closed it with a smile then packed it carefully in a large cardboard box with *Keep Here* scrawled on the side. He was surrounded by several such boxes and plastic crates; and a long roll of brown paper, another of bubble-wrap and packs of sticky brown tape. Elsewhere in the room were the tools, machines and accessories of creative endeavour: an easel and drawing board; a small table with desktop computer components on and under it; an open chest revealing tubes and brushes; flip charts; a small mixing desk; an electronic grand piano; a synthesiser and drum machine together on a stand; and a reel to reel tape recorder. Two large speakers hung on the wall. A chrome stand held a microphone and pop-screen, a pair of headphones draped over the boom. There were wires and cables everywhere; some taped to the floor, others dangling loose.

Soon, people would arrive to carefully dismantle all this paraphernalia, place it in special cases and carry it away.

James looked from the window in to the leafy, grass-lined avenue beneath. It was empty save for a few parked cars and, as he watched, a van appeared causing James to tut in exasperation that they were early. But it sailed past, a rat running.

He was in a large first floor room at a house in Weybridge. At some point in its history, this space – The Studio as he knew it – had been created from two other rooms. Despite its size, and that it had once been fit for purpose, the room was needed for other things. Change was coming.

He went to make peppermint tea with which he returned to The Studio. As he sipped the insipid watery beverage, his thoughts returned to Laura and how she would have judged the things that had happened in the seven years since her death: things James had done; or had affected him; or he had failed in. There were many things for her to judge.

Such as his decision to move to France and create a mass of work in her honour: she'd have enthusiastically approved of that, and might even have accepted his disintegration at the end of it.

Such as the fact that during that French escapade, James and Philippa became a couple.

Such as the humility he showed in spending time and energy to rebuild his relationships with Carol and his parents once he'd returned to England.

Such as the undercurrent of problems connected with Roger Whitham.

Laura always told James he was soft and too forgiving. It turned out that he had missed so much that was obvious and that others had seen. It was Carol, while working on her contribution to the exhibition, who began to believe there was something indefinably wrong about Roger. Yet his charm usually persuaded her that there were no real grounds for concern and definitely no reason to say anything to James or Philippa. However, the nagging doubts continued so she mentioned them to Bill Drysdale who agreed to do some digging. He travelled to Richmond to see what he could learn as a stranger and potential customer in Roger's gallery; he viewed things; asked questions; haggled; walked away; and then agreed to buy things. He bought something James had painted, all the while learning Roger's way of working. He soon enlisted help from his colleague Jon Morgan and, as a team, they continued to test and probe how Roger behaved and, in particular, how he was selling James Clifton.

Their initial conclusion was that, probably, Roger was a bit of a shyster who played a game with customers and avoided paperwork if he could. But Bill and Jon didn't think that was the whole story and needed to get James involved.

Bill called James to find out what had happened to his back catalogue when he sold his flat and was delighted to hear that James had the signed and dated inventory. He was less pleased by the news that the list was not up to date and that James, consumed by his work and the build up to the exhibition, had no record of what Roger had sold, or what had been received for the sales. Bill was also unhappy about the original terms James had signed.

A cat and mouse game ensued. More visits to the gallery confirmed that Roger sold things in a haphazard way and without proper records. Nothing seemed to indicate that James' works, money and future were in safe hands. Finally, and a little more than a week before the start of the exhibition, James, Jon and Bill arrived together at the gallery as it was closing one evening. Roger became pale and silent: cat and mouse had become lions and wildebeest.

In the polite conversation that followed, Roger was encouraged to admit that the agreement for him to take thirty per cent of any sale was a massive over-statement of his contribution, and that ten per cent was more honest. He was shown the inventory of James' works and asked, for each item, to write whether it was sold or still in store. If it was sold, he had to write down the sale price, and how much he had given to James. When he said he couldn't always be specific, they discussed the deals he had done selling James' paintings to Bill and Jon. Roger couldn't explain why he had neither paid nor communicated any of that to James. He began to shake, and was clearly scared as he admitted he had no record of any transactions involving James' works.

Bill summarised the situation: Roger was a hustler par excellence. But he'd been stung by smarter operators, and James needed to be paid an agreed amount, including interest, for each painting Roger had sold. All of the works currently in his care were to be removed immediately but Roger would still stage the exhibition with Bill and Jon managing it as James' agents. In return for his work promoting the event, the use of his premises, the cost of utilities and the work needed to transform the gallery, Roger would receive a flat fee, payable from whatever he owed James.

Roger evoked a death-rattle protest. He had spent money helping James while he was in France. He'd sent cash, hired a van, leased special cases to safely transport the paintings, managed customs and excise issues and costs. He'd spent money on advertising and marketing James' exhibition.

But this was a flop. Asked for proof of what he'd paid, Roger admitted there was none. After a long, theatrical silence Jon told him to stop being ridiculous and to accept the fact that Customs & Excise, Inland Revenue, the police and the Office of Fair Trading (not to mention the local and national press and endless former and potential customers) would be left in ignorance of his misdemeanours if he simply followed their instructions, accepted their terms and kept very, very quiet.

Laura would have been horrified that James hadn't spotted even the possibility that Roger was dodgy. He was supposed to be a purchasing and supplier manager; how could he have missed such a crook? How did others see it and act on it, yet James had seen nothing?

She'd have been delighted by the success of the exhibition and the fact that every single work was sold before the end of the fifth day. But James had thrown a minor wobbler; he'd lashed out against everything, saying he'd become a commercial puppet. This quickly intensified into a more general bout of undignified sulking and idiocy that lasted too long and almost destroyed several relationships. He was living with Philippa at her home in South Kensington and she was carefully managing their relationship, as they had agreed during their time together in

Fréjus. In the weeks after returning from France they were apart more than they were together. James was travelling between Hereford, Bath and Richmond on a kind of rota. Philippa was busy with a new client. But in whatever time they had together, they worked on the evolution needed for their partnership. It was calm, focused and real.

Philippa was equally calm and focused when James imploded. She told him she loved him but he wasn't welcome in her home if his energy was being poured down a drain and he wasn't working on anything new. So he took flight and signed a short lease on a flat in Windsor, where he became secluded, kicking and spitting against just about everything. This reversion to type – living on junk food, coffee and beer – once again caused his weight to balloon and his mind to shrivel. After a momentous year of effort and achievement, James had crashed back in to himself.

He spoke daily with Philippa but, on each occasion, any small talk was concluded by her asking him what he was working on. The calls ended quickly when he said *nothing*. So, he sat in pubs listening; to suited workers who filled their lunch break talking balls over fizzy water and hot pot; to the suits, uniforms and overalls that dropped by in the late afternoon to gargle a couple of beers before heading home; to the evening crowd. James heard a great deal, but little that was of value and he grew weary of it. This was where he had been. He knew he was wasting everything but the undertow of drinking and failing was like a vortex, spinning and sucking him down and away. Whenever he tried to sketch or outline an idea, or think himself in to creative shape, he found no motivation, inspiration or strength.

In the spring of 1992, determined to stop being what he had become, James decided to vary the theme. He called a number he knew by heart and when a voice said: 'Hello, Gary Greig speaking, how can I help you?' James replied, 'Hello you old cunt, it's James. Remember me?'

They met that weekend at Covent Garden and set off on a long hard drinking session. From what they discussed, and how they discussed it, nothing seemed to have changed since they'd last been together. James told Gary what he'd been up to since his sudden, mysterious resignation the previous year, then heard all the dirt from the office. As Gary imparted these tales, James found no link to or empathy with those people or their situations and affairs. Then Gary revealed he hadn't made it as a musician. His band collapsed, amidst vitriol and name-calling, leaving Gary to focus on a Sunday lunchtime residency at a wine bar in which he brilliantly entertained people who weren't listening. Gary and Bridget had also parted, so these performances were an essential enabler for his love life.

James berated Gary for his lavish lack of ambition only to find the accusation returned with great force. The pleasure of their re-union was relegated beneath a serious, critical, and objective assessment of their respective failures.

After that, the event didn't seem such fun and ran out of steam. When they finally parted there was no urge or determination to do it all again. Absolute change had happened for both men; James saw that the changes affecting him were almost completely positive and to his advantage.

He took the tube to South Kensington hoping Philippa would be home and happy to see him. But she wasn't there and James had no key. He staggered back to the Underground and at Waterloo jumped on a train to Windsor. He slumped in his seat, warily watching assorted yelling drunks until he realised they were unthreatening and uncomplicated. The journey, through familiar stations where he'd lived and worked and played, gave James no joy of recollection. He couldn't understand what he'd gained from his time with Gary. He had no place in that history. This voyage was worthless.

When the train arrived at Windsor and Eton Riverside station, James was nearly sober but completely driven by the need to do new work. He walked the streets well in to the early hours, pacing out what he needed to do, switching off all the circuits that made him so fragile. He felt as if Philippa and Laura were walking with him up and down Eton High Street, Thames Street, Castle Hill, and Peascod Street.

Then later that day, when he had slept off the drink and fatigue, James made two phone calls. He told Philippa they had to meet so he could tell her about the work he was going to start. He said he wasn't asking to be immediately readmitted to her life and home but was going to prove to her that it could happen soon. She told him she was ready and he should come home to her as soon he could show where this was going. She was still calm and focused.

But when he spoke with Angela, she ripped in to him for throwing Bill's generosity and guidance back in his face. Bill had returned from the exhibition with a mission for his coming retirement; to be James' manager, mentor and agent. She said it had made Bill come to life after the pain and anguish of Laura's death and James was the biggest, worst kind of fool for behaving as he had done. Bill came on the line and James mumbled through another set of apologies and regret. By the end, he was sniffing and snuffling through tears.

Bill told him to get a grip and listen. James had a career. There was money from the exhibition and previous sales. People were expressing a desire to see James' work, old and new, and Bill wanted to convert that in to more sales. Potential clients wanted his talents but all James could do was break things. Bill had been controlling these opportunities so none was lost, but time was running out. James needed to change, forever, and find the energy and desire to be someone new, doing new work.

People were doing the right and necessary things. James, after all his years of reckless under-achievement, needed to engage with reality; to catch up with what he always should have been.

Bill travelled to meet him the following day and they booked into a hotel to spend the afternoon and evening talking in detail about James' future. As well as a review of prospects, Bill worked through what James was doing and thinking, where he was living, why he had to change, what had happened with Philippa and where that relationship was going. It was uncompromising and tough. James clung on.

The next morning they continued this planning and development session. Bill wanted to map out how they would use his existing works to maintain, then grow, the interest in James. Then he revealed a very specific opportunity: the offer of a commission from a council seeking to promote art as part of a programme of culture and diversity. The offer proposed that an artist was needed to do several things: design posters and flyers; create a giant frieze in the Town Hall with images from schools in the borough; and work with children in schools. It would be hands-on and challenging and it wouldn't be lucrative; it was about growth and evolution. In spite of Bill's scepticism about whether he could handle such a project, James was enthusiastic.

Within a week, they met the council's officials to express James' interest and suitability for the appointment. Bill led the negotiations and James was marginal in the discussions, even though he was exactly what the council wanted. But when the meeting was held to sign contracts, James insisted on the inclusion of an annual prize from his own pocket. Bill became agitated and tried to stop this but James persevered, saying the prize would go to the young person judged by him to have created the best portrayal of Love. James wanted this to be called the Laura Drysdale Prize and with that inclusion, it was James who concluded that the deal was done. When they left the council offices, Bill grabbed and hugged him.

Laura would have been delighted by the way James threw himself in to that project. He felt a new kind of vigour and soon had approval for poster art to be sent for printing and distribution. Next, he convinced the council that too much time would be wasted visiting schools to create images for the frieze.

Instead he proposed an alternative, that he would use a series of landmarks in the Borough. The original would be displayed in the Town Hall, with smaller copies provided to schools and council offices. The work would be used as a watermark or background image on council documents and signs. The officials accepted his logic, loved the idea and told him to proceed. The project gained traction and interest.

What James enjoyed most was the work in classrooms. He was, in equal measure, inspired and moved by the way children viewed art, from the simplest painting or drawing session to a discussion about perspective. He found that as an outsider he wasn't viewed as a teacher. He was young enough to be hip, old enough to be respected, talented enough to be quiet for. Children of all ages responded to him positively and James loved the attention and the notion that he was spreading the word.

Concurrent with this work, another opportunity surfaced. Bill called James and told him to get on a train to Aldershot where they would meet this new client. An Army regiment, recently returned from the Gulf, wanted a painting for their officer's mess to honour those who had died in Iraq; a small number, but lost to their pals and loved ones. They had no image in mind but this meeting with the regiment's commanding officer was to review options and agree next steps. To Bill, this was a simple commercial exercise; but James' pink-tinged politics and liberal stance on warfare made him uneasy as they drove to the barracks.

The meeting with the CO put him at ease. The man was more like a marketing executive with none of the military stereotypes James expected. Colonel Peters had seen James' exhibition and referred to several of the works as being in the right direction. Surrealism was off limits but the finished product didn't need to be a bland portrait. He seemed to know his stuff and James was hooked.

They were given a tour of the barracks and met some soldiers who were polite and reserved and dutifully answered any questions he asked. But James sensed their indifference, both to him and the planned memorial.

When he left Aldershot James had no idea what he would do for this client. Two days later he was still bereft, so he asked some of the kids he was working with what *army* meant to them. It started with silly crudities and clichés, but when he stuck with the subject he heard a theme emerging around four things: guards; guns; crosses; poppies. It took James a few days to transform those into: readiness; resolution; remembrance; rebirth.

He pencil sketched an outline idea and faxed it to Colonel

Peters. A broad circle comprising four images, each blurred in to the other: a sentry with his rifle presented; a mortar firing, surrounded by dust covered soldiers; a mass of white crosses in carefully tended patterns; poppies, wild and plentiful in sunlit fields. He faxed this with a scribbled cover note to the effect that he would probably go with watercolours to achieve the effect he was after and that he would call the Colonel the following morning for feedback.

The initial response was cool but James was too busy to be defensive. Instead, he did a colour version of the sketch using pastels and posted it, this time suggesting the Colonel should ask some of his men for a reaction. The response was positive. James spent a day at the barracks absorbing the details of uniforms and weapons then began work on the painting. It took him a week and he was soon back at the barracks signing off the finished painting. He returned one last time to see it, framed and hanged in the officer's mess, before joining Colonel Peters and his team at a mess dinner where James was formally thanked and toasted, then presented with a regimental crest. He smiled bravely and hated every minute.

Cash was banked and more people were interested in his services. Bill was managing a string of clients who wanted James to do things: portraits of children or pets or houses; corporate images; civic scenes; or just the desire to have an original James Clifton hanging over the fireplace. Bill guided all this and carefully weeded out the least lucrative or most pointless options. James kept in touch with the schools he'd worked at, and found there was an overwhelming interest in winning the Laura Drysdale Prize. He was torn to pieces by having to choose its first ever winner.

By the autumn of 1993, a more personal project had become pre-eminent for James. Philippa was bored by the confines of being a musical servant for others and had decided to invest her time and money in work of her own. From a network of contacts, she had a small advance against potential sales of an album she wanted to do even though what she planned would be pretty uncommercial. She asked James to provide artwork for the CD sleeve and they started working together.

The formula for creating complementary music and image was not easily found. Philippa believed she could give James an overview of how the music flowed together then he could go away and create pictures. That didn't work and nor did the provision of lyrics. In the end, what worked was when James sat unobtrusively in the background while Philippa played, arranged and recorded her music. As it grew from simple piano backing tracks to soaring paeans of ambient glory, James was engrossed and inspired. After each recording or rehearsal session, Philippa and James went to a pub or restaurant where James found he was able to map out ideas that would fit. They agreed with his concept that simple pencil sketches would work brilliantly; he proceeded on that basis.

This process had the effect of making them intimate; it renewed their raw emotional drive and made them more powerfully and deeply in love.

James completed his work and Philippa enthused that his drawings, one per song on the album, were evocative and simpatico. Critical acclaim endorsed her view and the album sold modest volumes that created new offers of work.

It became clear that working together like this was a business ready to be run and they pitched the idea to a network of connections. Feedback was positive and, after months of planning, they formed their company; *Sound&Vision*. They had input from Bill Drysdale in a non-executive role. It gave them a vehicle to fulfil work, either singly or as a unit, and soon found that the proposition of combined music and image was an attractive one. Business bloomed: corporate work; presentations; conferences; software and gaming; media; advertising; television shows. *Sound&Vision* was a small, nimble proposition and it delivered quickly, effectively and cheaply. It had no unique selling point, but it gained a reputation for winning where others failed. Their success frustrated bigger agencies, who sought to swallow this talented partnership and quash its potential. They resisted the mainstream, continued to be busy and between times, were hopelessly happy in love.

Just before Christmas 1995, James Clifton and Philippa Fletcher married in an unostentatious and discreet civil ceremony in South Kensington. It was a select, very small gathering that moved from the Town Hall to a private room in a local pub where champagne and finger food were waiting. The happy couple was calm, focused and real. Their guests saluted this union. James gave a short speech and Philippa made an even shorter announcement that their first dance was imminent. Expecting *Still in Love with You*, and wondering how they could possibly dance to it, James didn't know whether to laugh or cry as the intro to Carly Simon's *You're So Vain* throbbed from the speakers. They danced closely and tenderly and as those three minutes drew to a close, Philippa whispered to James: 'You've got me now James Clifton. Don't you dare fuck this up.'

They had no time for any kind of honeymoon for something huge was in the pipeline. They'd recently completed work on a popular television drama, a three-part serial shown on consecutive nights that autumn. Philippa's theme music was the same for all three shows, but James had created three different sets of graphics and animation so each episode had the sense of being somehow new, yet joined to the last. This had captured the attention of an American film director and after some initial exploratory communications they met on a conference call to discuss his film and the terms being offered. After hearing outlines of the plot and main characters, *Sound&Vision* agreed to review contracts to compose the film's score and design its title sequence. Negotiations and agreement followed then Philippa and James flew to Los Angeles and were soon immersed in their respective roles. James identified scenes in the rushes that he wanted to use. Philippa wrote and recorded her ideas, assuming the final version of her score would be played by an orchestra. After hearing it, James suggested it would be perfect performed by a string quartet, an idea approved by the director and producers.

Several weeks of effort ended with their music score and title sequence signed off. *Sound&Vision* received the pre-agreed advance allowing its owners to have a belated honeymoon in New York before returning to England. On its release, the critics hated the film but loved the music and Philippa's status as a composer was massively enhanced.

Within two years of its inception, *Sound&Vision* was stable enough for its owners to move to a discreet avenue in Weybridge and a house with an enormous first floor space that became the studio for their respective equipment, aspirations and inspirations. They asked Bill Drysdale to be executive chairman which he happily agreed to do and guided them to new ideas and bigger business opportunities, including ones that would seal the security they now craved for their financial future.

One opportunity was a new exhibition by James. He'd been working diligently to complete a collection of pieces on the theme of Corporate Greed and, when it was announced, there was anticipation and expectation in advance of the opening. Bill suggested they should hold the event outside London and they soon agreed terms with a gallery in Leeds where the show opened late in the autumn of 1996. It was a success with the punters, who came in increasing numbers, and with buyers. But the media's cognoscenti was less enamoured and one gave the exhibition a terrible drubbing in his column. He also decided to wade in to James in quite personal terms.

Since he was no longer able to fall from a cliff on to a shoreline of frailties, James called the critic and invited him to lunch. For two hours, he plied the man with chat, charisma, claret and cognac. They shook hands and parted with quite genuine warmth. The critic left the restaurant with a piece of paper stuck to the back of his coat saying:

I am a pissed-up twat.
I write meaningless nonsense in the Sunday Courier.

James told Philippa he was hugely ashamed of his actions.

Philippa told James she was more proud of him than she had ever been.

Success meant the company had to expand and Bill took charge of a project to move them to a business location. Their Weybridge studio had been a wonderful place to start their creative outputs but a bad place to expand in to new deals. They needed additional skills and people, and while those might not be employees, they couldn't all work together in two converted bedrooms. Above all, they needed a place that could be identified as the home of *Sound&Vision*.

James was sorting through boxes and cupboards when something lying behind the desk caught his eye. As he reached for what looked like a photo frame, the telephone rang. Angela's voice greeted him loudly.

'Hello darling James. We're desperate for news about Laura.'

'She is fine. I'm waiting for these removal guys to get here so I can get down to the hospital.'

'Well? Come on, give me some vital statistics.'

'Laura Rosanna Clifton. Born May 12th 1997 at just under eight pounds and at just after eight in the evening. Popped out without a murmur, smiled uncannily like a drunkard and then howled. Philippa's loving attention soon stopped all that. It was quite wonderful and beautiful.'

'Eyes?'

'Green and tigerish.'

'Hair?'

'Not enough to tell.'

'We can't wait to see you all. This is so wonderful and we're so proud.'

As Angela talked, James picked up the framed object; he walked with it and the phone on to a landing then in to a small room bedecked in pink and mauve. A series of pictures, showing an acer through the seasons, hung on the wall above a cot. A mobile, that he had made himself, tinkled as he walked by. A small silver teddy bear dangled as the central feature of this creation.

'And is Philippa okay? Any physical problems?'

'None. She was very serene and calm and only swore once. She also called me a tosser. But, and admittedly I'm a novice here, everything looked pretty straightforward.'

He headed back to the studio and, as the conversation with Angela drew to a close, realised what he was holding. It was the only newspaper review of his debut exhibition, framed for posterity. It ran:

'And so to Richmond to fulfil an invitation to Roger Whitham's welcoming Insight Gallery.

Since I have known him (many good years), Roger has uncovered some interesting talent, so his enthusiasm for James Clifton deserved attention.

The exhibition of Clifton's works, under the title 'Brittle Dreams', was nicely managed and carefully staged. An accompanying pamphlet was a helpful addition to the display, but I sometimes found it got in the way of how I saw the sequence. 'Brittle Dreams' takes the viewer through the phases of a relationship. It shows progress from incompetent competence, to the pain of failure and final critical appraisal by a jury of peers. In style, Clifton is probably closest to Edvard Munch. And he seems safest as an Expressionist. But when he stumbles in to other genres, the theme and projection become veiled or even lost. In 'Look, Listen and Learn' there are hints of Impressionism and it left me cold. 'Raged Ragged' had a baffling Abstract style that appeared unrelated to almost everything else in the sequence. The Realism of 'Over Exposure' was nice, and technically brilliant. The Surrealism of 'Gran Turismo' was clever but again, I saw no link with the whole. I found 'Smashed', an image of a disembodied soul floating in a sea of blood, most unpleasant and an unnecessary intrusion on the generally less vivid scenes that preceded it. So one has to presume that the jury of peers reached 'No Verdict'.

It is certainly the case that James Clifton has talent and, when he digs deep, can be inspiring. But the general lack of a sustained style and the cold, impassive subject matter of 'Brittle Dreams' left this critic feeling too empty to enthuse. Perhaps Clifton needs to re-appraise where he is coming from to fully realise that talent.'

James read the review again, with a small smile and a resigned shake of his head.

'He was right. You are a charlatan.'

James frowned and with a shrug dropped the frame into a tea chest full of other discarded memories.

'And all of this?'

The doorbell rang.

'It's all I ever wanted.'

CPSIA information can be obtained
at www.ICGtesting.com
Printed in the USA
BVHW081019050919
557659BV00016B/1286/P